John Drake trained as a biochem[...] before realizing he was no good at [...] the television department of ICI un[...] writer. John's hobby is muzzle-load[...] British history, British politics (as a spectator) and current affairs. He is married with a son and two grandchildren.

PRAISE FOR THE TRAITOR OF TREASURE ISLAND:

'From the taverns and manor houses of early eighteenth century England to the decks of the ships and the tropical islands of the Caribbean, the authenticity is palpable, the story engrossing, the characters completely human.' – James L. Nelson, author of *The Only Life that Mattered* and *Fin Gall*

'A novel and refreshing take on a classic, *The Traitor of Treasure Island* is instantly captivating with a well-crafted plot that definitely keeps the pages turning.' – Alaric Bond, author of the Fighting Sail series.

PRAISE FOR JOHN DRAKE:

'Broad comedy, high drama, plenty of action, a pinch of sex... the genre has room for this cheerily debunking outsider' – *Daily Mail*

'John Drake writes beautifully, and you'll be torn between savouring the words and quickly flipping the pages.' – Nelson DeMille, #1 *New York Times* bestselling author

Those who would like to know what happened before *The Traitor of Treasure Island* will find the full and previous history of Flint, Silver, Selena, Billy Bones and the rest in the following John Drake books, published by HarperCollins:

Flint and Silver
Pieces of Eight
Skull and Bones

Likewise, those who would like to read the Jim Hawkins account of the Treasure Island expedition will find it in *Treasure Island* by the immortal, magnificent and incomparable Robert Louis Stevenson.

THE
TRAITOR
OF TREASURE
ISLAND

JOHN DRAKE

LUME BOOKS

LUME BOOKS

First published in 2019 by Lume Books
30 Great Guildford St,
London, SE1 0HS

ISBN 978-1-83901-171-9

Printed and bound in Great Britain by
Clays Ltd, Elcograf S.p.A.

www.lumebooks.co.uk

In memory of Councillor James Cecil Edwards, OBE, JP, Mayor of the Metropolitan Borough of Bethnal Green 1939–1941.
My books deal with fictional heroes: Jim Edwards was the real thing. In 1940 he was asked to find volunteers to train as civilian bomb-disposal officers, since the number of unexploded bombs left live after German air raids was too great for the Royal Engineers to defuse.
He put up a list in Bethnal Green Town Hall inviting volunteers to add their names.
His own name was first on the list.
He was my dad.

Introduction

I wrote this book because I was inspired by the following words, from a letter of 18 March 1790, sent by the captain of an outbound convict ship, to his wife:

'The boy Jim Hawkins of Treasure Island, has grown to become the notorious Sir James "Slippery Jim" Hawkins, perpetual member of parliament for Trelawney West, who — following his recent trial — is to be transported to Australia for crimes too depraved to be named.'

I wrote the book because of those words and because of an uncanny experience that I had in the summer of 2017, when I felt that one of the un-dead was out of its grave and knocking at my door. I felt this because a certain object was delivered to my home by FedEx: a seaman's chest, very old, and much like any other seaman's chest, except that it had the initial 'B' branded into the top surface with a hot iron, and the corners were smashed and broken by rough usage. But it shocked and amazed me — because I knew whose chest it must be, and I could barely believe it.

The chest was sent on spec by a dealer who was familiar with my books on Long John Silver, and the asking price was not cheap. But once I had seen the documents inside, I paid up without question. Indeed, the very first paper I handled was the letter mentioned above, and it seemed uncanny in itself, that I should glance at this document before all the rest, because there were plenty of them.

It and all the other papers were collected by Dr David Livesey, ship's doctor on the Treasure Island expedition, and placed in the sea chest with Livesey's journal of the expedition. Finally, in 1758, Livesey instructed Lucey and Lucey, solicitors of Polmouth in Cornwall, to safeguard the chest for one hundred years, before publishing its contents using money left by Livesey for the purpose. Livesey added more papers to the chest in later years, including a copy of the Treasure Island map commissioned by Squire Trelawney, who gave the original to Jim Hawkins, and Flint's map of perils to navigation north of the treasure island.

But Lucey and Lucey went out of business in 1847, by which time Livesey's instructions were lost, so the chest sat in a vault for 259 years, until it came to me.

What follows is therefore Livesey's own story, taken from his journal, and interspersed with chapters written by me describing wider events based on sources in the sea chest. These chapters are merely my own efforts, but they are as accurate as I can make them, and I have placed one such chapter right at the beginning of the book to give details of Jim Hawkins' parentage, which is unknown to modern readers.

One last point before I stand aside: inflation has done such ghastly work that one golden guinea of George II's time was worth — in theory — over one thousand twenty-first century pounds. But gold was scarce, with much business done on credit at high prices, so ready money was worth even more. Thus Jim Hawkins' 'silver fourpenny' (see Chapter 4) sounds miniscule but was worth over twenty modern pounds, while Flint's treasure, which was in gold, silver and precious stones, had colossal buying power, which must be valued, in modern terms, in billions.

John Drake, Cheshire, England, May 2018.

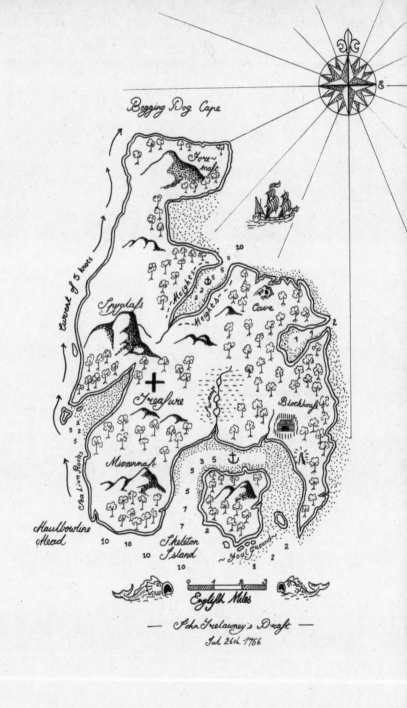

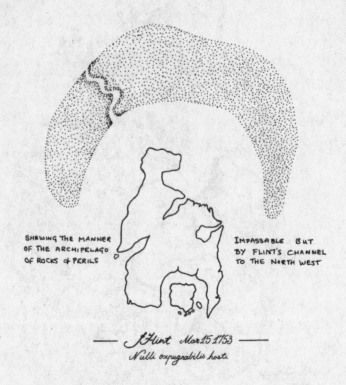

SHEWING THE MANNER
OF THE ARCHIPELAGO
OF ROCKS & PERILS

IMPASSABLE BUT
BY FLINT'S CHANNEL
TO THE NORTH WEST

—— J Flint Mar 15 1753 ——

Nulli expugnabilis hosti

CHAPTER 1

1740

Squire Charles Trelawney blustered and roared, but he kept one beefy arm around the slim body of sixteen-year-old Charlotte Tavistock, who clung to Trelawney and gazed up at him as her protector.

'You libertine!' yelled a middle-aged, respectably-dressed man, 'You rogue! You swine! You villain! You damned seducer!' He yelled it straight into Trelawney's face, and the three young men that stood with him, yelled right along with him.

'You tell him, Pa!' cried his eldest son.

'Tell him!' said the middle son.

'Tell him!' said the youngest.

The four men were Charlotte's father — Daniel Tavistock, cooper of Polmouth — and his sons Absolem, Iziah and Zachery. Worked up in anger, they made a formidable team, and even Trelawney took a pace back from them. He stepped back even here, in the great hall of his own house: flagged with stone, lined with portraits, hung with arms of the civil wars and brightly lit with sunlight that flooded through the Tudor glass of the windows. He stepped back even before the whole staff of the house — two dozen of them, men and women, boys and girls. They had turned out and were now gaping and goggling. The male servants, led by Redruth the gamekeeper, were deep in their loyalty to the House of Trelawney and eyeing the basket-hilt swords that hung on the walls in case it should come to a fight.

So Trelawney did not step back because of fear. He was a huge man, bred up to field sports and prize fighting, so he stepped back only because he knew he was in the wrong. But still he blustered.

'Damn your bloody impertinence!' he said. 'I'll have you out of your house and begging in the street!'

'No!' said Charlotte Tavistock. She said it firmly and reached up to seize Trelawney's strong chin, turning his face towards her. 'They're my father and my brothers,' she said, 'and they are innocent and we… are not!'

'Oh…' said Trelawney, hit fair and square. He was indeed a libertine. He was indeed a seducer. He was a man who revelled in the rich, red meat of life. He loved food and drink, games and sport, music and dancing, the playhouse, the alehouse and any other kind of house where lights burned late and there was fun to be had. But Charles Trelawney was not a rogue, not a swine, definitely not a villain, and he knew right from wrong even when he got on the wrong side of them.

More important still, although his own mother would not have said he was clever, he was kind and generous when sober, and now he was morbidly burdened with guilt over getting a girl as sweet and lovely as Charlotte Tavistock into the family way. He looked down at the smooth oval face, the big eyes, the sleek hair and the luscious, slender form. He could lift her with his two hands on her waist and hoist her up to the full length of his arms as she filled the room with laughter, and he tingled with the joy of it. All that, and now she was two months pregnant with his child.

'Oh…' he said again, and he bit his lip and folded Charlotte in his arms, 'I'm so sorry, my little dear,' he said, but so softly that nobody heard. Nobody heard, but all present saw the change in him. A second ago he'd been ready to fight the world, and now he stood with head bowed.

'What was that?' said Charlotte's father, smelling advantage. 'What did you say, sir?' Trelawney mumbled something, but the words were lost in his tears, because now he was weeping with remorse. 'Bah!' said Tavistock, 'Enough of that, sir! What will you do for my girl? What will you do for my child?'

Trelawney gave a great sigh, and his audience watched in raptures of fascination as he kissed Charlotte's brow, and took her hand and kissed that too. He did so with such reverence that his affection for her was obvious.

Then he stood back and bowed to Charlotte, and then bowed to her father.

'I'll do what I can,' he said. 'I'm married already, as all the world knows. Married a creature that I do not love, and which my father chose for the land she'd inherit, and which creature lives apart from me in London.' He turned to Charlotte again, and he sobbed in such sincere emotion, and kissed he hand so sweetly, that all the female onlookers dabbed at their eyes with their aprons. 'I'll find her a good husband,' said Trelawney, 'and a good living, and I'll settle a monthly allowance on her for life, to take care of her, and it shall be in my will besides, should she live longer than me.' He paused before the final admission of guilt. 'Her… and the child, too,' he said, 'for it'll be mine by blood even if born out of law.'

*

In all these matters at least, Squire Charles Trelawney kept his word. Thus, well before Charlotte's child was born, she was decently married to one Andrew Hawkins, a widower in his forties and of acceptably pleasing appearance, who previously had been landlord of a modest inn on George Street, Polmouth. But with the money granted Charlotte by Squire Trelawney, Hawkins purchased the splendid Admiral Benbow inn, off Black Hill Cove, which was well patronised by the villages all around, and a thriving business.

Squire Charles arranged all this out of his own goodness of heart. But his goodness was goaded and guarded by the great number of witnesses that had heard him acknowledge Charlotte's child as his own, and his tremendous promises regarding her future. All this tasty gossip was spread far and wide, but one person of considerable importance — who was not apparently present at the time — managed to hear everything for himself... because he was hiding in the minstrels' gallery at the upper end of the great hall.

That person was Squire Charles' fifteen-year-old son John; a hulking great boy as wild as his father, who ran away to sea shortly afterwards. But ten years later, Squire Charles was thrown from his horse in a thundering gallop in pursuit of a stag across Bodmin Moor, and thereby broke his neck such that his son became the squire and had to give up seafaring.

Thus John Trelawney — the Squire Trelawney of *Treasure Island* — knew from his youth that Jim Hawkins was his half-brother.

CHAPTER 2

1754

From Dr Livesey's journal:

From the moment I saw her, everything in my life revolved around Mrs Charlotte Hawkins. She was barely out of her twenties and in full flower of beauty: small, dark, neat and gloriously radiant of face. She was also a woman of perceptive intelligence — in all but one matter — and I was smitten and fell, and could never look at another woman thereafter. It is for that reason that I shall not publish this writing during my lifetime or hers, because I shall never do anything that might make her unhappy: not to one degree, not to one inch, not to one hair of her head.

So I must keep silent regarding the monstrous calumny of lies and distortion that has been published by Jim Hawkins, concerning Squire Trelawney's expedition to the treasure island. Likewise I must be silent regarding the personal character of that selfish, lying, traitorous little monster that, beyond all understanding, is the beloved son of Mrs Charlotte.

The boy had indeed inherited her fairness of face, because the little swine was smooth-skinned and bright-eyed, with lustrous hair and the same grace as herself in his manner and bearing. Even his laughter turned heads and made women smile, and men too because they thought him a jolly young fellow and a good companion, even if a small one, because at the time of the treasure expedition he was fifteen years old, yet slight of stature and appearing younger. More than that, he appeared innocent despite having — in full degree and to excess — the carnal appetites of a full-grown man, and spent his Sundays not in church, but in beastly fornication with the whores of Polmouth. Even on weekdays he could not stroll down George Street, the main thoroughfare of Polmouth, without receiving knowing winks from every strumpet that passed him by, since they all knew him as a client.

This I have seen with my own eyes, while walking with him, and I have endured the shame of these same women greeting me, with a 'Good day, Doctor!' as if I too were their familiar. So if any reader should sneer at my embarrassment, perhaps imagining that I have led a sheltered life, let me advise you of the following. First, that the practise of medicine — and more still that of surgery — does not breed weakness of spirit, and second that I was a mature man in my late thirties when I met Jim Hawkins, having served under the Duke of Cumberland and lived the roaring, cussing, debauched life of a solider. I saw action too, at battles including those of Dettingen and Fontenoy, receiving a wound at the latter, which persuaded me to give up killing and return to earlier studies of the healing arts.

But to pursue to my narrative, by 1754 I was a single man, though firmly settled near Polmouth in a good house with servants. In addition to being a doctor I was a magistrate, and known to all the folk of the area, including Squire John Trelawney, who became a great and true friend. Like his father he was a large, strong man, a famous sportsman and a marksman who frequently won wagers that he could hit a silver dollar at one hundred paces within five shots of his American long rifle.

Thus I was used to calling on him, and at the Admiral Benbow, which lay near the centre of the land where I practised and was a convenient stopping-off point when I rode out to visit my patients.

All this was true, but the real reason that I went so often to the Admiral Benbow was to seize any chance to meet, to gaze upon and to have conversation with the woman of my dreams, even though she could never be mine; because my Charlotte was married to Mr Andrew Hawkins, supposed father of their darling boy Jim. Alas my tragedy! Alas my addiction to the unreachable! But I could not keep myself from at least seeing the lady while making best attempts to keep decent cover over my feelings.

As for the inn itself, it was a stone building, close to the sea, with a broad view across the red sands of Black Hill Cove. It had two floors and an attic, with walls three foot thick and a roof of stone slabs, having been built in Queen Bess' time when it was wise that if a house were close to the sea, then should be stout as a castle for fear of the Barbary pirates who raided the coast for slaves. Likewise, the doors and shutters of the Admiral Benbow were inches deep of seasoned oak, and pierced with loops for musketry.

Which did not mean that the interior was old or decrepit: far from it! Under the hand of Mrs Charlotte, the inn was spotless bright, fresh-painted and cheerful, and furnished with every convenience of domestic husbandry. It also had a fine cellar of French wines and brandy, even if — as a magistrate — I never asked if any customs duty had been paid on these liquids. This because half the coast were smugglers— and I had to live among these pretended fisher-folk and not become their enemy.

So, all was well with the fabric of the Admiral Benbow. But all was *not* well with the landlord, who became dazzled by the monthly allowance which, as all the county knew, flowed every month to Mrs Charlotte from Trelawney House, tempting Mr Andrew Hawkins into laziness and the bottle. This brought despair upon his wife, who stood wringing her apron at the sight of her husband's debauchery, and it wrung my heart besides to see the tears in her eyes. Yet in bizarre perversity, a comic-drunk landlord was good for business, because his behaviour was relished as entertainment by the young folk of the villages all round, and I give the following story as proof.

One hard, freezing winter night I stayed over at the inn, having ridden myself and my poor mare Dulcie to exhaustion in order to arrive in time to deliver twins at a nearby farm. By God's will the infants lived and the farm rejoiced. But I could go no further, and took a room at the Admiral Benbow and saw to it that Dulcie was well stabled, since even then I did not trust the boy Jim Hawkins, who was ostler as well as pot-boy, to look to a horse unsupervised. But Jim gave me his pretty-faced, oh-so-charming smile as he rubbed down the horse — *'Yes, Doctor. No, Doctor. Three bags full, Doctor,'* — always smiling and smiling. So I bade Dulcie goodnight and went upstairs to wash in my room.

Later I came down to the big parlour, to find it blazing with light, roaring with noise and sweltering in heat from a huge fire in the grate and from the mass of country folk filling benches around tables and even sat upon the floor. Jim was busy serving out drink and food, as were the two young servant girls that had been taken on as business grew, and Mrs Charlotte was working hard beside them. But Mr Hawkins ——husband of my idol, and landlord of the Admiral Benbow — was not working, because he preferred dancing on a table in the middle of the room.

The sight was grotesque in the extreme. He was a fat man, over sixty years old, with lank hair around a bald pate that now nudged dangerously against an iron ring of candles slung from the ceiling by chains, which spattered him with hot grease and gave every suggestion of falling down on him at any instant. He was dancing to the music of a local band: two whistles, a flute, a fiddle and a drummer. He was red-faced, sweating from his exertions, his shirt torn open at the neck. He clutched a quart pot of drink as he staggered and stumbled, and at every step the audience roared in glee as he so very nearly fell off the table and came down among them.

'Go it, sir!' they yelled. 'Go it Mr 'awkins!' And they laughed and laughed, and so did the boy Jim, who was so entirely unworried at the sad spectacle of his father deep in drink, that the little rogue had the gall to wink at me as if he and I were sharing the fun. But all I cared about was his mother, who was trying to hide herself in a corner, with the tears burning in her eyes such that a man only a little worse than myself, and who felt for her as I did, might well have contemplated the murder of her wretched husband. Then several voices cried out together.

'Give us a song Mr 'awkins!' they yelled. 'Give us the old song!'

'Yes!' cried the boy Jim, in his clear little, dear little, cultured voice. 'Give us a song, papa!'

Hawkins the senior grinned, muttered something in a slurred voice, then waved to the band — who struck up a tune — and began:

'Fifteen men on the dead man's chest ...' He paused and the audience roared out the chorus:

'Yo-ho-ho! And a bottle of rum!'

'Drink and the devil have done with the rest ...'

'Yo-ho-ho! And a bottle of rum!'

'But one man of the crew alive ...'

Then the mood changed like a squall at sea, as an enormous voice thundered out over all other noise.

'Belay there! Belay there, I say!'

Everyone fell silent, the music ceased, and we all looked to a table by the fire, where a monster of a man had been seated alone, but was now stood up. He was a master-mariner from head to toe, in a long blue coat with brass buttons, and a cocked hat on his head even here in the heat of the parlour. He was big and bold and wore his hair in a tarred pigtail that fell down between his shoulder blades. He was ugly of face and broad of hand, and his skin was much darkened by the sun and weather. He was a virile man in the fullness of strength, but he looked old, and was scarred down the face in a white line against the tanned skin. He was Mr Billy Bones, known to all as 'The Captain', who was resident at the inn as a paying guest. He stood out from the table, with a naval cutlass slung under his coat-tails, though he made no move to draw it.

'I'll have no more o' that song!' he yelled, 'For it's Flint's song, and a bad song, as brings bad luck!' And he added foul oaths that I will not repeat.

There was silence except the crackle of the logs on the fire, and then a great muttering as the name of *Flint* went round the room, which name some knew and some did not. So those who knew told those who did not, that Captain Flint was the most sadistic and atrocious pirate who ever sailed, and was now, most fortunately, dead.

But then Mr Hawkins recovered himself. He frowned, and took a gulp from his tankard, and surely it was raw spirit that went down his throat because it gave him courage.

'Who the damnation are *you*?' he said, and stumbled and staggered, and with gleeful help from the folk, managed to get down from his table and advance upon Billy Bones, with the crowd all eager for the fun. 'Who are you to tell me what song to sing?' said Hawkins, 'What man shall say what song I may sing in my own house, indeed?'

'Aye!' said some voices.

'Go on Mr 'awkins!' cried others, and Andrew Hawkins, puffed up with support from all around — or so he thought — slammed down his tankard on a table, spilling half the contents, and made a great pantomime of pushing the people apart to clear a space.

'Back!' he cried, staggering and sweating.

'Back! Back!' cried the company in mockery, and they heaved benches and tables, scraping and groaning, aside, and people stood shoulder to shoulder, jam-packed staring inward, holding their breath for what might follow.

'So, you villain!' cried Andrew Hawkins. 'You'll tell me what songs to sing, shall you? Oh no you shan't, by Heaven, because I shall pummel sense into you! So put up your fists and fight like a man!' And to a resounding cheer, he took up the ludicrous imitation of a man at fisticuffs: legs bent, arms raised and his belly hanging over his belt, such that he looked more like a man straining at stool, than ever he did a pugilist. So everybody laughed, everybody but his wife, myself and Billy Bones, who calmly laid a hand on his cutlass hilt. At which Andrew Hawkins, in his drunken anger, stamped and roared defiance and pulled a large clasp knife from his pocket, opened the blade, and stood with it poised in his hand as if to throw it.

All present gasped and I knew that I must act.

This, because I could see that Billy Bones was a practised killer. He was like others that I had known in my military service; some men take kindly to killing and become easy in the doing of it. They are disturbed and wounded creatures, corrupted by the horrors they have seen. But they are deadly dangerous, and I knew that Mr Bones would cut down a man like slicing bread. So I knew that I must act, and yet I held back because the Devil whispered in my ear. *What if you did nothing, Dr Livesey?*

What if there were a fight?

What if Hawkins died?

Who then would comfort his widow?

I confess that I paused and listened. But by the Grace of God I put temptation behind me and pushed into the middle of the room. 'Make way,' I cried, taking advantage of my reputation among the people, 'make way for the doctor!' I took advantage of that my professional clothes: black coat, knee britches, white stockings and the powdered wig that proclaimed my status.

In all modesty, I was not the worst doctor in England, and had done my best for many of those present. So there was a change in mood on all sides, with men tugging forelocks and women making curtsies in my honour, and the noise of the room fading away.

Soon I stood between Mr Hawkins and Mr Bones and looked at each of them in turn and delivered a resounding speech that had more certainty in its words than ever was present in my mind. 'Now, sirs,' I said, 'all present know that I am a magistrate as well as a physician.' I looked around and everyone nodded. 'Thus I cannot stand by and see violence done in this house! Know that, and know that I stand for the law, and command forces that will rout out and prosecute all those who break the King's law!' I looked around again. 'God bless King George,' I said, then paused, and added in a strong, deliberate voice: 'God... save... the... King!' It was only a modest device, by the standards of parliamentary rhetoric, but it worked on these loyal folk.

'God save the King!' they all cried, and I was victor of the field from that instant, with the people growling agreement with everything I said.

'Now, Mr Hawkins,' I said. 'You run a good house here, and I am sure that you wish to keep your license and your business. So put away that knife like the good fellow that you are.'

'Yes, Doctor, indeed Doctor,' he said, and mumbled much apology in a brandy-soaked voice, and he did indeed put away the knife before raising a respectful finger to his brow for myself and Mr Bones, because now that he was calmer, Hawkins realised what an abysmal idiot he had been in attempting to challenge such a man as he. So I turned to Mr Bones.

'And *you*, sir,' I said, 'I do not rightly know, but I see from your dress that you are a seaman, and from your speech that you are an Englishman.'

'Aye,' he said, 'I am both o' those,' and he dithered a second, licked his lips, frowned in thought and slowly raised a hand to his hat in salute, acknowledging the authority that he supposed me to represent.

'Ahhhhhh!' said our audience, in a communal sigh at seeing the bear chained up and obedient to his betters.

'So,' I said, 'Mr Hawkins and Mr Bones! As Englishmen both, I call on you to shake hands and bring this matter to a close.' This they did, with more willingness on Mr Bones' side than Mr Hawkins', but Hawkins was fuddled with drink, and Mrs Charlotte instantly came forward and led him away to his bed without a single glance at me, which stabbed me with pain because I had spoken out only for her, and certainly not for Hawkins.

After that, the people decided that the fun was over for the night and they left, pulling on mufflers and greatcoats and breathing steam into the black, cold night outside the door. Soon I found myself and Mr Bones stood facing each other, and myself weary from everything that had passed that day, and badly needing to sit down, and take a bit of food and drink. Since Bones was staring straight at me, and because we should soon be the only men in the parlour, it seemed ill-bred to turn my back on him and sit down by myself. Also I must confess that he intrigued me as a man who must have a fascinating past. So I addressed him.

'Will you keep company with me a while, Mr Bones? And perhaps take a glass at my expense?'

'Right kind of your honour,' he said, touching his hat again, 'I'd be obliged.'

So we took a seat by the fire, with Jim Hawkins smiling and rushing forward to drag tables and chairs to our convenience in anticipation of the tip I usually gave him. Billy Bones and I sat down and I know not what he made of me, except that he was polite after a fashion. As for my impression of him, I saw that I was looking into the face of a deeply sad, deeply troubled man, who sighed heavily from time to time, as if dreadful matters weighed upon him, which indeed they did as I later discovered, confirming the truth of my first impressions. Meanwhile, the malicious imp that was Jim Hawkins was standing at my elbow, with a white cloth over his arm and an eager expression on his face.

'What might by your pleasure, Mr Bones?' I asked.

'Rum!' said he. Jim smirked at that, and winked at me in his familiar way.

'As usual, Captain, sir,' said Hawkins to Billy Bones, and gave a little bow.

'Have you eaten, Mr Bones?' I asked.

'Aye,' he said, 'I always haves me supper at the turn of the after-noon watch.'

This meant absolutely nothing to me other than the fact that he had eaten.

'Then will you forgive me if I dine?' I said. 'I am famished.'

'Get to your vittles, Doctor,' he said, 'and never mind me.'

So I ordered food and a bottle of wine, and off went Jim through the door that led down a passageway into the kitchen, to make up my order.

'And leave that door ajar!' said Billy Bones to Jim, 'for I'll have no ears to keyholes!'

'Of course not, Captain,' said Jim, as if the thought had never occurred to him.

'Huh!' said Bones. 'Discipline is the thing for boys, Doctor. Discipline!'

And so we sat talking over the food and drink: Billy Bones telling of the sea life, and I recounting my experiences as a soldier, which greatly interested him, since for all the violence of his seafaring life, he had never seen a battle on land between formed troops, with cavalry on the wings and cannon balls bounding across the field and smashing poor devils into minced meat. I think he saw me as a kindred spirit when I told him that, after being wounded at Fontenoy, I was so horrified by the scale of human misery brought by warfare that I gave up soldiering.

'Hard times, Doctor,' he said, and he shook his head heavily. 'But I seen worse.' He paused and looked at me, and I had the feeling that I get when a patient hesitates to take me into his confidence.

'Go on, Mr Bones,' I said, with a little smile and a nod of the head, such as I might give to a man who will not list his symptoms for fear of being sentenced to surgery. On these occasions a good doctor must show a little kindness and a great deal of sympathy, and by this means Billy Bones was persuaded to speak.

'I done bad things, Doctor,' he said, 'things even Jesus won't forgive.'

'Come now, Mr Bones,' I said, 'there is salvation for those who repent.'

'Not for me, Doctor. 'I burned ships, and I killed men in their beds, and all because I sailed along o' Flint.'

I would have asked more, but I heard movement on the stairs, and there came Mrs Charlotte, down from putting her husband to bed. This time she looked straight at me with a nervous smile and I forgot Mr Bones and my half-eaten dinner. Indeed I forgot all the world but her. She smiled and walked across the room and into the kitchen passage, and there she stopped and looked back at me as if to say something, but despaired of words and merely raised her two hands in helpless appeal.

'Beg pardon, Mr Bones,' I said, and was across the room and at her side in an instant, and the pair of us whispering, since Billy Bones was watching, and the boy Jim lurking somewhere.

'Can I be of assistance, ma'am?' I said, finding no better words.

'I could not speak earlier,' she said.

'I understand, ma'am.'

'How can I thank you, Doctor? My husband was such a fool tonight.'

'You never need thank me for anything, ma'am. I am forever in your service.'

'I know,' she said.

Those were all the words that passed between us: all the words that could — or should — pass between a decent married woman and a doctor who thought himself a decent man. But a wealth of meaning was within the two words 'I know', because Charlotte Hawkins made clear in those words that she understood my feelings for her. More than that, I knew that my feelings were returned, because — to my sublime delight — she reached out one small hand and touched my cheek. Then she turned with a sob, ran off into the kitchen and busied herself clattering pots and pans.

I must have walked back to my chair, though I do not remember doing so, not with such emotions inside me, and being so tired that I could barely keep awake. But eventually I was sitting opposite Billy Bones, who was speaking of a girl he'd once loved, surely guessing what had passed between myself and Mrs Charlotte.

'Sweethearts we was,' he said, 'after I saved her and her pa from pirates, aboard the West Indiaman *Isabelle Bligh*, homebound for England. Her name was Olivia Rose: *Livvy* Rose, I called her, and I promised her I'd be a good boy.' He sighed and looked down at his boots. 'But I weren't no good boy, 'cos I sailed along o' Flint.'

So powerful was the name of Flint that it brought me back to my surroundings.

'Do you mean Flint the pirate?' I asked.

'The very same,' he said.

'Did you know him?

'Aye! I knew him. And that was Flint's own song that the swab Hawkins was singing this night. The song that Flint sang through London when they took him to Tyburn for hanging.'

'And *was* he hanged?'

'No, not Flint! Not him! Not my jolly rascal! Not my bounding boy! He escaped to sail again.'

'And you sailed with him?'

'Aye!'

'Then were you too… a pirate?'

Billy Bones paused and thought, and called for more rum, which Jim Hawkins brought with such speed that he had surely been listening from somewhere.

'Leave the bottle,' said Billy Bones.

'Aye-aye, Captain!' said Jim, with the mockery of a seaman's salute, and as he turned to go, Billy Bones caught him such a fine kick up the breech that I had to smile. Then Billy Bones took a pull of rum straight out of the bottle and looked at me.

'Was I a pirate, says you?' He put his head on one side. 'Are you asking as a man or as a magistrate?'

'As a man.'

'Then yes. I was a pirate. I was Flint's first mate, and one of the worst aboard, and my only hope is that even the Devil won't take me when the time comes, 'cos Saint Peter won't let me come aboard. Not him! Not no-how! Not Billy Bones.'

'So what happened to Flint?

'Dead. It was me that put the penny pieces on his eyes, to close 'em.'

Billy Bones' words made my own eyes even heavier than they already were. I was longing for my bed and for sleep. But I had just one more question before I got up and climbed the weary stairs to find my room.

'*How* did he die?' I asked, 'how did Flint die?'

'Too long a tale for tonight, Doctor. But it were one man's doing.

'Who?'

'The only man that Flint was afraid of.'

CHAPTER 3

'Silver?' said the gentleman. 'Long John Silver?' You ask about him?'

The gentleman smiled at the four young seamen who stood opposite him with their hats in their hands, while he sat at ease beside Mr Douglas Seagrove, owner of the liquor shop which was cleared of all other persons for this meeting. In addition, the table in front of the gentleman and Mr Seagrove was covered with a black cloth, to hide what lay beneath.

The liquor shop was a long timber shed full of benches and tables and with an earth floor. There were store-rooms and a cook-house, and a row of jugs and barrels at one end from which drink was served, with a dozen girls to do the serving. But today there were no girls, in order to secure the privacy that comes from the absence of their pretty little ears. Rough as it was, and such as it was, it was the best liquor shop in Savannah, and it was protected from the sickly heat by a good thatched roof and broad veranda shades over the doors and windows.

Meanwhile, the four young seamen stood awaiting the answer to their question, while gazing respectfully at Mr Seagrove — because he was one of the great men, not only of Savannah, but of the entire Royal Colony of Georgia. So they looked closely at him, but they did not look closely at the gentleman *beside* Mr Seagrove, and they certainly did not look straight into *his* eyes, because if they did, then even though the gentleman was the most civilised and mannerly of gentlemen, and spoke in cultured tones... despite all that, if they looked into *his* eyes they saw something unholy, they saw something occult. To be precise, they felt the chilling paralysis that grips a man who faces a maniac. And yet and withal, the gentleman had charisma. He fascinated and dominated the four young seamen, and had filled their minds with wonderful tales of adventure and loot, and riches and women, and fine living and grog, and every last, single thing that seizes hold of a young man's imagination and drives out all else.

In return, the gentleman was fully aware of the effect that he had on other men. He knew it very well indeed. But he merely smiled and sat comfortably, and took another sip of the Spanish wine in the glass in front of him. There was a bottle of the same and a full glass of it in front of Mr Seagrove. But Seagrove had not taken a drop, even though it was the best wine in the house. It was the best because the gentleman chose only the best. Thus, he was the best-dressed man in Savannah. His linen was white, his fingernails clean, his clothes fresh — and he was smooth as a cat, with an olive, Mediterranean skin. He moved like an athlete and had a beautiful, brilliant smile. He was slim-built and only of average height, but men always thought of him as tall.

'Long John Silver?' said the gentleman, 'Do we speak of a one-legged man with the green parrot?'

'Aye, Cap'n,' said one of the four seaman, 'one leg and a parrot. That's what they say.'

'But do they, now?' said the gentleman, leaning forward as if in diligent inquiry, 'and are they accurate in their description? Do they say that his face was broad and blond, and that he was taller than other men? Do they say that he was always clean and neat? Do they say that he leans upon a crutch but is, none the less, a devil in a fight? And do they say that it was the *left* leg that he lost? Up close to the hip? And do they say that the parrot can nip off fingers at a bite, and constantly cries *Pieces of eight! Pieces of eight! Pieces of eight!*?' The gentleman was ranting now, and his eyes blinked fast and his fists clenched. But then he relaxed, and he laughed and nudged Mr Seagrove, who smiled uneasily.

'Well, my boys,' said the gentleman, 'you may be reassured that — whatever you may have heard — Long John Silver has lost all interest in our enterprise, and even if he had not,' and here the gentleman's face lost its smile and became, for an instant, extremely ugly, 'even if he had not,' repeated the gentleman, 'then you may rely entirely upon me, to deal with him.'

Then, the gentleman smiled again and stood up so smartly that everyone jumped, and he laughed. 'Come with me,' he said, and walked to one of the windows: a mere hole in the wall, closed with shutters against the sun. He threw open the shutters to reveal a grand panorama of the squalid settlement that was Savannah; a collection of greasy log-houses, laid out on a Roman-style, right-angled grid some eight hundred yards wide by six hundred yards long, with a massively ditched and palisaded fort at one end, from which a Union Flag hung limp in the still air. It was noon, and the streets were empty, with the citizens sheltering from the heat. The gentlemen turned and beckoned to Seagrove and the four young seamen. Then he swept a hand at the view.

'I give you Savannah!' he declared. 'Capital city of Georgia: youngest and most southerly of the thirteen colonies of British America. I give you Savannah, home of the General Assembly of Georgia where democracy rules, headed by His Grace the Governor. But of still greater interest, my boys, look just over there,' and he pointed, 'where we can see the topmasts of the ocean-going vessels that have come up the Savannah river from the Atlantic, and are now anchored beneath our sight, because here the river runs deep and muddy, through a channel forty feet below the town.' The four young seaman looked at the cluster of masts.

'Which is yours, Cap'n?' asked one of them.

'Why, that one, dear boy!' replied the gentleman. 'See there? The one wearing British colours over Spanish? Do you not see her topmasts, over there to the right?'

'Aye, Cap'n!' they chorused, and nodded to each other.

'That is my ship *Revenge*,' said the gentleman, 'a brig of two hundred tons, mounting eight six-pounders and already well manned.'

'With a tasty Spanish prize astern of her,' commented Seagrove.

'Indeed, sir!' said the gentleman. 'And now, *brother*s…' he said to the four young men, 'because I hope I may soon call you that?'

'Aye, Cap'n!' said the four, knowing the significance of the word, and so keen to become *brothers* that the gentleman sniggered at their eagerness while inwardly chastising himself for the one and only fault which he acknowledged in his person: the compulsion to laugh at the gullibility of others, on occasions when it was best that he kept his face serious. So he controlled himself and continued.

'Brothers-as-you-soon-shall-be,' he said, 'take careful note that the weather in Savannah is so very hot and steamy that it causes things to rot.' He paused and gazed earnestly at his listeners, none of whom knew what the devil he was talking about. Again he felt the urge to laugh, as they nodded without understanding. But he crushed the laughter and continued. 'In similar fashion, 'the geographical position of Savannah — so close to the Spanish Main and West Indies — causes *the morals of men* to rot, especially when a ship comes up-river with a prize, but without the legal papers to prove that the prize was legally taken.'

'Oh!' said the four, and they grinned as they began to understand.

'Thereby,' the gentleman went on, 'in Savannah, King George's law runs only on Sundays.' Mr Seagrove nodded at this. 'Today is Thursday,' said the gentleman, 'and there is business to be done!' The gentleman placed a hand upon Mr Seagrove's shoulder as if in friendship, yet Mr Seagrove cringed. 'Or at least, dear boys,' said the gentleman, 'there is business to be done by men such as myself who are well-connected.' He smiled at Seagrove. 'Isn't that so, my dear sir? Assemblyman as you are, and future *President* of the Assembly as you aspire to become?'

'Yes,' said Seagrove, putting profit before fear.

'Good!' said the gentleman, and he walked back to the table covered with the black cloth, which he whisked away like a matador working his cape, and the four young seamen goggled at what was revealed: four brace of heavy, sea-service pistols with a half-dozen of cartridges for each, and four cutlasses with scabbards and baldrics.

'There, my jolly boys!' said the gentlemen, 'If you would become brothers and sign articles, then equip yourselves with the tools that turn a common seaman into a gentleman of fortune! And after that? Why! Say goodbye to all those who might care for you, and present yourselves aboard the good ship *Revenge* with all your traps and baggage, by the turn of the first dog watch.'

'Aye-aye, Cap'n' said the four young seamen, stamping feet and raising fingers to brows in naval salute, before falling upon the luscious goods laid out on the table.

The gentleman and Mr Seagrove stood back and smiled as the four young seamen laughed and joked and stuck pistols in their belts and cartridges in their pockets, then slung baldrics over their shoulders while constantly turning to the gentleman and saluting, over and over again.

'On your way now, lads,' said the gentleman, 'and don't be late, because we sail this day with or without you. We sail for England to begin our great enterprise.'

'Aye-aye, Cap'n!' they said once more, fairly grovelled in their joy and finally backed out of the gentleman's presence before running off with whoops and cries of delight, slamming the big front door behind them.

'Huh!' said Seagrove, 'Will that be the last of them?'

'Yes,' said the gentleman, 'with those four. I have all the men I need, provided you can get me a first mate to work a chart and quadrant.'

'You'll have him tonight,' said Seagrove. 'His name is Edward Arrow. He's a good navigator, and has detailed local knowledge of Cornwall, where you're bound. But as for his character — you must take him as you find him, for he's the best I could get, for such work as yours.'

'Accepted,' the gentleman replied.

'And now, by God, I'll take a drink and a damned bloody big one!' said Seagrove. So the two men sat down again, and Seagrove drained his glass and filled it again from the bottle on the table. The gentleman watched him and took another tiny sip. Seagrove felt better with the wine inside him, and asked questions that needed answering.

'Can you control your crew? This isn't an ordinary voyage. Not even by your standards. So, can you manage them?'

'Oh, I think I can do that,' smiled the gentleman, then he put his head on one side and looked steadily at Seagrove. 'Have you ever seen a man disembowelled?' he asked. 'And more than that, *forced by his own efforts* to draw out his bowels… in punishment?'

Seagrove hesitated.

'No,' he said.

'Well,' said the gentleman, 'this is how it is done. You must take a hammer, a nail, a hook and a sharp knife. Then tie the offender to the mainmast, and keep a flaming torch ready…' The gentleman continued, giving such details that Mr Seagrove felt sick by the time the gentleman was done, ending with the words: '…and any man who has seen this procedure, never dreams thereafter, of disobeying my orders.'

He reached for the bottle. 'More wine, my dear Seagrove?'

'Yes,' said Seagrove, and finished the bottle. Then he changed the subject, seeking anything to rid his mind of what he had just heard. 'How's your wound?'

'Fully healed,' said the gentleman, 'thanks to an excellent surgeon.'

'But you nearly died.'

'Indeed I did.'

'And you've bounced back something wonderful since then.'

'Indeed I have.'

Seagrove looked at the empty bottle.

'I'll get another,' he said. 'Do you want more?'

'No,' said the gentleman, 'but I shall not stand in the way of your pleasure.'

Soon after, and fortified from within, Seagrove resumed his questions.

'Was it Silver that shot you?'

The gentleman's eyes began to blink, and his fists clenched. Seagrove knew he was treading dangerously, but there were things he had to know before funding the expedition this gentleman had in mind. So Seagrove waited nervously until the gentleman replied.

'It was not Silver himself who shot me,' he declared. 'It was his wife.'

'Selena?' said Seagrove. 'The black girl?'

'The transcending lovely black girl,' said the gentleman, 'the incomparable, wonderful and luminously *glorious* black girl.'

'*She* shot you?'

'Yes.'

'Everyone thinks it was Silver.'

'Everyone is wrong,' stated the gentleman, and Seagrove drank more wine. He needed it.

'Does Silver know what you're going after?'

'He cannot know. He thinks I am dead.'

'And is he really not after it himself?'

'No. He is not after it himself.'

'And how do you know that Billy Bones has the papers?'

'I was listening when they all thought I was dead, and I have made enquiries since.'

'So you *do* know about Billy Bones — and Silver don't?'

'Yes,' said the gentleman, ' I know, and he does not, and I am therefore a better man than he.' The gentleman smiled. 'Well,' he said, 'at the very least, I am the better placed.' And he laughed, suddenly and loudly, and Seagrove flinched, as he tried to understand this profoundly disturbing man, who might become the source of immeasurable wealth.

'But you were so close in all things,' said Seagrove.

'Yes,' agreed the gentleman, 'it was always the two of us.'

'Long John Silver as quartermaster,' said Seagrove, 'and yourself as captain… Captain Flint.'

CHAPTER 4

From Dr Livesey's journal:

I called at the Admiral Benbow frequently that winter, because Mr Andrew Hawkins was drinking himself to death, and the process was exacerbated by a congestive hypertrophy of the heart. This condition I diagnosed by the methods of *palpation, auscultation and percussion*, as we doctors say in our pompous dignity, but which in the King's English means feeling the chest, pressing an ear against it and tapping with a finger.

So I was frequently able to see Mrs Charlotte, which caused me both delight and despair, and likewise I was frequently in the company of Mr Billy Bones, who became a great source of information to me on all things seafaring, though he would never return to the subject of Flint's death, nor the only man that Flint feared.

I found Mr Billy Bones to be a plain and simple man, much wounded by adversity. But he had been a navigating officer aboard the King's ships until he fell into piracy, and had enough education 'to take my noon observation and plot a course' as he put it. So he was no mere hand before the mast, and he had the big fists and heavy boots that drove lesser men to their duties.

I know that he liked me, because there were occasions when the weather was clear and I had time to spare, when he would invite me to take walk along the headlands, bringing a big, brass telescope so that we could spy out the ships passing down the coast. He always treated me with politeness, and he sought to explain the bewildering differences between one ship's rig and another, touching his hat in salute, with words such as:

'Beggin' your pardon, Doctor, but if you'd take the glass and cock an eye on that 'un there, why, you'll see she ain't a *brig*, not properly, but what we calls a *snow*.'

It was his way of offering instruction and also — if I do not probe beyond reason — I think that it was his way of finding someone whom he could respect and admire, because although he would not discuss the death of Captain Flint, it was obvious that he had admired the man enormously, and would have followed him down the cannon's mouth. Because Billy Bones was a man who had need of an idol. He needed someone set before him: someone whom he would follow with the devotion of a faithful hound. It made me uneasy to think that he saw me as such a man, but I suspect that he did.

'He was a roaring boy was Flint,' Billy Bones said once, 'he had the Devil in his eyes, and there weren't no man as could face him... no man but one.'

'Who was that?' I asked, but he shook his head and turned away.

Meanwhile Mr Andrew Hawkins deteriorated such that the boy Jim would be sent by his mother to fetch me at unconscionable hours of freezing, winter nights. But I always turned out of bed gladly, and threw on my heavy clothes and mounted up in haste, at the thought of seeing Mrs Charlotte.

One vile night, I was riding towards the Admiral Benbow, relying entirely on the native sense of my good Dulcie who knew the ground well, since all that I could see was the cliff edge to my right, with the gleaming black sea beyond, and frozen white fields on either side. The roadway in the lane was near invisible, with only a thin moon giving light and the hedges throwing deep shadows. So Dulcie was galloping on animal instinct, and she was galloping only because Jim Hawkins was ahead of me on one of the inn's horses, which he was whipping as if to skin it alive, and I was determined not to be left behind by the likes of him, which was wrong of me, but still I pressed on.

At the inn we dismounted. I trusted Dulcie to Jim Hawkins and hurried in through the front door, where Mrs Charlotte stood dressed in an Indian silk banyan and turban against the cold, and the two serving girls beside her in mop-caps and dressing gowns. They stood blinking and worrying and looked to their mistress in alarm. Lights were burning, there was a fire in the parlour, and I stopped briefly to throw off my greatcoat, hat and scarf and warm my fingers — which would have been useless to a doctor, as cold as they were. It was so late that there was no company in the house, only Mr Billy Bones — fully dressed — sat in his accustomed seat by the fire, and tipped his hat at me as I entered.

'Doctor,' said Mrs Charlotte, coming close, 'he fell in the tap room! My husband fell! He was smitten with the apoplexy, and the girls and I couldn't move him, and we'd never have got him to bed without Mr Bones' help, who carried him upstairs.'

'Aye,' said Billy Bones. 'Couldn't let him lay there in the cold. Not a shipmate.'

'Thank you, Mr Bones,' said Mrs Charlotte.

'Pleasure, ma'am,' was Billy Bones' response.

'You did well, sir!' I said, and Billy Bones saluted.

'And now my husband fights for breath,' said Mrs Charlotte, 'and I fear for his life, and so we sent for you, Doctor.' She looked at me, and laid a hand on my arm, and the longing for her came over me. But I kept my feelings close, and I nodded at her words, though I already suspected that if Hawkins had fallen in the tap room, then drink was heavily involved.

'Take me to him,' I directed her, and she did, lighting the way with a candle, to the upstairs corridor and the room where Hawkins slept. As ever — in the shame of my envy — I was glad to know from common gossip that Hawkins and Charlotte no longer shared a marriage bed. Then I was at his bedside, with the stench of rum assaulting me every time Hawkins breathed out. He was blue in the face, mouth wide, throttling for air, and his pulse thudding and bounding. But he was alive and in no imminent danger, so there was little I could do, other than call for more pillows to get him upright in bed so he should not drown in his own spittle, and as Mrs Charlotte and I heaved him about, her arms brushed mine and I thrilled at the sensation.

'Shan't you bleed him, Doctor?' asked Mrs Charlotte, gazing into my eyes, when we had her husband sat up to my satisfaction. 'Shan't you let him some blood? Won't that help?' As she spoke, I looked down at Andrew Hawkins' forearm, where a good fat vein stood out just waiting for the lancet. I could indeed have let him some blood. Almost every doctor in England would have done the same, since it was universally acknowledged that blood-letting was of great benefit in cases of congestion of the heart.

'Please, Doctor,' said Mrs Charlotte, 'I know that my husband is imperfect…' and she paused, seeking safe words, 'and I know that you are… at my service…' She paused again, and the two of us looked at one another over the rum-soaked, stinking, snorting hulk of her husband.

'I know all that,' she said, 'but ...' and words failed her and the Devil tempted me again.

What if you let some blood, Dr Livesey, as everyone says you should?
What if you let enough for Hawkins to slip away?
Who would know that you acted deliberately?
Who would even care?

So I looked at my instrument case and I even reached a hand towards it. But right prevailed.

'No,' I said. 'That won't help him. He's breathing easier now. Keep a fire in this room to warm him, and have someone come in regularly to make sure he has not slipped down from his pillows.' So we left him, and Mrs Charlotte asked if I would take some food and drink against the cold night, in her private parlour. It was common politeness that I accepted, and with one of the serving girls close by, there was no impropriety. Thus I enjoyed a quiet hour with Mrs Charlotte, in a cosy room, over some warmed-up pigeon pie and a tankard of brandy and hot water, brought in by the girl. Mrs Charlotte sat on one side of a small table, and on the other, and I looked at her in the candle light and was stabbed with her loveliness. Then she made me smile.

'You look strange without your wig, Doctor,' she said.

'No time to put it on, ma'am,' I said, 'and it doesn't fit well under a fur hat.'

'You look younger without it,' she said, and I was ludicrously flattered.

'Why didn't you bleed my husband?' she asked. 'I saw you look to your instruments, and yet you didn't bleed him.'

I sighed. I could not possibly tell her all that had been in my mind. 'I have reasons, ma'am,' I said, 'but they are tedious to recount.'

'Perhaps not,' she said, and smiled, and I could not resist her.

'Then do you know that I was once a soldier, ma'am?'

'Yes. Folk talk about that.'

'But I was a doctor first: trained first by my father and then by Cambridge University. I was a doctor until I was twenty-six, when my Uncle Williams — *General* Williams — filled me with the nonsense that a young man should be a soldier, and bought me a commission in the foot guards.'

'And did you serve?'

'Yes, for five years, and fought as a major at Fontenoy, where I was wounded.'

'Oh!' she cried in concern, and I was delighted to see that she cared.

'It was nothing,' I said, 'I was cut by a French sword.'

'Oh!' she said and reached out a hand to touch mine, which thrilled me to my bones.

'Nothing to dwell on, ma'am, ' I said, 'the surgeon sewed me up, and God healed me.'

'And does this bear on your not bleeding my husband?'

'It does ma'am, it does indeed, because I lost so much blood on that occasion and became so very weak, that I took it as a sign from Almighty Providence, that no good comes of opening a man's veins, and so I never do it. Indeed the very thought of it revolts me.'

'And yet you are a fine doctor,' she said, 'and a fine man.' She looked at me with such admiration that I weakened and would have taken her hand in mine, but the servant girl came in to clear away my plate and cutlery. So I sat back and behaved myself, even though she repeated the words when the girl was gone.

'You are a fine man,' she said.

'I do my best, ma'am,' I said. 'I try.' Which indeed I did: I tried very hard and later it was even harder because as I left the inn, there was nobody in the main parlour but ourselves. Billy Bones had gone to bed, one of the girls was washing my plate, the other attending to Mr Hawkins, and the boy Jim was gone to the stable for my horse. So I stood beside Mrs Charlotte with none to see.

'Thank you, Doctor,' she said. 'Send your bill and I will pay at once.'

'Yes, ma'am,' I said. Our words were formal but we stood so close that the desire to take her in my arms was unbearable, and it was my sure judgement that she would welcome the approach. But we stayed apart, because the burden of being decent folk sat so heavily upon us. So I never kissed her, nor swept her up into my arms and rode off with her, as I so much wanted to and as my very soul was longing to. The philosophers say that there is nothing so galling as the memory of temptation resisted, and so it was for me, and probably explains what happened next.

Thus I said goodnight to Mrs Charlotte, and walked off with torment inside me and went round to the stables, since the boy Jim had not appeared with my mare. At the door to the stables I found him waiting, with Dulcie beside him saddled up and ready for the road and her reins tied to a ring-bolt in the wall.

'Hallo, Doctor,' he said, and grinned. 'We need to have a word, you and I.' He spoke so pert and saucy, that I very nearly knocked him down then and there. But he was too small for a man of my size to do that. Also, his next words intrigued me.

'Do you know of a tall, seafaring man with one leg?'

I frowned. 'No,' I said. 'What do *you* know of such a man?'

He grinned again.

'Well, Doctor,' he said, 'it's not a matter of what *I* know, but what your friend Billy Bones knows.' And he stood smiling and silent, to season my appetite.

'Go on,' I said, 'let's hear what you have to say.'

'Well, Doctor, Mr Bones is so afraid of this man that he pays me a silver fourpenny on the first day of each month, to keep lookout for him, and warn Mr Bones if I see him.'

'And so?' I said.

'And so, Doctor, we come to yourself. We come to *yourself and my mother*,' and he gave a leering, sniggering wink, 'my mother, my own dear mother, upon whom you gaze with such hot desire as would melt pewter pots into puddles. And we come to the fact that I won't go telling all the neighbours, provided you pay me…'

I never did find out how much he wanted, or how often he wanted to be paid, because I fell upon him in that instant and took him by the collar, and dragged him into the stables, and slammed the doors to keep the noise inside. Then I found a horse-whip and gave him the finest thrashing of his life. By George, but he yelped! And I didn't stop till my arm was tired. Then I dropped him in a heap and leaned over him.

'Listen, you little monster,' I said, 'if ever I hear the like of that from you again, you'll get the same again, only ten times over. Do you hear me?'

'Yes,' he said, in a tiny voice.

'Yes, *Doctor*!' I said. 'Yes, *sir*!'

'Yes Doctor. Yes sir.'

'Good!' I said, and walked out. But then I turned and went right back.

'And if you say a word of this to your mother,' I said, 'you'll get it *a hundred* times over!' and I gave him a few more for luck , and good, strong, fine ones they were too!

Then I threw aside the whip and rode home, feeling oceans better than I had when I left Mrs Charlotte un-kissed — because even a decent man cannot be decent all the time. What's more, and despite all that happened later, I cherish the memory of the whacking that I gave Jim Hawkins, and of his outraged, terrified and incredulous expression as the blows fell down upon him. Served him right. Served him right indeed, and it worked too, because I heard no more of blackmail from Jim Hawkins.

But I heard *much* more of the seafaring man with one leg.

CHAPTER 5

The Spyglass Tavern was neat, bright and prosperous, and being on the waterfront of Bristol's docks, it was much favoured by seafaring men from the vast ocean-traffic that flowed through that great port. Thus the likeness of a giant telescope hung outside as a sign, fashioned in wood and painted up like brass, and windows ran down the sides of the main room, with pretty red curtains and a fine view outside to the quayside. There, seamen and stevedores mixed with clerks, tarts and merchants, and everyone was talking, and the cart-wheels rumbling, and the horse-hooves clopping and the masts, yards and rigging rising thick as a hedge from the anchored ships. It was life and commerce writ large. It was the thriving trade of a maritime nation, and a joy to see.

Meanwhile inside the Spyglass, the floor was cleanly sanded, there were doors wide open in welcome, and there were clouds of tobacco smoke, and a growl of conversation in many languages besides English, such that all in the same day a visitor might hear Dutch, Spanish, Portuguese and Breton, and French too — because even with another French war coming just around the corner, the profits of trade drew men to Bristol from every port of Europe.

But all these conversations stopped as a man came in through one of the doors, with a hand on the shoulder of a street-urchin, and a porter behind with a sea-chest. The man was plainly blind, because he tapped before him with a stick, and wore a green shade over his eyes and nose. But he was well-dressed and cared for, with a laced hat and a good boat-cloak over small-clothes, and he was sure of himself. He sniffed the smoke as he entered.

'Baccy!' he said, and shook the urchin's shoulder. 'Will this be the Spyglass Tavern, boy?' His voice was high and thin, and it was Welsh.

'Yessir!' confirmed the urchin.

'So,' said the blind man, and raised his voice. 'Would my old shipmate Israel Hands be aboard and within hailing?'

'Mr Hands is in the cellar, sir,' said one of the waiters. 'Who shall I say is asking?'

'Pew!' said the blind man, 'Emanuel Pew the sail-maker,' and the waiter went below, while Pew felt for an empty chair with his stick, and men moved away to avoid contact with him. Then he took off his cloak and sat down, folding the cloak on a chair beside him, and all the while fumbling with searching hands and un-seeing eyes, in a manner as eerie as the crawling of a spider. Finally he opened his purse and drew out coins, fingering them to make sure which was which, and gave payment to the urchin and porter who touched forelock, and went out leaving the chest beside Pew. 'Grog!' said Pew, loudly, 'and mind it ain't more than three-watered!'

With that, the conversations started again, and men minded their own business until Mr Israel Hands, host and proprietor, came up the cellar stairs and looked around. He was a small, wiry, intelligent man; quick and active in his movements. He saw Pew and bore down on him and the two men stood, and first they shook hands, but then they smiled and embraced like old friends.

'Brother Pew!' said Hands.

'Brother Hands!' said Pew. Then the two of them feared they'd been indiscreet and they looked round the room. But the company merely nodded and smiled, mostly being too young to know what *brother* might mean.

'There's a back room where we can talk,' said Hands, then he called to a waiter. 'Here's Mr Pew come aboard,' he said, 'so heave his goods aloft and make all fast in a good room.'

'Yes, Mr Hands!' said the waiter, and Hands took Pew's arm, and spoke quietly.

'Come along o' me, shipmate,' he said, 'there's a clear way between the tables and no steps nor stairs to trip you.' Soon they were seated in a small room with the door closed and a jug of grog and tankards on the table.

'Here's luck!' said Hands and raised his tankard. Pew nodded and raised his own tankard and gave a toast.

'Here's to ourselves, and hold your luff: plenty of prizes and plenty of duff!'

'Ah!' said Hands, 'that were Long John's favourite toast. The man himself!' and he repeated the words, and they both drank.

'So! Where is he?' said Pew, 'I thought you'd summoned all of us?'

'I did,' said Hands, 'and he's expected any day now, and I thought you'd be here yourself, a week ago, for I'd sent you a letter long since.'

'I would've been sooner,' said Pew, 'but I lives with my sister, see? And it's her that reads for me, but she's been sick abed, so sore as can't even read, and I couldn't let the maid read a letter from Israel Hands, for fear of what she might see inside of it. So it was only the day before yesterday my sister was fit and could read.' He took another drink. 'So here I am!' he said.

'Aye,' said Hands. 'We'll all have to keep traps shut on this,' and he shook his head. 'Maybe we should've seen it coming. Maybe we got soft.'

'Soft we are,' said Pew, 'We've lived fat on the money, see?'

'Aye,' said Hands, 'but it were well meant, 'cos Long John shared out the gold, fair and square. Him that set it aside years ago: a bit here, a bit there, all safe in banks, so's when we gave up the sea we could live rich.' Pew nodded.

'He even gave you this house to run,' said Pew, 'though it had to be you, see? Since you were the only one as could keep accounts and reckon up.'

'Aye,' said Hands, 'a master gunner has to keep records aboard ship. He can't be a common hand that signs with a cross. So I got this house. But we all got fair shares.'

'So what's going forward?' said Pew. 'Who's been asking questions about who?'

'It's Billy Bones,' said Hands, 'they're asking about Billy Bones. They know his name, they know what he looks like, and they say he's here in the west country.'

'Who are *they*?' said Pew. 'Seamen?'

'Aye.'

'That's bad,' said Pew, 'very bad.'

Hands nodded. 'It's worse,' he said. 'They know who Billy Bones sailed with.'

'Bloody buggery,' said Pew, and then his mouth fell open because no oath that he knew was strong enough, 'They ain't sent by...' he began, and he hesitated before speaking because Pew believed that to speak the unholy, is to summon it up, 'they ain't sent by... *Flint*?'

He uttered the name and in that unholy moment the two men jumped as if scalded, when feet rumbled and the door burst open.

'We've found him!' said a loud voice, 'He's at the Admiral Benbow Inn, off Black Cove outside Polmouth.'

'Tom Morgan!' said Pew, who could tell a man by his footsteps, let alone his voice.

'Pew!' said Morgan, 'Shipmate!'

'Pew!' said another voice.

'Blind Pew!' said a third, and Pew named them both.

'George Merry! Black Dog!' he said, and there were smiles and reunion, and more grog and tankards. But then back to business as all sat down together.

'Is it Billy Bones you've found?' said Hands.

'Aye,' said Tom Morgan, 'them other swabs had asked already and folk knew the answer quick by now, what with being asked before, and Billy Bones is an easy man to spot.'

'What other swabs?' said Pew.

'Them who was asking after Billy Bones before us,' said Morgan.

'Aye!' said the rest.

'And who sent 'em?' wondered Pew, and this time he came right out with the name. 'Was it Flint?'

Tom Morgan sniffed. He looked at the rest and said nothing.

'Oh Jesus and Mary,' said Pew, 'Tell me it ain't Flint.'

'Aye,' said Israel Hands, 'cos Flint's dead.' He looked at Morgan. 'Flint's dead, ain't he? You know that Tom Morgan, 'cos you was there.'

'So I was,' said Morgan, 'I saw him dead, and Billy Bones asked me for pennies to close his eyes, and I gave him two pennies.'

'So he's dead,' said Pew.

'Aye,' said Israel Hands, but Morgan said nothing.

'So *is* he dead or *ain't* he?' cried Pew.

'The thing is, shipmates,' said Morgan, 'when we was asking folk about them who went round before us...'

'Go on! Go on!' said Pew.

'Well,' said Morgan, 'some said there was a special one among 'em. One in charge who wore fine clothes. One that smiled and spoke soft, but no bugger dared look him in the eye.'

'Hellfire and bloody damnation,' said Pew, 'It can't be him, 'cos he's *dead*.'

'Aye!' said Tom Morgan.

'But what if he ain't?' said Israel Hands, 'and he's after Billy Bones?'

'Then we got to warn him,' said Pew, 'once a shipmate, always a shipmate, see?'

'But he parted bad from us,' said Tom Morgan.

Then all fell silent as there came a polite knocking.

'Who is it?' cried Hands, and a waiter put his head round the door.

'Gentleman and a lady to see you, Mr Hands,' he said. Then he looked over his shoulder and turned back with an awestruck expression. 'A wonderful lady,' he said. 'Such a lady as I never saw in all my life!'

'Ah!' said Hands, standing up, 'Fetch 'em in!' Then all stood, including Pew because he'd heard the waiter step aside, then the rustle of a woman's gown, then one heavy footfall followed by the thump of a wooden crutch.

'Long John!' he said. 'Thank God you're here. Thank God and all his angels!'

CHAPTER 6

From Dr Livesey's journal:

Much more happened, and it happened very fast, in the weeks after Andrew Hawkins suffered his first stroke. It all came in a mad jumble, one thing on top of the other.

First, on a stone-hard day with frost on the fields, Hawkins had a second stroke, though this time up in his bedroom where he had been sleeping off a hard morning's drinking. It seems that he came down with a thump that shook the rafters below, and Mrs Charlotte and the girls rushed up, found him on the floor and put him back to bed. Then the boy Jim was sent, mounted, to fetch me.

By the time I reached the Admiral Benbow the business was nearly done. Hawkins was going out like a guttering candle: pulse dimming, breath slowing, legs cold from foot to thigh, and — as Shakespeare says of the dying Falstaff — his nose was sharp as a pen. Since Hawkins had been made comfortable there was nothing I could do, and soon he gave the death rattle and was gone, and I covered his head with the bed sheet.

Later, I took satisfaction that I was so filled with sympathy for poor Charlotte, that no demon entered my mind to rejoice that her husband was gone. Rather I was in pain at her distress, as she stood with one of the girls hanging on to her arm and weeping.

'He wasn't such a bad man, Doctor,' she said.

'No, ma'am,' said I.

'He never raised a hand to me. He was just weak.'

'Yes, ma'am.' Then she looked at me, as ancient guilt arose.

'And he was the best I could ask for, after my sins,' she said, and thinking of her pregnancy by the old squire, she burst into tears which so stabbed my heart that I would have taken her in my arms, except that from downstairs there came the howling of Jim Hawkins in terror.

'Mamma! Mamma!' He's killing me!'

So we ran down into the parlour to witness a scene as if in a play. The sun was setting, the shadows long, there was some company sat down, and Mr Bones was in his chair by the fire though rising with an oath, as through the open door came the sinister figure of a blind man with an eyeshade, and a great boat-cloak with the hood thrown over his head against the cold. But what seized our attention was the blind man's grip — a wrestler's lock — on Jim Hawkins' arm, which he twisted such that Jim nearly fainted with pain.

'You little swab!' cried the blind man. 'You little bilge rat. Knock my stick away, would you? Mock a poor blind man who's just asking for the Admiral Benbow inn? Take that, you louse,' and he twisted again.

'Ow! Ow! Ow! Mother! Mother! Mother!'

'My boy!' cried Charlotte, who never could — nor would — see ill in him.

'What's this?' I said. 'Let go of him!' But the blind man merely stamped in anger.

'Is this or *ain't* this, the Admiral Benbow inn?' he demanded. 'I summons all hands to speak up, or I'll wring the limb off this here chicken!' And he twisted again, and Jim yelped. Then Billy Bones spoke up. He spoke big and loud, because he knew the blind man.

'Pew!' he said. 'Who sent you? Was it Long John?'

'Aye, that it was,' said Pew, and shoved Jim Hawkins away such that the boy fell to the floor, before getting up and clinging to his mamma. Then, as Billy Bones stepped forward, Pew pulled a disc of thin card from his pocket and held it at arm's length towards Billy Bones and stopped him dead. The disc was two inches across, inked black on one side and had writing on the other.

'Avast!' said Pew. 'It was Long John that sent me, 'cos even you, Billy Bones, wouldn't meet a blind man with a blade or a pistol, while contrariwise you'd kill any other one of us! So I brings this, and you must take it.'

Bones dithered and licked his lips, then snatched the disc from Pew's hand, peered at the writing, and staggered as if from a blow.

'Rum!' he cried, 'Rum, for the love of God!' Then he looked at Pew and frowned, and his chin came up and he uttered another foul oath. Then:

'How long have I got?'

'You're an hour ahead of them at best,' said Pew, 'and they knows the bearings of you where you lies at anchor.'

'Then I'll cut my cable and run!' said Billy Bones, and turned to me. 'Doctor,' he said, 'can I take your horse, 'cos I hear she's a good 'un.' With that everyone looked at me, and here was a foul mess and no mistake: Mr Hawkins fresh deceased, the women in tears, half a dozen country folk and a blind madman in the parlour, the formidable Mr Bones quaking in terror, and unknown numbers of evil men about to fall upon us at any minute. But the crisis awoke the guards officer that slept within me, because someone had to take command, and so I did.

'Mr Bones,' I said, 'how good a horseman are you?'

'Don't know, Doctor,' he said, ''cos I've never put me leg across a nag.'

'In that case, we'll stand fast here and send for help,' I said, 'because this inn is built like a fort, while you'd be thrown in half a mile from my horse. 'So I need volunteers,' I said, 'one to ride to the Preventive Office and another to Trelawney Hall.' I looked round the room. 'Jim?' I said, knowing that whatever else he was, he could ride excellently, but he just buried his face in his mother's arms. Then one man raised a hand, and then another raised a second, though most of the company fled out of the door and ran for home. That left only myself and Billy Bones in defence, together with two odd little, wrinkled little, grizzle-haired brothers: Jamie and Ernest Woolacombe, who were notorious poachers and who grinned at the prospect of a fight. Meanwhile, blind Pew would not be caught behind locked doors.

'Beg pardon all, but I'll sling me hook,' he declared, 'cos if Flint's coming, and he catches us, then them as die'll be the lucky ones!' And with magical sense of location, he seized Jim Hawkins and twisted his arm again. 'Put me on the road for Polmouth, you little rat,' said Pew, 'and I'll let you go.' And he hauled Jim out of the door like lightning, with Billy Bones too stupefied to stop him, the two volunteers beyond reach on the far side of the room, while as for myself; what did I care for Jim Hawkins? Besides, there was much to do.

'Horses!' I said. 'To the stables!' And I ran outside with the volunteers behind, putting one on my Dulcie and the other on Jim's horse, both of which were still saddled, and each man got up like a horseman born and bred. 'You to the Preventive Office!' I said to the first man, 'and you to Trelawney Hall!' to the other. 'Say that you act in my name, and that they must come at once with all the armed men they can muster!'

'Yes, Doctor!' they said, and were off with hooves sparking the cobbles. Then I looked in the opposite direction along the Polmouth road. The sun was gone, but the moon was out and I saw Pew and Jim a hundred yards off, scuttling towards a two-wheeled, single-horse cart and driver that I supposed had brought Pew from Polmouth, because how else could a blind man have got here? But then came the thunder of hooves and the grinding of wheels as a heavy wagon laden with men, and the driver cracking his whip, came roaring down the road towards the cart and the Admiral Benbow.

Pew screeched, Jim shrieked and the two fought violently: Pew to hang on to his sighted guide and Jim to get free, as the wagon gathered a frightful speed, delivering a broadside of pistol fire into the cart as it passed, every shot of which missed — but the terrified horse bolted, dragging the empty cart bounding and swaying towards Polmouth, leaving Pew and Jim right in the path of the waggon.

Desperate with fear, Jim broke free and I cannot know if it was *deliberately* that he pushed Pew into the path of the wagon, but push him he did, then sped towards the Admiral Benbow, while Pew staggered blind and helpless and was run down: mashed, smashed and pulverised, by iron hooves and iron wheels. The two big draught horses reared up in fright, and the wagon slewed off the road, with men roaring and shouting and the driver hauling on the brake, and the wagon grinding to a stop, which gave time for Jim to reach the inn, and all of us to get safe inside, and to slam and bar every door and shutter in the house, where everyone looked to me for what we should do next.

'What arms have we got?' I asked, and Mrs Charlotte pointed to the brass-barrel blunderbuss that hung over the parlour fire: a huge example of its type that would fire a quarter-pound of shot.

'There,' she said, and I seized it.

'Is it loaded?' I asked.

'I don't know,' she said, so I opened the pan which was un-primed, then probed the bore with the ramrod, striking empty metal.

'Never mind, Doctor,' said Jamie Woolacombe, seeing my expression, 'we got our guns in the tap room where Mr Hawkins make us leave 'em, and we got the loadings too.' The brothers drew powder flasks and shot bags from their pockets and grinned right merrily.

'And I got two brace o' barkers in my sea chest,' said Billy Bones, stirring out of his daze, 'with powder and ball besides.'

'Well go to it, my boys,' I cried, 'you Woolacombes get to your loading, and you, Mr Bones, be so good as to stand guard at the door, and you, Jim Hawkins, fetch Mr Bones' pistols and powder — and be quick about it!'

'Here!' said Billy Bones, pulling a loop of string with a key attached from around his neck. 'This'll open my chest.' He threw it to Jim, who dithered and looked at his mother.

'Fetch the pistols!' I cried. 'Our lives are on it!'

So up the stairs he went at the run, while Mrs Charlotte gathered the two girls in her arms, the Woolacombes dashed into the tap room and emerged with a pair of fowling pieces, and Billy Bones spat on his hands, drew cutlass and stood ready.

'Goose shot, Doctor!' said Jamie Woolacombe, charging his gun, 'We'll get two or three of 'em at once with that.'

'Good man!' I said, and I gave him the blunderbuss. 'Load this too,' I said, and turned to Billy Bones. 'Have you plenty of pistol balls, Mr Bones?'

'Aye-aye, Doctor!'

'So! Mr Woolacombe?'

'Doctor?'

'Put a whole handful of balls on top of the powder in the blunderbuss, and ram well home with wadding!'

'Yes, Doctor!' said Jamie Woolacombe, and grinned at the thought.

'Mrs Charlotte,' I said, 'how best can we get sight of the ground outside the door?' She blinked and paused, and then — like the brave girl that she was — she nodded firmly.

'Upstairs front bedroom, Doctor, through the window!'

'Good!' I said. 'Then Jamie, get upstairs to cover the door, and Ernest, stand fast and wait for orders.'

'Yes, Doctor!' they said, and Jamie was off, nimble as a terrier, even as Jim Hawkins came down with an armful of pistols, powder and shot.

After that things fell silent for quite a while, as we doused lights so our enemies could not see in, and busied ourselves in the red glow of the fire, and while Mrs Charlotte and the girls kept watch through the loop holes, Billy Bones, Ernest Woolacombe and I — with precious little help from Jim Hawkins — loaded the blunderbuss and Mr Bones' pistols. These proved to be two exceptionally fine, silver-mounted pairs by Brudatour of Marseilles, beautifully made with crisp, sharp locks and long barrels.

Then there came shouts from outside and a clumping running of feet, and a great beating on doors and shutters.

At this, Jamie Woolacombe hailed me from upstairs.

'Am I to give fire, Doctor?' he asked. 'They're gathering round the front door and getting something from the wagon.'

'Not yet,' I said, 'we must not do murder, and perhaps they have no deadly intent.'

Which words I barely spoke before there was a smashing of glass as pistol barrels were thrust in through the loop-holes of the parlour windows, breaking the panes behind, and bellowing fire and smoke into the very room where we were standing. Some four or five shots were fired, then the pistols withdrawn, but by God's will none of us were hit, though we coughed in the smoke and the girls shrieked and clutched at Mrs Charlotte. And this they did, those villains outside, without even a warning or a demand that we open up!

'Fire at will!' I cried, and Jamie Woolacombe let fly, while Ernest Woolacombe blasted goose-shot out through one of the loopholes, and Billy Bones and I fired pistols through others, causing the most appalling shrieks and oaths from outside because, despite firing blind, we struck lucky.

'What sport!' cried Jamie Woolacombe from upstairs. 'Three laid dead on the ground, and another one limping as he runs!' But then a voice was yelling outside: a strong voice and a passionate voice; a voice that made men obey.

'Fall back!' it said. 'No further move without my command. Fall back and gather round me.'

Feet pounded, silence fell, we re-loaded and waited, and then our attackers grew clever. There were no more close-in attacks, instead there was careful, aimed fire at the loop-holes, causing balls to hammer and smack the woodwork all around them, such that we were indeed driven to retreat from them. That was bad, but worse followed. Up in the front bedroom, Jamie Woolacombe fired. His gun boomed and he laughed. 'Got you, you dirty dog!' he cried, then; 'Doctor?' he said.

'Yes?'

'I fired at the flash of his gun, and got the rogue! That makes four!'

'Well done Jamie!' I said. 'But don't show yourself.'

'Not me, Doctor!' he said. But then he did. A single shot came from outside, then Jamie returned it, and at least a dozen shots came in return, co-ordinated by some clever commander to concentrate on the window from which Jamie had fired. And so there was a great smashing and battering of shot on Jamie's window, and we downstairs heard Jamie's cry, then the dull rumble of his body falling to the planks of the floor.

'Oh no!' cried Ernest and ran upstairs, and we heard him weeping and sobbing but had no time to pay heed because there came another and serious attack, this time on the oak of the front door, where a pair of men were striking alternate and deliberate blows with heavy hammers. *One, two! One, two!* Dust and splinters leapt off the woodwork.

'Stand by, Mr Bones!' I said.

'Aye-aye!' he replied, and faced the shivering door with a pistol in one hand and a cutlass in the other, as I gave Mrs Charlotte a pistol and tried to give one to Jim Hawkins. But he just shook his head, even when one of the little serving girls spoke.

'I'll take it, Doctor,' she said.

'Good girl!' I said, and looked to Mrs Charlotte. 'I'm off upstairs,' I said, 'to see what I can do.'

'Be careful, Doctor,' she said, 'be careful, my dear man.' And this time I had no strength left to resist, so I kissed her on the lips not caring who might see.

'David!' she said.

'Charlotte!' I said, and I was hers and she was mine for ever... provided only that we survived the night.

So up the stairs at the run, fumbling in the dark for the front bedroom, and there lay Jamie Woolacombe in his brother's arms, shot twice and ugly through the head, and gone beyond aid. But I had brought the blunderbuss and a pistol, and, keeping my head well down, I crept to the window and fired one of Monsieur Brudatour's weapons at the stars. This produced the expected volley from the enemy outside, after which I stood up and gave fire from the blunderbuss with a dozen pistol balls over four drachms of black powder. I aimed where I guessed our enemies stood; the weapon thundered and kicked, the flash lit the night, scraps of wadding smouldered and fell, and men groaned and shrieked.

So they paid dear for Jamie Woolacombe.

But again, the strong, clear voice sounded, and as I ran downstairs again I heard the front door being smashed in, and men roaring and bellowing and firing pistols into the woodwork to break the door still further, which indeed they were doing, as nails yielded and timber groaned, while vigorous arms could be seen through the gaping planks, swinging hammers in the moonlight.

'Charlotte!' I cried, 'Get into the tap-room with the girls!'

'Take care, David!' she said, and she fell back, as did the boy Jim: miserable wretch that he was, he took no part in the fight.

'Stand by, Mr Bones!' I said.

'Aye-aye!' he said. Then, since I had not asked before:

'Who *are* they, Mr Bones? What do they want?'

'It's *him*,' he said. 'Out of his grave. And he's after what I've got.'

'Who is?'

'Flint,' he said, and no more words were possible, as the door fell down in shards and wreckage, and Billy Bones and I fired our pistols, and a fusillade came from outside, and Billy Bones was stumbling, and men were falling, and there came a great rushing of bodies over the ruined planks, and Billy Bones roared like a lion and laid on left and right with his cutlass, and I struck out with the fireside poker for want of anything better.

So it was Hell and Bedlam, and while I did my best, it was only the huge and furious Billy Bones that saved us. It was him, together with three shots fired, close-range at our enemies, in the wavering moment when either side might have prevailed: a charge of goose-shot from Ernest Woolacombe, come downstairs with his gun, and two rounds from Charlotte who would not cower in safety, but stood forth with the pistols I'd given her and the serving girl.

Then the enemy screamed and fled, and Billy Bones was out into the night, swinging one final and enormous blow that would have cleaved his victim from scalp to collar-bone, except that the cutlass thumped into the swinging sign of the Admiral Benbow, leaving a notch that survives — with great fame and reputation — even to this very day.

I followed fast behind Billy Bones, and only then realised that there was yet another reason why the villains were in flight. A pounding of hooves was approaching, as a body of horsemen charged down the road towards the Inn. I recognised Squire Trelawney in the lead with many others behind, hallooing as if on a hunt. Then Trelawney was upon us and out of the saddle, and embracing me and asking questions, while Mr Dance, the Supervisor of Preventives, was trying to master his leaping horse and yelling at Trelawney:

'Guard the inn, Squire!' he cried. 'Me and my lads'll run down the smugglers!'

*Smuggler*s he called them, thinking that was what they were, and off he galloped with his men in a thundering roar and a cloud of dust, down the Polmouth road after the wagon-load of our enemies.

Trelawney was high with excitement and swung me off my feet, so pleased that I was safe, and his followers cheered and all the horses bucked and whinnied, and I pushed free of Trelawney and threw my arms around Charlotte in such joy as I never felt in all my life.

'Oh-ho,' said Trelawney, to me. 'What's *this* then, you old dog?' But Charlotte was struggling and pointing.

'Look!' she said, 'Mr Bones!' and we all turned to see Billy Bones on his knees with a hand to his chest and his dinted cutlass fallen to the ground.

'Damnation!' I said — may I be forgiven such profanity — and we all of us fell upon poor Mr Bones and carried his great weight into the parlour, and the fire was made up and water on to boil, and my instrument case brought, and tired as I was, I was cutting open Billy Bone's' shirt and finding: damnation, damnation, damnation — I care not if I say it — a bullet wound in the centre of the broad chest.

He had been hit at the very outset of the fight but had refused to fall until his duty was done, God save the brave heart of him!

'Livvy Rose?' he said, but so softly that all of us — some dozen or more — leaned in to listen.

'What's he saying?' said Trelawney.

'Livvy Rose?' said Billy Bones, 'Is that you?' And everyone frowned in puzzlement.

'She was his sweetheart,' I said. 'Years ago. Before he fell into piracy.'

'Was he a pirate?' said Trelawney, 'I didn't know that.'

'Livvy Rose?' said Billy Bones, in a desperately sad voice. 'Where are you?' And nobody spoke. But then dear, kindly Charlotte leaned close to Billy Bones' ugly face.

'I'm here,' she said. 'It's Livvy Rose.'

'Ah!' said Billy Bones, and smiled.

'I'm sorry for all that I done,' he said. 'But I was a good boy at the last, wasn't I?'

'Yes,' said Charlotte. 'And nothing else matters.'

So Billy Bones gave a great sigh and died in peace.

CHAPTER 7

The longboat bumped alongside of the stern quarter of the brig *Revenge*, in the moonlight, in the wallowing swell, with the big vessel looming above and the black-dark inlet all around.

'Boat your oars!' said Flint, and the shaken crew obeyed, while up above, men leaned over the rail, eager for news.

'Did you get it Cap'n?' said Mr Arrow, the first mate, calling down. He was a large man, who affected ponderous dignity but was unclean of person, with lank hair and the smell of sweat wafting out of his tight-buttoned clothes, and fingernails as black as coal. He had little control over the men but was a gifted navigator, as indeed he had to be — or he'd never have been first mate. But now Flint was looking up from the stern sheets and shaking his head as if in sorrow.

'Mr Arrow, Mr Arrow,' he said, 'you may go to hear the dogfish bark. You may seek to find your arse with a hand mirror. You may do those things and many more. But do not repeat the question you have just asked.'

'Oh,' said Arrow, and flinched.

'Oh,' said all hands, clustered by the mainmast among the disciplined clutter of a sea-going ship: capstan, gratings, masts, yards, rigging and furled sails, plus a most considerable battery of guns for a supposedly honest merchantman. The men looked at each other in dismay, but they had no time to brood.

'Stand by to haul lumber aboard,' ordered Flint from the boat. 'For certain blockheads have managed to get themselves wounded.'

'Oh?' said all hands aboard the brig.

'Step lively!' said Flint, which was all the word needed from him to produce a stampede of action, as slings were rigged and lines lowered, and three badly-wounded men hoisted aboard and taken below for the attentions of what passed for a surgeon aboard *Revenge*: a tar named Gilbert who'd once been a sick-bay swabber in the King's navy.

Then there was a busy time rigging triple blocks to the mainstay tackles and yard arms, and hoisting the boat aboard, while Flint himself went swiftly up the side by the main chains and gave one further order.

'Make sail!'

'Where away, Cap'n?' said Arrow.

'To Polmouth, Mr Arrow, and come below so soon as the anchor is catted and fished, bringing Mr Hitchin and Mr Kelly in your wake.'

'Aye-aye, Cap'n!' said Arrow, who knew what was good for him. But there was a surly murmur from the hands, especially those out of the boat who were whispering to the rest.

'What's this?' said Flint, and his teeth flashed in a smile. 'Would any brother choose to dispute my orders?' He walked among them, pinching cheeks and twisting noses in the most genial way, and he smiled and smiled. But no man dared challenge him. So Flint went below, where very soon he was joined by Arrow, who knocked on the door of the stern cabin, and took off his hat before going in.

'Ah, Mr Arrow!' said Flint, sitting in the gloom where more shadows than light were cast by the lantern swinging from the deck-head. He was comfortable on the padded bench that ran across the cabin beneath the stern windows, with a large table in front of him, and Arrow was pricked with dismay to see that Sam Hitchin the quartermaster, and Pat Kelly, the bosun, were already snug in chairs with glasses in hand, and rum in the glasses, and turning to leer at him as the last to obey their master's summons. They leered because that was the behaviour of men who served under Flint, with every one exerting himself to be the most pleasing to their captain. They did so because even a very few days under Flint soon convinced all aboard that this was the only safe way to behave.

Arrow reflected on this, and had to admit that such a system did indeed result in a smart ship: hands leaping to obey, lines running smooth in the blocks and no rust, taint or tarnish allowed. But even Arrow knew that there were flaws in Captain Flint, flaws that prevented him from becoming a good officer as recognised by the King's navy, in which navy Arrow had himself served, until his own flaws were found out. But he pondered too long.

'Mr Arrow,' said Flint, 'are you truly with us? Or is your mind elsewhere?' He laughed, and Hitchin and Kelly laughed with him. 'No matter,' said Flint, and slid a bottle across the table. 'Do help yourself,' he said, and stared in such a way that Arrow felt obliged to search his conscience for derelictions of duty. He searched so hard that his expression gave him away.

'God's boots, Mr Arrow!' said Flint. 'Have you been at the pickles and raisins again?' Arrow blushed and Flint laughed, because there were worse sins in a first mate than thieving the men's rations. There was, for instance, the great interest that Mr Arrow took in the ship's boys. However, Flint thought Arrow was the best to be had in Savannah, and Arrow knew Cornwall very well indeed.

'So,' said Flint, 'tell me about this wife of yours, Mr Arrow.'

Arrow frowned, and glanced sideways at Hitchin and Kelly, who grinned.

'My wife?' he said.

'Your wife, Mr Arrow, because here I am, come aboard, without the map.'

'The map, Cap'n?' said Arrow.

'The map, Mr Arrow,' said Flint. 'The map which surpasses all other maps. *That* map — and certain papers appertaining thereunto.'

'Papers, Cap'n?'

'Those that I have, this night, failed to grasp,' said Flint, 'at cost of five men dead and three bad wounded.' He sighed in regret. 'And Blind Pew too — killed by chance!' He shook his head. 'You never knew him, Mr Arrow, but he was a clever one, and I would have welcomed his counsel.'

'Pew?' said Arrow

'Pew,' said Flint. 'Sent to give warning to Billy Bones, I suppose.'

'Warning?' asked Arrow.

'Which caused my attack to fail such that we must turn to other ways.'

'Other ways?' said Arrow, and Flint paused.

'My dear Mr Arrow,' he said, 'if you do not refrain from repeating my words in that moronic fashion, then I will come across this table and cut out your tongue.' Flint smiled as if joking, but Arrow knew better — and so did Hitchin and Kelly, who did not laugh. 'Good!' said Flint. 'Now, Mr Arrow, the fellows we sent out seeking Billy Bones, came back with much gossip about the Admiral Benbow inn, and the boy Jim Hawkins.' Flint looked at Arrow, who was still profoundly silent. 'Speak up, Mr Arrow,' demanded Flint. 'You've heard of the boy Hawkins, haven't you? He who is half-brother to Squire Trelawney?'

'Aye-aye, Cap'n,' said Arrow

'Aye-aye,' said Hitchin and Kelly.

'And what have you heard of Jim Hawkins?'

Arrow frowned and adopted an attitude of censure. 'I have heard that the wretched boy has carnal connection,' he said, 'connection with the fallen women of Polmouth.' Hitchin and Kelly sniggered but Arrow frowned again and pressed on. 'He is obsessed with such practices,' he said, 'and cannot resist them.'

'Shocking!' said Flint, in mockery. 'And now… tell me of your wife, Mr Arrow.'

'My wife?' said Arrow, vastly displeased at such a juxtaposition of conversational topics. He glanced again at Hitchin and Kelly, who nudged one another.

'Your wife,' said Flint, 'with whom you do not live, since it suits the pair of you that you do not.' Arrow fidgeted in his chair, wanting greatly to discuss anything other than this. Flint laughed and relented.

'But when you *do* meet the lady,' said Flint, 'How do you find her to be situated?'

'Ah!' said Arrow, and smiled. He sat upright and spoke with pride. 'My wife owns The Exchange in Polmouth!'

'Which is?' enquired Flint, although he already knew.

'Which is the best gaming house in the west country,' asserted Arrow. 'With faro, hazard, rouge-et-noir and roulette. All that and fine dinners — free to the public on Sundays — with French furniture, silver plate and—'

'Yes, yes, yes, ' interrupted Flint, waving Arrow to silence, 'as you've told me many times on this dreary voyage from Savannah.' Hitchin and Kelly nodded agreement, and Flint smiled and leaned forward. 'But what of the whores, Mr Arrow… the famous whores of The Exchange? Why do you not speak of them?'

Arrow frowned heavily. 'I know nothing of such matters.'

'Do you not?' said Flint, 'though everyone else does?' But Arrow remained silent. 'Never mind,' said Flint, 'Mr Arrow, you will get out pen and paper and write — in your best round writing — a letter to Mrs Arrow introducing myself to herself, and asking for her special assistance, and some particular clothes for myself, against the promise of a very large sum in pure gold.'

'Then are you going ashore again, Cap'n?' enquired Arrow.

'That is my intention, Mr Arrow.'

Arrow hesitated, knowing that he was about to step on hot coals with bare feet.

'What about... *him*?'

'Aye,' thought Hitchin and Kelly, though they dared not speak it. '*What about... him*?'

'Him?' Flint began to blink, which Arrow knew was a very bad sign, but he'd gone too far to back off.

'*Him*, Cap'n. Him that you said was the most dangerous man in England.' Flint blinked hard, and Arrow avoided his eyes.

'Do you mean Long John Silver, Mr Arrow?' said Flint, and Hitchin and Kelly nodded.

'Aye, Cap'n. Him! What if *he* was to find out you was alive? Which he might, after tonight.' Flint blinked and blinked. He took a deep breath and spoke.

'Then, as I have told others,' he said, 'you may leave Mr Silver to me.' In which bold words — and with unique rarity — Flint spoke with a confidence that he did not have. Instead, he had the unshakable conviction that he would never have peace in this world unless he found Silver and killed him once and for all.

After which, he would take hold of Silver's wife.

*

'So it *is* Flint,' said Selena, 'we only thought it was him before, and now we know!'

In the back room of the Spyglass Tavern, the men sitting round the table looked at her and nodded agreement. They nodded because she was Silver's wife and respected for it, but also because she fascinated them as a woman of exotic beauty, born a black slave but now a free woman in a gown fit for a duchess. She was young, neat and shapely, with large eyes and much grace of movement, but more than that she had the wondrous, indefinable quality that makes men worship one woman while another — equal in face and figure — is regarded merely as pretty.

Selena and Silver made a striking pair: she so dark and small, and he so fair and large, for he was far taller than most men, with fair hair, a broad face, fastidiously clean and with big, strong hands. When standing, Silver leaned on a crutch to take the place of his left leg, which had been cut off at the hip. But now he sat at the head of the table for this meeting of himself and the leading men of his crew from the old days: Israel Hands, Tom Morgan, George Merry and Peter Black, better known as Black Dog. Silver and those four sat with Selena because she was too far in to be kept out, and there was also the green macaw parrot on Silver's shoulder, big as an eagle, and gently nibbling his ear with a beak that could split brazil nuts or take off a finger.

For years the parrot had been thought male until she laid an egg, so she bore a male name, which was the name of the man who'd owned her before she came to John Silver. She'd borne that name so long, that all the spite was drained out of it as far as she was concerned. But now the poison was boiling again — because her name was Captain Flint.

'It's got to be him,' said Silver. 'The news is up and down the coast of how they went hammer and tongs at the Admiral Benbow. And as for the wagoner they got the cart from, he told the likeness of Flint, as plain as print: *not specially tall*, says he, *fair-faced and speaks like a gentlemen, and moves like an acrobat. But mad in the eyes, and all his men afeared of him.*'

'That's him,' exclaimed Israel Hands.

'Aye!' said everyone else.

'So what does he want, John?' asked Selena.

'Well,' said Silver, 'he wanted Billy Bones, didn't he?'

'And now Billy Bones is dead,' she replied, 'and Blind Pew as well!'

At this all present fell silent. Then Silver took hold of his crutch, shoved back his chair and stood up.

'All hands on deck!' he said, and the company stood. 'Charge your pots,' he told them, and the bottle went round. 'Here's to Blind Pew the sail maker,' said Silver, 'him as lost his lights in the same broadside that took my leg,' and he raised his tankard. 'Blind Pew!' he said. 'Shipmate, messmate and brother!'

'Shipmate, messmate and brother!' they chanted. They drank and sat down, then sat in silence a while, until Israel Hands spoke.

'You were still right to send him, John,' he said. 'Billy boy slaughtered all round before he fell, 'cos that's the kind of man that he was, and he'd never have parlayed with any other than Pew.'

'Aye,' said everyone but Selena.

'I'd have gone,' she said. 'I told you so.'

'No!' said Silver, 'Not while there was any chance of *him* bearing down on us. And I was right, 'cos he was!'

'I'd still have gone,' she said. 'I can pull a trigger as well as any man, and—'

'No, no, no!' cried Silver. 'No! No and never!' and he slammed a hand on the table. 'You *know* what he wants from you, my lass, and what he'd do if he don't get it! So never the risk of that shall you take, and there's an end of it, and never another word shall I hear!'

Nobody spoke for a while, then Israel Hands looked at Silver.

'So, what did he want from Billy Bones?'

'Pah!' said Silver, 'The map of course. The map and papers. What else?'

'Aye,' said everyone.

'When did you see the last of them, John?' asked Israel Hands, and Silver thought hard.

'Flint had the map,' he said, 'he had it somewhere about him, but the map itself ain't no good without the notes, of which he had half and I had half, and I laid the two halves on his body, as he lay dead in Savannah,' he looked at Selena.

'Because you were done with piracy and murder,' she said, and Silver frowned.

'No lass,' he said, 'we wasn't pirates nor murderers: we was *gentlemen of fortune!*' He said it with pride and all the rest agreed.

'Aye!' they said.

'And what might be the difference,' she asked, 'between pirates and gentlemen of fortune? Because whatever they are, you've sworn to not be either of them again, and I will not—'

'Belay!' said Silver, 'This ain't no time to fight old battles,' and he put his hand on Selena's. 'I threw down my half, because you wouldn't be with me if I didn't, and I'd already got gold enough put by for all of us, and I was sickened with being one such as Flint.'

'So what shall you be now he's come back?' she said, 'you can't look to the law, because we'd all hang beside Flint if the truth were known.'

'Aye!' said everyone.

'And Flint won't give up,' she said, 'not if he knows Billy Bones had the map and papers.'

'Which he does,' said Silver, 'else he'd never have dared return to England.'

'In that case he'll try again,' she said. 'He'll go after all those at the Admiral Benbow and we have to stop him.'

'Why?' asked Israel Hands. 'Why don't we sheer off and keep mum?'

'Aye,' said Morgan, 'don't see how it's any of our business.'

But Silver sighed and sighed. 'No, Tom lad,' he said, ''cos gossip spreads both ways. If *we've* heard about Flint being in Polmouth, who's to say *he* ain't heard of *me* and my lass in Bristol?' He smiled at Selena, then tickled the parrot's feathery head. 'Not to mention this here bird, 'cos the three of us together is easy to spot and hard to forget.'

'Pieces of eight! Pieces of eight!' said the parrot, which usually made everyone laugh. But not today.

'No, my jolly boys,' said Silver, 'we'll have to face him or he'll come after us! We'll keep sharp lookout, see how the wind blows, and then set course accordingly.'

'But *can* we face him, John?' said Israel Hands. '*Can* we face him if it comes to it?'

'You can leave Mr Flint to me!' said Silver, and he smiled as if with confidence, even though Silver had no confidence in this respect. Instead, he had the unshakable conviction that he would never have peace in this world unless he found Flint and killed him once and for all.

And that went double for Selena. He looked at her, and thought of Flint, and he shuddered.

CHAPTER 8

From Dr Livesey's journal:

In the days after the fighting at the Admiral Benbow, there was much to do. First, the reckoning and clearing away of the dead. Aside from Blind Pew, who was found on the Polmouth road, there were five men left abandoned outside the inn, stripped of their weapons and anything that might identify them. They were all young, and all seamen by their clothes and weather-stained faces. But none were known to the locality, and from their features they might have been of any nation from Norway to Portugal. After a brief inquest in Polmouth Town Hall, they were heaved into a pauper's grave, with the fewest words spoken over them that decency allows.

Pew was buried in the nearest village churchyard, since the balance of opinion thought him innocent of active villainy. But Mr Bones was laid to rest — at my asking — in a grave dug up on Black Hill Cove, where I hoped that his spirit might keep watch on the passing ships. So, I made sure that his telescope was at his side, and I paid for the casket and headstone. The parson was uneasy at a burial in such a place, but the people approved and Squire Trelawney insisted, so a proper service was given with a surprising number of folk standing by.

Andrew Hawkins was buried in the cemetery of St George's Church, Polmouth, after an elaborate service with a great attendance of villagers, citizens of Polmouth and relatives from as far away as Bristol — though many of the younger folk seemed to have come for a carnival, not a funeral. Thus I distinctly heard voices at the back of the crowd, singing *Fifteen Men on the Dead Man's Chest* as Hawkins was carried to his grave, and since truth delights the angels, I confess that on hearing this song — delivered mocking and slow, in time to the footfalls of the coffin-bearers — then even though I was walking with Charlotte on my arm, and herself draped in mourning, I was gripped with the most appalling urge to laugh.

But all this came in due time. On the night itself, every soul in the Admiral Benbow was stretched like a cable before it snaps, with two dead men in the house, door and windows smashed, blood on the floors and the fear that the attackers might return, and so — as can happen when the actual fighting stops — a tiredness came over me and I was happy for Squire Trelawney to take command, which to his credit he did.

'You! And you!' he cried to two of his men, as we stood round Billy Bones' body. 'Outside to keep watch on the road and give warning of any danger!'

'Aye, Squire,' they said, and out they went.

'And the rest of you, search this house, for fear any villain might still be hiding!'

So a clumping of boots rumbled up the stairs and over the boards, in every direction in a great noise of searching, and of slamming and banging without the least return, because all our enemies had gone. Meanwhile, believing that danger had passed, Jim Hawkins bucked up something wonderful, and stood forward boldly, telling Squire Trelawney's men where to search.

'Don't forget the cellars!' he cried, 'and all the upstairs bedrooms, and I'll see to the tap room myself!' He gave a respectful nod to Squire Trelawney, and went on his way with measured tread.

'There goes, my brave Jim!' said Trelawney, who was the old squire's son in all respects, including his limited intelligence. 'A man, not a boy!' he said, and he turned to me. 'I don't doubt he stood beside you when the shot was flying!'

'Hmmm,' I said, since Charlotte was close by.

'And now, said Trelawney, 'You shall none of you stay here this night, but must come to the Hall and be safe from all harm. And as for you, David Livesey: well done, sir, for the good soldier that you are!' And I blushed because Charlotte was gazing upon me with adoring eyes.

But Trelawney was still speaking. 'What did they want, David?' he asked. 'What has happened here?' So I drew him aside, because there were too many ears listening.

'John,' I said, 'I think I know who was here and what he was after.'

'Tell me!' he urged.

'It was the pirate Flint. Him and his men. They were after something that Mr Bones had.' Trelawney shook his head. 'Can't be,' he said. 'Flint's dead. Everyone knows that.'

'Do they?' I asked. 'Billy Bones didn't think so.' And I paused as a thought came to me. 'Wait!' I said, and went over to the body of Billy Bones, stretched out on the parlour table. He was grey and stiff with his mouth hung open. Trelawney shivered as I went through the dead man's pockets. 'Look!' I said and drew out the disc of card that Blind Pew had given to Billy Bones. Trelawney and I went to a stand of candles now burning over the fire, and looked at the disc: one side inked, the other with writing. It said:

Flint is risen

And is coming for you.

'May I?' said Trelawney and took the card from me and peered at it. 'D'you know what this is?' he said.

'No,' I said.

'It's a black spot.'

'What's that?'

'It's a summons among pirates. It's a solemn warning, such as they might pass to a captain before they depose him.'

'Depose him?' I said. 'How can they depose a captain?'

'By voting!'

'What?' I exclaimed. 'Do they have elections on pirate ships?' I smiled because the idea seemed absurd; but Trelawney was emphatic.

'Most certainly they do!' he said. 'They have Athenian democracy. They sign articles, which are a constitution giving every man a vote.'

'God bless my soul!' I said, and was never more amazed in all my life.

'So,' said Trelawney, 'some company of pirates — of which Mr Bones was once a member — has given solemn warning that Captain Flint is alive and after him.'

'That's certainly what Billy Bones thought,' I said.

'And Flint was after something that Mr Bones had?'

'Yes,' I said, and lowered my voice still more. 'I think we should go and look at Mr Bones' possessions, in his room.' Trelawney nodded, and looked around. His men were done searching and were stood awaiting orders, while Charlotte and the girls were sat by the fire with shawls over their shoulders, trying to keep warm in the door-less, window-less parlour in the freezing night. But the boy Jim was standing upright, as though immune to cold, with one hand on his mother's shoulder, as if he'd defend her even from the fiends of Hell.

'Good lad, Jim,' said Trelawney, and then to his men: 'Stand guard, you fellows! The doctor and I have business upstairs.'

'Aye, Squire!' they chorused, and up we went with candles, and into Billy Bones' room where the first thing we saw was his old sea chest, pulled into the middle of the room. It was like any other seaman's chest, except that it had the initial 'B' branded into the top of it, and the corners were smashed and broken by rough usage. It had a lock with the key still in it, so we threw it open and a strong smell of tobacco and tar rose from the interior, which had been much disturbed by Jim Hawkins in searching for pistols. But we found a suit of very good clothes, carefully brushed and folded, which looked as if they had never been worn. Under that was a quadrant, a tin cup, several sticks of tobacco, a piece of bar silver, an old Spanish watch and some other trinkets of little value and mostly of foreign make, then a pair of brass dividers and five or six curious West Indian shells. Underneath there was a fine boat-cloak, also never used, then a substantial canvas bag that gave forth a pleasing jingle, and finally a bundle sewn up in oilcloth, and looking like papers.

On impulse, Trelawney picked up the largest of the shells and turned it over.

'Look,' he said. 'It's got words scratched on it.' Which indeed it had:

To William
from Olivia Rose
Beau chevalier sans peur et sans reproche

'What does that mean?' asked Trelawney, who had no French. So I translated.

'It means: *Fair Knight, fearless and unsullied.* It's poetry. It's famous.

It was said of the Seigneur de Bayard, who was a French knight in the time of Henry VIII.'

Trelawney nodded. 'And this Olivia Rose: she said that of Billy Bones?'

'Yes,' I said. 'She was the Livvy Rose he spoke of.'

'And he kept it all these years,' said Trelawney, then picked up the canvas bag, and opened the drawstring at the top. 'Stap my vitals!' he said. 'It's gold coin.' He hoisted it up and down and whistled. 'There must be twenty pounds of weight here,' he said, and looked at me. 'What's that in value?'

'Enough for a house with servants,' I replied.

'So is this what Flint was after?'

'No,' I said, 'it's not enough. Not nearly enough.' I picked up the oilskin package. 'I think it's this,' and I looked round. 'But I don't think we should open it here. I think we should get ourselves safe inside Trelawney Hall at best speed, and right away.'

So that's what we did, leaving five men to guard the inn, and myself happily taking up Charlotte behind me on my horse, and her needing — of sheer practicality — to clasp me tightly round the waist. To judge from the squeals and cries, some of Trelawney's men were likewise enjoying the task of taking up the servant girls, while Jim Hawkins, now mounted on his horse, found courage and cried out: 'I'll go ahead, Squire, and give warning that we're coming!'

'That's my boy!' said Trelawney. 'View halloo!'

'View halloo', cried Jim, and laid on with his whip, thereby contriving to get his beloved self out of any danger and into the arms of safety at the utmost speed, and getting credit for the doing of it.

Off he galloped, thunder and lightning into the night, but the rest of us rode at the speed of the slowest to enable all to keep up, making our way through the blinding cold in a tight body. Then, finally, we passed through iron gates, and up the gravel drive to the bright-lit Hall, with its roaring fires, woken-up kitchens and good warm beds for us all. All that, and Jim Hawkins standing in the lobby at the head of a great body of house-folk.

'Squire, sir!' he said with a noble bow. 'Mother! Doctor Livesey!' He greeted us as if he were heir to the house, which I don't doubt he aimed to become, since all the world knew he was the present squire Trelawney's younger brother, and Trelawney was unmarried and had no son — none that he acknowledged, at least.

'Good boy, Jim!' said Trelawney, then there was busy work as all dismounted, myself taking Charlotte in my arms to help her down. Then everyone was taken inside to be warmed and fed, and the women of the house took care of Charlotte and her girls, while Trelawney and I went straight to his library, where he stopped just outside the big, double-doors and shouted to the servants.

'Send us some dinner! Something good and hot, and some bottles of the best!'

'Ah!' I said, thinking well of him. But there was more. 'And send Jim Hawkins,' he cried, 'send him at once!' And he smiled. 'Jim must see what's in that package of yours, Doctor,' he said, 'he's won the right!' I was struck so dumb with surprise that I said nothing, because I could think of nothing to say. I add in my defence the true fact that I was exceedingly tired, and had just fought a deadly action with men killed all around me. None the less I must share the blame for allowing Jim Hawkins to join us, and be party to all that followed.

Thus, when the servants brought food and drink on silver trays, we let the food go cold and the wine un-poured, being enwrapped with what we discovered. And this is how it was:

The library was huge, with books by the furlong, a massive fireplace burning pine-logs that by themselves gave bright light, and candles besides. There was a long table that Trelawney cleared of the books scattered on it — all of them concerning blood-stock and horse-racing — so that we could take chairs and sit down, then open the oilskin package in comfort. It was about a foot square and an inch thick and was sewn up tight. So, Trelawney found a pen knife.

'Here, Doctor,' he said, 'stitching is medical work!'

I nicked the threads and opened the package, which crackled and creaked, and we found four objects.

First, a small notebook with stiff covers, much battered and stained; second, a sealed paper packet; third, another and smaller packet; and finally a slim, silver porte-crayon such as gentlemen use to contain a pencil.

'Shall we try the book first?' I suggested.

'Yes!' said Trelawney and Jim, so we went through it page by page.

First there were some scraps of writing that a man might make for idleness or practice, mostly misspelt: *Mr W. Bones Qwater Master, Offe Palm Key he got itt,*' and some single words and scribble. But I could not help wondering who had *got itt* and what *itt* was that he got.

'Not much instruction there,' I said, and we passed on, finding the next dozen pages filled with a curious series of entries like those in an account book. Thus, there was a date at one end of each line and a sum of money at the other. But instead of explanation in between, there was only a varying number of crosses. On the twelfth of June 1750, for instance, seven pounds had been entered, and there was nothing but six crosses to explain the cause. In a very few cases, the name of a place was added, such as *Offe Caraccas* or a latitude and longitude, but that was all. This record lasted several years, the sums of money growing larger with time, and finally a grand total had been made — after five or six wrong additions — and beside it the words *Bones, his pile.*

'I can't make head nor tail of this,' I said, but Trelawney could.

'It's clear as noonday,' he said. 'This is Mr Bones' account-book. The crosses stand for the names of ships or towns that he and his fellows plundered. The sums are Bones' share, and where he feared ambiguity he added something such as *Offe Caraccas*, which I take to mean some unhappy vessel boarded off that coast, and God help those aboard her!'

'Ah,' I said, 'what a fine thing it is to have been a seaman!' But there was little else in the book, other than — towards the end — a table for equating French, English and Spanish money.

'And now,' announced Trelawney, 'for the packets.'

The biggest had several wax seals which I opened carefully, and out fell another, smaller package, and a map representing an island which I thought looked like a fat chicken laying an egg. The egg was in fact an islet labelled *Skeleton Island*, enclosed within the southern end of the mainland. The map had latitude and longitude, soundings, bays and inlets, and it showed the island to be about fifteen miles long and ten across. There were two land-locked harbours, and a hill in the centre marked *The Spy-glass*. But before all else, there was a red ink cross, and beneath it was the word: *Treasure*

'Treasure?' said Jim Hawkins, like a hound on a scent.

'Rot!' said Trelawney. 'Gammon and nonsense.'

'Oh,' said Hawkins, disappointed.

'Wait,' I said, 'let's see the rest.' So I unsealed the lesser packet, and found five small paper triangles, that must have been made by tearing apart a stack of five squares measuring some three inches on each side. The squares must have been folded and torn along the diagonal, and the triangles were dense with writing, but made no sense because each was only half of an original whole page.

'Look in there!' said Jim, pointing at the porte-crayon. So I did, unscrewing the cap at the end, and inside — tight rolled — I found the missing halves of the triangles. Then, putting together the first pair of them, we read:

An Aide Memoire of Bearings and Distances
J.F. Sept 5 1752
Let not me be laid by and never heard of.

'Bearings and distances?' said Trelawney, 'And what's this here? *Let not me be laid by and never heard of.*'

'It's from a play,' I said: *The Duchess of Malfi.*' I shook my head. 'And a sad, miserable work it is too, with the horrible strangulation of a poor woman at the end of it. It's not a work I'll ever see again.'

'Well *somebody* liked it ,' said Trelawney. 'Flint, I suppose, black-hearted villain as he was.'

'Never mind that, look here!' exclaimed Jim Hawkins, laying out the papers to form legible pages. 'Look!' he said. 'It's detailed directions!' He read out snatches at random: '*From Anvil Rock twenty-four paces north-north-west … cross uneven ground much fallen into swamp … six paces from the biggest tree,*' his voice grew shrill with excitement as he read the final words, '*…here dig six feet deep to find the treasure…* Squire! Doctor!' Jim cried, his pretty, greedy eyes shining in his pretty, greedy head. 'These are detailed directions leading to buried treasure!'

'Nonsense,' said Trelawney.

'Why?' I asked. 'Why should there *not* be buried treasure?'

'Because pirates never buried their treasure,' he said, 'they lived short lives and fast, and the moment they had money they went ashore to spend it on whores, drink and dinners. And then they beat about and got more, until the navy caught them, and hanged them from the yardarm without trial. I know. I've seen it done. And anyway the size of Flint's treasure — in rumour at least — was vastly too great to be real.'

'Did none of the pirates keep their riches?' I said.

'None! They didn't live long enough. Take Blackbeard, the greatest of them all. D'you how long he lasted pirating?'

'No,' said I and Jim together.

'A year and six months. Then the navy got him and shot him and cut off his head. So he didn't leave any treasure, believe me.'

'What about Captain Kidd?' I asked. 'Didn't he leave buried treasure on Governor's Island off New York?'

'Bladderwash!' said Trelawney. 'Half a world of fools has dug up Governor's Island and found nothing. Kidd only pretended he had treasure to buy his way out of a hanging, but he danced on air in the end.'

'Squire,' I said, 'I cannot argue with you, for you were a seaman and I was not. But here's Flint the pirate himself, come ashore in Cornwall and risking his life to get hold of the papers that were in Billy Bones' chest, and which now lie here.' I tapped a finger on the table. 'So answer me this: why would Flint do that if there's no treasure to be found?'

Trelawney said nothing. He frowned and thought. He got up, and looked into the fire a while, then he went over to the bottles we had ignored, and he drew a cork and poured for the three of us.

'Here,' he said, handing out glasses. 'David, your question is a right good one and I can't see my way around it,' and he grinned and winked, 'so you've turned me about, and now I say that if Flint *did* keep what he took, then it'd be a fortune vast beyond counting. So I am resolved that the three of us should go and find it, and I'll fit out a ship in Bristol for the purpose. So, gentlemen, I give you the toast: Flint's treasure!'

'Flint's treasure!' we said, and I raised my glass — though even then, I had doubts.

CHAPTER 9

'Tell me of Flint's treasure,' said the beautiful gentleman, and Jim Hawkins gaped at the gentleman's magnificent clothes. Coat, waistcoat and britches, embroidered in brilliant silks that wove patterns of interlocking flowers; and the gentleman's fine calves in white silk stockings; and his silver-buckled shoes and spotless white wig. All this, and a countenance so handsome, and with such fine eyes and teeth, that even Jim Hawkins — who was vanity incarnate — knew that he was second in face and figure to the man who sat opposite on a padded sofa by Gobelin of Paris, in a richly-draped, private room on the second floor of The Exchange, Polmouth.

The gentleman sat with a luscious female on either side — trollops, of course — but from the top of their trade, with fine clothes, gleaming shoulders, laughing eyes, and one with a naked, gartered leg hooked over the gentleman's knee, which leg he stroked: sliding his hand beneath the folds of her skirts, to find the upper reaches of her thigh.

'Oh! Oh!' she gasped, as the hand explored, and Jim Hawkins licked his lips. He sat in an exactly similar Gobelin sofa, with an exactly similar trollop to one side of him, and Madame herself, Mrs Frances Arrow, on the other — because he was a favoured customer who paid in gold. Thus he loved The Exchange, and The Exchange loved him. Even Madame loved him, because he had once asked for her own personal services, declaring that whatever her age — which was fifty-one, though he never learned it — she had the figure of a girl of twenty and was a wonderful woman. At this, Madame had been so charmed that she seriously considered the request. But finally she concluded that not only were there limits to duty in any profession, but she was old enough to be his grandmother and she had the good name of the house to consider.

'Tell the gentleman what he asks,' she said, 'tell him, *you naughty boy*,' which made Jim smile, since all the girls called him that, and he liked it.

On balance, Jim Hawkins did not hate the gentleman, as he was very close to doing. Instead — and with rare grace — he acknowledged a superior. Having a cunning little mind, he resolved to make a friend of the gentleman so as to learn from him and become like him.

'Mr Stone,' he said, because that was the gentleman's name as introduced to Jim Hawkins by Madame, 'I am sworn by my comrades to be silent in this matter.'

'But you told *me*, naughty boy,' said the trollop beside Jim Hawkins.

'Yes,' said Hawkins, frowning, 'but that was in a loose moment after too much drink.' And everybody laughed. But then the sounds of conflict came from the short corridor which linked the side room to the gaming room. 'What's that?' said Jim. 'Do let's see!'

Madame nodded to one of the girls, who got up, sauntered to the door and swung it open. 'Ah!' said Jim Hawkins.

'Oh-ho!' said Mr Stone, and everyone laughed, because a fight was well under way in the middle of the gaming room, around the odds-and-evens wheel. Thus gold guineas, gambling counters, wigs, hats and pairs of spectacles flew in all directions as gentlemen tumbled over each other in a dense-packed, tumbling fury: punching heads, biting ears and bellowing loudly, while one taller than all the rest — a man of advanced years but wielding a heavy stick — was systematically hitting everyone within reach and without the least discrimination.

The company in the side room laughed and laughed, enjoying the fun and drinking wine, until Madame's bully boys came charging upstairs into the gaming room, and comprehensively battered all present, and threw them out, then bowed respectfully to Madame when they were done.

'Close the door,' said Madame finally, and the door was closed.

'Did somebody dispute the accuracy of the wheel?' enquired Stone, smiling, and Madame merely shrugged. 'It is, of course, an honest wheel and an honest game,' said Stone, making a question of the statement.

'Of course!' said Madame.

'Of course!' said Stone. Then he looked at Jim Hawkins. 'But *I* have a better game.' He smiled at the girl with the gartered leg. 'Oblige me, my chicken, by fetching me that small table,' he said, 'and who can lend me a fan?'

So, a small, gilded-wood table was set before Mr Stone. It was about two feet high, on three ornate legs supporting a disc of fine mosaic about a foot across, and Mr Stone sat himself on the floor with the table between his knees, and placed on the table a fan that Madame had given him, having first closed it. 'Now!' he said. 'We shall play my game: Stone's game,' and he looked at Jim Hawkins. 'Will you be first, sir?' he asked, and his smile was so fine that Jim Hawkins nodded. 'Good fellow,' said Stone. 'So, sit opposite me, and everyone else stand close so that there can be no trickery.'

Everyone was intrigued. Everyone stood round the table.

'Here is the game,' said Stone, 'do you see the fan where it sits on the table?'

'Yes,' said Jim Hawkins.

'Yes,' said everyone.

'And here I sit,' said Stone, 'with my hands in my pockets.'

'Yes,' said everyone.

'While you, Mr Hawkins, shall place your hands on the table.'

'Yes,' said Jim Hawkins, and did so.

'Good man!' said Stone and Jim smiled.

'And all that you must do now, Mr Hawkins,' said Stone.

'Yes?' said Jim.

'All you must do now, in your own time and at your own choosing…'

'Yes?'

'Is pick up the fan before I can seize it, but with the warning that I shall beat it upon your fingers if I am quicker than you.'

Jim Hawkins frowned.

'But you have your hands in your pockets, while mine are on the table.'

'*Precisely*, Mr Hawkins. So let us begin when you are ready, and for this first attempt we shall make no wager. Are we agreed?'

'Yes,' said Jim, and everyone nodded, and Stone smiled like a wolf that smells a lamb. But Jim Hawkins held his breath, and everyone else did, and then he snatched… and the fan was in Stone's hand, rapping Jim's knuckles, and everyone gasped because a gun-lock could not have struck faster than Stone.

'Ouch!' said Jim Hawkins, hit by the riveted end of the fan.

'Again?' suggested Stone. 'Perhaps I was lucky?'

If so, he was lucky a dozen times in a row, though each time, by just a little. Stone slowed in his movements until finally, with excitement growing and the girls and Madame cheering, *finally* Jim snatched the fan. Then Stone sighed, and shook his head, and Madame served champagne — several glasses going to Jim Hawkins — while Stone sat back and smiled.

'Well done, sir!' he cried.

'Thank you, sir!' replied Jim.

'Though of course,' said Stone, 'this is not the real way to play the game.'

'No?' asked Jim Hawkins.

'Oh no,' said Stone, 'because, properly, and *between men*,' he paused, 'the game should be played with a hammer.'

He smiled and toasted Jim Hawkins. 'To you, sir,' he said, 'a bold, brave winner!' After that, Stone studied Jim Hawkins very carefully, and judged that he was now sufficiently full of wine, and sufficiently drunk on praise, and entirely surrounded by women whom Stone needed to impress.

'So I make you a wager,' said Stone.

'Which is?' said Jim Hawkins, and smiled at the trollops, who blew kisses in return.

'Which is,' said Stone, 'that we play the game once more, and for a wager.'

'Which is?' said Jim Hawkins, laughing.

'That if *you* win, then I must pay you one hundred guineas,' said Stone, and everyone gasped at the amount. So Stone turned to Madame. 'Dear lady,' he said, 'pray assure Mr Hawkins that I am good for that sum.'

Everyone looked at Madame, who thought, and thought, and finally nodded. 'Thank you, Madame,' said Stone. 'Meanwhile, Mr Hawkins, if *I* should win, then we must play the game with a hammer,' he smiled, 'until you tell me about this treasure of yours…'

*

Later the gentleman sat alone with Madame.

'Latitude and longitude are safe in my memory,' he said, 'but the detailed instructions are not, and the boy has seen them. So I shall need him again.'

'Never fear, ' she said. 'He'll be back of his own accord. He can't keep away.'

'Good! And since all the world comes to your house,' he said, 'you will know the men who run that world. Including Squire Trelawney?'

'Oh yes,' she said. 'We know him well.'

'So, someone must sell Trelawney a very good ship at a very good price, to gain influence over him. Do you know someone who might do that?'

She nodded. 'Mr Matthew Blandy, West India merchant and deacon of the church.' She smiled. 'I know things of him that his church does not.'

'Then with his help,' said the gentleman, 'I shall put men among Trelawney's crew, including a first mate.' He smiled. 'Would you mind if he were your husband — Mr Arrow?'

She laughed.

'And,' he said. 'You must sift the gossip that flows into this house to seek a seafaring man with one leg, and a green parrot,' he breathed deep, 'and a negress wife of great beauty.'

CHAPTER 10

From Dr Livesey's journal:

I did my best to kill off the expedition; at least I tried. On the morning after our ride to the Hall, I spoke to Trelawney after he had consumed an enormous breakfast with a quart of small beer to wash it down. He was in merry mood and I got him into the library, although it was so early that the servants were still clearing up from the previous night. So we stood and waited as they finished at high speed and ran out bowing, closing the door.

'Are the papers safe?' I asked, looking at the table. Trelawney smiled.

'Do you take me for simple-minded?' he said, which was a trying question, so I said nothing, and he smiled. 'Locked safe in my Chinese cabinet,' he asserted, pointing to a huge and hideous piece of oriental carpentry, covered with lurid lacquer work in black and gold.

'Good,' I replied, 'now can we sit down? Because I have something to say.' So we sat.

'Now, sir,' he said, 'what's this about?'

'The expedition for treasure,' I said.

'Ah!' he responded, with such a smile that I knew my arguments were doomed. But still I tried.

'Squire,' I said, 'John! Why we should risk our lives attempting to recover pirate treasure, when we — both of us — already enjoy every good thing that life can offer?'

He just gaped. 'Why?' he repeated, with an expression of profound incredulity. 'You ask *why?*

'Yes,' I said, 'I have a fine practice, a good house, money in the bank, and will soon have everything that I could dream of.' Whereupon perhaps he wasn't such a dull blade after all, or perhaps he knew me better than I did myself, because he slapped his thigh and laughed.

'A-hah!' he said, 'I see it now, you sly rogue: you have a most exceedingly pretty wife coming your way, and by George I don't blame you if you want your honeymoon, because who wouldn't with such a tasty lady? So what we'll do is this: we'll delay sailing until after—'

'No,' I said, 'it isn't that. It's yourself besides. You have the greatest mansion in the west country, a fortune, fine lands, good tenants and an honoured place in society. So why should you risk all that, for a pile of coins and stones that you don't even need?'

I thought I had him there, because he gaped and spluttered and spread his hands wide in disbelief. But no: his amazement was entirely at myself, for not seeing what was so obvious to him.

'For the adventure!' he cried. 'For the thrill of it! For setting sail, out into the wide seas and the world of wonders!'

'But we could be facing Flint and his pirates,' I said, 'they'll never give up and they might come after us!'

'YES!' he said, in a great roar, 'Let 'em come, the rogues, and we'll meet 'em with drawn swords and hot shot!' And he leapt up, threw his arms around me, hoisted me to my feet and danced me round the room so that I had to smile. Then he stopped, gasping and panting.

'Anyway,' said he, 'aren't you a follower of Dr Johnson, the dictionary writer?'

'Yes,' I said, 'I admire him as a scholar and philosopher.'

'Well then,' said Trelawney, 'your Johnson said: *every man thinks meanly of himself for not having been a soldier, or not having been at sea.*'

'Bless my soul!' I said. 'How do you know that? You don't read philosophy.'

'Parson said it in church,' he said, 'and preached a damn boring sermon on it.' And I laughed and laughed, and that was the end of it. He was a dear friend and a good man, but he was stubborn, and I could not shift him, even on the subject of Jim Hawkins.

'Well at least let's not bring Hawkins,' I said.

'Why not?'

'Because he can't be trusted.'

'Nonsense! I love him for the rollicking, bouncing boy, that he is!'

'Who spends his money on whores — the money *you* give him.'

'Well done him! If he weren't poking tarts, it'd be innocent farmers' daughters.'

'Could he not behave and control himself?'

'Oh David!' said Trelawney. 'Don't be a dull dog!' And he began to stamp round the room, clapping his hands and singing: 'Fifteen men on the dead man's chest ...' and he was so happy, and so innocent in his joy that I could not resist him, and in the end I joined in and sang that wretched ditty with him: *I*, who should have known better, but did not.

So the expedition went forward and various practicalities had to be observed because, in the first place, Flint and his pirates were still at large somewhere. Mr Dance, the Supervisor of Preventives, later confirmed that what he still called *the smugglers* — and we thought it best not to say otherwise — had escaped in their wagon, and very likely gone on board of a brig that had been lurking in Kitt's Hole but disappeared on the night of the Admiral Benbow attack.

Thus for a while, Trelawney Hall became our fortress, where we could stand guard over each other, shoulder to shoulder with the men of the house-folk, armed from Trelawney's gunroom. Also, and with extreme grudging on the squire's part, Mr Bones' gold was sent to the crown court at Bristol, for adjudication. As a magistrate I insisted on that, though Trelawney grumbled, wishing to spread it among the needy of his tenants.

But then, when no pirates appeared, life became normal. Thus funerals were held and Charlotte went back to the Admiral Benbow where all damage had been repaired by Trelawney's generous kindness, but conversely, Jim Hawkins was again sneaking off to Polmouth, with Trelawney's connivance and the best horse in his stables.

On the day of the return to the inn, I drove Trelawney's dog cart with Charlotte beside me and Jim and the serving girls behind, because I was still nervous that the pirates might strike. So my case of instruments was emptied of everything except a pair of dragoon pistols borrowed from the gun room. But I kept that to myself, and fortunately there was no need for them.

When we drove up to the inn, we found a most touching assembly of local folk waiting for us at the door, who cheered and waved, and rushed forward to help down Charlotte and the girls, and who thumped me on the back and proclaimed me a hero

'Well done, Doctor, sir!' they cried.

'You showed it them smugglers!

'Hurrah for England!'

It would have been immensely flattering, except that they also cheered Jim Hawkins, who waved and smiled and who — I later discovered — had spent much time at the Hall with the younger female servants, feeding them a tale of the Admiral Benbow siege which differed remarkably from the truth, and they had spread the tale. Still worse, after we got down, Charlotte placed a hand on my arm, and nodded towards Jim, who was giving the most wonderful affectation of modesty before a circle of admirers. She smiled, and whispered to me.

'My boy,' she said, 'I am so proud.'

She said that! She who had actually been there and seen everything. She whom I could deny nothing. So what could I do, other than smile?

'Doctor?' she said. 'David?'

'Charlotte?'

'You *will* take care of my darling boy and bring him back safe to me?'

At this, the devil visited me again. He came up grinning and chuckling from below and filled my mind with visions: visions of Jim Hawkins going overboard in a storm, or falling from a precipice, or hit by accidental gunfire, or tripped within reach of a hissing serpent, and in all these visions a pair of hands was pushing Jim Hawkins into danger. But I recovered myself, and spoke as a gentleman should.

'Your servant, ma'am,' I said, 'in all things, and for so long as I shall breathe.'

'Oh David, ' she said, and the gratitude in her eyes wrung my bowels with guilt.

But then we were inside, and Charlotte and the girls were about to take off their coats and make busy to serve the crowd, when we noticed there — standing forlorn with his box of belongings beside him — a skinny little boy who was touching his brow in salute of Mrs Charlotte.

'And who are you, my lad?' she said.

'Please, missus,' he said, 'I'm Robin Sidmouth, missus, sent by Squire to stand in for Mr Jim Hawkins while he be away, and mother says I'm to be a good boy and do as I'm bid.'

'Ahhhhh!' said everyone as if contemplating a kitten, while Charlotte stepped forward, put her arms around Robin and kissed him on each cheek.

'Well bless you, my boy,' she said, 'and if you do what your mother says, you'll prosper in this house.'

'Ahhhhh!' said everyone. But something — perhaps the Devil's work again — caused me to glance at Jim Hawkins, and there on his pretty face was an expression of malice fit to sour the milk, because the boy Jim was jealous, and was minded to make life a Hell on Earth for poor little Robin.

And so the visions came back, and I saw Jim Hawkins going over a cliff, and I saw the hands pushing him, and I knew whose hands they were.

Then, later that afternoon there was a quiet time, when the girls had got the kitchen and parlour in hand and Jim Hawkins was not to be seen. In fact he was busy tormenting Robin Sidmouth in the barn, which I did not know at the time or I would have kicked him round the house and back again. But innocent as I was, I sat alone with Charlotte in the back room and enjoyed a moment very precious in memory, because at last I was able to take my lady in my arms, and kiss her dear lips and stroke her hair, and in that little room, we agreed to pledge ourselves — each one to the other — in marriage.

'We'll wait a year for decency,' she said.

'Six months!' I said. 'That's quite enough. Or when I'm back from the expedition.'

'Just come back to me, David,' she said, 'and bring my boy with you.'

Then I had to go to London to find a locum tenens doctor to take my place while I was chasing treasure, which — given the location of the island — must mean my absence for at least four months and possibly far longer. Meanwhile, Trelawney was mad eager to begin the business, even in winter, and wanting to be off to Bristol to get a ship and crew. So after my return from London I dined at the hall, and later we talked, over brandy and tobacco pipes.

'We surely we can't sail until spring?' I said.

'Rot!' he said. 'What if the pirates get there first? To the island?'

'How can they,' I said, 'without the map?'

'Ah,' he said, 'they have ways!' And he winked, as if privy to mysteries beyond the wit of landmen like myself. Then he laughed. 'David,' he said, 'anyone would think you were afraid of these pirates, and you that was a soldier. Why, they're only men like us!'

'There's only one man I'm afraid of,' I said.

'Name the dog!'

'You, sir! Because you cannot guard your tongue and you'll blab to all Bristol.'

Good fellow that he was, he took not the least offence, but just laughed.

'Never!' he said. 'I shall be silent as the grave.'

CHAPTER 11

The public room of the Spyglass was busy, even on a vicious, cold day with frost on the windows and ice on the cobbles outside. But the public room was snug, with fires in the grates and chatter and noise and the waiters going to and fro. At the innermost end of the room, Selena stood on tip-toe to kiss Silver, who was heavily dressed in greatcoat, muffler and gloves, as was Israel Hands beside him, while Tom Morgan and the rest stood by.

Silver put an arm around Selena and smiled. But then the fear came on him again.

'Have you got your pops,' he asked her, 'primed and loaded?'

She sighed and stood back. 'Yes,' she said, and slipped her hands through the slits in her gown and petticoat, to the fashionable pocket-hoops that shaped the gown: linen bags stiffened with cane and ideal for the little things ladies carried: purse, handkerchief, scent-bottle, patch-box... and a pair of box-lock pistols by Godsall of Birmingham, each one taking a ball that would knock down a man, stone dead. These were swiftly displayed then slipped back inside the pocket-hoops before anyone should notice. Silver nodded.

'And do you know to push forward—?'

'Push forward the trigger-guard,' she said, 'to take off the safety catch, before I cock the lock and give fire.' She shook her head. 'And have *you* got a nice warm coat against the cold?'

Silver smiled. Israel Hands smiled.

'Well and good,' said Silver, and turned to Tom Morgan, Black Dog and George Merry, 'but I'm leaving this lass in your care, shipmates,' he said.

'We know that, Long John,' said Tom Morgan, 'and we're ready with barkers and blades.' He patted his coat for what lay beneath.

'I'm relying on you, lads,' said Silver.

'Go on, John,' said Selena, 'get about your business.'

'And you look after that old bird o' mine,' said Silver. 'She don't like the cold, remember.'

'She's in the kitchen where it's warm,' said Selena. 'Now, is there anything else before you go?'

Silver sighed. He was in horror of Flint. Horror of what he'd do to Selena. He could barely bring himself to leave her. But Israel Hands shook Silver's arm.

'Come on, John,' he said, 'I've spoke to our man, and said we can get him a crew. But he's got no patience, so he might go elsewhere if we don't look lively.'

'Just remember, John,' said Selena, 'you must stand behind Mr Hands and give respect, because you're to be ship's cook.'

'Cook!' said Silver. 'Cook, by thunder?' And everyone laughed.

'Cook it must be,' said Selena, 'otherwise it'd be plain that you're a leader of men and dangerous, while no man fears a cook!'

'But I *can't* cook!'

'Don't matter,' she said, 'Tom Morgan'll do that, won't you Tom?'

'Aye,' said Morgan.'

'Come on then, *Cooky!*' said Hands, and laughed.

'I'm coming,' said Silver, and thumped and bumped his way down the long room, and out of the door on to the quayside, with Israel Hands beside him. Then the two of them made their way over the slippery ground — most troublesome for Long John with his crutch — with few folk about, and hardly any hand-carts or wagons, since the great port was shut down by the freezing weather, and as near quiet as Bristol ever was.

'Hell's bells!' said Silver, pointing to the icicles in the rigging of the ships in harbour. 'There's not a vessel that'll sail this day. None with any good sense.'

'Aye,' said Hands, 'not till the spring.'

'But Mr Trelawney would sail tomorrow,' said Silver.

'*Squire* Trelawney.'

'Squire?' said Silver. 'What's that then? What's it mean?'

'Don't mean nothing, rightly,' said Hands. ''Tis what they calls a *courtesy* title. It ain't like a lord that sits in parliament. But this one, Squire Trelawney, is the biggest man for miles and is precious rich.'

'Then why's he off a-hunting for treasure?' asked Silver.

'Don't know,' said Hands. 'But once he gets drink inside him, he talks about it to anyone that'll listen.' He looked at Silver. 'And make no mistake, John, it's our island he's bound for, with a map and everything. I know 'cos I've listened to him.'

'Can't he keep a hitch on his jawing tackle?'

'Not him, John. He'd tell it to the parrot, given the chance.' Hands looked at the sign hanging over a splendid, large building in yellow brick, four stories high. 'Ah,' he said, 'that's the one: The Old Anchor. Best hotel in Bristol.'

'Very nice, I'm sure,' said Silver, and he hopped up the steps leading to a pillar-and-pediment entry, with beggars clustered around it, and a servant in livery and laced hat to open the door leading into a bright, high lobby. There, Silver and Hands were greeted with a bow, by a most superior servant in fine clothes.

'I'm here for to see a Mr Trelawney,' said Silver.

'*Squire* Trelawney?' asked the servant.

'Aye,' said Silver.

'A-hem,' said the servant, and looked to one side, into a large room where some gentlemen and ladies were gathered around the fireplace, listening to a large man, full of swagger, dressed in the blue coat and bright buttons of a master mariner. He had a loud voice.

'… to which purpose,' he declared, 'I now have a fine ship: *Hispaniola* by name, which shall have a fine crew, and fair winds and a swift passage, enabling me to astound the world with the cargo I shall bring home on board of her!'

'That's him,' confirmed Hands.

'God help us,' said Silver.

CHAPTER 12

From Dr Livesey's journal:

Perhaps I should have gone with Trelawney when finally he left for Bristol: perhaps, or perhaps not, because in the end he was no more deceived than I should have been. But my locum tenens was delayed in London, and I had medical duties that could not be ignored, so Trelawney went alone, and we heard nothing until a letter arrived in the mail, and was brought to my door. I reproduce it here in full, leaving readers to gasp at the content just as I did.

Sunday April 27th 1755
The Old Anchor Hotel, Bristol.

Dear Livesey,,

The ship is bought and fitted. She lies at anchor, ready for sea. You never imagined a sweeter schooner, and a child might sail her: two hundred tons, name Hispaniola, built yankee-style for speed, and fitted out as a privateer and therefore mounting twelve broadside guns throwing six-pound shot, and a long gun throwing nine-pound shot, as bow-chaser. I got her through the most splendid fellow: one Blandy, who sought me out, knowing my need, and has proved himself the most surprising trump. The admirable fellow literally slaved in my interest, as did everyone in Bristol, as soon as they got wind of the port we sailed for: treasure, I mean.

Blandly himself owned the ship, and sold her for the merest trifle, such that every class of man in Bristol is astounded at the bargain I made.

So far not a hitch. The workpeople — riggers and what not — were most annoyingly slow; but time cured that. It was the crew that troubled me.

I wished for thirty men, in case of attack by natives, buccaneers, or the odious French, and Blandly again stood forth, and found me half a dozen, including a first mate with quadrant and dividers — Arrow by name — till the most remarkable stroke of fortune brought me the very man that I required.

The word of our expedition having spread, I was approached directly by a veteran of the King's navy, one Israel Hands, who has served his country as a master gunner, and is a scholar able to keep accounts. He is a man of property, being owner of a substantial tavern, and brought with him his cook, a most tall and impressive fellow, who has lost a leg in Britannia's service but who, to the shame of our nation, was discharged without pension. His name is Long John Silver, and a finer seaman never breathed.

Being tedious of the shore life, these two sought berths in our expedition and I was monstrously touched, as you would have been yourself had you been in my shoes, and I engaged Hands and Silver forthwith, thinking that I had found only my gunner and cook. But it was a crew I had discovered. Between these two and myself we have a company of the toughest tars imaginable: not pretty to look at, but fellows of the most indomitable spirit, and I declare we could fight a man o' war.

I am in the most magnificent health and spirits, eating like a bull, sleeping like a tree, yet I shall not enjoy a moment till I hear my tarpaulins tramping round the capstan. Seaward ho! Hang the treasure! It's the glory of the sea that has turned my head. So now, Livesey, come post; do not lose an hour if you respect me.

Ever your friend and comrade-in-arms,
John Trelawney..

Postscript. I did not tell you that Blandly is to send a consort after us if we don't turn up by the end of August, and has found us a sailing master: Captain Alexander Smollet — a stiff man, which I regret, but supposedly fit for the work.

Also a most interesting item concerning Silver. On visiting Hands' tavern, which is called The Spyglass, I met Silver's wife — a woman of colour — who is to manage the establishment, during Hands' absence. And by George, and by Heaven, and by all the angels, never in all my life did I see a lovelier woman!!! So God alone knows how Silver can bring himself to part from her since I could not, and would not, if she were mine.

Yours,
JT

There was nothing to be done about Trelawney's indiscretions, so the party of us who were to go with him gathered our baggage and said our farewells. When I went to the Admiral Benbow to say goodbye to

Charlotte and collect Jim Hawkins, I was almost moved to sympathy for him. He genuinely loved his mother and was sincerely sorry to leave her.

'Oh, my little one,' she said.

'Oh, mamma, mamma,' he said, and wept real tears.

But then I spied little Robin Sidmouth standing with the serving girls; they with their arms protectively around him and looking grim at Hawkins, while Robin had bruises on his face, together with sheer relief to see his tormentor going out of the door. So I wondered if he too had visions of the boy Jim and a pair of pushing hands...

*

Thus our adventure began, with five of us picked up at dusk outside The Royal Oak, Polmouth, aboard the mail bound for Bristol. Myself and Jim Hawkins, with Tom Redruth and Rob Hunter, who were Trelawney's gamekeepers — fine marksmen both though Redruth was now quite old — and Mr Joyce who was Trelawney's secretary. I was wedged between Redruth and Hunter, and in spite of the swift motion and the cold night air, being tired from the exertions of the last days I must have dozed from the very first then slept solid, uphill and down dale, through stage after stage. When finally I woke, it was by the cessation of motion, since I opened my eyes to find that we were standing still before a large building in a city street, and that the day had long since broken.

'Where are we?' I asked.

'Bristol, sir,' said Redruth, 'Time to get down.'

So down we got, and found porters to carry our luggage and take us to The Old Anchor Hotel, which was far down on the docks, with a magnificent view of all that went on there, and had been chosen by

Trelawney so that he might keep charge of the work on our ship: the schooner *Hispaniola*. On the way there, to my fascination, we passed along quays which — with the return of clement weather — were now full of a great multitude of ships of all sizes and rigs and nations. In one, the tars were singing shanties at their work; in another, there were men aloft high over my head, hanging to threads that seemed no thicker than a spider's; and on a third, there were craftsmen laying paint and gold leaf on wondrous figureheads of mermaids, tritons, stallions and admirals, which had been far and wide across the oceans.

Having been a landman all my life, aside from crossing to Flanders as a soldier, I was entranced by all this, and by the smell of tar and salt, and the sight of sailors, with rings in their ears and whiskers curled in ringlets, and tarry pigtails, and their swaggering, clumsy sea-walk. Indeed, if I had seen as many kings or archbishops I could not have been more delighted.

Trelawney was away, aboard of our ship, when we reached the hotel. So we put our traps into the rooms made ready for us, and sat waiting his return in one of the grand public rooms where Joyce, Jim Hawkins and I were most comfortable. But Redruth and Hunter stared nervously at the velvet curtains, Indian carpets and crystal chandeliers, because they were plain country men in plain country clothes who feared that the high-nosed hotel servants might turn them away. So I told Redruth and Hunter to rest easy, and put a Spanish dollar in the hand of the chief servant, who became my friend forever, and who bowed low and brought rum punch and smiles for us all.

Later, Trelawney arrived, bellowing and blowing, in a long blue coat and sea-officer's hat. He advanced into the big room with a noise that caused every eye to turn, and delivering such a wonderful approximation of a mariner's sea-walk, that I had to smile.

'Livesey! Jim! Redruth!' he cried. 'And Hunter and Joyce!' He went round shaking hands, yelling for pots of ale and pouring out words, of which I remember only him insisting that I go at once to the Spyglass tavern, because — reading between his words — I deduced that he was not entirely sure of some of the men he had engaged. Thus he drew me aside.

'Doctor,' he said, whispering low, 'you know me: a straight judge of a man's character, and not one to be bamboozled?'

'Hmmm,' I said.

'Mr Hands and Mr Silver,' he said, 'are grand fellows. Seamen born and bred. And such as strike fear into England's enemies.'

'Yes?' I said, and ever so slightly, the smile faded from his face.

'I'd be grateful — not that I'm unsure — if you'd go along and meet them.'

'Of course,' I said. 'But to what purpose?'

'Oh, nothing special... just run the rule over them... have a few words...'

'Of course,' I said, 'if that is what you wish.'

'It is, Doctor, it is indeed.' Then a thought came to him and he smiled. 'And take Jim with you. He's a sharp 'un. He'll see at once if anything's not... well... take him with you! You'll find the Spyglass easy enough. Just follow the line of docks, and look for the sign of a large brass telescope.'

So out I went with the person whose company I least desired, and I was not pleased. But Jim was overjoyed at this chance to see some more of the ships and seamen, and we picked our way among a great crowd of people and carts and bales, for the dock was now at its busiest, and intensely fascinating. So, young Mr Hawkins turned on me his famous charm, and he smiled and chattered and asked my opinion of everything, thereby seeking to ingratiate himself.

'What might that be, Doctor, sir?' and 'Why are they called the *West*

Indies, sir?' and 'Where does tobacco come from, sir?' That and much more. Cunning little toad. But soon we reached the Spyglass, which was a bright enough place of entertainment, all neat and fresh-painted, with long windows, and a large room full of company, mostly being seafaring men. As we entered, a waiter in a long apron approached and gave a polite nod.

'Your pleasure, gentlemen?' he said.

'I am Doctor Livesey,' I said, 'friend of Squire Trelawney, and come to ask after Mr Hands and Mr Silver.'

'Ah!' he said. 'Be seated gentlemen, and I will fetch Mr Hands at once.'

So we sat at an empty table near the door, and the waiter went within the premises to a corridor at the back. He returned almost at once, and stood aside as three persons came out and walked down the room towards us. The last was a very tall, neat man, who had lost a leg and went on a crutch. This I knew must be Long John Silver, and before him came a sandy-haired, intelligent-looking man of middle size, dressed in gentleman's clothes: a broadcloth ensemble in modest grey. They were men in the prime of life: perhaps in their thirties. But nobody would have given them a glance compared with the woman who came first.

She was dark-skinned and young, and slim but with a full figure. She had the most penetrating eyes, fine teeth, the deportment of a dancer, and a gown worth a matched pair of carriage horses. Every man in the room gazed at her, and the boy Jim was transported into wonder, with eyes as round as bullets. So I suppose she was a lovely lady, but there was one such already in my heart and room for none other.

'Doctor Livesey?' enquired the sandy-haired man. 'I'm Hands, Israel Hands, late master gunner and now owner of this house.' Jim and I stood and we all shook hands. 'And this lady is Mrs Selena Silver,' said Hands, 'wife of Mr John Silver, my cook.'

'Good day, ma'am,' said Jim Hawkins, insinuating himself between myself and the lady, whose hand he took, and managed the astounding feat of kissing that hand with passion while gazing at its owner in adoration, and yet doing so with such decorum and propriety that none of us could take objection, not even her husband, John Silver! It was a master work of deceit, and everyone smiled but me.

'You cunning, sly, devious, clever little toad,' I thought.

'And who are you, sir?' said the lady, much flattered.

'Jim Hawkins, ma'am, forever at your service,' he said, and the little devil managed a swift leer at myself, having heard me use the same words to his mother.

After that, we sat together and drink was fetched, and Mr Hands recounted much of what Trelawney had already told me, with Silver and his wife nodding, and taking little part in the conversation.

'So it's pirate treasure we're after,' said Hands, eventually, 'Flint's treasure.'

'Do you know anything of pirates?' I asked him. 'Or of Flint?'

There was the briefest silence then Hands and the lady glanced at Silver.

'Long John knows a little,' said Hands, and Silver reflected before he spoke.

'Flint?' he said. 'He was the blood thirstiest buccaneer that sailed. Blackbeard was a child beside Flint! The Spaniards were so prodigious afraid of him, that I was almost proud he was an Englishman. I've seen his top-sails, sir, with my own eyes, off Trinidad, and our cowardly son-of-a-rum-puncheon skipper, he put back into Port of Spain.'

So we passed a while in conversation, then I left with Jim Hawkins: he making yet another fine performance of his goodbye to Selena Silver, and afterwards chattering about her all the way to our hotel. But I ignored him, thinking of the people we had met.

The lady was correct and mannerly. Who knows what her upbringing had been, but somehow she had been given the deportment and speech of an English lady. Mr Hands was exactly what would be expected of a master gunner: thoughtful, measured and calm, because only such a man could be entrusted with the keys to the powder magazine, where one mistake will blow a ship to splinters and kill every man of her crew.

Those two I understood, or thought that I did. But Silver — Long John Silver as they called him — was a puzzle. He was quiet, saying nothing without prompting, but I had the feeling that Hands deferred to him, and I certainly thought that even crippled as he was, Silver had a strength and virility that spoke more of the soldier than the cook. Nonetheless, I detected no dishonesty or fraud, and I accepted the two men as shipmates. I was therefore, and in every way, as totally deceived as Trelawney had been.

But at that time, there were too many preparations to consider for me to ponder my decision. Thus we were soon out of the hotel and berthed aboard *Hispaniola*, making ready for sea. I recall being rowed out in a shore-boat, with Jim Hawkins, Redruth, Hunter and Joyce, past anchor cables, hulls and dense thickets of masts, and taking first sight of the ship, and what a pretty thing she was! She was a Maryland-built, two-masted, gaff-rigged schooner: flush-decked, steered with a tiller and with topmast and t'gallant on the fore-mast, and stay-sail and flying jibs before that. This rig, on a sharp hull, made her very fast, and she was pierced for a battery of guns. Of course I knew none of this technical vocabulary at the time. But what I did know was that *Hispaniola* was most pleasing to the eye, and I hoped that she sailed as well as she looked.

So the boat went alongside, and we passengers made our clumsy, landmen hash of climbing out of the rocking boat, and up what passed for a ladder: mere battens nailed to the ship's side, and which side rose like a mountain above us.

Then we got ourselves over the bulwark rail, and stepped into the tar-reeking, salt-spray world of timber, hemp, brass, iron and canvas which is an ocean-going ship. We stared at everything: the soaring masts, the incomprehensible web of rigging, the lines bound round the pin-rails and the rows of guns under their tarred-canvas covers. We did that while the seamen swiftly hoisted our luggage out of the boat, and doubled bare-foot across the deck to stow it below, knowing where everything went without being told.

We also stepped into a fierce argument between two men in the dress of ships' officers. One was Squire Trelawney, and the other was a thin, sharp-looking man with the dark-wrinkled face of the veteran seaman, though he was much the same age as myself. This man was Alexander Smollet, who was to be captain of *Hispaniola*.

'I tell you *no*, sir!' said Smollet, stamping his foot.

'I tell you *yes*, sir!' said Trelawney in such rage that I thought he might knock down Smollet on the spot. But then Trelawney saw me.

'Come aboard, Doctor!' he said. 'Come aboard and put this fellow in his place.'

'Fellow,' said Smollet, '*Fellow*? You must damn well touch your hat and call me *sir*!'

'Come below, both of you,' said Trelawney,' and he found a hatchway and went down a ladder without another word, and Smollet and I followed him into the stern cabin. The cabin was low, but most neatly furnished, with brass lamps, and cupboards, and shelves secured with wiring so that nothing should fall off. Meanwhile Trelawney slammed the door, closed the stern windows and turned on me.

'Doctor,' he said, 'tell this fellow—'

'This *what*?' demanded Smollet.

'Tell *Captain* Smollet,' said Trelawney with sarcasm, 'tell him that we have a true map of true treasure, and all details needed to find it!'

'Map?' said Smollet, with a sneer. 'Papers? More likely bog-house bum-wipes! There never was such thing as pirate treasure.'

'I see,' I said, understanding, and I held out my hand to Smollet. 'Captain,' I said, 'I'm David Livesey, and I'm to be ship's doctor.'

'Are you now?' said he, and shook my hand with little warmth.

'Your servant, sir,' I said, 'and I hope to start on good footing, by stating that Squire Trelawney himself once had the very same doubts as you in this matter,' and I looked at Trelawney. 'Isn't that so, Squire?'

'Oh…' said Trelawney, recollecting what he had so obviously forgot, and it is to his credit that his natural good nature conquered his temper. 'Well I'm damned,' he said, 'damned and roasted,' and he laughed. But Smollet still frowned. So I stepped in, and swiftly gave our reasons for believing that it was real treasure we were after; Flint's treasure, with Flint's map, and Flint himself on the trail of it.

'I see,' said Smollet when I was done, 'and is that why we shall have a master gunner, Mr Trelawney? Shall it be powder and shot? Shall it be *stand by to repel boarders*? For that's not what I understood when I took this commission!' And the two of them began to argue again, just as they argued about everything, ever after, through the sheer cussed collision of their particular personalities.

'I don't like the crew,' said Smollet.

'British tars every one!' said Trelawney.

'We'll stow arms and powder aft,' said Smollet.

'For'ard!' said Trelawney.

'We'll sail on the Monday tide,' said Smollet.

'Tomorrow!' said Trelawney.

'The first mate stinks something foul,' said Smollet.

'He does not!' said Trelawney.

'Gentlemen,' I said finally, 'can we at least agree that we are aboard a fine ship?'

'Ah,' said Smollet.

'Ah,' said Trelawney, and that is as near to unity as I could bring them, and in the end I left them to it, and I hope they enjoyed their quarrels because they never ceased.

That was my introduction to *Hispaniola*, and — victory for Captain Smollet — it was decided that we should sail on the Monday, once the last of our crew had come aboard, these being Israel Hands, John Silver and three others: Tom Morgan, George Merry and one 'Black Dog'. These five proved to be close friends, which at the time I did not remark upon though indeed I should have done, considering all that followed.

CHAPTER 13

Bidding farewell before going aboard *Hispaniola*, Silver embraced Selena, though it was as formal as the lord mayor embracing an alderman. It had to be like that, because they were in the public room of the Spyglass, with half Bristol crammed in to see him off, and stamping feet and drumming fists on tables to mark the event. But Silver and Selena had said their goodbyes in private and this was just for show, with Israel Hands and the rest stood by with sea chests on hand carts, and porters waiting.

'Three cheers for Long John!' cried someone, 'and may he bring back all the treasure in the Indies!'

'Aye!' bawled the company.

'Now,' said the first voice, 'hip-hip…'

'Huzzah!' they cried, and twice more to the word of command.

'Thank you right kindly,' said Long John to all the grinning faces, 'and there's free beer for all hands at my command.' Thus there was a joyful charge to the deep end of the room, where barrels and tankards were lined up in rows.

'Remember what I said, my girl,' said Silver, as the press surged past. Then he looked at the waiters in their aprons, 'and they'll be with you, and the girls in the kitchen.' But she laughed. The serving staff were good folk to carry a tray or roast a chicken, but not for fighting. Nobody would expect it of them.

'Don't worry, John,' she said, 'I'll sleep with pistols by the bed,' and he sighed as the guilt came surging over him that he must leave her unprotected.

'I have to go, lass,' he said. 'He'll come after me. I'll take the danger with me. He'll know Trelawney's got the map, and he'll come after that — by thunder he will!' He shook his head in emphasis. 'He'll come like the Devil after a soul,' which words were unfortunate when spoken to Selena, who had been born on a South Carolina plantation with a mother who believed in voodoo, the zombi and the midnight ton-ton man who stole children. Selena's fine education sat on top of that, but did not remove it.

'What is he, John?' she asked. 'Is he a man or something worse? I shot him, remember? In Savannah. I shot him fair and square, but he came back.'

'I don't care what he is,' said Silver, 'I only know I have to finish him.' He held Selena close. 'I'll skin him and gut him,' he said, 'I'll cut off his head and tear out his heart, and when I've done with him — I take my Bible oath on it — there won't be no coming back!' He kissed her once more before parting. 'Just be thankful he'll go after the treasure first. That before all else. First the treasure, then me, and I'll be ready!'

'So be ready,' she urged him, 'and be ready for that island.' She looked at Israel Hands, Tom Morgan and the rest. 'Because we all know it from the old days, and it's as rotten as Flint. It's a wicked place where wicked things were done. So all of you — take care.'

*

'We're bound for Bristol, Mr Hitchin,' said Flint, standing by the ship's wheel, and his quarter-master risked a glance at Pat Kelly the bosun, while all hands stood mustered in the waist, with hats off in respect, as Flint's standing orders required. The ship lay easy at anchor, the gulls called, the sun shone, and busy little boats pulled to and fro between the many vessels anchored in Polmouth harbour, second biggest of the West Country.

Hitchin raised hand to brow in salute.

'Why Bristol, Cap'n?'

'Why, Mr Hitchin?' said Flint. '*Why?* Because I say so! Do you require further explanation?'

Hitchin licked his lips nervously, remembering the last occasion that anyone had questioned Flint's orders: one Frederic Pitman, a shaven-skull bully-boy who had been a professional cudgeller at county fairs, and thought himself swift of hand. Flint had responded to Pitman's questions so skilfully that Pitman found himself playing *Flint's Game* to settle the matter. The game involved a small table, a carpenter's hammer and every one of Pitman's fingernails smashed bloody, while Flint made merry jokes and the crew roared with laughter.

Hitchin was an intelligent man, literate and numerate, and who — with Mr Arrow gone — was now first mate. Thus Hitchin understood just how powerful was Flint's mixture of sadistic brutality and wild humour, in delivering an obedient crew. But Hitchin still had private thoughts:

'He's touched is Flint… he ain't quite there… not by a long sea mile…' On the other hand, Hitchin believed everything he had been told about the biggest treasure ever put together in one place. So he shrugged and spoke.

'Aye-aye, Cap'n!' he said. 'All hands to up-anchor and make sail!'

Later, with the hands singing as they heaved the capstan round and brought in the anchor cable, and with Flint gone below, Hitchin spoke to Pat Kelly.

'Who was it came aboard before Flint gave orders to sail?'

'Dunno,' said Kelly, 'some bugger of a landman, in Flint's pay.'

'What did he want?'

'To talk to Flint. Then off ashore in his boat.'

'What did they talk about?'

'Dunno, but my guess is that he was telling Flint that Silver's sailed aboard *Hispaniola*, out of Bristol.'

'Aye,' said Hitchin, 'that'd be it. He's been waitin' on that, has Flint.'

'So why ain't we after Silver?' said Kelly. 'Flint knows where the island lies, 'cos it was him as drew the map in the first place. And he knows who's got the papers telling where the treasure's buried, 'cos he got that out of the boy Hawkins. He told us that when he come back from that buttocking-shop, and he was laughing fit to split, and all hands cheered.'

'Aye, matey,' said Hitchin, 'that's Flint for you. He knows how to tickle the hands. He says what he wants us to hear, and no more. So if you want to go below and ask him why we're bound for Bristol, then down you go and God speed to you! But I shall steer a safe course, and do as I'm bid.'

Meanwhile Flint sat in the stern cabin, enjoying a bottle of wine; something he very rarely did. But now he raised a glass.

'To Long John Silver!' he said. 'Whose company I shall seek out with utmost determination, even though it is not the first duty that lies before me.'

*

Selena woke up and began to worry. It was only the second night after Long John had gone with Squire Trelawney, and a griping fear was tormenting her, though she tried to deny it. So she lay in the darkness

117

and listened to the sounds of the house: creaks and groans of old timbers and a loose window rattling in the wind. There was noise from outside too, because ships sailed when the tide was right and not by the clock, so dockyard preparations might go on all night. Thus a wagon rolled past with a clopping of hooves and a rumble of iron tyres, and stopped nearby, even at this hour.

Selena tried hard to explain away her fears. Long John said he'd given up the pirate life — all of it. He'd promised! He was come ashore and would stay ashore, and he'd given up the map and treasure in Savannah. He'd done so because she'd told him that he must choose *her* or the old life. And so they'd come to England and lived clean and comfortable... until now.

Because Flint wasn't dead, Trelawney had the map, and it would be a race for the treasure, and surely end in a fight. Then maybe Flint would win? Or maybe Trelawney would win and Long John would have the treasure in front of him, and he'd be on the island and changed by the island , with all its memories, and what would he do then? She worried and worried, because she knew Long John very well indeed. She knew how deeply he believed in his 'articles' and his 'gentlemen of fortune' and how much he loved the sea life. She knew what a leader he was among men, such that they'd follow him not out of fear, but for trust and admiration. She knew how great would be the temptation to go back to the old ways once he was out of her sight. Finally — reaching bitter conclusion — she knew that if he did go back to the old ways, he would betray every promise he'd ever made her and she would have to—

Clunk! Something sounded outside the bedroom.

Selena stared blindly into the night. She listened hard. No more noises came. She shifted in her nightgown. She turned over. She made the pillows comfortable. She tried to sleep. But now her fears for Long

John were replaced by primordial fright, as the fantasy monsters of childhood — finding her to be alone in the dark — crept out of memory and howled to be recognised. She attempted to remind herself that she wasn't really alone, because three kitchen girls and a waiter slept in the house, and all the doors and windows were bolted, so the house was safe. That's what Selena *tried* to believe, but it didn't drive off the night-time horrors, because she'd been bred up among folk who were steeped in supernatural belief — believing it to be proven reality — and even the strongest mind struggles to throw off the lessons of childhood.

So Selena was consumed with fear, and wanted to curl up under the bedclothes and not move, for fear of provoking some monster to pounce. Worse still, she was *sure* that there were more noises down below, and *sure* that the door had creaked open, and *sure* that something was slithering across the floor towards her.

Then Selena fought back. She was not a terrified child, but an intelligent woman: one who'd seen storm and shipwreck, battle and death. So she dismissed her fears as infantile and reached for the pistols on the bed-side table, seeking their comfort in the dark night.

But as her fingers touched them… a hand seized her wrist and held it tight.

CHAPTER 14

From Dr Livesey's journal:

Hispaniola proved to be a most splendid seafaring ship, though somewhat wet as was explained to me by Captain Smollet on our first day at sea, while land was still in sight and a traffic of ships about us on the grey waters.

''Tis all compromise, with ships,' said Smollet, as we stood by the helmsman on the tiller, and I had to hang on to the rail to keep my footing, with the ship heeled over under a press of sail and myself not having acquired my sea-legs. 'Take your east-coast collier,' he continued, 'broad in the beam and round in the belly, such as rises to the waves and barely breaks them. But she's built for cargo not speed.'

'I see,' I said, even though my attention wandered because a delight had appeared further forward — or for'ard as I must now say — and which was the boy Jim Hawkins, with a face as green as grass, clinging to the capstan and heaving his stomach dry.

'Urrrrrgh!' he cried. 'Yuuuurch!'

'While so fine a ship as this…' Smollet was still speaking.

'Urrrrrrrrgh!'

'…cuts the waves like a knife, and heaves the spray back over her shoulder, but runs like a racing stallion!'

'Urrrrrrgh!

'Oh!' said Smollet, seeing why I smiled, and he looked at me. 'Are you not feeling the motion yourself, Doctor?'

'No,' I said.

'Then you're a lucky man,' he said, 'for there's few, even among seaman, as don't.' And then he frowned and let loose a masthead-hailing bellow. 'You there! Ship's boy! Swab up that mess or you'll get my boot so far up your breech, it'll come out your mouth!' He nodded at me. 'I'll have no favourites aboard *my* ship!' he said, and by Jove but I began to like Captain Smollet, and when I laughed he began to like me too.

After that, with the ship charging out into the deeps beyond the shore, there was a most wonderful process of trimming sails and heaving on lines, and the entire setting-up of the ship into the plan Captain Smollet wanted. Then credit again to Trelawney, who stood beside me to observe, and had the sense to make no comment, other than:

'See, Doctor,', pointing to the very numerous deck-hands who ran to their duties, instantly working together, as seamen do. 'See the wisdom of a large crew. I wanted thirty to fight pirates if we have to, but *many hands makes light work* as the saying goes, and every task is done all the quicker.'

Later I had further initiation into seamen's ways, as Mr Arrow came up to take over the watch from Captain Smollet. Arrow was a man I never liked, because he did indeed stink, and I suspected other uncleanliness within him. Also he seemed constantly to be nervous: which in fact he had good reason to be, as we eventually found out. Nonetheless he was a skilled navigating officer. Thus Arrow approached Smollet, and touched his hat in salute.

'Cap'n, sir,' he said. 'I'm come on deck, sir.'

'Your watch, mister,' said Smollet, 'course: south, south-west, with a touch of weather helm, and running hard at eleven knots.'

'Aye-aye!' said Arrow, which is as much as I understood of their conversation, because Smollet chose to stay and chat, perhaps feeling out the manner of his first mate, and I do my best here to represent some of their speech.

'I've tried for years taking in sail with the weather clewlines,' said Smollet, 'and I'd have given my oath that nothing serves like the weather clew. But now it's lee clew first!'

'Aye!' said Arrow, 'For in the first place the sail gets over the lee yardarm, and then if your weather brace should be carried away taking in a top-sail, then your lee rigging strains nigh to breaking.'

'So it does,' said Smollet, 'and bear in mind that in hauling up the lee clewline first: you have a heavier but steadier strain.'

'Whereas hauling the weather clew…' said Arrow. Then on, and on, ad nauseam. But every discipline has its gobbledygook, as anyone may see who looks into a medical journal. So I listened a while longer, Trelawney nodded as if in understanding, and at last — when I could bear it no more — I went below to order my things in the little cabin I had been given.

The whole schooner had been overhauled for our purpose, with six berths made astern, out of what had been the after-part of the main hold. This set of cabins was joined to the galley and forecastle only by a passage on the port side, and the berths were given to Trelawney, myself, Jim Hawkins, Joyce and Arrow, with Redruth and Hunter sharing one. Meanwhile, Captain Smollet slept in a round-house on the main-deck. It was very low but with room to swing a hammock, and it was as close to the tiller and binnacles as any shipmaster could wish, in case of emergencies. As for John Silver and the rest of the hands, they slept for'ard as was normal practise aboard any ship.

In the next days a ship's routine was established, with each twenty-four hours divided into watches, wherein half the crew was on duty and half not, as is the fashion at sea, and the reckoning of each day began not at dawn, but at noon, with the sun at its highest. At this time the navigating officers, Smollet, Arrow and Trelawney, would take their 'noon observation' with quadrants, such that the ship's position might be found by calculation. Noon was also the time for the men to go to their dinners, and receive their first allowance of grog. So noon was a happy time aboard ship.

In addition to the normal routine of a ship at sea, Trelawney insisted on weekly gun drill, as if we were a man o' war. Captain Smollet disapproved; partly because it was nonsense in the merchant service, but mainly because it was Trelawney's idea.

'Wasteful of time,' he said, 'for we're at peace with both France and Spain.'

'What about pirates?' asked Trelawney. 'Considering what we're going after?'

'Pirates?' said Smollet, 'Only if they get word from a man with a loose jaw.'

'Meaning who?'

'Meaning him that has a loose jaw!'

'D'you mean me, sir? How dare you, sir!'

'I dare because it's a waste of money to burn so much powder!'

'My money, sir!' said Trelawney. 'And worth every penny!'

As ship's owner, Trelawney prevailed, and each week one of the ship's boys took up a drum and the ship beat to quarters, and Mr Hands took command of this drill most competently and our battery was made ready, and run out, and a few rounds fired for practise. Then what a surprise it was to see how much the men liked it! I suppose that with the great noise and huge smoke clouds it was like letting off fireworks. Trelawney had certainly spent money on equipping the ship with a full powder magazine, so I suppose he was determined to use it.

He also took time to educate me on the manner of our crossing of the Atlantic, which we had to do since our treasure island lay off the South American continent, north of the Brazils. Thus I had assumed that a ship crossing the Atlantic steers westward from Britain and sails to its destination — but no! Trelawney explained what must be done, one day as we sat on the main-deck after dinner, leaning against one of the aftermost guns ,with our bellies comfortably full.

'A ship can't steer direct for the Americas,' he said, 'since in our English latitudes, the winds blow mostly from the west.'

'I see,' I replied.

'So a mariner has to go south, with the wind on his beam, and find the trade winds.'

'I've heard of those,' I said, 'but what are they?'

'A mighty disturbance in the air, Doctor, just north of the Equator, whereby steady winds blow westward to carry a ship to the Caribbean, and the American colonies, and all the wonders of the new world.'

'So how far south must we go?' I asked.

'Depends on the season,' he said. 'Not so far in summer, but somewhere in the region of thirty degrees of latitude, and north of the Portuguese Canary Islands.'

'So the trade winds take us westward,' I said, 'but how then do we come home across the ocean?'

'Easily,' answered Trelawney, 'we go north to find the westerlies, to carry us home.'

So much for my education, though now I allow myself a little pride in my own application of science — not so much for its intended purpose as for a happy accident which occurred later. Thus before embarking on the expedition I had read widely on the medical perils of seafaring, and was worried by the risk of scurvy: a disease endemic among those on preserved rations, and which killed thirteen hundred men on Admiral Anson's great circumnavigation of 1740–1744. I had also read of the Scottish physician James Lind's experiments with the prevention of scurvy by lemons, and was resolved to try something similar. But I could think of no way of persuading seamen to eat lemons, and hoping that some other fresh fruit might serve, I paid for a great barrel of apples to be taken aboard *Hispaniola*, and left open by the mainmast, where any man who fancied, might take one. And Trelawney approved of this.

'You're wise to offer them free-willingly,' he said, ''cos Jack Tar don't like being told what to eat, and if you ordered him, he'd say no just to spite you.'

Otherwise, aboard ship, the hands settled into their messes and the rest of us into ship-friendships, myself taking a glass now and again with Captain Smollet, and Joyce — whom I found to be a wide-read and educated man — while Smollet and Trelawney avoided one another when they could, and behaved with formal politeness when they could not. Meanwhile Hunter and Redruth kept together, and Mr Arrow dined alone because nobody wanted him in their company. This was a sorry portent of what was to come, though he did spend some time talking to two of the hands that, like himself, had been introduced to Trelawney by his friend Blandy. These were Alan McGuigan, an Ulsterman, and Louis Baudry, who was French on his father's side. The three were an odd mixture — not actually friendly, since a first mate could not sit down to eat with deck-hands, but at least it gave Arrow someone to speak to.

Then of course there was John Silver and his followers: it was soon obvious that that is what they were, even if Israel Hands affected to be the master among them. This little group spent their off-watch time together, down in the galley during foul winds, and usually accompanied — to my great surprise — by Jim Hawkins, whom they obviously liked, especially Silver.

Thus early in the voyage, with Jim recovering from his sea-sickness, I saw him meet Silver for the first time aboard ship, during one of the quaintly named 'dog watches' which ran for two hours each, in the afternoon and early evening. The boy was up on deck, now looking grey rather than green, and just about able to make his way without hanging on. Silver was on deck to smoke a pipe by the lee rail with Israel Hands, and he looked at Jim and smiled, and Jim smiled back, because for reasons of personal alchemy that are beyond my understanding, the two of them liked one another. My best attempt to explain this is that Silver and his wife being childless, perhaps Silver saw Hawkins as the son he might have had? He certainly treated him like a son; because as Hawkins stumbled, Long John reached out a hand in concern.

'Steady as she goes, lad,' he said, 'back your topsail, and parlay.' So they fell to chattering, and Jim Hawkins perked up, and the colour came back to his face, and Long John nodded.

'Good lad,' he said. 'Smart as paint you are. I saw it the moment I clapped eyes on you.'

The result of this, over the next days, was such a change in the character of Jim Hawkins that I began to think I had misjudged him. Thus he took to the sea life something wonderful, and would join in with the hands at their work, and would run from one end of the ship to the other, and up the shrouds and into the rigging, in competition with the younger seamen, some of whom were little older than himself, though roughened and toughened by their calling.

'Skylarking!' said Trelawney the first time I watched Jim run up the shrouds. 'There's a sea-word for you Doctor: *skylarking*.' Trelawney smiled, and looked up and raised his voice.

'Go on, Jim-lad! Go on, my hearty!'

'Aye-aye, sir!' cried Hawkins.

'Ah,' said Trelawney, 'there's my bold, brave boy!' and he winked at me. 'He comes of good stock, does our Jim!' And he laughed, and for once I laughed with him. And all was due to the influence of Long John Silver upon Hawkins, for he admired Silver greatly, as we all did, because the man was a phenomenon.

I saw this for myself, from the first moment he came aboard, with his crutch slung round his neck on a line to leave his hands free. He was out of the shore-boat, and up the side and over the rail at a speed, and with a nimbleness that put shame on my own efforts. He was likewise agile with the ship under way, moving across the decks and up and down companionways, just as well on his one leg and crutch as any fit man on two legs. The crew respected him to a degree that was remarkable, touching their hats to him, even as they called him 'Barbecue' which was the West India seaman's name for a cook. In fact the only way in which he was inferior to others was during a strong blow, with the seas coming over the rail, when his crutch slipped in the wet and the crew therefore rigged some lines across the deck for him to cling to, and which were known as 'Long John's earrings'.

Beside that there was the great, green parrot that he brought aboard, and which clung to his shoulder, and would never be parted from him except to perform her offices, taking flight such that no droppings ever sullied the decks.

'Ah, she's a sea-bird from head to tail,' he would say, as the hands gathered around to pet the bird and hold out pieces of food. 'And old?

Why, such as her is only babies at one hundred years, and they lives forever mostly,' and he would tickle her head, and she would gently nibble his ear, and then cry out:

'Pieces of eight! Pieces of eight! Pieces of eight!'

'Aye!' said Silver, on one of these occasions. 'Hark to her! She saw the Manila galleon took, did this bird. She saw it took, and the Spanish dollars pouring on the decks like waterfalls. She's seen that and worse,' and he sighed, and took off his hat as if in church. 'Sweet Jesus save the souls that died, 'cos this old bird's seen such wickedness as would shrivel the heart of a stone statue.' Then he smiled and put his hat on his head, and looked at me standing by, as if he'd just noticed me. 'Doctor!' he said, touching his hat in the most respectful manner. He was a great puzzle to me, was Long John Silver, with his appeal to 'Sweet Jesus'... and I wondered if he were mocking me.

Then we suffered a mystery, and the mystery was Mr Arrow, who took to coming on deck with clumsy feet and slurred speech as if he had been drinking. Captain Smollet took him aside several times for interrogation, attempting discretion so the crew should not know — which of course they did, since they were looking on with eyes like hawks and ears like donkeys. On these occasions, Mr Arrow would shake his head vigorously and deny everything. Once, Smollet even appealed to me, waiting for a moment when the two of us were below decks in the half-dark, where the deck heaved under our feet, the timbers creaked and a square of light came from the hatchway above. He stopped me with a polite word and we peered at one another.

'Doctor,' he said. 'A word in private. Can a man *seem* drunk, and yet not be?'

'Perhaps,' I said, 'if he has a fever.'

'And can he smell of drink if he's not taken any?'

'Not to my knowledge.'

'Damnation!' he exclaimed.

'It's Mr Arrow, isn't it?'

'Yes,' he said, 'and he's just made me search his cabin for drink, to prove he's got no bottles hid, and he ain't — not in there, leastways — but there's rum on his breath and no mistake.'

So we puzzled over our mystery and I even looked in the few books I had with me, to see if there was any known illness, any imbalance of the bodily humours, that might explain Mr Arrow's behaviour. But of course I found no medical explanation because the truth was — or at least I supposed it to be — that he was seeking refuge in drink because nobody liked him and he had no authority over the men. As Trelawney said of him:

'A first mate should be a bulldog, and he's not even a pup.' And Trelawney was right, because Arrow had no physical dominance what-soever. I had only to remember Billy Bones to know that: Mr Bones with his mighty fists and thundering brow! But I thought there were deeper reasons, because while Arrow could navigate and knew his sails and rigging, even setting aside his personal dirtiness, he never seemed at home aboard ship, and would have been happier ashore in some arithmetical employment: perhaps as a clerk in a counting-house. So I wondered... what had driven him to sea at all?

Aboard *Hispaniola* the crew agreed with me in all this, and said so with the vigour of sea-language. But although I was once a soldier, *full of strange oaths* as Shakespeare says, I cannot bring myself to write down what they said of Mr Arrow — even though it was very funny.

CHAPTER 15

'Arrow?' said Tom Morgan. 'He'll never shit a seaman's turd!' and everyone laughed: Silver, Hands, Merry and Black Dog, but then the ship's bell sounded.

'Eight bells,' said Silver. 'Turn o' the watch, and he'll be down for his quantum, so all hands to stations, and leave me clear seaway.'

All but Silver got up and left the galley; the snuggest place in the ship, carpentered to a nicety with cupboards, counters and folding tables, and with an iron stove, and pots, plates and knives lined up like the Prussian Guard. All that, and a wholesome scent of good food, and cram-packed casks and jars of provisions. So, as the last men went out, Silver propped his crutch against a bulkhead, and got up and drew out a big gallon jug from behind a line of casks. He put the jug on a table, found a pair of horn cups, and got himself seated, while from above there came the rumble of bare feet on the main-deck as the larboard watch stood down, and the starbolins ran to their duties.

Soon there was the sharper sound of leather shoes, and Mr Arrow came through the hatchway, and Silver smiled.

'Mr Arrow!' he said. 'Drop anchor, and take a noggin with Long John.'

'Thank you right kindly, Mr Silver,' said Arrow, who slumped down on a stool and took off his hat. 'Such oafs and blackguards I have to deal with!' he exclaimed. 'There's no discipline among them.'

'It's the times we live in, sir,' said Silver. 'You can't get proper seamen no more, only pups that's run away from their mothers.' And he drew the cork from the jar with a resounding *boomp* that brought a smile to Mr Arrow's face, and an even greater smile when Silver poured a generous measure into Mr Arrow's cup. Then Silver poured a tiny drop into his own cup, and raised it, and leaned across — braving the smell — and whispered to Mr Arrow as if to a friend.

'This is the stuff for kings and princes! Near twice the strength of common rum.'

'Oh yes?' said Arrow.

'Aye,' said Silver. 'So: here's to ourselves, and hold your luff: plenty of prizes and plenty of duff!' Then more toasts were drunk until Mr Arrow — barely capable of standing — made his way to his cabin and his hammock, to sleep until his next watch. As he went, Silver, who had barely wetted his lips, put away the jug, and sat waiting until Israel Hands and the rest returned. It made a tight squeeze in the narrow galley, but there was need of a council.

'Now then, brothers,' said Silver, 'we've got him prepared, and accustomed to the drink, but are we sure of what he is? Are we *sure*, before we give him his dues?'

Everyone looked at Black Dog. 'Step forward, brother,' said Silver. 'We've heard it before, but we'll hear it again, 'cos we're gentlemen of fortune, and shall act under articles.'

'Aye-aye!' said Black Dog, touching his brow. 'Well I heard,' he said, 'I heard the bosun — Job Anderson — talking to Arrow. Anderson was talking about the men what was sent round by Flint, to ask for Billy Bones.' Everyone nodded. 'He said — Job Anderson said — that he was in Polmouth when them men was going round, and he saw Arrow among 'em, and Arrow was givin' orders to the rest.'

'And what did Arrow say to that?' asked Silver.

'He said it weren't him, and he weren't there, and he'd swear it on the Bible.'

'And what did Job Anderson say?' said Silver.

'Well,' said Black Dog, 'he said — Job Anderson said — if it weren't *you* Mr Arrow, it was someone that *smelt* like you, and Job Anderson laughed.'

There was a silence as everyone looked to Silver, who nodded slowly.

'He's Flint's man,' he said, 'and we'll have to do what's needed.'

'What about Baudry and McGuigan?' asked Israel Hands. 'They're close with Arrow, and they're the only men aboard ship that is. What about *them*?'

'I don't know,' admitted Silver, 'but I do know that them two together ain't right; not from what I hear, 'cos the one's a Pope's catholic and other's an Orange protestant!'

'Aye, but it don't make them Flint's men,' said Hands.

'No,' agreed Silver, 'so those two may stand easy until proven guilty, but for Arrow, my brothers, then I propose to this council that we shall move as follows. First, we shall get alongside of all hands aboard this ship, as will steer a course with us.' Silver looked around, everyone nodded, and he continued. 'Then, regarding Arrow, we shall wait for the first good storm of wind, and...' but Silver fell silent as footsteps sounded. 'Ah!' said Silver, smiling. 'Come aboard Mr Hawkins, these lads here was just leavin' and you and I can have a good old yarn.'

So there was a scraping of stools, and the rustle of men getting up, as, taking their lead from Long John, Israel Hands and the rest smiled at Jim Hawkins and made way for him.

'Don't go on my account,' said Hawkins, but they all grinned and went out.

'Sit down, lad,' said Silver. 'Sit down along o' Long John and take a bunch of raisins and a glass of Madeira — you're man enough for that by thunder!' They both laughed, Silver served food and drink, and a most pleasant conversation followed; at least for a while, as Silver told of the sea life, and the lands he had seen, and eventually of pirates.

'What were you saying about the old days, Mr Silver?' enquired Hawkins. 'The last time we spoke?'

'Long John!' said Silver. 'Call me that, 'cos I answers to no other name!'

'Then… Long John,' said Hawkins.

'Well, lad, it's like this,' began Silver, shoving another bunch of raisins towards Jim. 'In them days there was pirates and there was gentlemen of fortune.'

'And what's the difference?' asked Hawkins.

'I'll tell you,' said Silver. 'Because in old England — which thinks itself free — barely one man in every hundred has the vote to send members to parliament, while among gentleman of fortune, them as has signed articles and bound themselves together: why! Every man votes as good as any other.'

'And what about respect for women?' said Hawkins.

'Ah, that's my lad,' said Silver. 'You remembers what I told you, don't you?' Jim Hawkins nodded. 'So,' Silver went on, ' according to articles,' and he touched his brow in respect, 'no brother shall lay hands on a woman that ain't willing.' And Hawkins nodded, much impressed, because despite his own greed for women, he imagined his mother aboard a captured ship and dependant on the mercy of her captors. Thus the more Silver spoke, and the more time Jim Hawkins spent with Silver, the more he nurtured the good within Jim Hawkins, of which there was some, since all creatures are a mixture of good and bad.

Thus the life of a gentleman of fortune, as Silver told it, was a life of honour, brotherhood and subservience to rules. But then the conversation took a sharp turn as Silver's parrot woke up from dozing on her perch in a corner.

'Pieces of eight! Pieces of eight! Pieces of eight!' she said, and Silver and Hawkins jumped.

'Be still you old fool!' cried Silver, and threw a pocket handkerchief over her head, so she squawked and wriggled to get rid of it, before hopping onto Long John's shoulder where she stood and rubbed herself against his chin, and he stroked her feathered head.

'Why's she called *Captain Flint*, Long John?' asked Hawkins, and Silver was so relaxed, petting the bird, that he spoke without thinking.

''Cos Flint had her before me,' he said, then '*Ah!*' as he recognised a mistake in admitting closeness to so notorious a pirate. But Long John was not a man to dissemble or deny, and looked straight at Hawkins. 'So, my lad,' he said, 'you heard what I said, and now what do you make of it?'

Jim Hawkins thought very hard before replying.

'Did you know him, then? Flint?' he said finally.

'Aye,' said Silver.

'What was he like?'

'Bad. Worse than you can dream of.'

'Was he a monster? Was he ugly?'

Silver laughed out loud. Then he got up and found the jug of special rum and poured some into a horn cup. 'You'll pardon if I don't share, my lad,' he said, 'as this is more medicine than drink.'

'You were talking about Flint, Long John, and how he was ugly.'

'Ugly, says you?' Silver closed his eyes, remembering, then looked at Hawkins. 'No! He was smooth as a panther! He was handsome as

Lucifer!' Silver drained his cup and poured more. 'He was handsome, quick as lightning and vicious besides.'

'And soft spoken,' said Hawkins.

'That he was,' nodded Silver, and stared hard at Jim Hawkins. 'But how did you know that?'

'Billy Bones told me,' said Hawkins, in a fluent lie. 'He was at the Admiral Benbow when the pirates attacked us.'

'Billy Bones?' said Silver, and this time he guarded his tongue as memories came in on the flood. 'He'd have been a seaman I suppose? One that knew Flint?'

'Yes,' said Jim Hawkins, 'he knew Flint.' And in that moment the brief period ended, when the life of Jim Hawkins might have been changed for the better by his admiration of Long John Silver. It ended because — all in an instant rush — Jim Hawkins understood several things, which fitted together like the pieces of a broken pot miraculously re-joined.

Thus he realized that he too knew Captain Flint, and that Silver was the one-legged seaman Billy Bones had feared, and that Flint was more powerful than Silver. Even beyond that he realized that he — Jim Hawkins — knew things that Long John Silver did not: not Silver, nor Squire Trelawney, nor Doctor Livesey, nor Captain Smollet, nor any of them.

So Jim Hawkins smiled and made new plans.

CHAPTER 16

From Dr Livesey's journal:

We were ten days out from Bristol when the first of the events occurred that signalled dangers beyond those we had expected.

First, Mr Arrow's behaviour grew worse and he regularly turned out with hazy eyes, red cheeks, stuttering tongue, and all the marks of drunkenness such that time after time Captain Smollet had to order him below in disgrace. Then sometimes he fell and cut himself, sometimes he lay all day long in his hammock, and sometimes he would make the effort of coming on deck and attempt to give orders to the men. But that was the worst of it, because they openly jeered, and even laid hands on him, turning his hat back-to-front, or — in the rough humour of seamen — attempting to trip him, at which Captain Smollet or Squire Trelawney would roar out in anger, cursing the hands for their impertinence, and receiving in reply such ugly looks as threatened the foundation of ship's discipline.

Then, our ship having found the trades, and sailing gallantly westward at great speed, we ran into a mighty storm of wind, with a head sea and a black sky, with rain coming down like iron rods, and such terrifying claps of thunder, and such violent, lurid lightning, that the whole universe seemed an apocalypse of sensation. Or at least it did to me, because when the storm came down on us, Trelawney hauled me out of my cabin and on deck with him to see the storm, and he grinned and yelled into my ear.

'Catch a look, Doctor,' he said, 'it's worth seeing, though it ain't nothing compared with the typhoons of the Indies.' He was yelling into my ear because the noise of the wind was so great that conversation was possible only if one man bellowed into the ear of the other, as we clung to hand lines with the sea and the rain streaming off our oilskins, and Captain Smollet was likewise shouting into the ear of Job Anderson the bosun.

Here I must pause to state, that while it would be insufferably dull to repeat constantly that we shouted into one another's ears, I stress most emphatically that it was only by that means that we communicated at all. So we bellowed and yelled, and I direct readers to understand that conversation aboard a ship in a storm does not proceed as it does in a gentleman's library, but only by the utmost and heroic exertions of the larynx. So:

'See now, Doctor,' cried Trelawney. 'We shall have to lie-to.'

'What's that?' I asked.

'It's bringing the bows of the ship as close to the wind as can be,' he said, 'and look aloft! See how our brave fellows strike sail!' He nodded in admiration of their seamanlike skills, combined with Smollet's ship-handling. 'She'll bear only a reefed topsail in a blow like this,' he continued, 'with all other canvas struck. So she can't steer her course, but must ride out the storm as best she may.' Then, 'Yes! Yes!' he cried, 'that's the way lads!' as up aloft the top-men worked with marvellous dexterity to take in most of our sails and reef the topsail, and all in the most hideous blast of wind, and performing such feats of acrobatics as would have brought applause on the London stage. I laughed too at the joy of my friend, and his confidence drove off some of my anxiety, at least until his next words.

'This way she'll bear the oncoming seas,' he said, and he pointed ahead. So I looked and saw what he meant by 'oncoming seas,' which was an endless succession of colossal waves: waves the height of our main-mast, waves like wet black mountains, waves that drain a man's courage and pump him with fear, as they bear down like a charge of the Devil's dragoons. But Trelawney never wavered.

'Ah!' he said, 'feel how she rides!' And *Hispaniola* proved her worth because even with her sharp bows she rose to the waves and refused to let them drown her. 'She's Baltimore built,' said Trelawney, 'a Marylander out of Chesapeake Bay!' and he seized my arm and shook it. 'Now ain't this the life, Doctor?' and he laughed and laughed, 'ain't this why we left home?' Then, 'Whoa!' he cried, as the ship lurched, and Captain Smollet shouted orders and made corrections accordingly.

'See, Doctor,' said Trelawney, 'the ship can't do everything herself, or she'd be turned beam-on, and be rolled and dismasted, or worse still, she might be driven stern-on to the weather, with the waves breaking down on us and driving us bodily under.' So I watched and wondered, understanding little of the seamanship, other than to marvel at it, noting only that Captain Smollet had four men on the tiller at all times, and lines rigged — like Long John's earrings — giving us something to cling to on a canted, heaving deck, that one second was drained of water and the next was waist deep.

This monstrous gale of wind lasted two days, with Captain Smollet leaving his post only when relieved by Trelawney, or by the bosun Job Anderson when both Smollet and Trelawney were exhausted, and the best of this is that Trelawney and Smollet finally saw some good in each other as fellow seamen, and so they ceased their bickering.

Note, that I have not mentioned our first mate, Mr Arrow, who should have taken his turn on watch. But he did not do so, because at first he was drunk, and after that because he entirely disappeared during the first night of the storm, and was never seen again. At the time, the obvious-seeming explanation, that he had been swept away by the storm, was accepted by those whom I will now call the 'loyal hands', in distinction from the great bulk of the crew who seemed to regard Arrow's loss as a merry joke. Thus, on the first day of good weather after the storm, Captain Smollet mustered all hands and attempted a few words of farewell for Mr Arrow. But the crew would not follow his lead.

Mr Smollet had a Bible in his hand, and wore his best hat and coat, and I think would have attempted divine service if the manner of the men had permitted. But even though the sea was now benign, with a good fresh wind, clear skies and bright sunshine, and even with *Hispaniola* forging along like a mail-coach, the crew were in an odd mood. They had distinguished themselves with exemplary behaviour during the storm, but every seaman does that out of sheer self-interest, and he accepts discipline for the same reason. So now that the storm was gone, there were other things working in their minds

So we stood by the tiller at the stern: me, Trelawney and his followers, with Jim Hawkins beside them, just behind Captain Smollet, who faced for'ard towards the rest of the crew, every man of them, other than the lookouts on the maintop and the helmsman at the tiller.

'Men!' said Smollet. 'We have lost a shipmate, as can happen at sea, but we must needs remember him, and say some words.' Even at that there were sneers and murmurs, and I noted the further oddity that the men did not stand in a body, but in three groups. The biggest formed around John Silver and Israel Hands, with a smaller group to one side, while McGuigan the Ulsterman, and the half-French Baudry stood together, alone. I noted that, and the looks that passed between these groups. Thus Silver's group were grinning at everyone other than McGuigan and Baudry, who received only scowls and disdain, while the rest who were not part of Silver's band, stood wondering and uncertain, and muttering to one another and paying scant heed to Captain Smollet. 'Come now, lads,' said Smollet, 'we've lost a comrade and as true Britons we must give respect for Mr Arrow.'

'Not for his fat arse!' said a voice at the back.

'Nyaaar,' said another, and there would have been more, except that John Silver stood forward and saluted Captain Smollet, and glared at all the rest.

'Avast there!' he cried, 'hats off for Mr Arrow!' and there was a dithering and a muttering, but then — led by Israel Hands and Tom Morgan — there was a rustle as the crew took off their hats. 'Aye!' said Silver, and saluted again. 'Beggin' your pardon, Mr Smollet, sir,' he said, but some o' these lads was born under a three-ha'penny planet, and their brains was laid bung-upwards.'

'Thank you, Mr Silver,' said Smollet. 'All hands dismissed to your duties!'

'Aye-aye, sir!' said Silver, and glared at the rest once more.

'Aye-aye, sir!' they said, but with little warmth.

Later Smollet spoke to Trelawney and me, privately at the taffrail astern of the tiller. He spoke softly.

'This is bad, gentlemen,' he said. 'I don't know what's working among the crew. If it weren't for John Silver I believe we'd have had mutiny. I've knocked men down for such looks as I got this morning, but I didn't dare today, not with so many of them in the same mood.'

'It's Arrow,' said Trelawney. 'They don't like — didn't like — him, and there's no loss there because the man was a lubber.'

'Yes,' nodded Smollet, 'but *I* didn't make him a lubber. It ain't my fault he'd got drink hid somewhere. It can't be that. So why the foul looks?'

'Who knows?' shrugged Trelawney. 'We have a fine ship, the men are well paid, they've good food, good drink — Navy rations of that — and even a barrel of apples to take as they choose.' He looked at me. 'What do *you* think, Doctor?'

'It's the treasure,' I said, 'it doesn't take Socrates to see that! It has to be the treasure, because chasing treasure doesn't make a normal voyage.' Then I looked at each of them in turn. 'Or does it?' I asked them. 'You gentlemen are the seamen, not I!'

'Of course it's the treasure!' said Smollet, 'I knew that! What I meant was: what's brewing among the lower deck *in that regard?* Are they resolved to take both ship and treasure, and do away with us?' And with those words, Captain Smollet expressed the fears that all three of us had carried, worrying in the backs of our minds, for some days. So there was relief to have the matter in plain view, and the three of us nodded and sighed, and we all looked for'ard to see what the men were up to, which in fact was no more than their duties. 'Then let's be grateful,' said Smollet, that the arms are stored aft with ourselves, and that we are six loyal hands to bear a musket each, and a brace of pistols.'

'Six?' said Trelawney, 'Surely seven: that's ourselves, which is three, plus Redruth, Hunter, Joyce and Jim Hawkins. That's seven!'

'If you count Jim Hawkins,' said Smollet, 'which I do not because he spends too much time with John Silver.'

'What,' said Trelawney, 'you don't trust Silver? But you said he stopped a mutiny.'

'So he did: for this morning,' said Smollet. 'But he ain't no cook, as all aboard this ship knows, 'cos it's Tom Morgan does the cooking, and I don't trust Tom Morgan, nor Black Dog, nor George Merry, and they're Silver's men.'

'But Jim!' said Trelawney. 'Not Jim! He's one of us,' and he looked at me. 'Come Doctor, you must admit that?' But even as he looked at me he read my expression, and doubtless thought of my past arguments against bringing Jim Hawkins at all. So I did not have to say a word. 'Oh,' he said, and he was near tears.

'Hold hard, Squire,' said Smollet. 'I'm not saying Hawkins is a mutineer. It's just that he's too close to those that are, or might be. I'm saying that we shouldn't tell Hawkins anything unless we want Silver's crew to know.'

'Silver's crew?' said Trelawney. 'His *crew*! Is *that* what we've brought aboard?'

'No,' I said. 'Captain! Squire! Did you not see how they were divided? Did you not see that two of them stood alone, and there was a whole group that weren't with Silver? They aren't one crew but two, at least, and I think that six loyal hands with firearms can still be the masters aboard this ship.'

'Spoken like a soldier!' said Smollet.

'Which he was!' said Trelawney.

'So we shall tell Redruth, Hunter and Lewis what's afoot,' said Smollet, 'but not Jim Hawkins.' He looked at Trelawney. 'Squire?' he said, and Trelawney nodded.

'Not Hawkins,' said Trelawney, 'we shan't tell him,' and he sighed deeply.

'Then,' said Smollet, 'if the crew really do turn nasty, I shall open the arms locker, and we shall walk the deck together, with brown bess in our arms and pistols in our belts.'

'Shouldn't we do that at once?' asked Trelawney.

'No!' said Smollet. 'Because we may have judged them wrong, and if we stand forth armed for a fight, we might bring on the very thing we fear, and would be forever watching of our backs, in fear of a knife, for the rest of the voyage. So it's the last resort of all, to go to the arms locker.' He looked at each of us. 'Do you agree, gentlemen?'

'Yes,' we said.

'What's more,' he went on, 'I want all hands pulling together, at least until we reach the island. You saw how the men worked together during that blow?' Trelawney and I nodded. 'Well then,' said Smollet, 'we may need them to do that again, and do it right willingly. So I don't want them dragging their feet like pressed men in fear of the lash.' He looked at the two of us. 'Do you agree?'

'Yes,' said Trelawney and I together.

'Good!' replied Smollet, 'and there's gun-drill in the afternoon watch, which never fails to put a smile on their dirty faces. So, Squire,' he said, and he smiled, 'I agree with you on the virtues of burning powder, and I praise your wisdom in bringing so much of it aboard.'

So we laughed and made the best of a bad job, and things went in this fashion for a considerable time, until we had almost reached the island. As Captain Smollet put it, in sea parlance: 'we've run up the trades, and got wind of her, and now we must run her down,' which meant that we had now reached the latitude of the island, as any competent mariner could do, and were somewhere to the east of it. However, since no man knew how to find a ship's longitude at sea, we must needs run along the line of latitude, heading westwards, until we came upon our destination.

This, we had almost done, and were hour-by-hour awaiting sight of the treasure island, when Jim Hawkins surprised us all.

CHAPTER 17

Flint slept uneasily. It was the dream again.

An admiring company sat all round. Fine people, richly dressed. They cheered and applauded. They loved Joe Flint. They gaped as he totally disrobed. They gasped as the basket came in. They stared as Flint removed the lid. They held breath as his naked arm drew forth a live serpent which wriggled and tried to strike.

But Flint was too fast!

He juggled the snake. Again, and again, it tried. But it missed every time. At last it sank, limp and exhausted. The applause was tremendous. But the snake stirred. The small, scaled, evil head turned up. It looked Flint in the eyes.

And Flint was paralysed.

The snake moved slow and easy. It opened its mouth. Sharp teeth dripped venom. It looked once more into Flint's eyes. *Then bit him!* It bit strong, and deep, and hard. It pumped in all its poison.

Flint woke up. Four bells of the morning watch had sounded and it was past dawn. He gripped the bedding hard. He sought reason or sense within his dream, as any decent man might when a nightmare is fresh in mind. But Flint was *not* a decent man. He was neither decent nor normal, nor at all like other men; not most of them anyway, because just as some men grow to be seven feet tall, some are rare in different ways and grow to be like Flint. But fortunately they are few. So Flint laughed at himself, and laughed at the dream, then he threw away the memory like emptying a chamber pot.

So he was out of his hammock and into his clothes, and — without conscious effort — noting the heel of the ship, the mood of the ocean, and the bearing on the compass in the cabin, because whatever else he might be, Flint was a fine seaman. Then he was out and up on deck, and breathing the breeze and the spray, and feeling the wind, and then running his eyes over every fathom of line and inch of canvas, to be sure that the ship was trimmed to rights, which fortunately it was: fortunately for the officer of the watch, Mr Hitchin the quartermaster, now acting first mate.

As captain, Flint stood on the weather rail, with his ship's people deferring to the lee side. He grinned at them, and they nodded in relief that his mood seemed fine, though you could never tell with Flint. But nobody dared speak before him.

'Good morning, Mr Hitchin!' said Flint, when he was quite entirely sure that the ship was as smart and clean as he wished; lines coiled, decks white, brass gleaming, guns secured with sheet-lead aprons over the touch-holes.

'Cap'n!' said Hitchin.

'Cap'n!' cried all hands, and gave the full seaman's salute: one finger to the brow and the right foot stamping hard on the deck. So many stamping feet reminded Flint of the applause in his dream, and he laughed again, where lesser men would have shuddered.

'Course is a point south of west,' said Hitchin, 'three spokes of weather helm, making nine knots at the last casting.'

'Well and good, Mr Hitchin,' said Flint. 'And has the supercargo yet appeared, this morning? Has it allowed the grace of its countenance once more to shine upon us?' Flint smiled, so everyone smiled: Hitchin, the helmsman, the watch on deck, even the ship's boys.

'No, Cap'n,' said Hitchin, '*it* ain't. *She* ain't,' and Hitchin grinned. 'But I suppose she ain't slept much?' he said, and there was laughter from those standing nearby. But then, even though Flint never said a word, and never even looked his way, Hitchin knew he'd said something wrong, and was very afraid.

'Mr Hitchin?' said Flint.

'Cap'n?'

'You may consider yourself relieved, and may take yourself below, and stay there until I send for you.'

'Aye-aye, sir!' said Hitchin. 'Aye-aye, Cap'n. Goin' at once, Cap'n. Goin' this very instant.' And Hitchin ran below at utmost speed, relieved that things had not gone worse.

Meanwhile Flint stood quite still, braced against the cant of the deck, with some part of him noting the run of the ship, the course steered, the change of the weather and the set of the sails. He even gave occasional orders. But mostly he was within himself in dreams as delightful as his nightmare had been hideous.

The business of the Spyglass Tavern had been well planned: the wagon, the finding out of who'd be in the house and where, the burglars' tools, the stockinged feet, the warnings of utmost silence to the chosen men, and finally and before all else, the actual moment of entering her bedroom in the dark, in secrecy, when Joe Flint had experienced the most tremendous erotic arousal, which he relished to such degree that he prolonged it until the utmost last second. Then came the warmth and feel of her, and breathing deep the scent of her, and letting none touch her but himself, and carrying her out and away, with a hand to stifle her cries, and warnings of what would happen if she struggled too hard. He lived again the memory, and smiled at the oddities of reality. Thus she'd come away with just her night-gown and a slipper that got itself on to one of her feet. Just one slipper. Then he laughed again.

'*Did the Romans enjoy it so much*,' he thought, '*when they took the Sabine women?*'

'Cap'n!' said a voice. 'Cap'n, sir!'

Flint woke up again. He looked round. One of the hands was calling him because she had come on deck. She had come out of the cabin he'd given her, next to his own. He looked at her. He looked and looked. She wore boys' clothes since there were no women's clothes aboard, nor men's that fitted. She wore a shirt, with britches and a belt, and a red scarf round her hair. No woman would have chosen such garments, but the crew were awestruck and Flint's emotions were profoundly stirred.

But the mood did not last. She was walking towards him and shouting.

'What have you done?' she cried. 'What do you think I am? What do you hope to get from me?' He could see that she was trembling and very afraid, as any woman would be, alone on a ship full of men, so he admired her courage in coming up on deck. He admired it greatly. But she was angry too.

'Ma'am,' he said, 'I did what I did only because—'

'Ma'am?' she said. 'Don't call me that! I've got a name. I'm John Silver's wife, and you know that I can never — *ever* — have anything to do with you! So what are you doing? I ask you again, what are you doing? Why am I here? What can you hope to gain by taking me out of my bed and bringing me here?'

Flint was lost for words, and his crew looked on amazed. But then Flint spoke from the heart.

'You are here because I want you here,' he said, 'and because I cannot be without you.'

'And you think that's *enough*?' she demanded, leaning forward and shouting into his face. 'What *you* want? Just *you*? Am I a cat or a dog? Am I a piece of china? What about what *I* want? D'you think I don't have a mind and a will?'

'I meant only,' said Flint, 'that...'

'I don't care what you meant! Damn you and damn what you want! Go to Hell Joe Flint, and don't ever touch me, or you'll get a knife in the ribs or a pistol ball, and remember this!' She raised her voice in a shriek. 'I'd rather jump into the sea than have *anything* to do with you, and I swear I will do so if you come anywhere near me!'

*

John Silver and Israel hands sat leaned against Dr Livesey's apple barrel, by the mainmast. Six bells of the middle watch had just struck, and it was dark. All was well with the ship, and the apple barrel was a favourite yarning place among the crew, so there was nothing suspicious in choosing to sit there. Even so, Tom Morgan, George Merry and Black Dog were on watch, to give warning in case Smollet, Trelawney or any of the others might fancy an apple.

'So what are we to do with them,' asked Israel Hands, 'and what course are we steering at all? When we set out, John, it was to settle accounts with Flint, and we weren't after no treasure, because we don't need it, and because you — beggin' your pardon — you promised your lady most faithfully that you was done with the old trade.'

Silver shifted in the dark, perhaps because it was uncomfortable for a one-legged man to sit on bare boards, or perhaps he was uncomfortable in his mind.

'I'll explain,' he said, and chose formal speech. 'If you'll let me, brother?'

'I do, brother,' said Hands.

'We has to think step by step,' said Silver, and Hands nodded. Silver continued. 'We've a good ship under us, and praise be to the blockhead Trelawney that he fitted her out man o' war style, with a battery of guns! And praise be that he has all hands to exercise the guns every week, which is more than we could have hoped for, and will be the saving of us should we come alongside of Flint.'

Hands frowned. 'D'you think he'll come ready to fight?'

'What, him,' said Silver, 'Flint? By the powers! He'll have a ship and a crew, and he'll give us round shot and musket balls. Leastways we has to plan for that, 'cos we'd be blockheads ourselves if we didn't!'

'Yes,' said Hands, 'that we would. Go on, brother.'

'So,' said Silver, 'if we're to fight Flint, we'll need a full crew, and one that answers to me and not to Smollet or Trelawney. So we has to sign up all aboard as is willing to be brothers, and brothers under articles, 'cos I'll have it no other way than free-willing volunteers and jolly companions!'

'Yes,' said Hands. 'So be it!'

'But,' said Silver, 'we shan't have no free-willing volunteers if I don't promise each man a share of the treasure, and that's the truth, as plain as print!' Hands said nothing. 'And so,' said Silver, 'We has to plan on taking command of the treasure, as well as the ship, so's we can divvy out the loot fair and square among them as joins us.'

But Israel Hands was still unhappy.

'Yes,' he said, 'but beware of some of them, as joins, and be sure you can keep a leash on 'em, 'cos the word's gone as to the manner in which Mr Arrow went over the side, and some o' the new lads thinks it should be the same for Smollet and Trelawney.'

'Some do,' said Silver, 'I grant that. But most thinks like me, and wants to let Trelawney find the treasure with his map.'

'But you know that island, John. We all know it: you, me, Tom Morgan, George Merry and Black Dog. We know it, and we know the things that were done there.' He shook his head. 'And bad things they were too. But we know the island, so even *I'm* wondering why we need a map.'

'We needs a map, 'cos who's to say where the diggings is?' said Silver. 'Who knows where Flint buried the goods? We needs his map and papers for that, and Trelawney's got 'em, but I'll not do murder to get the map off him. I'll be true to my lass in that at least, 'cos I'm a gentleman of fortune and not a pirate.'

'Well and good if we keep control of the crew,' said Hands, 'but what about afterwards? What'll we do with Trelawney and the rest, once we've got the goods?'

Silver thought long and hard but said nothing, and was much relieved when three seamen came up to them very politely, and very respectfully, with their hats in their hands.

'Ah!' he said, and smiled. 'Sit down, my lads. Sit down all hands as wants to be brothers.' And there was much more discussion: right up until dawn and a loud hail from the mast-head.

'Land-ho!'

CHAPTER 18

From Dr Livesey's journal:

'Land Ho!' cried the lookouts and every man of us came on deck in a rush, and the ship rolled heavily as we landmen ran to the rail, and the seamen up into the shrouds for the best sight of our destination. It was just after dawn, with the new sun's light on the island, and driving off a great bank of fog such as was often found in those waters. I was standing with Captain Smollet and Squire Trelawney, who gave a great shout of joy and thumped Smollet on the back. Also Jim Hawkins joined us, running up from somewhere all excited and staring, though I barely noticed him at first.

'Damn fine navigation, sir!' cried Trelawney, 'Francis Drake himself couldn't have done better!' and he turned to the crew. 'Three cheers for Captain Smollet!' he said, and Long John Silver was the first to wave his hat in the air and encourage all the rest to cheer. So they did, and for a brief moment we were one crew again, united in purpose. But then we all looked at the island, and the very sight of it caused me to lose my good spirits such that I wondered if an island, an insentient collection of rocks and vegetation, can, of its own self, cause dismay? I wondered because I try to be a natural philosopher, but as Hamlet says to Horatio: *there are more things in heaven and earth than are dreamt of in your philosophy,* so perhaps an island can indeed be cursed? Who knows?

So we looked and pondered as we saw the profile of the island, distant by many miles to the north, and black against the sky. There were two low hills, and rising behind them was a third, higher hill, whose peak was still buried in the fog. All three seemed sharp and conical. But then Captain Smollet was giving orders such that *Hispaniola* was laid a couple of points nearer the wind, and sailed a course that would just clear the island on the east.

'And now, men,' said Smollet, when all was sheeted home, 'has any one of you ever seen that land ahead?' At this, the entire crew looked to Long John Silver — which I thought was ominous — who stepped forward with the green parrot on his shoulder and saluted Captain Smollet.

'I have, sir,' said Silver. 'I've watered there with a trader I was cook in.'

'The anchorage is on the south, behind an islet, I fancy,' said Smollet.

'Yes, sir,' said Silver. 'Skeleton Island they calls the little one, and the anchorage is between it and the main island. It were a favoured place for pirates once, and a hand we had on board knowed all their names for it.' He turned to the island and pointed. 'That hill to the north, they calls the fore-mast hill, since there are three hills in a row like the masts of a ship: fore, main and mizzen, sir. But the main hill; that's the big 'un with the cloud on it, they usually calls the Spyglass, by reason of a look-out they kept for fear of men o' war, when they was in the anchorage careening; for it's there the pirates cleaned ship of weed and barnacles.'

'I have a chart here,' said Captain Smollett. 'See if that's the place.' And Smollet produced a map which Silver seized with obvious hunger, and then with disappointment, because this was not the map we found in Billy Bones' chest, but an accurate copy, complete in all things — names and heights and soundings — but without the red cross and the written notes.

'Aye,' said Silver, and nodded. 'This is the same island to be sure, and very prettily drawed out. Who might have done that, I wonder? The pirates was too ignorant, I reckon. And here's the safe haven, sir, marked, above Skeleton Island, just as my shipmate said . There's a second anchorage to the north of the island, but beggin' your pardon most respectful, Captain,' and he saluted again, 'if you was to haul your wind and keep the weather of the island, you could enter and anchor to the south. For there ain't no better place on the island, and moreover there are great sand-banks to the north, and fogs and currents such as makes it death for mariners to approach from any other way than the south.'

'Thank you, Mr Silver,' said Smollet, 'I may ask for your guidance later.' Then he raised his voice and gave the orders needed to bring *Hispaniola* to the island.

'Aye-aye!' said Silver at this, glaring at the rest to compel obedience.

'Aye-aye!' they said, and went about their duties.

Then an odd little scene was acted out, as Silver came clumping up on his crutch and saluted me and the squire, then spoke to Jim Hawkins.

'Ah,' said Silver, 'this here is a sweet spot, this island. A sweet spot for a lad to get ashore on. You'll bathe, and you'll climb trees, and you'll hunt goats, you will. Why, the thought makes me a boy again, with ten toes instead of a timber leg,' he smiled greatly, 'so when you wants to go exploring, Jim lad, you ask Long John, and he'll put up a snack for you to take along.' Then he winked at Jim Hawkins, saluted again and went below; and never in all my life since have I decided whether he really liked Jim Hawkins or had other motives.

As soon as he was gone and the hands had dispersed, Jim Hawkins looked at me with a glittering excitement on his face, and I saw that he was intoxicated, as if with drink or fever.

'Doctor!' he whispered. 'Get the captain and squire down to the stern cabin, and then make some pretence to send for me. I have terrible news.' I did not trust Hawkins, not then nor ever, so I looked at Trelawney, who shrugged.

'Why not?' he asked, so we did as Hawkins asked, and what a tale he had to tell us though I wondered, even then, how much of it might be true. But it was all so grim, and so much in agreement with what we already knew, that we were obliged to believe him.

'I was in the apple barrel, gentlemen,' he said, as we sat round the table in the cabin. At the mention of the barrel, everyone looked at me. So I spoke.

'Why? What were you doing in the barrel?'

'The apples are nearly gone, sir,' he said, 'and I can't reach to the bottom, so I got right in to get one, and then I heard Silver and Hands come and sit down, and I stayed a while thinking to jump up and surprise them, but then I heard what they were saying and it's mutiny and murder, and our throats cut and the ship taken and the treasure too, and it's all John Silver's fault!'

'*What?*' we spoke in a single voice, and he poured out more words, all to the same effect: namely, that Silver was after the treasure, that he had recruited the ship's people to his plan, and that he would have the treasure map from us by any means.

'Murder!' said Hawkins, 'those were his words! He said — Silver said — that he'd kill us every one, if need be, just to get the map.' And Hawkins looked straight at Trelawney. 'As for you, sir, he promised that he'd wring the map out of you by any means if you don't give it up free-willingly!'

'By Jove!' said the squire, red-faced with anger and thumping the table. 'He'd better tread careful down that path! All hands to the arms locker!' And without further urging, Captain Smollet produced a key, and opened a long and heavy chest that lay under the table, so that a busy ten minutes was spent in handing out sea-service pistols to each of us, and a tower musket too; though not to Trelawney. He had aboard his Pennsylvania hunting rifle, which he fetched from his cabin, together with a canvas shooting bag with his loading tackles and kit, which thereafter he wore slung over his shoulder.

So we sat priming and loading, and setting flints in place, all of which came as a great comfort.

'Now then,' said Captain Smollet, turning to Jim Hawkins. 'First, young sir, you've earned our thanks!'

'Yes!' we all said.

'Second,' said Smollet, 'unless Silver is a bigger fool than I take him for, they aren't going to rise in mutiny until we're anchored off the island.'

'Why not?' I asked.

'Because they're only hands before the mast,' said Smollet, 'they can follow orders, not give them, and they'll need a master mariner to con this ship safe to anchor, in so treacherous an anchorage as this, what with shallows and sand-banks and currents, and if Silver really has been here before, which I believe he has, then he'll know that better than anyone. So he needs me, or Squire Trelawney, to pilot the ship to anchor.'

'Good!' I said, because that made sense.

'And there's another reason,' said Smollet, '*this!*' and he took a grip of his musket, where it leaned against our table. 'Because the time is come for us to parade in arms, showing Mr Silver what he'll get if he offers mutiny.'

'Good man!' said Trelawney, 'and if, sir, I ever doubted you before, then I was an ass!'

'No more than I was myself, sir!' returned Smollet and the two shook hands.

'But what do we do when we're anchored?' I asked.

'We hold the ship!' said Smollet. 'We get as many of the crew ashore as can be persuaded, and I think I know how. And then, if it comes to a fight — and it will, sooner or later — then we've got the powder and ball, and may God defend the right!'

'Well spoken, sir!' exclaimed Trelawney, 'and I'll send Hawkins to fetch Redruth, Hunter and Joyce, so's they can be told what's afoot and given arms.'

'By all means!' said Smollet, and though I looked at Jim Hawkins and hesitated, I did not act, and what a fool I was to sit there as he got up and rushed out, and how much I came to regret my inaction. So Hawkins was gone some while, but eventually returned with Trelawney's men, giving us six men and a boy, all armed and ready.

So we went up on deck in a body, and what growls and frowns we had from the crew! Tom Morgan instantly ran below to fetch Silver, who came on deck and stood with his close friends around him and glared, and thumped his crutch on the deck, where a two-footed man would have stamped. But that was all he did. That was all that any of them did, for although they had the numbers, we bore firearms. More than that, Captain Smollet was entirely right in his assertion that they — or rather Silver — needed a master mariner to bring *Hispaniola* safe to anchor. So there was an uneasy truce between all parties as Smollet gave the orders to bring us in to the anchorage and we all studied the island as we came closer and closer.

We studied the island, and none of us liked what we saw.

Grey-coloured woods covered a large part of the surface, with the grey broken up by streaks of yellow sand and by many tall, green trees of the pine variety, out-topping the others, some singly, some in clumps; but the general colouring was uniform and sad. The hills rose over the vegetation in spires of naked rock, especially the Spyglass. This monster was, by three or four hundred feet, the tallest on the island, running up sheer from almost every side, then suddenly it was cut off at the top like a pedestal for a statue.

That was dull enough, but then we were becalmed about half a mile to the south-east of the island, and there was dreary work before us, since with no sign of any wind, the boats had to be got out and manned, and the ship towed three or four miles round the corner of the island, and up the narrow passage to the haven north of Skeleton Island. It was deadly tedious work for the men in the boats, but at least it kept them busy.

While this went on, and with so little way on the ship, *Hispaniola* rolled scuppers-under in the ocean swell. The booms were tearing at the blocks, the rudder was banging to and fro, and the whole ship creaking, groaning and swaying. Very soon I remembered Captain Smollet's warning, that even seasoned seamen feel the motion sometimes, and indeed I did on that day.

So perhaps it was the sea-sickness that made me miserable, or perhaps it was the look of the island with its grey, melancholy woods, and stone spires, and the surf that we could see and hear, foaming and thundering on the steep beach. Because although the sun shone bright and hot, and the shore birds were fishing and crying all around us, and you would have thought anyone would have been glad to get to land after being so long at sea, my heart sank, and from that first look onward, I hated the sight of the treasure island.

Finally, *Hispaniola* was brought up to where an anchor was drawn in the chart, to show the best place for a ship to lie. We were about a third of a mile from two shores: that of the mainland to the north, and that of Skeleton Island to the south. The bottom was murky sand and the plunge of our anchor sent up clouds of birds wheeling and crying over the woods, but in less than a minute they were down again, and were silent, as we looked around.

The place was entirely land-locked: buried in woods, with the trees coming right down to high-water mark. The shores were mostly flat, with the hill-tops standing round at a distance in a sort of amphitheatre, with two stagnant, swampy little rivers emptying into this pond of an anchorage, with the foliage around that part of the shore having a poisonous brightness. It all looked so primordial and untouched, that if it had not been for the chart we should have believed that we were first that had ever anchored there since the island arose out of the seas.

Worse still, there was not a breath of air moving, nor a sound but that of the surf booming, half a mile away on the rocks of the beaches outside the anchorage. A peculiar stagnant smell hung over the whole area; it was a smell of sodden leaves and rotting tree trunks, and I sniffed at the stink.

'I don't know about treasure,' I said, 'but I'll stake my wig there's fever here.'

Then, Captain Smollet ordered the men out of the boats, and mustered before him on deck. We loyal hands stood behind him with our muskets and pistols, and if the men had been surly and grumbling in the boasts, they now became truly threatening, even with Silver and Israel Hands going from man to man, whispering in their ears to restrain them. In this foul mood, they listened to what their captain had to say, as he delivered the speech we had prepared.

'My lads,' he said, 'I've a word to say to you. This island is the place we have been sailing for, and since we've had a hot day, and are all tired and out of sorts, then a turn ashore'll hurt nobody. So! The boats are still in the water, and as many as please may go ashore for the afternoon. Then I'll fire a gun half an hour before sundown, for all to come aboard, and when grog and dinner will be served.'

It is often said that seamen are simple folk in matters other than seafaring. They are artful, brave, skilful and incredibly nimble if it be within in their chosen profession, but outside of it they are as gullible as children. Thus I think that most of our disloyal crew believed that once ashore on the island then they would bump into the treasure at the first footfall. Or at least, such belief would explain the raptures of joy that fell upon them at Smollet's words. They cheered and laughed and grinned, and having gathered what things they would take with them, and Tom Morgan having brought up some snacks from the galley, they swarmed down into the boats without a moment's hesitation — all but six of the biggest of them went, including Job Anderson the bosun, and were taken aside by Silver and Israel Hands, and given strict, though whispered, orders, and anyone could see the disappointment in their faces.

Indeed we paid such close attention to them that we missed something else as the crew went into the boats. It was something that must have been swiftly and cunningly done, and which would have alarmed us greatly, had we seen it.

Meanwhile, Anderson and the rest, hung their heads and all but wept. They were like children told there would be no birthday party after all. It was almost funny, except that when Silver finished talking to them, their surly looks disappeared, to be replaced by cunning smiles, and just before Silver went down into a boat, Anderson and the other five at first disappeared below, then came on deck again, and sneered at us loyal hands, then retreated to the foc'sle and stood looking at us. Then the boats were clanking and pulling for the shore, with the men bellowing a song to keep time: it was *Lilliburlero*, a cheerful soldiers' march and a good pulling-song for boatman, but one I have disliked ever since.

But I did notice something that would save our lives in due course. There was a sandbank in the middle of the anchorage, such that the mutineers had to steer around the left-hand side of it, to reach the nearest shore of the island, while on the right-hand side there was clear water, into the depths of the anchorage, to a more distant beach.

As soon as the boats had gone, all but the jolly-boat which was the smallest, and which Silver's men had not taken, Captain Smollet advanced along the deck followed by us of the loyal party. He stopped some twenty feet from Silver's men and made a final attempt at reasoning with them, because by ourselves: two seaman, four landmen and a boy, it would be a labour of Hercules to sail the ship even in good weather, and impossible if the sea rose up against us in another strong blow.

'Mr Anderson,' said Smollet, 'I am here to offer you a course back to salvation and an honest life.'

'Belay that,' said Anderson, 'I'll have no more gammon from you, 'cos I've had all I can stand already, and I'm to hold this ship until kingdom come, and she ain't sailing nowhere!' and he added a foul oath and spat on the deck.

'Aye!' said the other five, and a surprising peace of mind came upon our loyal party, because at last we were done with doubt and wondering, and facing plain mutiny, which we could fight.

'Job Anderson,' said Smollet, 'you're a fool. There's seven of us here with firelocks, and there's a hanging awaiting in England for all that won't obey orders.' Anderson cursed again, but one of his followers, Abraham Gray, was struck with doubt. He blinked and gulped and dithered, and Smollet saw his chance.

'Abe Gray,' said Smollet, 'you're a decent man within, so will you join us and be true to King George and old England?'

'I will, sir!' said Gray and ran forward to roars of anger from the rest. Then, led by Job Anderson, the devious swines reached inside their shirts, and each one produced a pistol — not the large sea service kind, but little pocket-pistols, which they levelled and fired at us, then dropped their empty pistols and sprang forward with sailors' knives.

They nearly had us, too, because the shock of facing fire is considerable, the noise alone strikes fear, and we stood with muskets aimed skyward, unready to fire. But Redruth and Hunter, marksmen since boyhood, cocked, levelled and fired. *Whoof-bang! Whoof-bang!* So down went Job Anderson with a ball in the breadbasket, and another man fell clutching his thigh. The squire was close after, clapping the muzzle of his rifle against the very brow of another mutineer and firing, even as the fellow attempted to grapple, such that lead, brains and flesh were blown out through the back of the tar-pigtailed head. But it was close work after that, and I was at hand-strokes with a fourth man, no chance to fire or draw pistols, and slamming the iron lockplate of my musket into his face, as he jabbed with his knife, and put the point through my shirt. Then the flash and bang of a musket came huge, alongside my ear, as Mr Joyce shot dead my assailant, while more guns went off, sending balls nowhere, and the matter was finally decided by Trelawney whirling his rifle by the muzzle, in a tremendous round swing, to clout the brass-bound butt so hard against the head of the final mutineer, that his skull cracked like a pistol shot.

Then we stood gasping and panting and sweating, with four dead men on the decks and another on his back, with knees bent, and blood on his hands where they clutched his wounded leg. He screamed loudly but got short shrift.

'Shut up you bloody villain!' said Trelawney and fetched him a great kick, then several more until he stopped screaming and lay there in terror looking up at us.

'Are we all safe?' asked Captain Smollet. 'Speak to me, lads!'

'Yes,' said Trelawney.

'Yes,' I said.

'Yes, sir,' said Hunter, and Joyce.

'Aye-aye, sir!' said Abe Gray. But Redruth the gamekeeper said nothing.

'Tom?' said Trelawney. 'Tell me all's well, Tom Redruth. Don't break my heart.'

'I'm sorry, Squire,' said Redruth, 'I did my best, sir. I really did.'

'Oh, no,' said Trelawney, and ran forward as Redruth sank to the deck with his legs failed under him. I dropped my musket and was down beside him, tearing his shirt open, and there I found, just as I had with Billy Bones, the small round hole in the centre of his chest. It was a mortal wound but I got up at once.

'I'll fetch my bag,' I said.

'I'd be grateful if you would, Doctor,' said Captain Smollet, 'since I'm afraid I'm hit myself.' And his fingers explored inside his coat, up by the left shoulder, and found blood.

'Jim! Jim!' I cried, feeling unable to leave two wounded men, 'go and get…' Then I realized that there was no Jim. He was not there. 'Hell fire!' I said. 'Squire, you take care of Mr Redruth! Joyce and Gray, take care of the captain!' Then I ran to my cabin, seized my box of instruments and dressings, and was about to get back on deck when the door of Squire Trelawney's cabin swung open with the ship's movement. The cabin was an anarchy of muddle: everything was turned out of boxes and cupboards, and thrown to the deck, and I looked and looked, then gasped as I guessed what had gone on. Indeed I knew it for truth, and I knew that I should never, never, never have trusted Jim Hawkins, and that in no small part I was a guilty as him, because I had allowed this to happen through indolence and hesitation.

Jim Hawkins had taken the map and papers, and gone into the boats, and gone treasure hunting with Long John Silver.

In short: Jim Hawkins was a traitor.

CHAPTER 19

'Good day, ma'am,' said Flint, and gave a graceful bow. He did it well. He would have made a fine dancer. Likewise he smiled, and since he was a handsome man, it was a handsome smile. But he was ignored. Selena walked past him, and stood at the weather rail and the crew all gaped and nudged, and wondered what Flint would do next. But Flint merely smiled, because he had long since decided what to do next. It was all a matter of patience.

'Ma'am,' he said, approaching her, in all deference and with quiet words, 'all is not as it seems, because those who you believe to be your friends, may be your enemies, while those whom you believe to be your friends—'

'D'you think I'm stupid?' she said, turning on him. 'D'you think I'll fall for such trash as *that*?' And she stood forward, mocking Flint's speech, manner and bearing: '*Those whom you believe to be your friends may really be your enemies*,' she said, and the crew sniggered. 'Can't you do better than that?' she asked. 'You've spent too much time watching pantomimes, Joe Flint!' This time there was actual laughter, incredulous laughter, and a lesser man than Flint would have been dismayed.

But Flint laughed *with* the laughter. He swept off his hat and bowed, he turned to his men and encouraged them to laugh. Then he struck back.

'And what is John Silver doing now, this very instant?' he asked. He said it in a whisper, for only her to hear. 'What's he doing aboard Trelawney's ship?'

She frowned at that, and he knew he had her attention. He said no more but just shrugged, and walked off and found ship's business to occupy himself as if no longer interested in her.

After that, Selena had nothing to do but wonder. She could do that and she could go where she wished aboard this ship, even among such a crew as this one; all of them young, all of them vigorous, and every one of them must be a pirate if he'd signed up with Flint. She could go where she liked because she was utterly safe from the crew, since no man of them would dare touch her for fear of Flint, while the three ship's boys followed her around gaping in admiration. In fact the entire crew did that, when Flint was not looking. They all stared and wondered and hoped. But that was all they did. So there was a certain entertainment here for a young woman, who was well aware of how much she was admired by men, and who could parade where she wished, and do as she pleased, entirely free of consequences.

Except for Flint.

Selena had to deal with Flint.

Who constantly contrived reasons for conversation.

So eventually they spoke.

It was not all at once, and it was not even all on one day, because Flint had made advances before, and would make further advances later. But this particular day was remarkable for the degree to which Flint found reasons for telling her the plain truth without attempting to deceive her — at least, not in any immediate sense.

All this because Selena was bored. At first, when taken aboard this ship by violence, and locked in a cabin, she had been afraid: *very* afraid.

She knew Flint from past times, because very much had passed between them. She knew Flint and his treasure island, and the vile things that had been done there. So she knew, better than anyone, his character and his obsession with herself and his hatred for John Silver. So at the very least she had feared brutal rape. But that had not happened. Instead she had her own cabin, and was treated with respect, and fed and clothed and even protected.

'God help the creature that offends you, ma'am!' Flint had said on the very first days of her being in the ship. 'God help him, because even the Devil won't treat him worse than I will!'

So now she was bored. Only the ship's boys dared to talk to her but had nothing to say, other than the grubby experiences of their grubby little lives. The men were polite, but terrified of being seen to take an interest. That had gone on for day after day after day. Worse still, and on every day, Selena had worried about John Silver. It was the old worry that never went away, because Selena had not been bred up in a safe or happy world. Her life had begun in slavery, which she escaped by violence, and she had lived among violence ever since, and among violent men. So she had done what any intelligent woman would do in such predicament: she had made the best choice of what was available, and...

'Ma'am?' said Flint.

'What?' she replied, away in her thoughts.

'Will you try?' said Flint, and laughed. She had wandered on to the quarterdeck by the helmsman and binnacle where Flint, and Hitchin the first mate, were busy with their quadrants.

'Try what?' she asked.

'It's noon, ma'am, and I have just taken my observation of the sun, and I wondered if you would like to do the same?' He held out the complex instrument.

'No,' she said, and he smiled again, and so they fell into conversation, and Hitchin and the rest fell back and kept clear.

'Why have you done this to me?' she asked. 'Why am I aboard this ship?'

'Because you are the woman of my dreams,' he replied, 'there is none other in all the world for me. You are my princess and my angel.'

Flint meant every word. It was pure truth. He could not help himself, and he was so intense in the delivery of these words that Selena knew that he was sincere. Whatever else he was — and he was many things and all of them bad — he really, truly was captivated with her. Meanwhile he stared at her with his uncanny eyes, waiting for a response.

'You know that I'm married,' she said, finally, 'to Long John.'

Flint sighed. 'I know,' he said, 'and I know that he's going to betray you.'

'No!' she said, 'Never!'

'Are you sure?'

'Yes!'

'Selena,' said Flint, 'John Silver is aboard the ship *Hispaniola* under command of Alexander Smollet, fitted out by Squire Trelawney, and they have *my* map and papers to find the treasure: *my* treasure!'

'How do you know that?'

'All Bristol knows! It's common gossip. Trelawney's a fool and he told all the world, and now *I'm* telling *you* that once John Silver gets near that treasure he'll take it and the ship from Trelawney, and he'll be a pirate once more.' He seized hold of her arm and shook it. 'I'm telling you, because we both know that you want John Silver to be an honest man, and remain ashore, and keep a tavern, and a cat and a dog, and a brace of children, and grow fat and be John Bull, and we both know that he'll never do it!'

Selena could not meet his eyes. She knew he was right…or feared it.

'So forget him, and come and see what I'm going to do,' said Flint, and threw his quadrant at one of the ship's boys. 'Here,' he said, 'stow that safe!'

Then he went below without even looking back to see if she was following, which she did, out of fascination and curiosity. Then, in the stern cabin, Flint pulled a chart from a cupboard, unrolled it and pinned it to the table with four chart-weights, one at each corner so it should not roll up again. He tapped a finger on the chart, where a pencil line — the ship's course so far — ended.

'We are here,' he said, then moved his finger, 'and the island — *my* island with *my* treasure — is here.' The finger stopped at a point on the map, off the South American continent.

'Now,' he said, 'look at this.' And he took a smaller chart from the same cupboard and laid it on the table. Selena stared: the chart showed an island, and a massive, semi-circular sand-bank to the north of it. She leaned over the map and studied it.

'It's the treasure island, isn't it?' she said, pointing at the chart, 'and that's the northern archipelago of rocks and sandbanks.'

'Well done, ma'am!' he said. 'I congratulate you. Though of course, you know it as well as I do, or John Silver does, because you've been there. But this is a little map that was never with the rest. This is one I kept privately.'

'And so?' she said.

'And so,' he said, 'having this map, I can land on the island to the north, passing through the safe channel among the sands, and the fog, and the rocks. I can thereby come safe to the island's northern anchorage, which is quite as good as the southern one, off Skeleton Island.'

She nodded, and Flint's smile faded, to be replaced by awestruck delight as he saw that she was impressed! She was impressed with his cleverness! He relished the thought, because even such small approval, coming from her, was a delight, and he wondered what he might do in future to cause the delight to continue? Or grow? He even reflected upon past behaviour, and wondered if perhaps he might act differently in the future…

On the other hand, he judged it wise not to point out, that in arriving secretly at the northern anchorage, he would be perfectly placed to inflict deadly surprise upon any other ship that might chose the southern anchorage.

*

Israel Hands sat with Tom Morgan, George Merry and Black Dog. Jim Hawkins was with them and another nine men sat close by. They sat in the green undergrowth, in the heat, under great spreading trees, some tropical, some not, and looked into a swampy clearing in front of them. It was about fifty yards across, with patches of dry ground, especially near to the side where the men were sitting. There was a nervousness among them, and those who'd been in other strange islands frightened those who had not, with tales of snakes, and of poisonous centipedes that grasped with a hundred hooked arms and could not be prized off with a crowbar.

'Brothers!' cried John Silver, who stood before the company with his parrot on his shoulder, 'I calls this meeting to order!' At this, Hands, Morgan, Merry and Black Dog immediately stood up and faced Silver. Jim Hawkins and the rest, unused to the formalities of a council, got up and grinned at each other, self-consciously. 'Are you ready and willing?' said Silver.

'Ready, aye, ready!' said Hands, Morgan, Merry and Black Dog.

'Ready, aye, ready,' said the rest, learning as they went.

'So,' said Silver, 'you've all spoke to me. You've all signed articles. You all know why we are here.'

'Aye!' said Hands, Morgan, Merry and Black Dog.

'Aye!' said the rest.

'But now, here we are, turned off the ship, and them lubbers aboard with their firelocks thinking they've got possession.'

'Aye!' they all said.

'So here's a little surprise for them, my brothers,' said Silver, 'cos didn't I tell you there's guns and powder on this island? Didn't I tell every man of you?'

'Aye!' they cried.

'And all stored safe over there,' he said, pointing towards high ground, 'in a timber blockhouse, built in Flint's time, where there's an arms chest as good as any aboard *Hispaniola*, and all within is wrapped in tarry canvas and sealed with pitch against the weather. So every man of us will soon be as fine a gentleman of fortune as ever stood forth to face the world, and the better of those swabs aboard ship!'

'Give a cheer, brothers!' said Israel Hands, and they did. Three times over and set the birds wheeling and calling, and every man grinned at his mates and was happy.

All except two.

'So now I charges you, as elected captain,' said Silver, 'to follow our master gunner, Mr Hands, who will lead you to the blockhouse, so's you can come back here with powder and ball, and the whole crew of us shall take to the boats, and go aboard *Hispaniola* for a reckoning!' There was more cheering. 'I'll rest here,' said Silver, 'since there's soft ground all the way and I'd be the slowest ship in the squadron. So off you go, and step out with a will.'

More cheering followed and the men formed up for the march, except for Jim Hawkins, Louis Baudry and Alan McGuigan, whom Silver detained — all three — for a private word. He did so even though Israel Hands spoke softly to him.

'Are you sure of this, John? I'd be happier if some of us were with you.'

'No,' said Silver, 'I want to the truth out of Baudry and McGuigan, according to articles, and I won't get it if they're looking over their shoulders.'

'Yes,' said Hands, 'but—'

'Get on with you,' said Silver, 'I've got this old bird, here, and the boy Hawkins too. So what could be wrong with that?'

'Pieces of eight! Pieces of eight!' cried the parrot as Silver stroked her.

'Just you watch your back, John!' said Hands, then off he went with the rest astern of him, and a great bother and noise of it they made, trampling the undergrowth and singing as they went:

'Fifteen men on the dead man's chest! Yo-ho-ho! And a bottle of rum!'

When they were gone, Silver took off his hat and wiped his brow with a handkerchief. Then he put all to rights again, and spoke to the parrot.

'Off you go, my girl, up in the trees!' and he hurled her into the air, such that she circled and squawked, then dived once over Long John's head and soared up to find a branch, where she sat and tucked in her wings and watched. 'Ah, she's a rare old bird, that one,' said Silver, 'more clever than most people, I shouldn't wonder.'

Then he turned to Jim Hawkins. 'You said you've got something to tell me, lad?' he said.

'Yes, Long John, I have indeed.' Jim Hawkins smirked and grinned.

'Well and good,' said Silver. 'But I has to parlay with these two brothers, here,' and he nodded in friendly fashion to Baudry and McGuigan, who nodded in return, though both were uneasy and looking for treachery or betrayal. 'So you go and sit over there, Jim Hawkins,

Silver pointed, 'by that big tree. That'un way over there, and I'll come to you when we've done here.'

So Jim Hawkins went and sat down, and reached inside his shirt to cuddle the map and papers hidden there, and he got himself comfortable and watched everything that followed, though he could not properly hear because of the oppressive, sound-deadening foliage all around and the fact that the tree Silver had sent him to was on the far side of the clearing. Jim Hawkins wondered why at first, though not for long.

Thus Jim Hawkins watched as Silver leaned on his crutch and beckoned Baudry and McGuigan to come close. Then he was asking questions, and they were slow to answer. Silver smiled and clapped Baudry on the shoulder in the most friendly fashion. But then Silver's questions grew more intent, and Jim Hawkins saw the change in manner among the three men. Baudry and McGuigan were leaning forward, making threats. Then they separated so as to get on opposite sides of Silver, who turned on his crutch, looking first at one and then the other. Then voices raised into shouts. Faces scowled, teeth glared. Then Silver let out a shout so loud that Jim Hawkins heard every word.

'Are you Flint's men or mine?' he roared. 'There's time yet to change!'

Then Baudry screamed, and McGuigan screamed, and both had knives in their fists making ready to leap. But they waited too long. Silver balanced on his one leg, whipped up his crutch and threw it like a spear, straight into Baudry's open mouth, such that teeth splintered and Baudry gagged, with the oaken shaft half way down his throat, even as Silver was spinning round, drawing a dagger and leaping at McGuigan as McGuigan charged. Then the two were on the ground and hands were working with blades, and McGuigan shrieking and Silver roaring. It went on for an age, until McGuigan's arm went limp and his knife dropped, and Jim Hawkins shuddered in fear and disgust as Silver got himself clear of McGuigan and dragged himself across the ground like a huge and hideous spider, too exhausted to rise on one leg. He went after Baudry who was still staggering and throttling, with eyes popping, and vainly trying to get Silver's crutch out of his mouth before he choked. In that desperate condition, Silver caught him by one leg, and Baudry tried to kick him off, but Baudry's strength was gone, and Silver hauled himself hand-over-hand up Baudry's body and thrust up, under Baudry's ribs, such that he died and fell without a twitch.

Silver rested a while, then slithered himself round to brace his foot against Baudry's neck, so that he could heave and lever on the crutch with both hands, to pull it out of Baudry's mouth. After that, Silver raised the crutch and hauled mightily on it, to drag himself upright. He got the crutch under his armpit, paused to catch his breath then went over to McGuigan, knelt down, and taking his dagger with his left hand, he put the point on McGuigan's breast-bone and beat down with the butt of his right hand, driving the blade into McGuigan's heart. He drove it in full and deep and proper, just to make sure that the Ulsterman wasn't going to get up for another round. Then Silver rocked the knife to and fro, to get it out of the bone, and finally wiped it on McGuigan's shirt. He wiped it most thoroughly until the blade was clean. Then he put away the knife and got up again, and hopped and thumped zig-zag across the clearing, keeping to solid ground.

At last he stood before Jim Hawkins, dripping in sweat, torn and dirtied, soaked in blood and looking like a fiend of Hell. His chest heaved so hard he could barely speak, and Jim Hawkins stared, and stared and stared.

'Now then, Jim lad,' said Silver, gasping and panting, 'what've you got to tell me?'

Jim Hawkins said nothing. He had always thought himself to be a most tremendous person; one who was more beautiful and clever than anybody else in the world… all except one special person whom he admired. So he had always looked down on others and laughed at them. But he was not laughing now, because — aside from the Admiral Benbow siege, when he had mainly closed his eyes and hidden in his mother's arms — he had lived a cossetted life, entirely free from ugliness and violence.

But now he had seen such an extreme display of ugliness and violence that his mind was refusing to believe it. He felt as if he had guzzled a colossal meal of outlandish food, and didn't know whether to digest it or heave it back up again.

CHAPTER 20

From Dr Livesey's journal:

With three wounded men to deal with, I had to choose who came first. The mutineer I set aside for the moment, as a villain who had just been trying to kill us, while Smollet waved away my attentions and pointed to Redruth. But sadly I could do nothing for the old gamekeeper, other than make him comfortable where he lay, supported by Trelawney, as if it were one of his own kin that was dying; which it truly was in all reality, since in such families as Trelawney's, generations of retainers serve for lifetimes, and are embraced as being *of* the family.

'Tom, Tom,' said Trelawney, 'Will you forgive me? I brought you here and I'm responsible.' Redruth could not speak by then, but smiled and patted Trelawney's hand as at last he faded, and closed his eyes in death, and Trelawney wept. So Captain Smollet gave a word of comfort, even wounded as he was.

'Bear up Squire,' he said, resting a hand on Trelawney's shoulder. 'There's nothing to fear for a man who falls in the honourable service of his country, or his ship, or his master. It may not be good scripture but it's fact, and the Lord above knows it.'

Since Captain Smollet would not be attended to, while another — the mutineer — was wounded worse, I turned next to this rogue, whose name was Norton: Noggy Norton to his mates. His femur was smashed by musket shot, and he bled heavily within the wound. With help from Hunter and Joyce, I pinned this rascal to the deck, slit his britches, explored the harm done by the ball and attempted to stop the bleeding. But the femoral artery itself was cut, I could not staunch the flow no matter how hard I tried, and Noggy Norton died howling and blaspheming, and cursing me as if it were my fault.

'Bloody sawbones!' he said. 'Bloody bastard! God damn your eyes!'

Those words and worse — very much worse — were his last. So considering the effect they had on Hunter and Joyce, who were country-bred men unused to such oaths, then I hope I may be forgiven for believing that while the Lord above welcomed Tom Redruth into Heaven, He sent Noggy Norton to another place entirely.

Then finally I got Captain Smollet sat down on a barrel, to open his coat and shirt, since he would not be persuaded to go below and lie down.

'Not me, sir!' he declared. 'Not aboard any ship under my command!' So I examined his wound and was dismayed, because it was serious. A ball had entered the pectoralis major and was surely lodged within Smollet's body, since there was no exit wound in his back. Worse still, noting blood on Smollet's lips, and a slight cough, I feared the ball might have touched the lung, and that any over-heroic actions on my part to remove the ball might do more harm than good. So I examined Smollet's coat and shirt, to seek any signs that portions of cloth had been driven into the wound, which event unfailingly produces a dangerous suppuration, such that a surgeon must remove the cloth if he can. But I found no obvious holes caused by the ball, and assumed that the fibres of the garments had merely been parted by its passage. So I took that as a small blessing on a bad day, and I bandaged the wound, and sent Gray down to the galley for a tot of rum for all hands.

The rum helped, but our captain was seriously weakened, and brave as he was, he could take no great part in our adventures, other than give advice. So he sat quiet, and since Trelawney was grieving for Redruth, I took charge.

'Gentlemen,' I said, 'we've six dead men here, on a hot day in the tropics, and they can't be left. We must get them over the side.'

'Never!' said Trelawney, looking up. 'I'll take Redruth ashore for decent burial!'

'Aye!' said Hunter and Joyce. But Abe Gray touched his brow and spoke to me.

'Doctor, sir?' he said. 'Beggin' your pardon, sir, but we ain't got time for no buryings.'

'Why not?' I asked.

''Cos them ashore,' he licked his lips as he thought of his own very recent behaviour, 'them mutineers, under Cap'n Silver…'

'*Captain* Silver?' repeated Smollet, in contempt. 'Never heard of him!'

'Aye-aye, Cap'n!' said Gray. 'But Silver, he knows where there's guns and powder in the blockhouse ashore, and he's gone to get 'em, and it was him gave us them little barkers,' he paused, and reached inside his shirt, and drew out a pocket pistol. 'Oh!' he said, and dropped it as if it were a scorpion, 'oh!' he said, 'they was Silver's, them little 'uns. He brought 'em aboard, he did…' and he faltered, overcome with his recent guilt

'Go on Gray,' I said. 'You're one of us now, so say what you will.'

'Aye-aye, sir!' said Gray and continued. 'Silver said we was goin' to take over the ship so soon as we was armed. So there'll be a shoal of them, comin' out from the shore, and we'd best make haste and be prepared!'

'Ah!' I said, as everyone looked at me, and I realised that I must make decisions because Smollet was beginning to swoon, Hunter and Joyce were entirely out of their element, and Trelawney was frowning massively.

'I'll not shift till we've given respect to Tom Redruth!' he insisted, and looked to Hunter and Joyce for support, but they avoided his eyes and stared at the shore where we could see the boats, clear of the water, and men on guard of them. In fact we all looked at the boats, and Gray spoke up again.

'They'll be pulling for the ship in no time, if we don't watch out.'

'Dammit!' said Trelawney. 'It's Tom Redruth first, or I'm no Englishman worth the name!' And he stamped a foot, folded his arms and glared at me. So I did my best.

'We'll wrap Redruth in British colours and consign him to the deep,' I said, well knowing that *the deep* in this case could not have been more than five or six fathoms.

'Yes,' said Trelawney, who was my dear and good-hearted friend, but not a man over-burdened with intellect. 'That'll be right. That'll be respectful.'

So we set to, and Abe Gray proved most wonderfully helpful, being anxious to prove his loyalty, and in fact he did most of the work. He found a union flag, sewed up Redruth's body in its folds, including a few round shot at his feet to take him down, and then he got a ship's plank, so the burial-at-sea could be done proper, with the plank balanced on the weather rail, and Redruth laid reverently on the plank wrapped in our nation's colours. Trelawney and Hunter held one side of the plank, Gray and Joyce, the other, and I stood with Smollet, who insisted on getting to his feet.

'Hats off!' I said.

'Aye-aye!' they said.

'We shall recite the twenty-third psalm,' I said, and we did.

The Lord is my shepherd; I shall not want.
He maketh me to lie down in green pastures,
He leadeth me beside the still waters.
He restoreth my soul.
He leadeth me in the paths of righteousness for His name's sake.
He restoreth my soul.
Yea, though I walk through the valley of the shadow of death, I
will fear no evil:
For thou art with me. Thy rod and thy staff they comfort me.
Thou preparest a table before me in the presence of mine enemies:
Thou anointest my head with oil; my cup runneth over.
Surely goodness and mercy shall follow me all the days of my life:
And I will dwell in the house of the Lord for ever.

'Amen!' we all said.

'Heave away, lads,' I said, and they slid Tom Redruth gently over the weather side, where kindly Providence preserved both Tom's dignity and the squire's feelings, because the shallow waters of the anchorage were too cloudy for us to see what lay at the bottom. After that, the mutineers went over the lee side without ceremony: each with a bread-bag full of shot tied to his ankle, and their nasty little pistols for company. We had time for nothing more, and they deserved nothing more.

'Now then, Doctor,' said Trelawney, putting his hat on, 'what next?' We all looked at the boats, still ashore, still unmoving.

'Can we use the cannon?' I suggested, going to the nearest six-pounder. 'Is there a gunner amongst us?' There was not, and we knew it. But Smollet spoke up.

'There's powder and shot in the magazine,' he said, though he was now sat down again, and looking ill, 'and all hands are exercised at the guns.'

'Aye-aye!' said Gray, still keen.

'Yes, but we need two dozen men to man the whole battery,' said Trelawney.

'We could load one at a time,' said Gray, 'and fire one at a time.'

'Good!' I said. 'But who's to lay the guns on target? Israel Hands always did that; him or the trained gun-captains, and they're all ashore.' Tthen I recalled what I knew of field artillery. 'What about grape-shot?' I cried. 'We could hit a boat with that. It's far easier than with round shot. Let's use grape-shot!'

'We can't,' said Trelawney, 'we've got none. There was none in Bristol and I couldn't wait for it to come from the Tower of London. I wanted to be off and away. I was impatient.'

'Oh my!' said Joyce. 'Look! They're getting into the boats!'

Once again everyone looked ashore, then they stared at me, and I thought of the Duke of Cumberland, with his staff around him, in lofty command of an army, and how much I had envied him. But now I realized what a horrible burden it is to take command, because sometimes it is impossible to act for the best, and only the least worst can be achieved.

'We can't hold the ship,' I said. 'No time to load grape even if we had any, and there's too many of them, and they've got muskets now, in plain view. So we'll have to take to the boat, and try to get safe away, by pulling to the left of that sand bank,' I pointed it out, 'so they can't come directly after us and must go round the long way, giving us time to get ashore.'

Trelawney looked at Smollet for his opinion. 'Sir?'

'The doctor's right,' said Smollet, 'we must abandon ship.'

'Quickly now, lads,' I said. 'Abe Gray! Fetch all the firearms, powder and shot you can find, and cutlasses too, and re-charge our arms and the squire's rifle.'

Gray frowned. 'Muskets and pistols, I can do, Doctor,' he said, 'but I don't know the ways of a rifle.'

'Leave that to me,' said Trelawney, 'it's an art.' And he patted the shooting bag hung over his shoulder.

'Aye-aye, Squire!' said Gray.

'Now, Captain,' I said, 'if you're able, fetch whatever charts and compasses you may need.'

'Yes, Doctor!'

'And the rest of us, fetch biscuit, salt pork, rum, tobacco, and whatever other vittles you can find, and get 'em down into the boat, and I'll bring all my medical gear. Quick now! There's little time!'

'And I'll fetch Billy Bones' map and papers!' said Trelawney.

'Ah!' I said, and Trelawney looked puzzled.

'What?' he said.

'I think they're gone,' I said. 'I think Jim Hawkins took them.'

'WHAT?' roared Trelawney — and it is a miracle he was not struck dead with apoplexy, so great was his rage. He charged off below to his cabin, where he turned over everything with great noise, and his roaring and bellowing confirmed my guess.

Then it was a mad scramble of cramming all we could into the jolly-boat without actually sinking it, and getting Captain Smollet down the side, which was hard with his strength failing. Then, with a fierce sun beating down and the oar-strokes of the mutineers sounding across the water, and their furious shouts as they saw us in the boat, with Gray and Trelawney at the oars we pulled for the shore.

At once, puffs of white powder smoke burst from the mutineers along with the crack of musket fire, and even the whistle of balls passing over our heads, causing us all to duck. But they were two hundred yards off, and beyond accurate fire from muskets.

'Pull, lads!' I cried.

'Gently!' said Smollet. 'Our gunnels are only inches above water.' And indeed he was right; the jolly-boat was barely afloat with so many of us aboard, and all that we had brought with us. 'Just keep steerage way,' said Smollet.

'Aye-aye!' said Gray and Trelawney together, which meant we were going so slowly that the villains were advancing on us, even with having to get round the big sand bank, and they were loading for another volley, besides. We could clearly see their arms going up and down, with ramrods. Then came muzzle-flashes and white smoke, and the evil sound of balls in flight.

'Enough of that!' shouted Trelawney. 'Here, Doctor! Take an oar, and unless anyone can see Jim Hawkins among our enemies, I'll see what can be done with my rifle!'

'He's not there,' I said, and with infinite care so as not to sink the boat, I took Trelawney's place while he looked to his priming, then lay flat in the boat with the long-barrelled rifle pointed towards the mutineers. It was precious awkward for him to do this in a small boat, laid as he was between myself and Gray, and with the muzzle-end of the rifle actually across Smollet's knees. But I knew he always laid flat for long shots, in the manner of the American colonists, because that was how he shot at Spanish dollars for wagers. I had seen him do it.

'Stop pulling,' I said, and Gray and I rested our oars to give Trelawney the smoothest possible platform. A brief silence followed, during which we clearly heard the clank of oars from our enemies, and even the cries of birds, then... *whoof-bang*! Trelawney's rifle fired, and a great, angry shout came from the mutineers as one of their number was squarely hit.

'Well done, sir!' I said.

'Well done!' all present chorused.

'No,' said Trelawney. 'I was aiming at Silver with his blasted parrot, and I hit the man next to him.' So we laughed, but it was uneasy laughter.

'Give way!' I said, and Gray and I resumed pulling. 'Can you reload, Squire?' I asked. 'Without oversetting the boat?'

'Yes,' he said. 'If I'm careful.'

'Then keep them under fire to put off their aim, because the hardest target is one that shoots back!'

This he did, and even though he did not hit another man, he sent balls shrieking among them, and knocked holes in their planks, for a rifle hits the mark at a range beyond that of any musket. Thus the mutineers became frightened and hung back on their pulling, and flattened themselves whenever they saw him take aim. Then, when finally our boat grounded in the sand of the anchorage, Trelawney splashed ashore towards a fallen tree, threw himself down behind it and rested his rifle over the trunk for a careful shot. He paused long over his aim, and we all watched in silence. Then the lock flashed, the gun roared, and we all cheered as a mutineer threw up his hands and fell back limp. Better still, a furious argument broke out among the men in the boats, and finally they gave up the chase as a bad job, and pulled for the ship. So we cheered again and helped Trelawney to his feet, brushing the sand off him and thumping him on the back.

'Well done, Squire!' we all said.

'Ain't no man in the county with a better eye than you, Squire!' said Hunter, who was a fine shot himself, and Trelawney nodded.

'It's easier on solid ground,' he said, 'and that's two more to Tom Redruth's account!'

So now we were ashore, and with our enemies gone we were able to unload our goods and make ready to march. We at least had Smollet's copy of the Billy Bones map, and that told us where we might find the blockhouse, so that is where we went, seeking strong walls for defence and having no better objective. In fact, the very top of the blockhouse roof was just visible from where we landed. It was not greatly far off and we soon made several journeys to get ourselves safe with all our goods.

This was just as well for Captain Smollet, because although he stoutly declared that he could march, he was soon so weary that Gray had to get an arm around him to help him move. Then, when we reached the blockhouse, it took our united efforts to get him over the palisade fence that surrounded it and had no gate nor entry, then once inside the house he fell deep into sleep, which was the best thing for him.

And so to the blockhouse itself, which was an oddity, because it was a mystery as to who might have built it and why. It could not have been pirates because they were nomads who did not defend fixed positions. But if one of the royal navies had built it — the British, the French or the Spanish — then it was surely wasted effort, because the only two anchorages on the island could easily be defended by batteries of guns, leaving no need for a fortification inland. None the less, there it was, and it was a considerable defensive work.

It stood where only trees had been before, in virgin forest where there was now a great clearing with a massive log-house in the centre, surrounded by the stumps of the trees that had been felled for its construction. The house itself was thoroughly well made, of whole logs, and was planted high up on sandy, rising ground and pierced with loopholes for musketry, to command a field of fire in all directions. Around the hill on which the house stood the palisade-fence, which had given us such trouble with Captain Smollet, ran six feet high, of logs pointed at the top and bound by horizontal beams, separating the uprights to leave a clear view between, but keeping them too close for a man to squeeze through. It was well placed to break up an assault, yet was too open for an enemy to take shelter behind.

The final virtue of the site was a constant supply of fresh water, from a spring that emerged from a point near the top of the hill, and which had been improved by the artifice of sinking an old, iron cauldron into the ground so that it was constantly filled to overflowing with running water, which then formed a stream downhill and ran off through the palisade into the jungle.

What is more, the blockhouse had seen active service at some time in the past, since on one side, a horizontal log had been knocked out of place by what looked like cannon-fire, there were shot-scars inside the building, and in some places the bottom tier of logs was inches clear of the sandy ground. So, some organised body of men had brought up a field gun to bear on the blockhouse for some reason now lost forever. Having stood siege myself at the Admiral Benbow, I found myself on the side of the defenders of this wooden fort, and I wondered what might have happened to them.

By the time we were settled in, having found the arms chest — now broken and empty — that Silver had known of, the short tropical twilight was on us. So I set watches, that we might not be surprised in the night. Then we lit a fire, since the island was remarkably cold at night, and I wanted all hands to have a hot meal rather than cold, of salt pork, with ship's biscuit and sauerkraut. I ordered rum served, besides, to warm us inside and out. Then after dinner I took another look at Smollet's wound, which showed neither redness, heat, swelling nor pain, but worried me deeply for fear of what might be damaged within, and I dared not ask myself whether or not he would survive.

After all that, Trelawney and I sat outside the blockhouse, listening to the night-time insects and gazing at the stars, each of us smoking a pipe.

We were silent a while, thinking over the events of the day, when Trelawney made an honest man of himself with regard to an important matter.

'How's Captain Smollet?' he asked.

'I don't know,' I said. 'He's in God's hands.'

'I hope he shall recover,' he said, 'because I have reasons.' He sighed.

'What reasons?'

'Well, David, it's just that I am, or was, a seaman.'

'And a fine, good one!'

'Thank you, David,' he said, but then dried up of words.

'What is it?' I asked. 'Tell me, John. Tell me as a friend.'

'Well,' he replied. 'I'm a seaman that can hand, reef and steer.'

'Yes?'

'I can do that, and I can take my noon observation.'

'Yes?'

'But after that, then Heaven help me, because I can't do the sums! I can't work out where I am at sea. Not by calculation. I can't do the reckoning and the numbers. It just ain't a thing my head can do, and that's why I never rose to first mate or captain.'

'Oh,' I said, and Trelawney looked at me as miserable as a bloodhound.

'So if Alexander Smollet don't get better,' he said, 'and with Mr Arrow long gone, there's no man among us that can navigate the ship back to England even if we had the ship, so we're doomed and anchored here, and Silver's doubtless got the treasure map from Jim Hawkins, and there's an island full of pirates, and what shall we do for the best?'

But then a gunshot sounded, somewhere in the woods, and Trelawney and I stood, and we took up our guns, while Joyce, Gray and Hunter came out with theirs, in case of attack. We stood a while, then nothing happened, and we all sat down again, and tried to be at peace. But it was precious hard to be peaceful,, and I for one did not know what to do next.

CHAPTER 21

Selena and Flint stood by the ship's wheel, with Hitchin the first mate and others who were awaiting orders. All were wrapped in heavy sea-coats because it was so cold, and a thick fog was everywhere. The sea was lively, the wind erratic, the ship carried no more than reefed topsails, and was barely under way, with a man in the fore-chains heaving the lead and chanting as the ship inched forward.

'By the mark five!' then another swing of the line, and a plunge of the lead, and 'by the deep five!' then another swing, all steady and slow, then a louder shout, in warning; 'by the mark four!'

'A point to larboard,' said Flint. 'There's shoal ground here.'

'Aye-aye!' said the helmsman, and glanced at the sails and would have nudged the ship closer to the wind. But the wind shifted, the sails shivered, the fog lifted, and suddenly, far ahead to the south, the island showed black against the horizon, and the sands, rocks and breakers of the archipelago were visible in between.

'Steady! Hold her steady!' ordered Flint, feeling the wind about to recover, which it did, and the sails filled, the helmsman steered his point to larboard and Selena stared at the archipelago. It was a death trap of swirling waters, vicious rocks, and hungry sandbanks, some displaying the wooden bones of ships: barnacled, weed-draped and rotting, and all the more dangerous because at any time the fog might come down again, thick and impenetrable, so that it was impossible to see more than the ship's own bowsprit ahead.

'Why is there fog here,' she asked 'in the tropics?' She looked at Flint and saw his smile, knowing he would explain, because he loved to explain. He was always explaining; always seeking to impress.

'It's due to a great upwelling of cold water, ma'am,' he said. 'It comes up through the archipelago, and is so cold it's almost freezing, and it meets the warm air and turns it into fog.'

'Where does it come from,' she asked, 'the cold water?'

'Who knows?' said Flint. 'From the icy north, or the icy south? Or perhaps the Devil sends it?'

'And is that what causes the currents?'

'Again, who knows?' replied Flint. 'But something does, because there're whirlpools and eddies that I've never seen the like of.' He paused and pointed. 'And rocks, too. See there!'

She looked and saw white water thrashing around gleaming rocks, off to the lee side of the ship. The rocks were covered with glistening, black monsters like giant slugs. They honked and barked, and they plunged into the deadly waters with easy grace and total assurance.

'What are those?' she said. 'Sea lions?'

'Ah, you remember, ma'am!' he said. 'Because of course, you've been here before.' He looked at her closely. 'We all have: you, me and John Silver.' She chose not to pursue that. She was unsure where it might lead.

'And how shall you find your way into the safe channel?' she asked.

'By sending a boat ahead,' he said, 'and sounding as we go.'

Later, Selena saw this for herself, having got up into the fore-mast shrouds for the best view. Flint was ahead of the ship in the long-boat with a dozen men at the oars, and a lead-line going in the bows, and even that was not quite enough for safety, because there were men probing to either side with boarding pikes, for fear of hidden rocks.

Once again, Selena was impressed because although Flint knew the channel, it was fearful hard work, and she could see the intensity of concentration as the boat's coxswain, at the tiller, gave pulling orders to keep the centre of the channel, while Flint stared everywhere and gave orders to Hitchin, in the bows of the ship, for Hitchin to bellow onward to the ship's helmsman at the stern. All of this chain of command was forged by men shouting, yet without the least confusion. Of course, it was not *actual* shouting, because the men sang out, with a tone to the sound, to help it carry and to ease the making of it. Selena thought it was like an opera, where many voices combine to make music.

'Back larboard, pull starboard!' from the coxswain.

'By the deep four!' from the leadsman.

'Starboard helm!' from Flint.

'Starboard helm, aye-aye!' from Hitchin.

'Starboard helm, aye-aye!' from the helmsman. Then on, and on.

'Pull together!'

'By the mark five!'

'Steady as she goes!'

All hands cheered when at last *Revenge* came out of the fogs of the channel and into clear water. They did so in spontaneous relief, and threw off their heavy coats. Then Hitchin saw advantage in currying favour.

'Three cheers for Cap'n Flint!' he yelled, and the crew cheered again, whereupon Flint glanced at Selena, and bowed to his men, and responded.

'Pipe spirits, Mr Hitchin!' he said. 'A tot all round for these good men.' Hitchin gulped. Everyone gulped. This was not the Joe Flint they knew. But they gulped with relish when the rum came up.

'Your health, ma'am!' said Flint, back aboard ship and offering Selena a cup, which she took... and smiled. The first smile she had given Flint, and Flint was deeply happy.

So was the weather. Once out of the archipelago, with the fog gone, the weather changed as if a curtain had been drawn back from the sun, and *Revenge* came down upon the island in hot sunshine, under easy sail, steering eastward.

'The eastern side is more sheltered than the west,' said Flint to Selena, 'and it's where the northern anchorage lies, and it's not so battered by the waves.' Selena nodded, and looked at the island with its jungles and its high pines, and found that there was something in the very sight of it that brought depression and — for her — bad memories of other days. Soon they were closing on the anchorage, up on the north-east of the island, and coming about to enter, where it opened about a mile wide at the mouth, running in between cliffs like a softer, southern version of the fjords of Norway. Inside, it widened somewhat and ran for a couple of miles to a sandy, white-and-yellow shore, with thick undergrowth and green-top trees bent over the beach. Behind that, the land rose fast and sharp to high ground on all sides. It was indeed a fine, safe haven where even ships of the line might rest at ease.

So the brig *Revenge* went in, and the island stretched out its arms to enfold her and all and all aboard of her, and it waited dark and silent and mysterious. The waters were calm, the wind was fair, and the ship glided on. But as ever with this island there were signs of past sorrows, because in the furthest end of the anchorage, there was the dismal wreck of what had once been a fine, three-masted ship, and a ship of war at that, as proved by its lines of empty gun-ports. It was green with weed, stripped of everything useful and heavily decayed. Flint looked at it so steadily that Selena was curious.

'What ship is that?' she asked.

'An ancient wreck,' he said, without looking at her.

'Did you know it?'

'Perhaps,' he said, and would not be drawn further.

Then, with the anchor cable flaked out on the deck and the bosun's crew at the cathead, the anchor was let go, dragging the heavy cable, that rumbled and shook the deck as it went over the side. But then the men fell to muttering with one another, and looking at the island, and shaking their heads such that Selena knew that it was not just herself who felt sad at the sight of the island.

But Flint was energised. He was re-born. He laughed! He snapped his fingers! He went round pulling ears, twisting noses, and playfully creeping up on the unwary with a swift boot up the stern.

'Gather round, my jolly boys!' he cried. 'Gather round and hear my words, and you, Mr Hitchin, send a hand down to my cabin for a chair. Quick sharp!'

'Aye-aye, Cap'n!' and a chair was brought, and Flint was inviting Selena to sit, and was so charming and smiling, and his crew so dazzled with such manners from their monster, that they smiled too, and so and once again, Selena smiled, and all hands cheered. They cheered because — secretly and in whispers for fear of Flint — she was the darling of every man aboard, which is hardly surprising, because even a plain woman becomes an object of desire when left alone among men for weeks, and Selena was very far from being plain.

'Now, my lads,' cried Flint, 'I have orders to give you, regarding our next actions on this island, and how you shall all become rich men.' All hands stirred and grinned, and nudged one another. 'Come close! Come close!' said Flint, and the men pressed forward and fell so silent that — in devilment — Flint waited till not a sound was heard, then clapped his hands to make them jump! He laughed and laughed. 'But first,' he said, 'we shall give honour to our princess.' And he turned to Selena, and gave a most graceful bow.

So did all hands, making their clumsy reverence with such obvious sincerity, that since many of them were fine young men, and since it is a rare women who does not bask in admiration, then Selena was exceedingly pleased and Long John Silver slipped down into to the cellars of her imagination.

*

There was actual fighting aboard *Hispaniola* when Long John refused to issue strong drink. But Silver, Israel Hands and the others, were the biggest faction among the supposed brothers, and a few heads were cracked with belaying pins, a few noses were broken with fists, and soon everything was quiet, and all hands sat in a ring on the main-deck, gasping from their exertions and fanning themselves with their hats, and dabbing at their wounds with their shirt-tails.

Silver looked down at them all, with his close followers at his back, and gave thanks that it hadn't been a real fight, and a wonder that it hadn't, since many of the crew now cuddled a musket. Silver looked them over, and shook his head because he knew that they weren't quite the real thing: not these lads. They weren't really gentlemen of fortune, but greedy young seamen lured away by gold. The hard men among them had been Job Anderson and the rest, who must have been killed in the fight with Smollet's crew — all hands had heard the firing — and then their bodies must have been heaved over the side. Either that or they'd sprouted wings and flown to fairyland, because there was no sign of them other than bloodstains on the deck.

But it was time for a speech.

'Now then, brothers,' he began.

'Huh!' said a voice in contempt.

'Oh,' said Silver, 'is there any man here that is *not* a brother?' Nobody spoke. Nobody dared speak. 'I asks because you've all signed articles,' said Silver, 'and I'm still captain, and ain't been deposed by the black spot, so here's article six, that you might have forgot, and it goes like this: any brother in dispute of the captain's orders when no black spot has been passed, shall meet the captain face-to-face, with cutlass drawn.'

With that, Silver drew the cutlass now hanging from his belt, and hopped into the middle of the ring of seated seaman, and threw the parrot into the air, which squawked and flew and settled in the rigging, and Silver looked in the eye of every man, and was absolutely prepared to fight.

'You, brother,' he addressed the nearest man. 'Do you want to dispute matters?' He turned to others. 'Or you? Or you?' He went to every man that dared look up, which most did not, because they knew what had happened to Baudry and McGuigan. They'd seen the bodies.

'So,' said Silver when he was quite sure of them, 'here's how it is, my lads. I'm sorry we've lost a few men, but that's how it goes for gentlemen of fortune. We ain't such pussy-cats as sits safe at home by the fireside. So we'll give thanks that we've got this vessel, with all the stores aboard her, and the guns and powder, all ship-shape and Bristol fashion. And we'll give thanks that we're four times the number of them swabs ashore, and are armed as well as them, and can screw what we want out of them, because without a ship they're marooned here forever! They can't get home without us, my lads, and they know where the treasure is, and we'll make 'em share it or die!' Silver looked at them closely, and saw the smiles, and knew he was half-way there. 'You can bring up the spirits now, Mr Hands,' he said, and the men cheered.

Later, in the evening, with the men pickled in rum and deep asleep, Israel Hands spoke to Long John by the apple barrel, where there were still a few fruits left. The ship eased gently at anchor, the sky was clear with stars and a moon, and a glow of red fire was distantly visible from the island where Smollet and Trelawney's party had taken refuge in the old blockhouse.

'What are we going to do with these lads?' said Israel Hands, 'D'you think they'll turn nasty now they've got firelocks?'

'Which they haven't got the stomach to use!' laughed Silver. But then, as if someone was listening, a gunshot sounded from the shore. Just one shot, but Silver and Israel Hands looked and wondered.

'Now, what might that be?' said Silver.

'Them ashore, shooting at something?' said Hands, and they waited for more shots, but none came.

'Bah!' said Silver, and returned to the discussion. 'We've got to make the best of what we've got, 'cos they're the only crew we've got. Or do you want to go round now, while they're asleep, to disarm them? What's your plan, shipmate?' Israel Hands still said nothing. Then a thought occurred.

'Where's Jim Hawkins?' he said. 'Where did he go?'

'Ah, he's no loss,' said Silver. 'I liked him at first, but he's just a boy with a girl's face, and he's a cunning little bugger besides, and hiding things.'

'What things?'

'He said he had something to tell me, but when I was done with them two ashore.'

'McGuigan and Baudry?'

'Aye. When I was done with them, then little boy Jim came over all green and wouldn't say nothing, and then I suppose he hopped off into the jungle.'

'Where did he go?'

'To the moon, for all I care.'

'I never liked him,' said Israel Hands. 'I didn't like the way he greased round Mrs Selena, back in the old Spyglass tavern.'

'Waste no time on that, Israel,' said Silver, 'my girl's true to me and no mistake.'

'That she is, John,' said Hands. 'You and none other.'

'And we got worse to worry about than Jim Hawkins,' said Silver.

'What?'

'Flint! We know he's coming. We know he'll come with a ship and a crew, and we've somehow got to make a fighting shipload out of such a crew as we've got, which is a parcel of boys that couldn't face a one-legged cripple, and are now drunk out of their senses, and Trelawney's got the treasure map, and who knows if he'll parlay 'cos he's pig-headed stubborn!'

'Oh,' said Israel Hands.

'Oh indeed, shipmate, 'so if you've got any good ideas then tell me, 'cos I've surely got none.'

'You'll think of something, John!' said Hands.

'Will I?' said Silver. 'Something that'll stop Flint?' And Silver was so downcast that a sudden doubt afflicted Israel Hands where none ever had before. It was hard, very hard, even to put this doubt into words.

'You're not... *afraid* of him, are you John? Afraid of Flint?'

CHAPTER 22

From Dr Livesey's journal:

We in the blockhouse were disturbed at dawn: disturbed by the unexpected arrival of a dear little, bright little, pretty-faced person who came to call, though he came in some considerable distress. Gray saw him first, being on watch.

'Doctor! Squire!' he cried, and we all got up from sleep — all except Captain Smollet who could not rise by himself — and we seized our guns and ran outside. The sun was just up over the trees to the east, it was very cold, there were long, morning shadows, and the low ground around the palisade was a yard deep in clinging white mist, while stepping through the whiteness that swirled behind him like the wake of a ship, and all dank and wet and soaking, was the boy Jim Hawkins. As we watched, he stumbled forward to the palisade, seized its timbers and moaned, and his fists clenched the bars like those of a monkey in a menagerie.

'Oh, sirs!' he cried. 'Oh, save me from monsters and demons because I've done a terrible thing, and I know it and I must be punished, and if only my mamma were here, and I know I shouldn't have, but I did, and I saw your fire last night, but didn't dare come to you until morning, and now I have, and I'm *so* sorry, and I only want to own up and be forgiven.'

I stress that the above is just a tiny portion of the lament and apology that Hawkins poured forth in self-pitying profusion. But he was so upset, and he looked so child-like, that even I was to some degree moved, while Squire Trelawney laid aside his precious rifle, and ran down the sandy slope with arms outstretched.

'Jim! Jim!' he cried, and reaching through the palisade bars he helped Jim Hawkins climb over, and picked up a sea-service pistol that dropped from Hawkins' belt, and stuck it in his own, and embraced him with kind words. 'Poor boy,' he said, 'poor boy. No harm shall come to you now.'

'Oh, sir,' said Hawkins, the cunning little devil, gazing into Trelawney's eyes in admiration and respect.

'Oh my poor Jim,' said Trelawney, adding, 'oh my poor little brother!' and thereby making public what everyone knew in private, and educating myself into how hopelessly he was deceived by the false contrition of Jim Hawkins. Then he threw an arm around Hawkins and got him up the slope to the house. 'Build up the fire!' he said. 'Let's get something warm inside this boy so he can tell us his story.'

So we did, and he did. We sat round the fire, some salt pork and biscuit was fed to Jim Hawkins, and a tot of spirit, and we listened to his story, which was indeed interesting, and we brought Captain Smollet out to listen when we realised its importance. Once again I give only a precis of the torrent that Hawkins delivered, but in essence it was as follows:

'I am so sorry, gentlemen, because a madness came upon me. It was Silver that led me astray, with tales of adventure and being a buccaneer. It was Silver and none other. Then when I was sent to fetch Hunter and the others, I went past the squire's cabin, and seeing the map and papers—'

'*Seeing* them?' said the squire. 'But they were locked in my chest!'

'It was broken open, sir,' said Hawkins, in a fluent lie. 'The mutineers must have done it.'

'Oh yes,' said the squire.

'Then why didn't they take the map?' I asked.

'They were disturbed, sir,' said Hawkins. 'I heard feet run away, which must have been theirs.'

'But how—'

'Never mind, Doctor!' said Trelawney. 'Let's hear what Jim has to say!'

'So I took up the map and papers,' said Hawkins, 'meaning to keep them safe.'

'Good boy!' said Trelawney. 'Well done!'

'And then I fetched Mr Redruth, Mr Hunter and Mr Joyce…' and Hawkins paused and looked round with such sorrow on his face that I almost thought it sincere, 'But where *is* Mr Redruth?' he asked.

'Fallen.' said Trelawney. 'Fallen in action like a true Briton.'

'Oh no!' said Hawkins and gave a most wonderful performance of grief, from which he was eventually extracted only by soothing words from the squire and another tot of rum.

'Go on, Jim,' said the squire, 'finish your tale.'

'Yes, sir,' said Hawkins. 'And then we were all armed with guns, and the captain,' he raised a finger to his brow like a seaman, 'the captain gave leave to the mutineers to go ashore, and Silver spoke to me, and I was persuaded to go with them, and I was such a fool as I cannot excuse, and so, entirely forgetting that I had the map and papers, I went with them until I was so confounded and horrified by what I saw, that I ran away and was lost in the jungle.'

'So have you still got the papers?' asked Trelawney.

'Yes, sir,' said Hawkins, and reached inside his shirt, and drew out Billy Bones' map, and Flint's papers, and offered them to Trelawney, who took them and studied them, then cheered loudly and waved them at us all. Then he embraced Jim Hawkins once more.

'My boy!' he said. 'My own, true boy. We never doubted you, Jim!' And he turned to the rest of us. 'We never doubted him, did we lads?'

'No!' said Gray and Hunter.

'Hmmm,' said Smollet, Joyce and I. But nonetheless, there indeed was the map, and there were the papers, and they were safe in our possession, and the treasure was as good as ours. So I moved half an inch closer towards welcoming Hawkins back again. But when Trelawney, Hunter and Gray had done clapping Hawkins on the shoulder, and he was done beaming like sunshine, I continued with my questions.

'You said you were horrified,' I said, and Hawkins nodded. 'What did you mean by that? 'What did you see?'

He looked at me, his expression changed, and I believe that what he said next was truth, because he gave a graphic account of how John Silver — unaided and in hand-to-hand combat — killed two men whom he believed loyal to Flint. The details are unpleasant so I omit them, but they were such details as I did not think were in Jim Hawkins' power to imagine. Neither was what came next, and it terrified Abe Gray and Hunter, and even gave Joyce and Trelawney a fright. In fact, I think that only Smollet and I truly sought some other explanation than the supernatural.

'So then I ran away,' said Hawkins, 'and I hid in the forest.' He paused and gathered strength to continue, and once again I believed that he was not lying when he spoke. 'I ran away and was hiding… and *it* found me and chased me.'

'It?' I said. 'What was *it*?'

'I don't know,' he said, 'but it wasn't human. It wasn't a man.'

'Was it a piskey?' asked Hunter, gone white in the face. 'Like them what we have in Cornwall? My dad saw one in the woods once, a great big 'un, and we had bad luck for seven years after.'

'There's no such thing, as piskies,' said Trelawney, though his fearful expression disagreed with his words. 'Leastways none that I ever saw.'

'Aye, Squire,' said Hunter. 'But my dad—'

'Let's hear from Hawkins,' I said. 'What did you see, Jim?'

So Hawkins tried to remember.

'It was dark,' he said, 'and the forest was all shadows, and I couldn't see properly, but it was like a man, only lower than a man, and it was ragged and stooping, and it ran so quiet I barely heard it, and however fast I ran to get away, it ran faster and it ran round me, and it kept reaching out to touch me and had claws for hands and long nails.'

'It must have been an ape,' I said, 'or some other simian.'

'No, Doctor,' said Hawkins, 'because it spoke to me. It kept asking questions.'

'It spoke?' I said. 'In English?'

'Yes,' said Hawkins, 'it did. It kept asking who I was and what I wanted, and it kept telling me to come back tomorrow.'

'Well, there you are gentlemen!' I cried. 'If this creature, this fellow, spoke English, then he was a rational being and not a goblin, a piskey or anything else that's magical.'

'Beggin' your pardon, Doctor,' said Gray, 'and it ain't my place to argue with such as yourself, but mermaids can speak, and they can sing an' all.'

'So can piskies,' declared Hunter. 'My dad told me that. They speaks the old, forgotten speech mostly, 'cos they's ancient, but they speaks proper words an' all.'

Looking at Gray and Hunter, I concluded that further argument was pointless and turned back to Jim Hawkins.

'He told you to come back tomorrow?'

'Yes,' said Hawkins.

'Why?'

'He didn't say, but he said to come back to the same place *at noon observation* tomorrow.' Smollet sat up, at that.

'Noon observation?' he said. 'Then he's a seaman! No landman would say that.'

'Beggin' your pardon, Cap'n, sir,' said Gray, 'but he might be a merman.'

'Bah!' said Smollet.

'Whatever he, or it, may be,' I said, 'he, or it, is a creature of this island, and he offered no violence, and since we are in dire need of allies, to gain some advantage over Silver and his men, then I propose that one of us goes to meet this creature, at noon today, to parlay — as the pirates say.'

'Ah,' said Trelawney, 'but who's to go?'

I laughed at that, because the answer was so obvious. It could not be the captain because he was wounded, nor Jim Hawkins who could not be trusted and who would never have gone in any case. It could not be Joyce because he was a clerkish secretary not a fighting man, and it could not be Hunter or Gray who were so burdened with superstition, that it would have been cruel to send them. In fact even Trelawney was wobbling on the edge, but more importantly he was our best shot, and was needed to help guard the house.

'I'll go,' I said, to relief all round, but I must admit that despite my protestations of rationality, I felt a touch of fright as to what I might meet in the forest, because we were not strolling through St James' Park in London, but on a tropical island full of mysteries. So even if the creature were not supernatural, it might still be something strange , or it might not be strange at all: it might simply be a maniac armed with a razor! So I pumped Hawkins for anything else he could remember of the apparition, and he managed to recall something else.

'Cheese, sir,' he said. 'It asked if I had any cheese.'

'*Cheese*?' The thought made me smile. But Hunter just nodded.

'It'll be a piskey,' he said, 'they always asks for food. That's a piskey and no mistake.' Again, I chose not to argue, and asked more questions of Hawkins.

'Are you sure it didn't try to harm you?'

'Not once I'd shot at it, Doctor.'

'You shot at it?'

'Yes, when it tried to grab me.'

'Ah,' said Trelawney, 'that'll be the shot we heard last night!'

'Yes,' we all said.

'So you were armed?' I asked Hawkins.

'Yes, Doctor. I had the pistols I was given on the ship. And then, when I was among the mutineers, Silver said I was to keep them. He said I was a brave boy to go with him, and I must keep my pistols, and so I had them in the forest, and I fired one at the creature.'

'Did you hit him?'

'No, Doctor. I was running, and my hand was shaking and I dropped the pistol after I fired.

'Or maybe you *did* hit him,' said Hunter, 'but the shot did no harm, being only lead, and it's silver you need for a piskey!'

'Aye!' said Gray. 'Or a merman.'

Later I discussed all this with Captain Smollet as I dressed his wound, inside the house while everyone else was outside. He was too weak to do much more than lie still, and I worried deeply as to what might be the outcome of his injury, but his mind was sharp.

'You were right not to argue about mermen and piskies,' he said, 'because you can't argue with seamen. You might as well try to turn a Jesuit against the Pope. No, Doctor, the fact is that with common seamen, what they believe, they believe and there ain't no shaking them, and I suppose country folk like Hunter are the same.'

'Yes,' I said, 'they are. But what do you think about the return of the boy Jim?'

'I don't like him and never did,' he said. 'He's too much the favourite, and I think he's a liar. He never did mean to keep safe the map and papers: he wanted them for himself!'

'Of course he did,' I said. 'But we have to pretend he's one of us, because we're a small company, and the squire dotes on him, and I don't want to divide our ranks because of him.'

Smollet nodded .'Is the squire really his brother?'

'Half-brother,' I said. 'Yes he is.'

'Then we've got to put up with the little swab, and meanwhile we need some help from somewhere, 'cos we're safe in this blockhouse, but we daren't go out, not even for treasure-hunting, for fear of Silver's men. So take care tomorrow, on that account as well!'

Next day, just before noon and with all these thoughts in my mind, I put a straw hat on my head, a pair of pistols in my belt and slung a musket over my shoulder, and went looking in the forest for Jim Hawkins' creature. I also took a good slice of cheese, wrapped in a handkerchief and stuffed into my cartridge pouch. Then I set off, trying to follow the directions I had received from Jim Hawkins, but mainly assuming that the creature was a better woodsman than I, and would therefore find me.

So I went on my way, and found Hawkins' directions were accurate, because after some while of walking through the trees, I found a path which I followed, and came across a ship's pistol on the ground, with its lock thrown forward after firing. So I was on the very spot where Hawkins had been, and I looked round in all directions. Everything was shades of green, and birds flew and called, and the surf boomed — as ever and always it does on that island — and the sun burned hot in the sky, throwing patterns of shadow through the great trees. All was still, and all was peaceful, though I could see nothing beyond ten or twenty feet in the dense foliage. I was surely alone, and with no creature anywhere near me. So I stooped to pick up the pistol... and started as I never had in all my life, because a voice spoke out in the silence. It was an odd voice that creaked like a rusty lock, but it was human.

'You've come then,' it said. 'Did the boy send you?' And the most weird and unimaginable being appeared before me, having been hidden behind a tree trunk.

He was a European, not a native islander, and certainly a man, not a monster. He looked skinny and tough, though I could not guess his age since his skin, wherever it was exposed, was dark-tanned and prematurely wrinkled by the sun. Even his lips were black, and the whites of his eyes looked startling in so dark a face, while his fair hair and beard were madly unkempt and straggled in all directions. As to his dress, of all the beggar men I ever saw or fancied, he was the chief for raggedness. He was clothed in old tatters of ship's canvas and sail-cloth, and all this extraordinary patchwork was held together by a system of the most incongruous fastenings: brass buttons, bits of stick and loops of tarry cloth. Round his waist he wore an old, brass-buckled belt supporting a large knife in a sheath. These were the only solid things in his whole accoutrement, and his posture was more that of a beast than a man. He leaned forward in a constant crouch, and his hands were indeed claw-like, with nails untrimmed, and cracked and stained.

He was watching me closely, because as soon as I got over my fright and took a grip of my musket, he first hesitated, then came forward, and at last, to my wonder and confusion, he threw himself on his knees and held out his clasped hands in supplication.

'I did no harm to the boy,' he said, 'I never touched him, for I'd not harm a fly, nor not even a goat if it weren't that I needs a bit of meat, now and then.'

'Who are you?' I asked. '*What* are you?'

'I'm Ben Gunn!' he said. 'Poor Ben Gunn what hasn't spoke to a soul in years, and nothing to drink than water, though I don't touch rum saving only a thimble-full for good luck.'

'How did you come here?' I asked. 'Were you ship-wrecked?'

'No mate, marooned!'

'Who did this to you?' I said, and he grew crafty.

'Who's to say? But I weren't no part of the mutiny.'

'What mutiny?' I asked, and his reply astonished me.

'Flint's mutiny!' he said, then corrected himself. 'Or maybe it wasn't his, but someone else's.'

'You knew Flint?' I said.

'No, no, no!' he replied, with great force. 'I never knew Flint. I never was in his crew, nor sailed under him, and I weren't no part of his mutiny, and it wasn't even on this island that it happened, and I'm poor Ben Gunn what's innocent of all charges, and was marooned with a bit of powder and shot and an old fowling piece, and some tools, and all of them worn out with digging. Poor Ben Gunn that eats fruit and berries, and has to chase goats for meat, and run 'em down and slice their necks.'

As he spoke he grew more confident, and came forward and ran his hands over my clothes, as if delighted to find something that was not ragged and torn; something that was whole and complete. Then a look of awe came over his face.

'Cheese!' he said. 'I smells cheese! I *dreams* of cheese — toasted mostly,' and he wrung his hands in grovelling supplication. 'Would you have a bite of cheese about you, matey? Would you now? Would you? For poor Ben Gunn what dreams of cheese, and who never was even *in* King George's navy, God bless him, let alone did foul mutiny against his lawful captain, nor took up arms against his mates.'

He rambled on in this fashion, until, becoming tired of it, I took out the cheese and gave it to him. 'Oh my! Oh my!' he said, and he bowed and genuflected before me and took the cheese, and consumed it in great bites and swallows until nothing was left. 'Ahhhhh!' he said, and smiled in satisfaction, showing strong teeth and a wet tongue, and breathing the stink of cheese into my face. 'May the Lord send favour upon you, sir,' he cried, 'for *God loveth a cheerful giver*, which we read in Corinthians two, chapter nine, verse seven!'

'So we do,' I agreed, surprised.

'Indeed, sir,' he said, and smiled and grew almost rational. 'Now you wouldn't believe, would you, sir, that I had a pious mother, and was Bible-reared, and could rattle off me catechism so fast, you'd barely know the words?' Then he stared at me and the wild man came back in his hungry eyes. 'Would there be any left?' he said. 'Of cheese?'

'No,' I said, 'but I know where there's more, if you and I can be friends.'

'Oh yes, God bless you, sir. And what might be your name, sir? Though I seed at once you was a gentleman.'

'You may call me Doctor Livesey,' I said.

'Aye-aye, sir, Doctor sir!' he said, and pulled back a little and attempted to stand straight, and he gave a seaman's salute, with a finger to his brow and one foot stamping.

'So you were marooned?'

'Aye-aye, Doctor sir.'

'And you've been on this island many years?'

'Aye-aye, Doctor sir, and don't know how many 'cos I lost count.'

'And you'd like to get off the island and home to England?'

He wept tears at that, and wrung his hands again, and nodded, and was so profoundly moved that he could find no words. 'So you know this island and its secrets,' I asked.

'Secrets?' he said, and turned the word over in his mind. 'Secrets?' he repeated. 'Things on the island and *in* the island?' He stared hard at me and emotions ran across his face such that first I read fear, then so deep a cunning that I felt I might need to take care with Ben Gunn. But I continued, because I had to.

'So, Mr Gunn,' I said. 'I can offer you a proposal.'

'Doctor, sir?' he said and saluted again.

'It is this: that I can offer you safe passage back to England...'

'God bless you, God bless you, God bless you!'

'...in exchange for your help as a scout, as a guide, and as a comrade-in-arms.'

'Aye-aye, Doctor sir! Comrade-in-arms, sir! Shipmate and messmate, sir!'

'Good,' I said. 'Now, Mr Gunn, have you seen the ship that brought me here?' I asked only to make sure that this poor man, with his disturbed mind, truly understood that a ship was nearby that might take him home. But his reply confounded me.

'Aye-aye, Doctor sir!' he said, and cocked his head to one side. 'I seen the ships, Doctor sir, I seen *both* of them.' Then he paused, and stared at me with round eyes, and he gathered strength as a man might before uttering the name of the Evil One, when alone and at night in a graveyard.

'But which ship is yours, Doctor sir, and which is Flint's?'

CHAPTER 23

John Silver was cheerful again. He hopped across the main-deck of
Hispaniola with Cap'n Flint the parrot on his shoulder, and his clothes
brushed and clean the way he liked them. He even had a feather in his
hat: a big, red ostrich plume, looted from Squire Trelawney's baggage.
So the sun shone hot and bright, the surf boomed, and the island was
clear of its morning mists. Thus a clear sight was to be had of beach,
jungle, hills and rocks, and the roof of the distant blockhouse where
Trelawney and the rest were fortified in their belief that they were safe.

'Mr Hands,' said Silver, 'you may take command of your guns!'

'Aye-aye, sir!' said Hands, and he walked down the line of six-
pounders, on the lee side, which was the side facing the target, to make
sure all was as it should be. Which it was, because each gun-crew was
ready with handspikes, rammers and sponges, while round shot was
ready on racks, and cylindrical cloth powder charges lay safe in their
lockers. Each gun was run out, with touchhole primed, and a man, as
trained by Israel Hands himself, was ready beside each gun with linstock
in hand and a smouldering match-cord dangling.

Thus Mr Hands saw that all was proper and good, and he was happy.
He was happy because he was a craftsman going about his work on a

sunny day, but he was especially happy because, when even Long John Silver did not know what to do for the best, it had been Israel Hands' idea — a gunner's idea — to bring Trelawney's party to reason with a bombardment. So Israel Hands stood to attention in this formal moment, and bawled out his orders in proper speech: navy speech, King's navy speech!

'Marking your target,' he cried. 'And as your gun shall bear! Guns one to six, in due order... FIRE!' Then he glared at his crew to make sure each man did what he had been taught, and was pleased to see that they did, because the one thing this collection of lubbers had always enjoyed, was gun drill, and Israel Hands had kept them hard at it, and they had taken note.

Thus the first-captain of gun number one bent over the breech of his gun, taking care to keep back where the recoil could not reach, and he took aim, noting the gentle roll of the ship which caused the muzzle to arc and curve, and ordering the handspike men to train the carriage a little to one side. Then he made his judgement, and nodded to the second-captain who dipped linstock to powder, and *WHOOF-BOOM*! The piece threw out a great cloud of smoke, and flashed and roared, and a six-pound iron ball was on its way to the blockhouse at many hundreds of miles per hour, while the gun itself rumbled back on its oaken wheels, more dangerous than the kick of a cart-horse if the crew did not keep out of its way. But they knew their work, they kept clear, then leapt forward with sponge, powder and shot, and rammed all home, and heaved on the gun tackles to run out the gun once more.

'In your own time, gun two!' yelled Israel Hands, ears ringing from the discharge of the first gun. 'Let the smoke clear, then take your aim!' He was determined that nobody should waste shot by blazing away in excitement, and without taking care.

'Aye-aye!' said the men of gun number two, and they waited as they'd been taught, and let the wind roll away the smoke of the first gun, which had comprehensively hidden the target from view. Then, *WHOOF-BOOM!* The second gun fired, and then the third, and so on, until gun number six fired, by which time gun number one was ready to fire again, and the whole sequence began afresh.

Israel Hands beamed in satisfaction, and so did Silver, even though the poor parrot had long since gone screeching up to the truck of the mainmast, a hundred feet over the deck, to get away from the noise and smoke.

'That's the way, Mr Hands!' said Silver, in the intense satisfaction that comes from actually *doing* something — especially something so bold as this — when previously all had seemed hopeless.

'Aye-aye, Cap'n!' said Israel Hands, and still dreaming he was a real master gunner again, he did not just salute, but swept off his hat and bowed.

'We'll give 'em a dozen rounds from each gun then go ashore to parlay,' said Silver.

So later, with the hands cleaning the guns and securing them with sea-faring tackles, Silver and Hands were rowed ashore with a strong escort, and the boat grounded among buzzing mosquitoes and draping foliage and the sand that was too hot to touch.

'Blasted island,' said Silver, as he got himself out of the boat and up the beach to the shade of the trees. It was heavy going for a one-legged man with a crutch, but he persevered.

'Now,' he said, picking a man at random: one Franky Grig, who'd once served in the Newcastle collier trade, 'you mind the boat, Franky lad, and the rest come with me and Mr Hands.'

'Aye-aye,' they said, then Grig stood by the boat and the rest followed Silver and Hands, grinning back at the man left behind, though he personally thought he had got the best of the bargain, since he could sit in the shade while they toiled through the jungle.

So he thought, in his happy innocence.

It was a while before they found the blockhouse, and they only found it at all because Silver had brought a little pocket compass to take bearings and keep direction, knowing from past experience how easy it is to be baffled in a jungle, and end up walking in circles.

'Ah,' he said, at last, 'here we are, my jolly boys,' and he turned to Israel Hands. 'D'you remember this, matey? Flint's blockhouse.' Hands pushed through the last of the greenery and came out beside Silver into the clearing, with its hill and its palisade fence, and the blockhouse on top. The air was fresher than it was among the trees, and he saw the sentry on guard at the blockhouse door, recognised Hunter the gamekeeper, and saw him run inside, shouting.

'Yes,' said Israel Hands, 'I know it, and it brings bad memories.'

'Huh!' said Silver. 'That's the past, shipmate, let's look to the future.'

'Wait!' said Hands. 'They've seen us and they're coming out.'

'Yes,' said Silver, and looked at the clump of armed men outside the blockhouse, some hundred paces from the trees, and thirty feet up on the hill. 'There's Trelawney, and Livesey, and that clerk of Trelawney's, and Abe Gray that deserted us, and Hunter as well.' He frowned. 'Hallo! Where's Cap'n Smollet? Where's he then?'

Israel Hands did not answer. He was looking around in disappointment, because there were shot-holes in the hill, and some of the trees had been hit, and there were three holes up near the peak of the roof of the blockhouse. But it was still intact and formidable, and the palisade fence was untouched. The bombardment had achieved nothing.

Silver looked at Hands and guessed what he was thinking.

'Never mind, shipmate,' he said, 'it were severe long range for six-pounders, and you were firing uphill at a mark you could barely see. I never thought we'd do more, and it don't matter. Just you hark to me.'

'John Silver!' cried a voice from the blockhouse. It was Livesey. 'If you've come in arms then beware. We have two dozen muskets ready loaded, and pistols for all, and will shoot you with ease if you try to climb the fence. Do you hear?'

'Aye-aye, Doctor!' said Silver, stepping out from the trees. 'But never fear, 'cos I'm come to parlay not fight.'

'Then put down your firearms and advance to the fence, and know that any treachery brings a volley upon you.'

'Aye-aye, Doctor!' said Silver. 'But shouldn't I be talking to Cap'n Smollet? Ain't he the man to give orders and take command?'

'The captain's safe inside,' said Livesey, 'I speak for him and for all.'

'So,' said Silver, quietly to Israel Hands, 'Smollet's either dead or wounded. That means there's only five of them.' Then he grinned, as a small figure came out of the house. 'Why,' he said, 'and who's that creeping out behind the men?' He raised his voice in a shout. 'Ah-ha, Jim lad! I see you there! Did you run away from old Long John?' He smiled and waved, then whispered to Hands. 'Little shit, I'll twist his neck if I get hold of him.'

'Silver!' cried Livesey. 'Make your mind up, or we fire!' And all five men up on the hill raised their guns. Even Hawkins levelled a pistol.

'Back your top'sl, Doctor,' said Silver. 'I'm a-coming. It's only me and the rest stays fast, except for Mr Hands, who I need to help me through this sand.'

'John,' said Israel Hands, 'can you trust them?'

'Oh yes,' said Silver, 'all but Jim-lad, and he ain't in charge.'

212

With that, Silver made a great play of laying down the musket that was slung over his shoulder, and taking pistols from his belt, and the cutlass from its scabbard, and Hands did the same, telling the men who had come with them to stay put at the edge of the forest. Then, with the help of Israel Hands, Silver got himself across the sandy ground and took hold of the fence for support.

'Well, Doctor,' he said, 'shall I stand here hailing, or will you lay alongside?'

In answer, Livesey put aside his musket and pistols and came down the slope to face Silver. Their conversation was brief and pointed.

'What do you want?' asked Livesey. 'What are you doing here?'

'Never mind what I *want*! It's what you *need* that matters!' said Silver.

'What *you* need is a hanging!' replied Livesey.

'No Doctor, it's me that wants the map and you that needs a ship to sail home.'

'A ship that you can't sail because you can't navigate!'

'And can you do that without Cap'n Smollet?' said Silver. 'Is he really inside, or is he dead?'

'He's wounded,' said Livesey. 'But he'll recover.

'Will he now?' chuckled Silver. 'Well it had better be soon, because Flint's coming, and I'm here with an offer for you, and for them inside.'

'Flint's coming?' said Livesey, who seemed not in the least surprised. 'He's coming, is he? And how do you know that?'

'Never mind how I know,' said Silver, 'but I do know, and I know that he means ill to every man on this island, yours as well as mine, and my offer is that your party and my party should act together in self-defence.'

'And how might we do that?'

'You give me the treasure map and papers, and I'll give you my word...'

'Your *word*?'

'My word of safe conduct back home to England.'

'And is that your offer?'

'It is!'

'Then listen John Silver, because this is mine: if you and all your men come here and lay down your arms, *then* we can begin to talk. Otherwise, there can be no trust between us.'

'Huh!' said Silver. 'Then I'll tell you my new offer. I don't doubt you'll have heard the guns firing from the ship, and felt the shot fall among you.'

'Yes, and to no great effect,' said Livesey, 'so you have no advantage there.'

'Aye,' said Silver, 'but that was just a warning. Next time we'll make field carriages, and drag the guns up here, and blow you all to pieces at short range.'

That was a serious threat. Livesey was worried. He was visibly alarmed. But then he thought, and smiled. He turned and called back up the hill.

'Squire, is your rifle loaded?'

'It is, sir!' cried Trelawney, and Livesey spoke again to Silver.

'You saw how well the squire shot, when you pursued us in the boats,' he said, and Silver said nothing. So Livesey first looked out towards the trees, then called to Trelawney. 'Squire?'

'Sir?' replied Trelawney.

'Do you see that stone, the size of a man's head, in the sand just where the trees begin?'

'I do, sir!'

'Do you think you could hit it with your rifle?'

Trelawney smiled, and lay down flat and took careful aim. Then a sharp crack, a puff of smoke, and a rifle ball smacked a shallow cavity into the stone and ricocheted off into the forest with a loud whine.

'There!' said Livesey. 'You can't shoot at what you can't see, and must bring your guns out of the forest to bear on the blockhouse, and if you do that, then Squire Trelawney will shoot down your gun-crews, man by man.'

'Damn you!' said Silver. 'Damn you to Hell!'

'I'd wish you the same, Mr Silver,' said Livesey, 'but I don't need to, because divine justice will do it for me.'

So John Silver turned and went away. He went back through the forest, grumbling and cursing and worrying. He was in a miserable mood until he got back to the boat, and the anchorage, and *Hispaniola* lying at anchor. Then things got even worse because Franky Grig was gone: Grig, who was supposed to be guarding the boats.

'Where is he?' said Silver. 'Where's he gone?' And he let out a great shout. 'Franky!'

Then they all shouted.

'Franky! Franky! Franky!'

But nobody answered.

'Leave him,' said Silver, 'he can swim back to the ship, or sleep ashore as he pleases.'

So they got into the boat, and once again Silver wondered what to do next.

*

Franky Grig woke up. His head ached. He thought it might be dark but he could not see properly because his eyes would not fully open; his eyelids were stuck together. So he tried to rub his eyes, but his hands would not move, and his wrists hurt. Then he tried to get up but he could not because his feet would not move. Everything hurt. Everything was different. He felt that he must be sitting up, because there was something behind his back.

'Ah,' came a voice, 'you have joined us at last. Might I ask your name?'

It was such a nice voice, and a soft voice, and a gentleman's voice, so that Franky Grig made the effort to speak.

'Franky Grig,' he said. Then, 'Where's all me mates and Cap'n Silver?'

'*Captain* Silver,' said the voice, 'how wonderful a promotion that must be for him.'

'What?' said Grig.

'Let's get you comfortable,' said the voice, and then somebody moved and somebody was wiping Franky Grig's face with a cool, damp cloth. It felt good. Grig sucked at the cloth.

'Are you thirsty?' said the voice.

'Aye!'

'Here,' said the voice, 'drink!' And a cup was put to Grig's lips and carefully tilted.

'Ahh!' he said, and blinked his eyes, which could now open properly, but which saw unclearly at first, and everything seemed blurred. But finally, Franky Grig saw five men sitting in a ring facing him, while a small fire burned to one side. They were seamen by their clothes, and one of them was obviously the leader, as he sat in front of them and was better dressed and had four pistols in his belt: one large pair, one small pair. They were silver-mounted, not common ship's issue, and he was a fine man with fine features, and the most powerful eyes. Grig found it hard to look straight at him, and the man laughed.

'I see that you are fully awake, Mr Grig.'

'Aye-aye, sir,' said Grig, recognising a ship's officer when he saw one.

'And are you entirely comfortable?'

'What?'

'I asked if you were comfortable.'

'Oh.'

'And are you?'

Grig thought about that, and looked about as best he could and realised that he was sitting with his back to a tree, tied to the trunk with his hands stretched behind him, and that his legs stuck out before him, with feet apart and securely fastened at the ankles to stakes driven into the ground. He also realised that while he was still wearing his shirt, his britches and drawers were gone. He began to be afraid.

'I see,' said the officer. 'So in order that we may proceed without time wasted or the least discomfort, would you like me to explain what has happened to you?'

The officer smiled and chuckled. He was greatly enjoying himself, and the four men behind him likewise laughed and nudged one another and waited to see what might happen next. 'So,' said the officer. 'I am Captain Flint, Joseph Flint. Perhaps you have heard of me?'

Grig trembled in terror. He had heard of nothing else than Flint all this voyage. He was the monster of the lower deck. Of things to fear, there was the risen dead, the Kraken, the Sea Serpent and Flint, and even Franky Grig knew that Flint was the sworn enemy of Captain Silver, and was worse than the Devil himself.

'Ah,' said Flint, 'I see that you know my name.' Franky Grig nodded. 'So to proceed, Mr Grig, these good fellows and I,' Flint indicated the four seamen sat behind him, 'we have come down from the northern anchorage, to establish precisely what Mr Silver and the rest are doing. We have therefore kept close watch on the good ship *Hispaniola*, observed with much interest the ferocious discharge of her guns this morning, then we lay in wait as a boat came ashore bearing Mr Silver and others, including yourself.'

'Aye,' said Grig, and instantly bit his tongue to remain silent, fearing that anything he said or did might be dangerous, as indeed it was — though keeping silent and doing nothing was equally dangerous.

217

'So' said Flint, 'we kept silent, there being too many of them for us to attack, and then once Mr Silver and his men were gone, I waited until you were dozing quietly beside the boat in happy dreams, and I came alongside of you and hit you with *this*.'

Flint displayed a cylinder of canvas about eighteen inches long, an inch-and-a-half wide, and neatly sewn up to contain a load of sand. It was limp and heavy in Flint's hand. 'Such an implement,' said Flint, 'if wielded by an expert hand, can stun a man without ruining him by the smashing-in of his skull. Do you follow me?'

'Hmmm' said Grig, faintly.

'And then we carried you some good long way from the beach, and came to this quiet place which I know from previous visits. It is an interesting place, since — as you can see — it is a deep bowl in the ground, fringed with thick vegetation that dulls the noise. It dulls the noise such that however hard a man screams inside of the bowl, then no other man can hear the screams outside of it. Do you follow me?

'Hmmm.'

'So can you guess why you are here, Mr Grig, situated as you are and dressed as you are?

'No.'

Flint reached to one side and picked up a small roll of canvas, tied up with cords. He opened the roll and laid it on the ground in front of him. Grig looked at the roll. It contained a pair of carpenter's pincers, a surgical knife and some sail-maker's needles.

'Since you do not know why you are here, Mr Grig,' said Flint, 'then I will tell you. Because in fact, Mr Grig, you are here to tell me everything you know about John Silver, and Squire Trelawney, and their expedition, and their map.'

'But I don't know nothing!' said Grig.

'Oh but you *do*,' said Flint. 'Everyone knows *something*. Indeed, they know far more than they think, and the real trick is to get it out of them.'

He picked up the pincers and leaned forward. 'We shall start with these,' he said.

CHAPTER 24

From Dr Livesey's journal:

I waited until Silver and Hands had disappeared into the forest, then climbed the hill back to the blockhouse.

'Good shooting, Squire!' I said, and he nodded, standing up with his rifle-butt rested on his shoe, for fear its brass-bound cap might be scratched by sand, as he went about the complex loading procedure: three times longer than that of a musket, using equipment and materials taken out of his shooting bag in a calm and ritualistic sequence.

First he poured powder from a powder horn into a thimble-sized measure, and tipped this exact charge down the rifle's bore. Then powder horn and measure were put away. Next, he took a penny-shaped patch of thin, greased leather and placed it over the muzzle, and put a lead ball in the centre of the patch, and took up a wooden tool, a *starter*, consisting of a small, fat handle attached to three inches of rod that fitted the rifle's bore. Gripping the handle, he put his weight on the rod to force patch and ball into the barrel. Then the starter was put away, and out came the rifle's ramrod, and a long thrust applied to seat the ball, all the way down on to the powder.

'A slow, steady pressure,' he said, heaving on the ram-rod. 'So the patched ball grips the rifling for a good shot, because the loading of a rifle is as important as the aiming. Then a charge of powder in the pan, a check that the flint is sharp and secure in place,' he smiled, 'and we're ready to fire.'

'If you say so, Squire, then who shall doubt you?' And we all laughed.

'Doctor, sir,' said Joyce. 'What did Silver want?' So I told them, and Trelawney frowned.

'So he proposed a union of forces?' he said.

'He did,' I answered, 'because he thinks Flint is on his way.'

'So he doesn't know Flint's already here?

'No, he does not.'

'If Flint really *is* here,' said Trelawney.

'We must assume that he is,' I said, 'and be prepared. We know from Ben Gunn that there's a ship in the northern anchorage, and that it is a brig: a fast vessel, heavily sparred and bearing a battery of guns, and it flies no flag.'

'That surely sounds like Flint,' said Trelawney, 'and we've known from outset that Flint might follow us. So what is Mr Gunn's opinion in the matter?'

'He *thinks* it's Flint,' I said, 'though he's seen the brig only from spyglass hill. He thinks it's Flint because he's afraid of Flint: deeply afraid, and he undoubtedly knows Flint from past times. So I asked if he would take a close look at the brig to see if Flint's aboard.'

'Will he recognise Flint?' asked Trelawney.

'Undoubtedly,' I said, 'Ben Gunn is like everything else about this island: he has a shared history with Flint and Silver, and all manner of dreadful things have happened here, and he's afraid even of the memories, and he's profoundly guilty besides.'

'Can we trust him?' asked Trelawney. 'Can we trust Ben Gunn?'

'Aye,' said the others, 'can we?'

So I thought long and hard. Ben Gunn was a wounded, damaged soul. In that sad predicament he reminded me strongly of Billy Bones. But finally, I nodded.

'Yes,' I said. 'He's not entirely sane, and he contradicts himself over and again, but he's too open to deceive. If he had any evil designs he would soon speak them, even if he then denied them.'

'So will you see him again?' said Trelawney.

'Yes. We agreed to meet in the same place each day: *sparing eventualities*. Those were his words, gentlemen, and it's past noon today, so I shall look for him tomorrow.'

'Beggin' your pardon Doctor,' said Gray, as I finished speaking.

'Gray?'

'It's the cap'n sir, Cap'n Smollet, he's took a turn for the worse.'

That was bad news indeed and I went at once to the captain, who was hot, and fevered and delirious. On examining his wound I found it swollen and red, and beginning to discharge a flow of pus. I sighed and knew that, after all, I would have to open the wound to probe for anything driven into it, and remove such intruders, including the ball itself. If I could.

'Gentlemen,' I said, because all were clustered around me with anxious faces, 'we must get the captain out into the daylight where I can see clearly, and also it is my experience that wounds treated in the sunshine do better than those treated in the gloom.'

So we took Smollet outside, with four of us bearing the load to move him as gently as possible, and then we laid him down in the hot, bright sun, and I fetched my instruments, and rolled up my sleeves.

'Squire,' I said, 'if you will kneel down to hold the captain's left arm, and if you, Gray, would hold his right, and if you, Hunter, would hold the captain's head, then he will be secure for the procedure.' I deemed these precautions necessary because even though Smollet was barely conscious, I had to guard against any sudden movement he might make at the feel of a knife, and which might be the end of him if he caused my hand to slip.

So finally I opened the wound with a lancet, since the puncture, made by the ball of a pocket-pistol, was tiny to begin with and now closed by swelling. Then I probed as deep as I dared, and working entirely by feel, and with a profusion of blood and matter flowing from the wound, I succeeded by God's grace in withdrawing the ball, together with a fair round plug of cloth, and Heaven knows how I failed in the first instance to guess its presence. But miss it I did, and now I had withdrawn it.

When finally, and in triumph, I held up my forceps with the ball and plug, and smiled at my assistants, I noted for the first time that all three had their eyes tight shut and were pale of face. Nonetheless they had kept Smollet still, who did indeed try to move, even though he never quite woke up. After that, I sponged the wound clean and dressed it, and we put the captain back inside the house, as comfortably as we could.

Outside I washed my hands and my instruments with water from our spring, and went to sit with Trelawney.

'Here, Doctor,' he said, 'well done, sir!'

I took a tot of rum. Trelawney took one too, and so did Hunter and Gray. 'Will he live?' said Trelawney. 'The captain?'

'I hope so,' I replied. 'A good bleed sweeps clean, and I've got out the seeds of the trouble.'

'And will you go tomorrow to see Ben Gunn?' asked Trelawney. 'With Silver's men on the island, and maybe Flint's too?'

'I have to,' I said, 'we can't stay here forever. We've stores for a while yet, but they are not infinite. And we couldn't even get to the ship without swimming, because we must assume that Silver has taken the jolly-boat.'

'Yes,' said Trelawney. 'I'd not thought of that.'

Then we sat a while, and Trelawney fetched the treasure map and papers for us to peruse and discuss. We had nothing else to do, after all. So Trelawney brought out his long, blue officer's coat, put it down, took the papers from a pocket and laid them on the cloth to keep them free from sand. Then we gathered round for a good look, especially Jim Hawkins, who was flushed with excitement and on his best behaviour, with his sunny-little face beaming steadily at the squire.

'Look, sir,' he said to Trelawney, 'here is the burial site!' And he looked at us all with wide eyes. 'Why cannot we sneak out one night and dig it all up and fetch it back here? What fun that would be!'

'Yes,' said Trelawney, in great approval, 'wouldn't it just? And that would confound Mr Silver and Mr Flint both.'

'Aye!' said everyone else, but I am afraid that I spoiled their cheerfulness with practicality.

'Wait,' I said. 'How great a load would it be?' I turned to Trelawney, 'You said once that Flint's treasure was fabulously great.'

'Yes,' he said.

'*How* great?' I asked. 'What does rumour say?'

'You'd never believe it.'

'None the less, what does rumour say?'

'It's a monstrous sum, sir!'

'Then name it, sir.'

'Well,' he said, and shrugged. 'The tale is, I've heard it said, and rumour has it... that Flint's treasure is worth 800,000 pounds.'

'God bless my soul!' I said.

'Well I'm damned,' muttered Hunter, though I trust he was not, and the others said the like, because such a sum was colossal. It would have built armies and navies, it would have bought rolling acres and mansions or whole streets and squares in London. It was money beyond belief. Most of us were stunned by the figure, but not Jim Hawkins.

'Let's go and fetch it!' he said, positively bouncing with excitement.

'That's my rollicking boy!' said Trelawney.

'Wait a bit,' I cautioned them, and smoothed a patch of sand on the ground. I made some calculations, writing my numbers with a bit of stick. 'If we were to assume that the whole value was in guineas…'

'Why?' said Trelawney. 'There might be precious stones or Spanish dollars!'

'Indeed,' I said, 'but we must start somewhere. So, let's assume that we have eight hundred thousand guineas,'

'Yes,' they all said, and looked at my calculations.

'Then since a guinea weights a quarter-ounce…'

'Does it?' asked Trelawney.

'Yes,' I said. 'That means we have 800,000 divided by four, which is 200,000 ounces in weight. Then dividing by sixteen to convert to pounds…' another calculation, '…gives 125,500 pounds, which divided by 2,240 gives… something over five and a half tons.'

'Oh,' they all said.

'Then, assuming that one man can carry one hundredweight for a few miles, and that there are twenty hundredweights to the ton… that means about one hundred and eleven journeys for one man, or about twenty-two journeys for five men.'

'Oh,' they chorused, disappointed.

'Perhaps fewer journeys,' I said, 'if the treasure were in diamonds or rubies.'

'Ah,' they said, looking up.

'But more if it were in Spanish silver.'

'Oh.'

'So this is not a job,' I said, 'that can be done swift and neat while our enemies are not looking.'

'Bugger!' said Trelawney, and I record the word because it so thoroughly captured the mood of all present. All except Jim Hawkins, that is, who was more dazzled by the worth of the treasure than dismayed by the labour of moving it.

'But, sir,' said Hawkins, and again his bright eyes were shining. 'If we *did* lift the treasure, just think what could be done with it!'

'Huh,' I said, looking at Hawkins, and the image came instantly to mind of him in a Parisian whore-house surrounded by naked trollops. I believe that he guessed my thoughts, because he gave me the look that kills, and then adopted — for Trelawney's benefit — a most sanctimonious expression of benevolence. The little rat would have made a wonderful actor.

'Sir,' he said to Trelawney. 'If one were in possession of a share of such money…'

'Yes, my boy,' said Trelawney.

'Then what profession should a man follow?' And Hawkins gave me such a sweet smile that I marvelled at his duplicity. 'What profession should a man follow, to become powerful,' he hesitated here, and glanced again at me, 'I mean powerful to do the most *good*?'

'Well,' said Trelawney, 'that would mean going into parliament, I suppose. What do you think, Doctor?'

'Yes,' I said. 'It would.'

'Thank you, sir,' said Hawkins, 'and thank you, Doctor.'

With that we abandoned discussion of the treasure for the moment, Trelawney put the map and papers in his coat pocket, and put the coat back safe inside the house. But later, in the evening when the others were elsewhere, Trelawney and I smoked our pipes together and he whispered to me.

'Doctor,' he said, 'I see we can't snatch up the treasure, but you've shown me that we might be able to get home, if we can take the ship.'

'Have I?' I said.

'Yes, because I've told you I can't work out my position at sea, haven't I?'

'Yes, old fellow,' I said, 'but the captain still lives, and we must hope for the best.'

'Of course!' he said. 'But here's my point. I know what the sums are, to work out position, but I just can't do the numbers, because the times tables are a box of mad frogs to me. They're all leaping and slimy, and I can't take hold of them, and never shall.' He smiled sadly and made a brave admission. 'David,' he said, 'I was over thirty before I realised that five times seven is the same as seven times five! But if we work together, and I show you the sums…'

'And I do the calculations …' I added.

'Then between us,' he said, 'we can fix position and sail the seas!'

We smiled and shook hands, and it was a happy thought in the deep of our troubles, and a small cause for hope.

Then next day, just before noon, I went over the palisade again. I was armed as usual and carried another piece of cheese from our stores, and went into the jungle. There, I imagined Silver's men or Flint's on every side, and at every twig that snapped or bird that called. But there was nobody there other than Ben Gunn, who surprised me as entirely and completely as he had before, having by years of practise become the most accomplished woodsman.

'Doctor, sir!' he said, and appeared from a bush where I would have given my oath that not even a robin could hide. 'I've come aboard, Doctor, sir!' he said, and stamped and saluted. So we stood in the steaming heat of the jungle, with sweat on my brow, and my shirt hanging sodden on my back, and unknown things creeping and crawling. There were ants the size of a thumb's width, and buzzing things that nipped and stung.

'Good day, Mr Gunn,' I said, and got straight to business.

'Is it Flint? Is he on the island?'

'Oh yes, Doctor sir, it's himself, and I seen him.'

'What's he doing?'

'Looking for the treasure, Doctor sir! What else?'

'So you know about the treasure?'

'No, no, Doctor sir, I wouldn't know about that. Only them as sailed with Flint would know about his treasure and how he argued with Long John.'

It surprised me that he knew of Silver, though it should not have.

'Do you mean Long John Silver?'

'Oh yes, Doctor sir, that'd be him: him what had the lovely black girl that Flint wanted, though I never knew him, not being one of his men, nor Flint's neither, though I suppose it might be him what came ashore yesterday, to talk with you after the cannonading.'

That was a vast meal of news all on one plate, so I pursued just one item.

'Did you say that Flint and Silver argued over the treasure?'

'Aye-aye, Doctor sir, 'cos Flint he wanted to bury it, and Long John said it were mad to bury it, and no gentleman of fortune had ever buried his goods, not in all of history, but then all hands voted and Flint won, 'cos Flint spoke so sweet, and so they buried the treasure.' He stopped in his flood of words, as if realising he had said too much. Then he shook his head. 'But it weren't on this island, Doctor sir, and

I ain't been searching for it all these years, not poor Ben Gunn. Not him. Not with spades and tools worn out.'

I needed time to think about all this, and concentrated on the practicalities.

'Can I rely on you to keep watch on Flint?' I said. 'Especially him, but on Silver too?'

'Oh yes, Doctor sir,' he said, constantly touching his brow, 'Ben Gunn'll do that. He'll do that, and he'll nip Flint's coat-tails too, if he can, 'cos Flint's the worst of the two, and Silver always was a gentleman of fortune what sailed under articles.'

'And shall we meet here tomorrow at the same time?'

'Aye-aye, Doctor sir!'

'And one more thing,' I said. 'Are there any boats on the island? I think Silver must have taken the boat we had.'

'Oh, yes Doctor sir, he's got your jolly-boat, and left you marooned!' He laughed at that. He laughed and laughed. Then he got cunning again. 'But he don't know about my boat, don't Silver, not Ben Gunn's boat.' And then the character of this bizarre person changed again, and he became almost a rational man. 'I have a boat, sir, and which I made with my own hands. Would you like to see it? It is not far.'

This was a puzzle because although I had declared to my comrades that I trusted Ben Gunn, he was so much my master in woodcraft, that I hesitated to follow him so deep into his own element. He moved so quick and silent that I imagined him getting behind me with that knife of his, before I could even cock and level my musket. But needs must, and the lure of a boat was very great.

'Yes, Mr Gunn,' I said. 'If you lead the way, then I shall follow.'

A'nd that is what we did, with myself keeping ready to fire if I had to. He followed paths — goat paths — that only he knew, and I was bitten and stung and smitten by the branches and soon lost all sense of direction. But then we came out of the jungle, and into the sands of the anchorage, so we must have gone southwards, and he turned and put a finger to his lips for silence, because *Hispaniola* lay at anchor some two miles to the west, but even at that distance some of her sounds came over the water. It was hammering mostly, as if carpenters were at work, and also — faintly heard — the chanting of men on hauling lines as something heavy was being moved. I doubted that the soft sound of voices would carry back to the ship, but I heeded Ben Gunn's advice and stayed silent.

Then I looked round and saw that we were far into the eastern end of the anchorage, on a low, sandy spit that is joined at half-water to Skeleton Island. Keeping to the cover of the trees, Ben Gunn led on, stooped and scampering and at such a speed that I struggled to keep up.

Then he stopped and pointed, and I saw, some distance further down the spit, and rising from among low bushes, an isolated rock of about twenty feet high, peculiarly white in colour. He pointed again at the rock in emphasis and I nodded, realising that this was Ben Gunn's landmark and sign to where his boat lay, and I began to grow excited, imagining something like a ship's long-boat that might bear a mast and sails, and enable us all to escape from the island.

Then, having again waved me to silence, and having looked and listened with animal senses, to make sure nobody was watching, Ben Gunn beckoned me down into a small hollow at the foot of the rock, quite hidden by a bank of green turf, and thick undergrowth, which we pushed through, and there Ben Gunn stopped and proudly displayed his boat.

In fact, what I saw at first was a large tent of goat-skins stretched over a wooden frame. But I followed Ben Gun into the hollow, where he lifted the side of the tent, and there was his boat. I was disappointed, but greatly impressed, because while it was too small a vessel to carry our party across the ocean, it was a fine work of hand craft, reflecting great credit on Ben Gunn, who in matters of boat building was nowhere near so mad as he looked.

It was a goat-skin boat on a wicker frame, with the black-and-white hair turned inward. It was some five yards long, quite narrow, with up-turned bow and stern, pegs on the gunnels for oars to pull against, and thwarts to seat five or six men. It reminded me instantly of boats I had seen in the west of Ireland and which the Irish call a curragh. So I asked Ben Gunn if he knew of such. But he just shook his head.

'I just made it, Doctor sir,' he said. 'Out of my own head.'

'Then yours is a clever head and an ingenious one!' I told him, and he touched brow in salute, and grinned at me with his wild face and hair. I smiled, thinking that if Hunter had been present he would have declared that Ben Gunn was indeed a piskey. So I gave Ben Gunn the cheese I had brought, and which he ate with relish, and I got him to show me the way back to my friends. There we parted, since he staunchly refused to enter the blockhouse which he said was Flint's and was cursed.

So I waved to Trelawney and the rest, and climbed the palisade. I had learned a lot more, and I was making a firm ally of Ben Gunn. But I still did not know how we should come safe out of our situation, nor what adventures we should have in Ben Gunn's curragh.

CHAPTER 25

Flint blinked. He blinked fast. It was a bad sign, which would have given warning to those who knew him well. But the two men standing in front of him did not know him well. They had been chosen because they were young and nimble, and best choice for a task which involved creeping silently: them and the other two.

So now Flint stood in the midst of the neat little camp they'd made the previous night. There was a fireplace ring of stones, a pot hanging over the fire on a frame of cut sticks, and the men's bedrolls were laid out in the clearing in the thick, festering jungle, with its never-silent insects and creatures, and always the rumbling beat of the surf that could never be escaped on the island and which, to Flint, was beginning to sound like the drip of the Chinese water-torture.

'Tell me again,' he said. But the two young men looked at each other in fear and said nothing. 'You first,' said Flint. 'You first Mr Elmore, then we will turn to Mr Kerr.'

'Aye-aye, Cap'n,' they both said, and they couldn't help but notice that a large fly crawled across Flint's brow, dipping its miniscule trunk into the sweat that ran there. Flint was in such a state of agitation that he ignored it.

'So?' said Flint, when Elmore remained silent, and he laid a hand on the hilt of his cutlass. Elmore took the hint.

'It was my watch, Cap'n sir, the morning watch, and I never was asleep…'

'Oh I do hope so, Mr Elmore,' said Flint. 'Just as I hope that your most beloved anatomical parts shall remain fast in place.'

Elmore shuddered deeply at the implied threat, having been entirely unable to watch, last night, as Flint had questioned Franky Grig. Not for more than a few minutes in any case, because after that Elmore had been obliged to go into the bushes to vomit.

'Do continue, Mr Elmore,' demanded Flint.

'Aye-aye, Cap'n!' said Elmore. 'I was going my rounds, like you said, pacing my steps so as to keep awake. So I went round that side of the fire,' Elmore pointed, 'and — as I hope for resurrection and salvation…'

'*Salvation?*' said Flint. 'You worry about salvation, Mr Elmore? Believe me, most truly Mr Elmore, your main task now is not hope of ascension, but avoidance of descent into the pit.'

'Aye-aye, Cap'n!' said Elmore. 'But as I hope for God's forgiveness, I hadn't more than turned my back, and I didn't hear nothing, but when I came round the other side, and looked down, and Grig was dead after what you done to him, and… and…' and here Elmore ran out of strength.

'And you saw two of my men,' said Flint, 'who had been alive and well seconds before, you saw them laid out with their throats cut, and the blood still pumping.'

'Aye-aye, Cap'n sir!'

Flint's eyes blinked, fast.

'And you heard nothing, and saw nothing?'

'No, Cap'n.'

'So do you suppose they cut their own throats, or that somebody came round on tip-toes and did it for them?'

Flint blinked faster and faster.

'I don't know, Cap'n. I don't know…'

'What *do* you know?'

'Nothing.'

'Then what use are you to me?' exclaimed Flint, and his temper snapped and the cutlass was out of its sheath and slashing at Elmore's neck so fast that Elmore had no time even to raise a hand. *Thump*! The head did not quite come off and the blade stuck in the meat and gristle. So Flint stood back and let go, and allowed cutlass and Elmore to fall. Elmore kicked quite a lot and his blood spattered Flint's boots.

Flint stepped aside and turned to Kerr. Flint was much calmer now, having discharged his temper upon Elmore. So he smiled.

'Now then, Mr Kerr,' he began. But Kerr was warned, and young as he was, Kerr had been on other voyages and was not a fluffy duckling. So Kerr pulled a pistol from his belt with his right hand, and tried to cock it with his left… only to find one of Flint's large-sized, silver-mounted pistols by François-Alexander of Paris, was already between his 'lips and tapping gently against his teeth.

'I would strongly advise that you take your hands from your pistol,' said Flint, and he laughed. Any man fears a madman, especially a madman with a gun, so Kerr let his hands fall to his side, as his bladder emptied itself down his legs.

'So,' said Flint. 'We turn to our prisoner, Mr Franky Grig, from whom it was my hope to extract further information.'

'Dead, Cap'n,' said Kerr, mumbling a little with the pistol muzzle in his mouth. 'Elmore woke me up and showed me. Grig bled a lot after you opened his belly, and he was dead like the other two.'

'And then, *and only then*, the two of you woke me?'

'Aye-aye, Cap'n. We wanted to be sure we knew everything that had happened.'

'And of course it had not happened on *your* watch, but on Mr Elmore's.'

'Aye-aye, Cap'n.'

'I see,' said Flint, and balanced the satisfaction of blowing out some of Mr Kerr's spine through the back of his neck, against the need to preserve as many hands as possible for future need. For a moment these points were finely balanced, and what saved Kerr's life in the end was the necessity that he should act as a beast of burden, carrying items of gear back to the ship, which otherwise Flint would have had to carry himself.

So Flint nodded. 'Good enough, Mr Kerr,' he said, and lowered his pistol and un-cocked the lock, then replaced it in his belt with its comrades. 'Now gather up our trappings, because we are returning to the ship.'

'Aye-aye, Cap'n,' said Kerr, and raised a hand to his brow. After that he had to go and sit a good while with his head in his hands and his heart thundering madly. But when Kerr stirred and looked up, his heart began to beat again, because Flint was sitting cross-legged in front of him and close enough to touch. But Flint was smiling.

'Calm yourself, Mr Kerr,' he said, 'because we have done rather well, you and I.'

'Cap'n?' asked Kerr, terrified to his bones that Flint might be mocking him.

'Oh yes,' said Flint, 'and I thank you for giving me these few moments of reflection.'

'Cap'n?' asked Kerr again, and Flint laughed.

'Oh do take that mournful look from your face, Mr Kerr. You look like a spaniel caught mounting the cat!' and Flint laughed again, but Kerr said nothing, because Flint had laughed when he was attending to Franky Grig and *that* hadn't been funny at all.

'So,' said Flint, 'I am going to take you into my confidence, Mr Kerr, and I want you to pay sharp attention.'

'Aye-aye, sir!' said Kerr, and Flint continued.

'The truth is, Mr Kerr, that when we set out from the northern anchorage to spy upon John Silver — yourself, myself and the others — I was in some state of alarm, because based upon the gossip of Bristol town, it was my belief that we should find Silver here, with a large crew and having taken over the treasure-map, and the schooler *Hispaniola*.' He raised his eyebrows in question. 'Did you know, Mr Kerr, that *Hispaniola* mounts twelve six-pounders, whereas *Revenge* mounts only eight?'

'No, sir.'

'Worse still,' said Flint, 'Silver would have the advantage of a first-class gunner in Israel Hands.' He smiled again. 'So there was cause for concern, should it come to a war of attrition.'

'Aye-aye, sir,' responded Kerr, who had no idea what 'attrition' meant.

'But now,' Flint continued, 'and thanks to Mr Grig, we know that Silver has only a small crew, greatly outnumbered by our own, and that our enemies are divided into two parties: Silver's aboard *Hispaniola* with all her guns and stores, and Trelawney's in the blockhouse with the treasure map and papers, but afraid to come out.'

'Aye-aye, sir,' said Kerr, who had no idea who Trelawney might be, or what the blockhouse was.

'And this is all good information, Mr Kerr,' said Flint, 'which entirely makes up for the loss of Mr Arrow, Mr Baudry and Mr McGuigan, all of whom I had ordered to come to me, once on the island, with whatever they had learned of Silver's plans, and the map and papers if possible.' Flint shrugged. '*Fortunes de la guerre!*' he said, and Kerr nodded. He knew about Arrow and the others, and now he knew that they were dead. Or he supposed they were dead. But he didn't mind that: they'd never been mates of his.

'So now, Mr Kerr,' said Flint, 'I shall capture *Hispaniola* and shall take such opportunity as may present, to be finished and done with John Silver.' He paused. 'Do you follow me thus far, Mr Kerr?'

'Aye-aye, sir.'

'I shall then persuade Mr Trelawney to give up the map and papers, or stay in his blockhouse and starve to death, and by this means I shall recover the treasure at last and make rich men of myself, yourself, and all aboard *Revenge.*'

'Ah!' said Kerr, scenting personal advantage at last.

'*Ah* indeed, Mr Kerr!' said Flint. 'But we now come to the reason why I am taking you so far into my confidence.' His smile faded and Kerr began to be afraid again. 'Can you guess the reason, Mr Kerr?'

'No, sir,' said Kerr.

'Then I shall tell you,' said Flint, and pointed to the bodies of the men who had been murdered in their sleep. 'Even your brain will have worked out that somebody crept in among us last night with a sharp knife.' Kerr nodded. 'But you will not have realised that it could not have been any member of Silver's, nor of Trelawney's, party because they would not have acted in such a way. You must trust me in that, because I know it to be true. Do you follow?'

'Aye-aye, sir.'

'And therefore we must assume, that there is some other agency working on this island which is opposed to us and which is silent, deadly and cunning, though we do not know who, or what it is. Do you follow?'

'Aye-aye, sir.'

'So here we come to the important matter, which is that I do not want my crew to know anything about that agency for fear of damping their spirits at a time when I need them high. Are you following me, Mr Kerr?'

'Aye-aye, sir.'

'Even more important is the fact that the girl Selena must know nothing of what has happened here, and she must know *exquisitely* nothing, *absolutely* nothing, *entirely* and *completely* nothing, of the means whereby Mr Grig was persuaded to talk. Do you still follow me, Mr Kerr?'

'Oh yes, sir. Oh yes, indeed.'

'Good. So, Mr Kerr, when we return to the ship I shall explain that we were attacked by Silver's men and beat them off, but that sadly we lost three of our comrades. I shall tell that story to your great credit and to mine, and you will confirm it. Do you follow?'

'Yes, sir.'

'I hope that you do, Mr Kerr, because if Selena learns anything else, then she can only have learned it from you, and in that case, Mr Kerr, I shall do to you what I did to Grig, except that it will be very much worse and will last very much longer.'

Kerr shuddered in terror.

'No, no, no,' he said. 'No need for that, sir. No need at all. No, no, no.'

'Good,' said Flint. 'Then let us pack up and be off, because there is much to do.'

*

The hammering and banging ceased at last, and Israel Hands mustered the sweepers with their brooms, to make all neat and tidy aboard ship, and the two guns were wheeled around to stand side by side in the sun. The carriages were not to be compared with those of the Royal Arsenal of Woolwich, but they were neat and practical, with wheels five-feet in diameter of solid pine plank, sawn to shape and iron-tyred with barrel-hoops cut to size. Each had a pair of ten-foot oak trails fixed to each axle, such that they could be towed by six men each, and trained by one man alone if need be. The cap-squares, ring-bolts and other metal fittings were all burnished with brick-dust and treated — as were the guns themselves — with Israel Hands' own formula stove-blacking, well rubbed in with a brush, then polished to a shine with rags.

More than that, further gear, including a hand-cart, was stacked neatly to one side of the guns to show just what could be contrived, with effort, determination and a bit of ingenuity. So the men stood back smiling in pride at what had been made.

'Fetch Long John!' Israel Hands told one of the men.

'Aye-aye, Mr Gunner!'

Silver was soon up from the cabin, and taking a tour of the guns with his parrot on his shoulder.

'Well done, Mr Hands,' said Silver. 'Well done indeed!' And he laid a hand on the wheel of the nearest gun. 'Nice and big,' he said, 'so we can haul the guns over rough ground and through the woods.'

'Oh yes,' said Hands, and opened the lid on the hand-cart. 'Powder and shot to go in here, and sponges and other tackles, and all proofed against the rain if we get any.'

'Good,' said Silver. 'And what about the shields?'

'Get 'em up lads,' said Israel Hands, 'and show the cap'n what we've made!'

The men doubled forward and raised up four large shields of ship's plank, with folding braces that could be rigged to keep them upright. Each shield was six feet high and four feet wide, and the men moved clear once the shields were up, to prove that they would stand fast on their own. As a further ingenuity, each shield had its own, detachable axle and wheels like those of the guns, so that they could be moved with ease.

'Very nice, Israel,' said Silver, 'but will they stop shot? Can that damned squire send a ball through them?'

'We'll have to see,' said Israel Hands, 'because they're two-planks thick as it is, and we don't want them any heavier or we'll never get them up to the blockhouse, and the main purpose isn't to stop shot, but to hide our men so he doesn't know where to aim.'

'Aye,' said Silver. 'So we haul the guns up at night, when the swab can't see us anyway, and be ready to open fire at dawn.'

'With the shields round the guns so only the barrels point through,' said Israel Hands, 'and we'll load and run-out behind them after that.'

Silver nodded. 'And all them as ain't serving the guns,' he said, 'shall fire with muskets on that blasted squire, to put off his aim — him and his rifle! And then, Mr Hands,' said Silver, raising his voice for all to hear, 'if we get these guns to the edge of the clearing, do you think you can hit the blockhouse?'

'I don't see as I can miss, Cap'n,' said Israel Hands.

'So let's get lifting tackles prepared' said Silver, 'and the guns and gear into the boats. And let's give Squire Trelawney a fine surprise tomorrow morning, and have the treasure map in our hands before dinner!'

The men cheered. Things were looking better.

CHAPTER 26

From Dr Livesey's journal:

The next morning, Ben Gunn surprised me.

He surprised me by appearing at the palisade fence and calling my name. Joyce was on guard and shook me awake.

'Doctor,' he said, 'it's your wild man. He's at the fence, calling for you.'

I stood up at once, pulled on my shoes and waistcoat, took up my pistols and musket and went out, with the rest of the company stirring around me.

'Doctor sir! Doctor sir!' It was indeed Ben Gunn, right at the fence gripping the bars with one hand and waving with the other. He was up to his waist in the morning mist, and beyond him the anchorage was covered with it. But that was the nature of this ungodly island: tropical one moment and frozen the next.

'Ben Gunn!' I cried. 'Come over the fence and inside!'

'Not I, Doctor sir,' he said, 'not for all my life and fortune, and I begs that you come down to me, for I won't set foot inside a thing what Flint made.'

Neither would he move a step, so I went down to him, and everyone stood to arms and peered into the forest for danger.

241

'What is it, Mr Gunn?' I asked as I reached him.

'Pirates, Doctor sir,' he said, and his words tumbled out in a jumble. 'It's Flint and Long John both. Flint's coming down from the north in boats, though I done two of 'em, and I'd have cut free the other poor lubber, which was horrible to see, but he was dead afore I got there, and Long John's coming through the woods, and he's coming alongside with guns run out and matches burning, and it'll be hot shot and slaughter if you don't watch out, 'cos I'll not give it to them what they're after, not Ben Gunn, so it's you they're after now and the papers, 'cos I heard 'em say so, and they're coming, Doctor sir, and you can—'

'Wait, wait!' I said, and laid a hand on his to calm him. 'I'm here, Mr Gunn, and my comrades are with me. So tell me plainly what's going forward.' He gasped and his face worked in great emotion, then he forced himself to speak slowly.

'Flint will attack from his boats, and Silver through the woods. Silver's got two field pieces and he's bringing 'em up through the woods. He got stuck on the beach, or he'd have been at this fence by dawn, but he's coming now and ain't far behind.'

'Ben Gunn,' I said, 'have you been keeping watch to protect us?'

'Aye, Doctor sir,' he said, 'that I have! Because' Ben Gunn is on your side, and all that he owns is yours to command.'

I was so touched by his words, and particularly by his quaint reference to '*all that he owns*' that I was speechless a while, and perhaps dwelt too long in my gratitude, because Ben Gunn was looking over his shoulder in alarm.

'That's Silver!' he said. 'He's coming! Him and his men.'

'Are they?' I queried his words because I heard nothing and saw nothing: only the jungle and the insects and the birds.

'They're bearing down on us, Doctor sir,' he said. 'So you'd best beat to quarters and summon all hands, and I'll be in the woods, acting your part whenever I may.' Then he was off and gone, moving like a greyhound for speed and an owl for silence. He truly was a beast of the woods.

But then, even I heard voices and the squeak of axles, and the trampling of undergrowth.

'All inside the house!' I cried, as I ran up the slope, because everyone but Captain Smollet had crept forward to hear what Ben Gunn had to say. 'Man the loopholes, and Squire, take your best position to cover this side of the house!'

So that is what we did, and at least we were under cover of the thick timbers, though there was no door to the house, but we had our muskets in our hands, and more loaded and ready, and cutlasses if it should come to that, and the squire was covering the woods with his American rifle. Even Captain Smollet had roused himself, and, sick as he was, had his back to a wall and a pistol in either hand. So did the boy Jim Hawkins, though I knew that he would be useless in a fight, and in practise he proved far worse.

Thus we waited, and the noises outside grew, and the foliage on the western side of the clearing stirred. Then someone shouted commands, and men burst from the trees with great wooden boards which they planted to the ground, and set upright with folding beams, yelling madly to encourage themselves.

'Go on, my lads!' cried a voice. 'Go on, my lovely boys!'

'Huzzah! Huzzah!' they cheered, and everyone in the blockhouse cocked and aimed. But I called out a warning.

'Don't fire!' I shouted. 'Give the squire a clear shot with no smoke!'

'Ah!' they said, then *whoof-bang*! The squire fired, and our people cheered to see one man fall beside the wooden screens, and the rest run back into the forest. Then a voice was bellowing, and men came out again to pull the screens into one line.

'Fire!' I cried, and our full volley sounded, then we were turning to our reserve muskets and the squire busy reloading. We hit nobody as far as I could see, but splinters leapt off the screens, and the man who had fallen, tried to drag himself into the jungle, which he failed to do. But John Silver — it was obviously him — threw himself to the ground, crawled swiftly to the fallen man and bodily dragged him towards the trees. I must admit that I held my fire as he did this; Joyce, Hunter and Gray did not, and who could blame them? But if they were aiming at Silver, they missed and did him no harm.

Then the squire was loaded again and seeking a target, which soon came, as two black muzzles were run forward between the lines of wooden screens. It was a pair of guns, just as Ben Gunn had warned: guns that he had somehow taken out of *Hispaniola*, hauled through the jungle on artfully-contrived land carriages, and brought to bear on us.

Whoof-bang!' went the squire's rifle, and somebody screamed behind the wooden screens.

'Aim between the screens!' said the squire. 'Don't matter what you hit, just give 'em cause to fear!' So we gave another volley and we fell to reloading, and in the middle of this work, there came the most appalling, thundering detonation as both guns fired and a pair of six-pound shot smashed into the blockhouse, knocking out one great beam and bringing death among us.

*

The blockhouse disappeared in the smoke of the latest volley from the defenders. Musket balls battered the shields, and one came right between the screens and hit, for the second time, a man who had been

244

wounded by a shot from Trelawney. The man cried out, and fell across the axle of the gun carriage.

'Get him clear,' cried Israel Hands, 'and gun crews stand by to train and elevate!'

'Hold hard!' cried Silver, still trying to haul another wounded man out of reach of musket balls, from where he lay outside the wooden screens. Silver was flat on the ground, half outside the screens, and pulling with both fists clenched on the man's shirt, while pushing against the ground with his one leg.

'Tom! With me!' said Israel Hands, and he and Tom Morgan crouched down and joined Silver. They pulled him and the other man well back behind the guns, with the trunk of a great tree for cover.

'Thank 'ee, matey!' said Silver. 'Where's me timber limb?' The crutch was brought and Silver stood up, but Israel Hands was shaking his head, and closing the eyes of the man they'd tried to save.

'Never mind, John,' he said, 'you did your best. You went out when nobody else did.'

'Aye,' said Silver. 'Now bring them bloody guns to action. Go on!'

So Israel Hands ran back to his guns, took up a powder horn and primed both touch-holes, and was in the process of training the first gun, when another volley sounded from the blockhouse, musket balls came smashing down again, and one took Tom Morgan clear in the belly as he was hauling on a gun-trail.

'Oh mother of mine!' said Morgan, and fell back and sat with his hands on his wounds. He sobbed and groaned.

'Get him clear of the guns!' shouted Israel Hands, and concentrated on his aiming. 'Left a bit, left a bit… hold hard! Right a bit… hold hard!' Then he aimed the second gun, made sure that both were elevated to maximum, and stood back. 'At my command…'

'Aye-aye!' said the gun-captains, just as Israel Hands had taught them.

'Give... *Fire*!' The linstocks dipped, the priming fizzed and the two guns bellowed and leapt and threw out jets of fire, banks of smoke, and two speeding round shot that battered into the blockhouse like the fist of God. When the smoke cleared, all could see that the blockhouse was hard hit, with timbers at a mad angle and holes gaping. So Silver's men stood out of cover, waved fists in defiance and cheered.

'Get back in here, you bloody lubbers!' cried Silver. 'Get back before...' and the whole side of the supposedly-ruined blockhouse disappeared in white smoke as the defenders gave another volley.

Black Dog's head jerked back on its shoulders, struck square in the brow, and he dropped lifeless. Another man howled as a ball smashed his left wrist, leaving his hand dangling by a strip of skin, while a third clutched his face, scoured down the cheek-bone and his ear torn to rags.

'Get behind the shields you sons of bitches!' said Silver, then he went out again, and dragged them all to safety. 'Didn't I tell you to take care?' he cried. 'And Israel, stand to your guns!'

'Aye-aye!' said Israel Hands, who would have done just that, being navy bred and knowing no other way. But only he, Silver and George Merry were like minded, and nobody else moved, because they had got themselves behind good strong trees and were determined to stay there.

'Come out, you lubbers!' cried Silver. 'Are you gentlemen of fortune or no-bollock eunuchs?'

'We ain't neither,' said a voice. 'We signed up as jolly companions and to share in the treasure.'

'Aye!' said the rest.

'And we ain't standing up for no sod with a rifle to make target practice!'

'Aye!'

'By thunder!' said Silver, and drew a pistol from his belt. 'Either you swabs will obey your lawful orders or I'll shoot you like the cowards you are!'

*

From Dr Livesey's journal:

A round-shot killed Joyce outright. The ball came thundering through the timbers of the house, spent its full force upon him, inflicting a dreadful wound that I shall not describe other than to say that the poor secretary, who never was a man bred up to violence or adventure, was instantly taken from this life to the next. But Hunter, Gray, Trelawney and I were still standing, in the dust and smoke, peering out through the holes blown in our wall, while the valiant Captain Smollet, now fully awake, was dragging himself across the floor to take hold of the musket Joyce had dropped, and which he ran out through a hole in the wall, and made ready to fire.

Again, the soldier within me spoke up, because I did not act out of any conscious intent.

'Give 'em another volley!' I cried, though my voice screeched with such fury as I had hoped was in my past, and which was no great credit to a doctor and surgeon. But we stood to arms, we cocked and levelled, and did so in a fortuitous moment because Silver's rogues came out from behind their shields and were dancing and mocking us in their delight at what their guns had done.

But they shrieked as we fired; one dropped dead, two were wounded and John Silver came out and pulled them all in behind their barricades. Thus we in the blockhouse might have cheered — but we did not, because Hunter was standing back from our ruined wall and looking down at his body, where his shirt was ripped from neck to waist, and blood was pouring from a wound where a great pine splinter, knocked off by the flight of a round shot, had laid open his torso. Even as we looked, he swayed and staggered, and down he fell, and once again Trelawney was on his knees beside another whom he regarded as family, and was tormented by sorrow.

Then there was silence, except for a voice from the forest, behind the screens and guns, which was Silver's, yelling something at his men.

But there was no more firing on either side; all parties were exhausted for the moment, and I became a doctor again. I dropped my musket, fetched my medical things and would have attended to Hunter, but he was already gone, held in Trelawney's arms all still and white. So I turned to our captain, who was, thank God, now sitting up and taking notice of all about him. Gray and I helped him back to the bed we'd made him of old timbers and blankets, and Smollet smiled at me.

'Didn't we give it them swabs? That'll learn 'em!'

'Your wound, Captain,' I said, and would have examined it, but he smiled again. 'No need, Sir,' he said. 'All shipshape and Bristol fashion: no blood, no pain.' So our next task was to deal with the remains of Joyce, which were in such appalling condition as even I found distressing.

'Hawkins!' I cried. 'Attend to poor Mr Joyce!' The little swine had played no part in our defence, and I thought it fair justice that he should have this task.

But Hawkins did not answer. I had assumed he would be cringing in a corner but he was not. 'Where's that bloody boy?' I asked, profaning in my anger, and we all looked.

'Sir,' said Gray, 'he's hopped ship! Look here: he's dug a hole and run!'

So he had. On the far side of the house, where the lowest tier of logs did not quite meet the sandy soil, a hole had been made, just big enough for a small person to squeeze through, and in my mind I imagined Mr Hawkins, grovelling on his knees and furiously scraping away with his hands, so that he might desert us yet again. Which thought stirred me to find Squire Trelawney's blue coat.

'May I?' I asked him, where he sat still holding Hunter's body.

'Oh no,' he said, guessing what I would find — or rather *not* find. So I searched the pockets, and the map and papers were gone, and seeing my expression, Trelawney uttered a number of great oaths and cursed the day that Jim Hawkins was born. Thus a great depression fell upon all of us, such that we sat a while and did nothing.

But then thirst drove us to action: the great thirst that falls upon men after a hot action.

'We need water,' I said, 'from the spring.'

'I'll go,' said Gray.

'No, I'll go,' said Trelawney. But I got up, and found a jug and went myself. I could not ask them to do what I would not. So I went outside, and was about to fetch water from the old iron cauldron, when I heard groans and cries from the jungle edge, and there came John Silver, out of the trees, with a piece of white cloth fixed to a stick. He approached the fence and stopped, and he waved the stick.

'Flag of truce!' he cried. 'Flag of truce!' He looked exactly as I felt: tired and miserable.

'What do you want?'

'A truce,' he said. 'A truce, Doctor, 'cos I've wounded men here that need attending.'

I looked at him, seemingly so crestfallen and contrite, and given all that had passed between us I might have hurled an insult and turned my back on him. But I had the odd feeling that I was speaking to a man like myself: burdened with authority, wondering what was best, and facing hard choices. So I did my best to act as a good general should, because we of the loyal party were now only three fit men plus the captain. We were outnumbered, had limited stores and would never survive further fire from the guns. Yet here was Silver seeking a truce, so what problems did *he* face?

'First lay down your arms,' I said, 'and stack your muskets against the fence. Pistols too.'

'Same for you in the house,' said Silver. 'All firelocks in plain view, and none in hand.'

'Agreed,' I said.'

'Aye-aye, Doctor!' came his reply.

'Then I'll talk to my comrades, first,' I said, 'and we'll see.'

Within a few words, the captain, Trelawney and Gray agreed. We gulped our water, stacked our guns — even as Silver and his men stacked theirs — then Trelawney and Gray set to work to bury our dead, while I climbed the fence with my medical bag.

Silver treated me with respect, saluting and calling me 'Doctor' and 'sir' and behaving as if we were still part of a united crew. His men followed in this, though I noted how surly some of them were towards Silver while ingratiating towards me, raising fingers to brow in defer-ence as if regretting the decision to mutiny, and seeking a way out. Meanwhile I had wounded men to deal with.

'We laid them together, Doctor,' said Silver, 'like going below to the cockpit in ship's action.'

'Good,' I said, but held back from saying *well done*.

'Tom Morgan's the worst,' explained Silver, as indeed he was, though there were three others for my attention. One with a hand hanging off at the wrist, one shot twice in the chest and one bleeding heavily from a ball that had not quite missed his face. So I did my best for all of them, though even as I cut open Tom Morgan's shirt, he died, staring at Silver to the last and mouthing words that none could hear, and I was amazed to see how affected Silver was at his death.

'Tom,' he said, 'old shipmate, are you going from me?' And he threw his arms around Morgan and held him close, exactly like the squire with his dying servants. The fellow with the chest wounds also died, being fairly pierced in the lungs, causing me to reflect how close the captain had come to death. But I left one other with a fine stump to take a hook in due course, and the last with his face and ear stitched, which would give him a scar to boast of.

Then I was done, and was so tired that I had not the wit to refuse when Silver offered hospitality. Or perhaps I had more wit than I supposed?

'Will you take a tot, Doctor?' he said. ''Cos you've fairly earned it.'

'Yes,' I said, and I sat down beside Silver, close to his contrived gun-carriages, with Israel Hands driving Silver's men to bury their dead, just as the squire and Gray were burying ours.

'Here's to ourselves, and hold your luff...' began Silver in what I supposed to be a favourite toast. But then he just shook his head. 'Thanks for what you done, Doctor,' he said, 'and I'll drink to Tom Morgan and Black Dog as was shipmates alongside of me, when we served under articles as gentlemen of fortune, in the old days.'

So he drank his tot, and then the great green parrot came fluttering down from wherever she'd been, and sat on his shoulder and nuzzled his ear, and he stroked her head.

'There you are, my lovely,' he said, 'you was gone away 'cos you don't like fighting, and now come back again,' and he shook his head in sorrow. 'Poor Black Dog, he lost two fingers to this old bird, did Black Dog, when she was Flint's and all hands hated her, and Black Dog tried to wring her neck!' He looked at me and I returned his gaze.

'Past times, Doctor,' he said, 'and old comrades gone.' And I realized that Silver cared more about his comrades than himself, and that in his own way he was an honourable man who served under rules — his *articles* — which were as binding to him as King George's law.

'I'll drink to comrades lost,' I said, 'to Joyce, Hunter and Redruth.' Then, remembering how I had once hoped to be done and finished with warfare, I spoke from the depths of my heart. 'So can we try to lose no more comrades, Mr Silver? Can we try to stop killing one another?'

'Aye!' said Silver, 'I think the tide's turning that way already, Doctor,' and he looked at his men, still busy with their burials, 'cos them lubbers won't fight, anyway, not even with a pistol to their heads!'

And so began the strangest friendship of my entire life. The friendship began, but the killing did not stop, because even as we raised our cups again, a man came running through the jungle from the beach. He gasped and shouted.

'The ship's under attack! They're coming to board and capture!'

CHAPTER 27

Flint stood back, to the admiring approval of all hands, having delivered his account of the recent battle with Silver's men. He nodded graciously to Selena, who was as wide-eyed as all the rest. He raised a hand for silence, and all that could be heard was the wind in the rigging, the creak of the cable as *Revenge* moved at anchor, and the distant calling of birds in this tropical fjord. That and the surf, of course: always the rolling, roaring surf. But all hands fell silent, and gathered close together on the quarterdeck for their captain's next words.

'In this way, my good brothers,' said Flint, 'we came away, barely preserving our lives: myself and brother Kerr.' He paused and shook his head. 'But I may not describe what was done to our comrades,' he said, 'I may not describe such things in the presence of a lady…' and he bowed to Selena.

'Ahhhh!' they all said and touched fingers to brow in salute of her.

'I may not report the torture which Silver inflicted on one of our comrades,' said Flint, 'to make him reveal where we are anchored.' All hands growled in anger. 'But I do commend to you,' he added, 'the tremendous vigour with which brother Kerr fought at my side, and without which we could neither of us have escaped.'

There came a great drumming of feet on the planks, then a growling and cheering, and finally, pistols were drawn and pointed skyward, and discharged in thundering acclamation of Captain Flint and of brother Kerr. So Flint smiled and bowed, and encouraged Kerr to bow, which he did with much embarrassment and without smiling. Then Flint waited for the smoke to clear and raised his hand again.

'So, here is what we shall do, brothers! A ship-watch will remain aboard, and we shall, the rest of us, embark in the long-boat and the launch, to pull down the eastward side of the island, coming about, and into the southern anchorage, and there...' He paused and then went among them, swaggering and prancing, and clapping men on the shoulder, and throwing out his chest, and stamping the deck with his shiny boots, and there was a great cheering and laughing, and Flint turned to smile at Selena, who could not help but be impressed. 'And there, my lads,' he said, 'and there, we shall, at dawn, enter, board and capture *Hispaniola* and deal with Mr John Silver. And after him: the blockhouse, the map, the papers, and...' He paused once more and spread hands and raised eyebrows in anticipation.

'The treasure!' they all roared, and Flint sneered inwardly, because they had swallowed whole the ludicrous, gushing, theatricality of a performance which was his own copy of that given by Thomas Sheridan playing the pirate *Captain O'Blood,* in *'The Irish Buccaneer'* at Drury Lane. 'Flint had once seen and admired it, for its tremendous and remarkable grip upon the emotions of the simple-minded.

I'f it worked for Sheridan, why not for me?' he thought, and laughed again. Then he raised a hand for silence, and this time Flint put on his serious face.

'Now brothers, we have a serious work to do.' He turned to his officers. 'You, Mr Hitchin, and you, Mr Kelly, will set all in motion to prepare the boats and our people for this expedition. Provisions aboard!

Blades sharpened! Every man with a dozen cartridges!'

'Aye-aye!' said Hitchin and Kelly, giving formal salute.

'Then to your duties, men,' he told them, 'because we leave at the turn of the afternoon watch!'

'Aye-aye!' they all roared.

'And now, my dear,' said Flint to Selena, 'a quiet word, if you please?'

'Yes, Captain.'

'In the cabin.'

*

Later, and over a bottle of wine in the neat, smart stern cabin, with its leaded lights open for the breeze, Flint told Selena everything he had learned about John Silver and his plans. He did this in such a carefully edited manner as to set Selena's mind on the proper course, and in this enterprise he was greatly aided by fact that John Silver *had* really and truly broken some of his promises to Selena.

'So he's gone back to the old ways?' she said.

'I fear so.'

'And he has used torture?'

'What can I say?' said Flint, and sighed, though keeping utmost concentration on Selena's expressions. He was careful to sit at the corner end of his table, while she sat on a straight side. That way he was not intruding, and yet she was within reach.

'Oh, Joe,' she said, tears forming in her eyes. Flint noted that and moved his hand towards hers: not so close as to be a threat, merely as an invitation. 'I'd hoped better of him,' she said, and being very much alone, and feeling betrayed and abandoned — and being very much deceived by Flint — she placed her hand on his.

'Never fear, dear lady,' he said. Then he raised her hand to his lips and gently kissed it. 'You may always rely on me, and trust me.'

He was an exceedingly handsome man, and exceedingly persuasive.

*

Later, the boats pulled away from *Revenge*. Flint sat in the stern of the launch with his quartermaster Hitchin steering and only a pulling-crew aboard, to act as a speedy vanguard if need be. Meanwhile the longboat followed, commanded by Kelly the boatswain and packed with men and stores, as the main strength of the expedition.

Flint turned and waved back at *Revenge*, noting the figures of Gilbert the sick-bay man, the three ship's boys and of course Selena, who saw him look back and waved. He waved to her, congratulating himself on having attempted nothing more than a kiss to her hand. The conquest would be a slow process, but Flint smiled — because everything was going his way.

Flint still smiled when the boats passed down the eastern coast of the island and found a landing place on a beach by the islets that fringed Skeleton Island. He smiled when he and his men spent a safe night, intending a dawn entry into the southern anchorage to take *Hispaniola*. But now Flint did not smile. Because at first light there was fog in the southern anchorage. The two boats crept forward with muffled oars, and the men damp with moisture.

'Why's there fog?' said Hitchin, steering the launch.

'Because there is, Mr Hitchin,' replied Flint. 'Sometimes there is, and sometimes there is not, because this island is a mad place for climate.' And he stared hard at the great hill to larboard, on Skeleton Island, and the lesser hill to port on the main island, which between them marked the anchorage entrance. 'A touch of helm, Mr Hitchin,' said Flint, indicating direction, 'or we'll be grounded. This anchorage is famous for its shifting sands, and the only safe way is with utmost care.' Flint frowned and looked ahead. 'A touch this way,' he said, and called back to the longboat following astern. 'Keep her in my wake, Mr Kelly!' he said.

'Aye-aye!' said Kelly.

This went on a while until Flint shook his head and gave up. It was too dangerous. He could follow the safe channel if there were no fog. But not like this. 'Ship oars,' he said, 'and drop anchor. We must wait for the fog to lift.'

'*Will* it lift, Cap'n?' said Hitchin.

'Yes,' said Flint. 'It always does.'

Finally, it did. The sun rose higher, the fog dispersed, and all hands gasped at the clarity with which the anchorage could be seen, with the topmasts of *Hispaniola* visible over Skeleton Island, and the birds circling over the jungles, and the warmth creeping back into men's bones.

'What did I tell you?' said Flint.

'Aye, Cap'n,' said Hitchin, 'but look to westward.' Flint looked and saw, far on the western horizon, a great mass of thundercloud in an otherwise perfect blue sky.

'Never mind that,' said Flint, we'll worry when we've got the map and papers. So pull, my hearties!' he said. 'Pull for *Hispaniola* because there she lies!' And the two boats were rounding Skeleton Island with the deep of the anchorage before them, when volleys of shots suddenly sounded from the main island.

'What's that?' said Hitchin.'

'That, Mr Hitchin,' Flint replied, 'can only be our enemies fighting among themselves, and a wonderful good thing too!'

'Aye!' said everyone.

'And there're their boats, on the beach!' said Flint. 'With only one man guarding; if we're quick we can take them and leave the lubbers marooned!'

'Pull,' said Flint, 'but follow my lead, for the bay's full of sand, and the tide's on the ebb.'

So, with *Hispaniola* in clear sight some two miles off, the boats shot forward. Then *boom-boom!* Two rolling, echoing cannon shots. Everybody looked at the island.

'There!' said Hitchin. 'Powder smoke over the trees!'

'That's where the blockhouse lies,' said Flint, 'so pull, my boys, let's get their boats while they're looking the other way!' That raised a cheer from the men and they pulled with heart, soul, mind and strength, and they beached, secured lines to the boats, and towed them out into the anchorage.

'Now,' cried Flint, 'cast off the tow, and the tide'll carry them out of reach of our friends ashore! And then, my boys, my very jolly boys, let's have their ship!'

Another cheer and the boats were let go, and the launch and longboat raced in a long pull to get alongside *Hispaniola,* where Flint led his men over the side by the main chains, howling and roaring, while the two men left aboard ship tried to train one of her guns at the boats.

But they failed in their clumsy panic, and being utterly terrified they merely ran below and hid, and were hunted out and butchered at Flint's insistence, and their bodies thrown over the side to shouts and jeers.

Flint laughed and laughed. He exulted in joy, he stamped round the deck pinching cheeks and twisting noses, rejoicing in all the ship's fine fittings: her guns, her masts, her rigging and her neat-furled sails, and all the fine stores and goods aboard this splendid ocean-going vessel. Everything from crockery to compasses, and from pickles to pork.

'Well done, my lovely lads!' he cried, and they cheered in delight, with not a scratch on any one of them, and a ship taken and all theirs.

'Cap'n Flint! Cap'n Flint!' they cried, and Flint's only problem, in that most happy moment, was keeping his crew out of the spirit room and sober. Then someone noticed action ashore.

'Cap'n!' cried a voice, 'Look on the beach!' And Flint shaded his eyes, and took a very careful look. A small group of men was moving out of the trees and on to the beach. They were far off but some things were easy to see.

'Well stap my precious vitals,' said Flint, 'isn't that a man on a crutch, all hopping and swaying? And isn't that a green bird flying over him? Now who can that be? Come on my boys, there's only a few of them. We've got their ship, and now we'll have them. We'll have their lights and livers, we'll have their ears for necklaces!' And he led the rush back into the launch and longboat.

CHAPTER 28

From Dr Livesey's journal:

Silver stood. I stood. The messenger rushed up to Silver and saluted.

'I was on lookout at our boats, Cap'n!' he said, 'and a launch and a longboat full of men came out of the mist, and has took our boats and is pulling for the ship!'

'It's Flint,' I said.

'How do you know?' demanded Silver. I hesitated a second before answering, then my last reservations went, and I decided to trust Silver completely: a course of necessity, since our loyal party had not a hope of fighting Flint alone.

'There's a wild man on this island,' I told him, 'who sees everything that goes on here.'

'Ben Gunn!' said Silver, 'Ben Gunn, by thunder!'

'You know him?'

'Aye,' said Silver, 'poor Ben Gunn that was ruined by Flint in the old days, and got marooned.' He sighed at the memories. 'Ben Gunn!' he said again, then looked at me. 'And did Ben Gunn tell you about Flint?'

'He did,' I said. 'Flint has a ship in the northern anchorage.'

'Then we'd best guard our own ship,' said Silver. 'All hands! All hands!' But his men were gaping and blinking, and aside from Silver, Israel Hands and another named George Merry, none looked eager for a fight. It was a dangerous moment.

'Well I'm with you, Mr Silver,' I said, 'and I'll bring my comrades too!'

'Hear that lads?' said Silver, and showed real cunning with his next words. 'The doctor and the squire are with us, and if we make a good show, they'll speak for us back in England and make all right!'

'Ahhh,' said Silver's men, and looked all the brighter.

'You'll do that, won't you Doctor?' asked Silver.

'Of course!' I said, and said it loudly because it was no time for understatement, 'I'll fetch the squire and Gray,' I said, equally loudly, but adding to Silver in a whisper, 'if they'll come.'

'Aye-aye, Doctor!' said Silver, saluting.

So I climbed the fence and ran to the squire and Gray, who had finished their sad work, and had heard Silver's lookout shouting.

'What's going on?' asked the squire, so I explained and though they worried over trusting John Silver, they agreed that we were obliged to join forces. So having checked that Captain Smollet could be left, and having put food and drink in his reach, we three, together with Silver's men, took up arms again and marched together to the beach. We made our way, dragging one of the six-pounders on its carriage, along with the hand cart of ammunition that Israel Hands insisted gave our only chance of dealing with Flint. We were about a dozen strong, including Silver with his one leg, and the fellow who had lost his hand, but who was lifted on the general excitement and declared he would not be left behind.

The anchorage sands were less than a mile off, the going was downhill all the way, and our trouble was not hauling the gun, but keeping it from running off. We would have made good time except that the home-made gun carriage hit some rock or root, and lurched and leaped and went over.

'Ware of her!' cried Israel Hands. 'Don't try to stop her!'

'Whoa!' cried another voice, as two tons of iron and wood slid uncontrollably among the trees, and down went the gun carriage and off came a wheel, where the linchpin had sheared from the axle.

'Bloody hellfire!' shoutedIsrael Hands, and knelt beside the gun, feeling the damage with his fingers.

'Can you fix her, Israel?' said Silver.

'Yes,' said Hands, 'timbers is split, but it's mainly the wheel, so leave some men, and the limber and tools, and the rest of you get down to the beach.'

'Quick as you can, shipmate,' said Silver, 'and call if you need more men.'

'Aye-aye!' said Hands, and we left him to his work. Silver and I, and the squire and Gray, went the fifty paces or so down on to the beach and out of the trees, where we looked at the anchorage to see what was happening, though Silver also looked at the sky to the west — and frowned.

'Foul weather coming,' he warned, and we all looked at a rumbling dark sky, far away. But we gave small attention to that, because our boats were cast adrift, way out in the anchorage, while a launch and longboat were alongside *Hispaniola,* with men clambering over her side, and their cries and cheers coming to us across the water. A man was leading them, up on our ship's bulwark, calling the rest to follow. He was a long way off, but his voice carried over the still water, which was especially calm that day.

'Flint!' hissed Silver, and we watched in utmost horror. We could do absolutely nothing as our ship was taken and captured, and the bodies of two men were later thrown over the side, with derisory howls and curses.

'That'll be my anchor watch!' said Silver. He cursed and groaned. 'Two more brothers lost!' But that was not all. Very soon, Flint and his men were getting back down into their boats and pulling towards us.

'Now what?' said the squire. 'What's this?'

'He's coming for us,' said Silver.

'Do we fight here?' asked the squire. 'There's a great many of them. Shouldn't we go back to the blockhouse?'

'No,' I said, 'we'd be starving in days.'

'Where's that gun?' said Silver. 'Israel,' he cried, 'are you with us, matey?'

'Ah,' I said, 'can we use the gun?'

'Aye,' said Silver, 'cos if that's Joe Flint, then he'll have seen me and he'll come after me. So I'm going to stand here while the rest of you go back and help Mr Hands, and let's give Joe a dose of round shot when he gets here.'

So Silver stood fast, and the rest of us plunged back into the forest, where Israel Hands was cutting off the broken tip of the gun carriage's axle, and shaping it from square to round, to take the wheel and pin. He did so with tools from the limber, but it seemed to take so vast a time, that we began to hear the chanting of Flint's oarsmen as his boats came closer and closer, and we fairly chewed our fists in agitation, because the work had to be done right, but time was short. At last the axle was ready, and with all of us heaving mightily we raised up the carriage, got the wheel back on and the pin driven home, and the gun was alive and ready for service.

'Down to the beach!' I cried.

'No!' said Hands. 'Load her first, so we're ready!' And he took up cartridge, wad and round shot, ramming well home. 'Now, lads!' he cried. 'All together now, and don't let her fall again!'

So we heaved the gun the few yards down the path and out of the jungle, and there was John Silver shouting in delight and pointing out into the anchorage, because after so much ill fortune, our luck had turned with the tide.

'Look!' said Silver. 'The swabs have run aground!'

We looked where he pointed and saw the big longboat, which had most of Flint's men aboard, had run full tilt into a sandbank, a hundred yards from the shore. The launch was still afloat and under way, but the men in the longboat were leaning on their oars trying hard to push themselves into deep water and get afloat again.

'Now then!' cried Israel Hands, and chose four men. 'You! You! You and you! You're my gun-crew. And you,' he pointed to another, 'get the linstock lit and hold it till I need it!'

I stood straight, eased my back muscles from the strain of moving the gun, and looked. The launch was trying to take off men from the longboat, with some wading through water only knee-deep to get aboard the launch. Then there was more shouting from a man standing up in the launch — Flint, I supposed — as the launch grew overloaded, and he drew and fired a pistol to hold back the rest. It was no mere warning shot, because I saw him take aim, and the pistol flashed and a man dropped. He shot down one of his own, to warn off the others, and the crack of the pistol sounded, and more yells and cries.

Meanwhile, Israel Hands was judging distance to the boats.

'Shall you aim at the longboat?' asked Silver.

'Yes,' said Hands. 'It's the bigger target, with more men.'

'Can you hit it?'

'Let's find out!' said Hands, and got behind the breech of the gun, and leaned over to sight down the barrel. His gun crew watched. He pointed left. They turned the gun to point left. He pointed left again. Another shift left. He pointed right and pinched thumb and forefinger together, to indicate a tiny degree. So the gun shifted that tiny degree, and Israel Hands primed the touch hole and reached for the linstock.

'Stand clear!' he said.

So we all got out of the way, and down came the linstock and the gun leapt and roared, and we heard the crunch and splinter of a direct hit, even before the smoke cleared and we could see the longboat torn open amidships and men killed and wounded, and pitiful fragments of men thrown up, to tumble and fall splashing into the water.

'Good shooting, Mister Gunner!' said Silver

'Lucky shot,' said Hands, then he and his men re-loaded and ran the gun forward, and took aim again, all steady and careful. About a dozen more shots went flying across the anchorage. Most missed, but two more went sizzling through the timbers and flesh in the longboat, doing dreadful harm and bringing shrieks and groans, with poor devils deserting the longboat and being fired on again by Flint, to keep them out of the launch, and men throwing themselves into the water in their fear.

But on the final shot, the six-pounder leapt back so hard in recoil, that it broke out of the already damaged carriage and crashed, smoking and hot and sideways, down across the axle, never to fire again: not on that day, at least. But that was not all, because one of the men not serving the gun, shouted out.

'Who's that?' he cried. 'Who's that over there? He's waving at the boats!'

We all turned and looked, and saw, far off up the beach and well towards the mouth of the anchorage, beyond *Hispaniola* and Flint's boats, a small figure was standing at the very edge of the water, with a great palm leaf in his hands, waving it to get attention, and just faintly there came the sound of his voice.

I guessed who it was even before I knew, because Silver and Israel Hands both took small telescopes from their pockets and focussed on the figure.

'As I live and breathe!' said Silver.

'Hell fire!' said Israel Hands.

'It's Jim Hawkins,' I said. 'Isn't it?'

'Aye,' said Silver, 'that's him, the little swab. He should've been drowned at birth, that one! He's waving at Flint.'

'Wait a bit!' said Hands. 'Flint's shouting back. He's nearer to Hawkins than we are and he can hear what the little swab's saying. And now what's this? The launch is moving.'

We all watched as the cram-full launch backed oars, and pulled away from the broken longboat and its yelling, frantic crew who were being abandoned, and we saw that the launch was coming towards us, towards the shore.

'What are they *doing*?' I wondered aloud.

'It's the low tide and the sandbanks,' said Silver, 'Flint's having to come round another big 'un, and then he can run along the shore and aim for where Jim-lad is standing, and pick him up.'

'*Pick him up*? Why should they do that?' I asked. But then I guessed. 'He's got the map and papers. He's told Flint that he's got them, and Flint is coming to get him.' I said that, and in all my life, including my time as a soldier, I never heard such a torrent of foul cursing as followed. But Silver spoke to the squire.

'Mr Trelawney, sir,' he said, touching his hat.

'Yes?'

'Have you got that rifle of yours?'

'I have.'

'Then could you put a ball into Flint?' said Silver. 'If his boat comes close enough?'

The squire frowned, and said nothing.

'Well, could you?' Silver repeated. 'Could you hit the swab?'

'Aye?' enquired others, and the squire still said nothing, even as

Flint's boat was coming into a range at which Squire Trelawney could hit anything he chose to, and Flint himself was standing up and waving and grinning in contempt, and we could hear the men in his boat grunting as they heaved the oars.

'Shoot him.' said Silver.

'I cannot,' replied the squire.

'Why not?' asked Silver. 'You shot my men!'

'But that was in hot action,' said the squire, 'and this would be in cold blood.'

'Flint's a *monster*,' said Silver. 'I'd kill him and gut him if I could!'

'So would I,' said Israel Hands.

'Shoot him, Squire!' said Silver. 'Shoot him and do the world a service.'

'Not if I am to consider myself a gentleman,' said the squire, 'no more than I could shoot a man who was running away.'

And he folded his arms, and that was that with so stubborn a man, because that was Squire Trelawney.

But then Flint smiled, and drew a pistol from his belt. He took careful aim at our group and fired. He missed, and we all flinched as the ball whizzed past. He drew another pistol and fired again, and George Merry fell dead, shot through the heart.

'Ah, George Merry!' came Flint's voice across the water, 'I've done for you at last, and I do most sincerely apologise, because I was aiming at John Silver,' and he laughed, and every man with a firearm, including myself, let fly in rage — and every shot missed.

So Flint laughed all the more, and his boat began to turn away from us along the shore, and he bowed to us all in mockery, then he waved to Jim Hawkins, and the men at the oars sent the launch charging away from us.

'Let's go after him,' I said, 'along the beach,' and I would have set off. But Silver grabbed my arm.

'Can't be done, Doctor,' he said. 'It's all quicksand between here and Hawkins, and there's weather coming that'll make it worse.' He looked up in despair as fat rain drops fell, and thunder rumbled.

But then, *whoof-bang*! The squire fired; we turned and saw him laid flat to aim over a mound of sand.

And out in the speeding launch, Flint fell over backwards — fairly and squarely hit.

CHAPTER 29

Flint looked at the men in the launch. They were surly and shaken. They were cram packed, with some on the thwarts, and some in the bottom of the boat, and they could see that a storm was coming, and they hated Flint. They hated him for shooting men to keep them out of the launch, and they hated him for leaving men behind in the smashed longboat, with Mr Kelly the boatswain dead, and their mates calling them by name.

'Can't we go back, Cap'n?' said Hitchin.

'Not if we want to survive,' said Flint, 'because that gun will fire again in seconds, and it might be aimed at us. So pull, you lubbers! Get us clear before they fire again.!'

But the men growled and refused to move.

'Oh God help us!' said Hitchin, looking ashore. 'He's aiming the gun again!'

'Pull, you swabs! Pull for your lives!' demanded Flint, and faced with dire need, the men pulled, though they pulled half-hearted and grudgingly. But then the gun on the beach boomed and jumped, and the ball went who-knows-where, because the gun broke out of its carriage, with the men around it running to get clear.

'Ah-ha!' said Flint. 'See boys? Flint's luck!'

'Ahhh!' said the hands. It was not a cheer, but every man wants to live. Then came even more of Flint's luck.

'Captain Flint! Captain Flint!' came a voice over the water. It was faint, but it could be heard. Everyone turned to look, and there on the beach up to his ankles in the water, was a lad waving a palm leaf and calling out to Flint, who took a careful look and smiled.

'*Why, it's Jim Hawkins!*' he said to himself. '*My little friend from Mrs Arrow's buttocking-shop. And he knows my real name. What a clever boy.*'

'Captain, sir!' cried Hawkins, 'I've got the map, sir. The map and papers, and I want to come aboard!'

Flint closed his eyes and sighed. He was saved.

'Did you hear that, boys?' he said. 'He's got the map and papers.'

'Ah!' said Hitchin, quicker than the rest to understand.

'What map?' said someone. 'What papers?'

'The map and papers that shall make every man of us as rich as a king!' said Flint.

'Ahhh!' they said, and this time it *was* very nearly a cheer.

'What's he doing, Cap'n?' asked Hitchin. 'What's he want? Ain't he one of Trelawney's crew?'

'In the first place, Mr Hitchin,' said Flint, 'never complain when fortune smiles, and in the second, Mr Hawkins is a devious little viper, so who knows what he's at? But I *do* know that I want him aboard this boat.' He turned to the men at the oars. 'So pull, my jolly boys, pull for the map and pull for the treasure!'

'Hurrah!' A cheer at last.

'Mind your steering, Mr Hitchin,' said Flint, 'there's another sand bank here, so take her round by the shore, then steer for Jim Hawkins.'

'Aye-aye!' said Hitchin, and the men pulled and the launch drove forward, and the shore came close, and Flint could clearly see each man standing by the wreck of the gun. There was John Silver. There was Israel Hands. There was George Merry. And there were others who must have been Trelawney and his party, and every man was armed. The distance was too great for muskets or pistols, but Flint sought a little amusement. His large pistols had already been fired, but he had the two small ones.

'Pull steady, my lads,' he said, and stood up and took aim at the group of men ashore. The pistol flashed and fired. 'A miss!' said Flint, and laughed as his enemies flinched. Then he replaced his empty pistol, drew the last, and aimed and fired. 'A hit!' he cried, at the pure, random chance of the ball hitting someone at such range, and a man fell, and Flint shouted his apology for killing George Merry instead of Silver. He even laughed as those ashore threw up their guns and took aim. 'Pull, my lads,' he said to his men. 'They'll not hit us from there.' And defying the possibility that the men ashore might *also* fire a lucky shot, he smiled and spread his arms to them as muskets flashed and roared, and he faced their fire in the sure and certain confidence of his own invulnerability, as musket shot whizzed past the boat. And only *then* did he turn and wave to Jim Hawkins.

Then the skies went dark in more ways than one, because the storm arrived and even as Flint stood triumphant, his luck failed. Because a hammer blow struck his knee and he fell among the oarsmen, hit his head on the gunnel and was stunned.

Hitchin took charge.

'Take hold of the cap'n!' he cried. 'Then pull for that bloody boy, and let's be out of here before them ashore can get to us!'

Those not at the oars grasped Flint and laid him among them on the bottom of the boat, while the rest pulled hard and strong, swiftly covering the distance to Jim Hawkins, and put the boat's nose half way ashore, and Hawkins splashed out to her and was hauled aboard. 'Back oars!' yelled Hitchin, and the launch cleared the shore. 'Give way!' cried Hitchin. 'Give way with a will, now!' and Hitchin steered southward, out of the anchorage. 'How's the cap'n?' he cried, and cringed as a thunderclap sounded above and rain began to fall. 'Is he alive?'

'Yes,' said Flint, and sat up and stared at his knee in disbelief. This was a new thing. A new thing on the face of the earth, and a shocking thing. Flint had never been wounded. Not ever. Not in all his life: never, never, *never*! He struggled to accept the fact that he too was mortal. The wound did not hurt much because it was numb. But it was undoubtedly a wound.

'Captain,' said Jim Hawkins, 'are you bad hurt?' He spoke with pure hero-worship in his eyes. But Flint ignored that and asked the only question of any importance.

'And have you really got the map and papers, Mr Hawkins?'

'Oh yes, sir. Yes, Captain Flint.'

'And are they safe and dry? Because even God won't save you if they are not.'

'Oh yes, Captain. They are safe in a waterproof package.'

'Good,' said Flint. 'In that case, well done, Mr Hawkins.'

'Thank you, sir!' said Hawkins. Flint nodded, but then his mind became as dark as the sky above. He looked at the wreck of the longboat, and thought of Selena, left back on board Revenge, and thought of men killed, men ruined, men lost, and just when he needed them! Worse still, he looked at the mess that was his left knee. He thought on those things, and knew that some proper vengeance was needed: some serious and heavy vengeance, and he was delighted to find the perfect victim.

'Pull for their ship, Mr Hitchin,' he said. 'Pull for *Hispaniola*.'

*

From Dr Livesey's journal:

The squire stood up. He brushed the sand from his rifle, set the butt on his shoe and immediately began reloading, with his coat wrapped around the rifle to keep off the rain.

'I see that you fired, sir!' said Silver.

'That I did,' said Trelawney. 'You were right, Mr Silver. The man Flint is full of malice. There was no reason for him to shoot at us, except wickedness. He did it for spite and he was laughing as he fired.'

'Well he won't laugh now, won't Flint,' chuckled Silver. 'Do you think you've done for him, sir?'

'Perhaps,' said Trelawney, 'but it was a long shot, and the ball may have fallen low.'

Then Silver was kneeling beside George Merry, and closing his eyes with two fingers, as Israel Hands knelt beside him.

'It's just you and me, now, Mr Gunner,' said Silver.

'Yes,' said Israel Hands. 'Pew, Tom, George and Black Dog. All gone.'

'Jolly companions in their time, shipmate,' said Silver.'

'We'll see George buried proper,' said Israel Hands, 'won't we, John?'

'Aye, so soon as we can,' said Silver, and got up. 'But what's Flint doing?'

We all looked. We saw Flint's launch take Jim Hawkins aboard, as the thunder rolled and a great storm came in from the west. We saw the launch steer for the mouth of the anchorage, but then it came about and headed for *Hispaniola*. The light was bad now, but we all stood in the rain, which was warm and tropical, not the cold rain of England, and we watched as the launch came alongside our ship. Men went aboard of her, then after a while, they came back into the launch, and the launch pulled hard —very hard — away and finally vanished in the gloom, clearly getting itself out of the anchorage.

After that, with nothing else to do and nowhere else to go, we decided on the blockhouse. But first we laid George Merry under the trees, and covered him with his coat, since Israel Hands and John Silver would not let him lie on the open beach. But as for whoever might have survived in the wrecked longboat, still firm on its sand bank, we did nothing. There were men still alive — we heard them — but the distance was too great for swimming, even if the weather had been calm which indeed it was not. Also, having seen the bodies of Silver's men thrown over the side like rubbish, we had little will to give assistance to their killers. So we turned our collars against the rain, and turned our backs, and headed for the blockhouse.

When we reached the clearing and the palisade, we climbed the hill to the blockhouse, and about a dozen of us, loyal party and mutineers combined, took shelter from the rain now coming down heavily, and from the thunder and lightning above. Inside we huddled together, and munched on cold salt pork and ship's biscuit, and each took a most welcome tot of rum. The rain came down with violence and streamed through the shot holes in the roof, but we had space to keep clear of that, and the sandy ground soaked up the rain, keeping us dry.

Then Abe Gray noticed a glow of light.

'It's the ship!' he said. 'Something's burning.'

We all stood and looked out from the doorway. The rain was tremendous, noisy and constant, but the black outline of *Hispaniola* was visible from our viewpoint up on the hill. Even the masts and yards could be seen. We could also see a red glow coming from the hatchways fore and aft.

'Is she on fire?' asked Trelawney. 'In such rain as this?'

'She can't be,' I said, and sought expert opinion. 'Mr Silver,' I said, 'can you see what's happening?'

Silver drew his telescope and looked.

'It's bad,' he said, 'she's well alight. She's on fire below decks where the rain can't reach.'

'That's no accident,' said Israel Hands, 'it's Flint's work. We saw his men go aboard.'

'Aye,' said several voices, and Israel Hands shook his head.

'That ship's got a powder magazine like a man o' war,' he said, 'and if the fire reaches it…' Then, 'Oh no!' he said, as a vast, bright flash tore the ship apart, with smoke and fragments, spars and planks, and blocks, pins, rails and even whole guns sent up into the air, lit lurid bright, and throwing long shadows. Then the heavy, dull, massive rumble of the explosion arrived, and the mariners among us groaned to see a good ship destroyed, as even *Hispaniola's* mainmast, a hundred feet long and weighing many tons, was hurled like a stick for a dog to fetch, trailing shrouds and stays and canvas, and fell wallowing into the anchorage with a great splash. It was hideous. We were as surely marooned as Ben Gunn, and though we still had our lives, we had lost everything else, and had surely failed in every possible way.

CHAPTER 30

The launch pulled out of the anchorage and headed north west. It was overloaded, with gunnels only a foot above the waves, and it swirled and swayed and all aboard her gasped as they were swept along by a tremendous current speeding north around the island. It was greater even than the normal current that ran there, being driven by the storm. So the sea ran smooth and flat and dark, and it moved so fast that even with the oarsmen merely keeping steerage way on the launch, it charged up the coast with the speed of a galloping horse.

'All hands to bailing duty!' cried Flint, as the rain came down in a flood, beating the waves into mist with a steady roar and seriously threatening to sink the boat, deep laden as she was. But the great numbers aboard helped save her, because not only did the men use bailing pans, but hats, hands and anything else that would scoop water and hurl it over the side. 'And you come here, Mr Hawkins,' said Flint to Jim Hawkins. 'You come and sit by me and keep those papers safe about you.'

Hawkins did as he was told, sitting at Flint's feet, all dazed with the noise and motion, as the men heaved slowly on the oars to give the helmsman control of the boat.

Fortunately, the journey was not prolonged. So fast was the current that inside two hours the launch came round the northernmost tip of the island, where despite the thunder and lightning, and the fierce rain, there were calmer waters on the eastern side, with the land mass giving shelter from the wind and storm. Then, inside the anchorage, with its high surrounding hills, the waves were gentler still, and this was a blessing because every man in the launch was exhausted. So the brig *Revenge* was a cheerful sight, even under a black sky, in bad light, and drenched dripping in water.

'Take her round the stern, lads,' said Flint, and the oarsmen brought the launch to where a plank-and-rope ladder was rigged, and one of the ship's boys was on watch. 'Get Mr Gilbert,' cried Flint, 'I am in need of his services.' So Gilbert was summoned and Selena with him.

'Joe,' cried Selena, 'are you hurt?'

'Shot, ma'am!' said Flint.

'Bad?' asked Gilbert.

'Hit in the knee.'

'Get him aboard,' cried Gilbert, 'and I'll make ready down below.' He looked at Selena, both of them in oilskins with the rain battering off their hats so loud they could barely speak, and running off them in streams. 'Will you help me, ma'am?'

'Yes,' she said, 'if I can.'

'And I'll need a bowline to haul me aboard,' said Flint, 'I'll not be climbing ladders today.'

Gilbert did his best, having many times seen how real surgeons worked. He rigged an operating table down below, from sailcloth and a bench. Then he lit every candle he could find, for light, and laid out his collection of tools and dressings. He also sent a pot of tar to the cook's stove with orders for the tar to be heated till bubbling.

Finally Flint was laid on the table, sunk deep in awareness of Gilbert's limitations. But whatever else Flint was, he was no coward, and he knew that Gilbert was all that he had. He had Gilbert, and he had Selena too, who was — by Gilbert's orders — sat astride the narrow table behind him, with her arms around him to restrain his movement. Flint thought that this, at least, was agreeable.

'You may proceed, Mr Gilbert,' he said, 'and be quick!'

'Aye-aye, Cap'n,' said Gilbert. But then he slit Flint's britches and saw what a fast-moving rifle ball does to a human knee.

'Dear me,' he said, and looked for his amputation knife. He picked it up, tested the edge, then put it down and reached for a stick-twist tourniquet. 'I'll have to get some men to hold this leg' he said.

'Why?' said Flint.

'So I can take it off, Cap'n,' said Gilbert. And Flint reached out and seized Gilbert by the throat.

'Mr Gilbert,' said Flint, 'if you take off my leg, then I will have you hung by the thumbs, and I will personally skin you with your own knives, taking care that you stay alive for the entire process. *Do you understand?*'

'Yes, Cap'n,' said Gilbert, 'but ...'

'But?' asked Flint.

'Joe,' said Selena, 'he's trying to help.'

'Is he now?'

'Yes!' she said. Flint paused and thought.

'Mr Gilbert?' he said.

'Cap'n?'

'This is my last word. You will save my leg by whatever means are within your skill. You will do so because your life depends upon it.'

'Aye-aye, Cap'n.'

So Gilbert probed with his clumsy fingers, and he cut with a knife to get properly into the wound, and he probed some more, and he pulled out bone fragments with forceps, and he snipped sinews by mistake, and he got blood all over his shirt, and he sponged and dabbed and finally, rather than sewing up, he sealed the complex wound and stopped its bleeding, by pouring in a boiling stream of ship's tar, which caused Flint, who had borne everything else in silence, to scream so loud that men put their fingers in their ears.

Then Flint was bandaged and carried to his cabin, and put to bed on the padded seat that ran from side to side under the stern windows. He was put to bed, dosed with laudanum, and Selena sat with him and fed him drinks and mopped his brow, relieved at intervals by Mr Gilbert. More importantly, she took careful note of the things Flint said while he was delirious. He talked about everything: of his past life, old shipmates, Jim Hawkins, and especially John Silver, and much that he said about Silver did not agree with Flint's earlier statements. It did not agree at all.

So Flint lay in his bed for over two days while the storm battered the island, and broke trees, and formed rivers, and forced those aboard *Revenge* to stay under hatches, because on deck it was hard even to breathe for the torrents of rain. Then the storm blew itself out, the rain stopped, the sun came up, the sky was blue and everything around *Revenge* steamed with mist, as the hot sun boiled off the rain. It dried every leaf, every bough, every square inch of sand. Then the birds began to sing, and the sea-turtles and dolphins appeared in the anchorage, as merry and bright as Jim Hawkins, who approached Selena as she took the first opportunity to get away from Flint and up on deck in the sunshine.

'Flint's no better than John Silver now, don't you think, ma'am? said Jim Hawkins. 'With his ruined leg'

Hawkins was fascinated by Selena. He had never seen a woman like her. So he adopted what he thought was a manly posture, with hands on the butts of the big pistols in his belt. But to Selena, Jim Hawkins was just a boy in a man's boots. So she said nothing and walked away from the ship's rail, intending to go below.

The air was not fresh at all. It was unbearably hot. The crew were lying in the shade of a sail rigged over the main deck to keep off some of the heat. They were mostly dozing, but some of them nudged one another, and whispered to see Jim Hawkins trying his luck with Flint's girl, such as none of them would even dare.

'Oooh!' they said, as she ignored him and would have walked away. But Hawkins grinned, and skipped around in front of her, taking advantage as he did so to kick one of the ship's boys hard up the backside as he passed. Hawkins smiled, inviting her to join in the fun. But Selena frowned. Shipboard humour was rough, but the kick was too hard, and the boy in tears.

'Oh, stop snivelling,' said Hawkins to the boy. 'It was only a joke.'

'Oi! You there!' said Hitchin the quartermaster. 'You leave them lads alone! You ain't no bleedin' officer!'

'No,' said Hawkins, with perfect confidence, 'but I have the captain's ear. So mind your manners or he'll hear about you.'

'Oh,' said Hitchin, and dithered, because Hawkins was Flint's pet who had brought the map and papers aboard. 'Oh,' he said again and looked away, and Hawkins laughed.

'Shall we take a turn about the deck, ma'am?' he said to Selena, and bowed. She stared at him in contempt. He was very handsome in a girlish, soft-featured sense, and no taller than herself, but more muscular. She guessed that Hawkins was perfectly capable of turning nasty with a woman if he could not get his way, and she was absolutely right.

'What are you doing here?' she asked him. 'Why did you desert your friends?'

'For Flint,' he said. 'I'd never seen anyone like him. So splendid, so well dressed, such command over other men.' He paused and searched for the right word. 'He made me *shiver*,' he said. 'He made me shiver to my spine and I wanted to be like him.'

'Oh,' she said, 'are you one of those who prefers men?'

He laughed and laughed at that.

'God bless you no, ma'am,' he said. 'You'd never believe the number of women I've had, and had them in every possible way!'

She frowned.

'You're a coarse-minded little boy,' she said. 'If I were your mother I'd be ashamed of you, and if you had a father, he'd tell you to become a man before you talk like that.' Hawkins laughed again.

'Well I'm a better man than Flint, now,' he said. 'He doesn't make me shiver any more. His leg's ruined, ' he shook his head, 'and he's spoiled.'

'So what will you do now?' she said. 'Desert again and go back to your brother?'

'My brother?' said Hawkins. 'You know about that, do you?'

'Yes,' she said.

'Then you must know that I can persuade him of anything at all, and that if I want to go back to him then I shall.'

'Shall you, though?' wondered Selena, and looked round the deck from mast to capstan, from pin rails to hatchways, and at the audience of men looking on. Then she smiled. 'Come here,' she said and offered her hand to Jim Hawkins, whose mouth went as round as his eyes in surprise, and he took her hand, knowing that his charm had worked as always it did. 'Come with me,' said Selena, and led Hawkins along the hot deck in the intense sun, and she smiled and turned him round.

'Would you like to kiss me, Mr Hawkins? she asked, and Hawkins could not believe what he had heard.

'What?' he said, and she smiled and put her two hands on his chest.

'I asked if you would like to kiss me.'

'Really?' he said. 'Here?' And he looked at the amazed and staring seamen.

'Oh yes,' she said, and for an instant, Jim Hawkins could not believe his luck. So he leaned forward most eagerly for the kiss… and his delight ended sharply, because Selena pushed hard and tripped him backwards into an open hatch, rumbling and tumbling down the companionway to the deck below. After that she walked off to cheers and laughter, because shipboard humour was indeed rough, except that this time the ship's boys were laughing with everyone else

Selena walked off and went below. Then she thought of real men. She thought of Joe Flint and John Silver. She wondered about them both.

Meanwhile Flint got better fast, because Gilbert's appalling treatment had at least killed any infection in the wound, and Flint was a fit man, strongly driven by will. So two days after the sun came out, he was up and about on a stiff leg that almost worked, and with a stick cut to length, and he paced the main-deck leaning on it.

'Gather round, brothers,' said Flint, and he smiled, and the hands drew close, wondering what to expect. 'Come close, ma'am,' he said to Selena, 'and you too, Mr Hawkins,' and he smiled to see her sneer at the boy, and he smiled even more at the bruises on Hawkins' pretty face, having been told by a gleeful Hitchin exactly how Hawkins got them.

So everyone gathered round and was merry, and the weather was fine, and the day was young, and Flint gave one of his great and inspiring speeches.

'Here are the map and papers,' he said, waving them, 'and because I have them, we shall every one of us ride in our carriages like lords,' he bowed to Selena, 'I shall ride with my lady beside me, and you,' he waved an arm at his men, 'you shall ride with a girl on either arm, and even you shall do the same!' he added, glancing to the ship's boys, and everyone laughed. 'Brothers!' he said. 'Think on it: golden guineas! Louis D'ors! Pieces of eight! Rubies, diamonds and emeralds! We shall all be rich because the treasure is so great that — even for such men as ourselves — it will be a week's labour to dig it up and get it all aboard ship!' They grinned in delight. 'But rest easy, lads, we have time aplenty because those swabs in the south can't move, even if they dared come after us. We took their boats, we burned their ship, and it'll be swamp for a month on their side of the island. So who's with Joe Flint to find the treasure — *this very day* — and dig it up?'

There was much cheering and enthusiasm, and Flint left it to Hitchin to fit out another expedition, with spades, picks and crow bars and provisions for the journey. The only time Flint intervened was to choose men to stay aboard ship, because every man of the crew was determined on treasure hunting.

'Mr Gilbert shall stay,' said Flint, 'because he is fat and slow!' Everyone laughed at that. 'He shall stay together with the boys, and whichever of the crew are the two smallest, because I want only strong men who can carry a heavy load of plate and coin.'

Flint said that loudly, the men cheered, and there followed a gleeful scrambling among them to compare size, with much shouting and struggling until the two shortest, and glummest, men were shoved forward with the rest cheering merrily, and the usual volley of pistol fire into the air. Then, over a dozen men, led by Hitchin, went down into the boats, with Flint embarking last by virtue of rank. But first he took Selena's hand, with a bow, and led her to the rail and the ladder down to the boats.

'You too, ma'am,' he said. 'Because I'll not be parted from you, and because when the treasure is raised, ma'am, my portion is yours to share with me because you are my lady, my delight, and I dream of no other.'

She tried to speak, but he gently touched a finger to her lips. 'I ask no decision, ma'am,' he said, 'not now, but know and believe, that you are in my heart until Heaven shall fall, and Hell shall freeze.' As ever, she could see that, in this at least, he was deeply sincere. But still she did not smile.

'When you were sick,' she said, 'you spoke of John Silver.'

'Did I?'

'You said he was a good man.'

'Did I?'

'Yes. You said he never used torture,' she frowned, 'while you threaten dreadful things. You threatened Mr Gilbert horribly. Did you mean what you said?' Flint said nothing. 'And you said that you were afraid of Silver. So are you? *Are* you afraid of him?'

Flint laughed at that.

'I fear nobody, ma'am,' he said, and Selena looked at him closely — and wondered.

Then he took her hand, and kissed it, and stood back as she climbed over the rail, as Jim Hawkins stepped forward, as if to follow her.

'Oh no, Mr Hawkins,' said Flint, 'not you!' Flint smiled. 'You will stay here with the boys. I'm afraid your reputation is somewhat spoiled.'

CHAPTER 31

From Dr Livesey's journal:

We spent two miserable days in the blockhouse. They were among the worst days of my life, and worst of all was the thought that I might never see my Charlotte again. In fact I was convinced of it, because one dark night, with the storm blowing and the rain battering the roof, I was sat leaning against the inside wall of the blockhouse with Trelawney next to me, and only our pipes for comfort. Then I had a happy thought.

'Well at least we shan't be here for ever,' I said, 'because your friend Blandy is to send a consort after us if we don't come home by August.'

'Ah,' said Trelawney, and said no more.

'Squire?' I said. 'John?' And I nudged him in case he had fallen asleep.

'Ah,' he said again.

'Blandy,' I said. 'Remember? Your friend who sold you *Hispaniola*?'

'Yes,' he said.

'He's to send a ship after us, isn't he?'

'Well,' said Trelawney, 'it was my intention — my very firm intention — to raise that matter with him, but what with the vast work of getting ready for sea…'

'Oh, John,' I said, and we never spoke of it again.

Then finally the storm ended, and the tropical sun came up. We were sick of the blockhouse by then, and sick of salt pork and biscuit, and went outside into the warmth, with thoughts of hunting for fresh meat, and trying the jungles for whatever else a man might eat, and I found that I was in command again. Captain Smollet was recovering, but weak, while the squire had the wit to know his limitations, and John Silver, Israel Hands and their men — if I judged them right — were resolved to become loyal servants once more, hoping that their mutiny might be forgotten, and that they might return to England, should ever we find a ship. So it was 'Aye-aye, Doctor!' and a respectful salute from all of them.

So I gave the orders that first morning, and we all took comfort from being organised and not helpless. Thus I set watches, sent out a hunting party, appointed cooks and water-carriers, and a man to be our master at arms to keep our powder dry and our muskets free from rust. Then we gave Tom Morgan a proper burial, with words from Captain Smollet's Bible, which I read to the assembled company, who stood with hats off. We also buried the bodies of a number of poor wretches washed up from the wreck of Flint's longboat, which was the last we saw of any of them, the rest — living or dead — having been taken out to sea by storm and tide, along with *Hispaniola's* boats.

But what depressed us most, was the sight of our ship, or rather its remains, far out in the anchorage and driven on to sand banks by the storm. It lay as the separate fore and aft portions — torn and blown apart — of what had been a beautiful a vessel, and there was much wreckage too, all along the beach.

'Perhaps we can make use of this?' said Israel Hands, though none of us were in a mood to imagine new ships built from old timbers. But later we were cheered by the hunting party, that came back without goats, but carrying great bunches of plantains and other fruit, which we ate with relish, accompanied with the last of our rum. So passed the first day after the storm, and without event. But the next did not, because just after dawn with the morning mist still on the ground, we had a visit from an old friend.

'Look,' said Trelawney, pointing to the edge of the forest, and there was Ben Gunn, not quite hiding among the trees, but not quite in the open either. Then he saw me, and stepped out, and saluted like a seaman and drew breath to speak. But then he shuddered in fright and ran back into the woods.

'Ben Gunn, as I live and breathe!' said John Silver, coming out of the house.

'And he's seen you, John!' said Israel Hands, and they both laughed.

'Does he know you?' I enquired.

'That he does,' said Silver, 'poor creature. He was a fine seaman once: a steersman aboard a King's ship, and was the pride of the lower deck.'

'Why is he afraid of you?'

'It ain't me he's afeared of,' said Silver, 'it's Flint. We was shipmates once, me and Joe Flint, and Ben Gunn thinks I'm the same as him.'

'I see,' I said, 'but I'll go after Ben Gunn. He's been a help in the past, and he knows the island, and we might need him again. He certainly knows how to hunt goats, which we do not!' Silver and Israel Hands laughed at that, but they touched hats deferentially.

'Aye-aye, Doctor,' they said.

So I took my musket and pistols, found a piece of cheese from our declining stock, and was off, over the fence and looking for Ben Gunn once more. I soon found him, or rather he soon found me. So I did not have to go far, and I could hear voices coming from the blockhouse even as Benn Gunn spoke.

'Doctor, sir,' he said, and before even a 'good-day', or any other explanation, he began apologising most abjectly. 'I done a terrible thing,' he said, 'such as I hope the Lord may forgive me for.'

'What is it Mr Gunn?' I asked, 'surely you can have done nothing bad here, alone in this place?'

He frowned and thought hard.

'Well I trimmed two of them what sailed under Flint,' he said. 'I trimmed their necks right proper!'

'What?' I said, not understanding what he meant until long after.

'But that ain't the thing, Doctor,' he said. 'I done a bad thing in keeping a secret, and it's a great secret and one that I should've told you and I didn't, 'cos I'm poor Ben Gunn and prays to see home again, and can't bear to be alone no more, and…'

With that he was off into self pity, and I had to take his hand, and attempt to comfort him, as I might with some poor fellow who'd lost a dear one and could not bear the grief. It is a doctor's duty to give comfort in such sorrows, and I had done so many times before, and I did now for Ben Gunn.

'Come, come,' I said, 'bear up, old fellow.' I patted his hand and smiled, because it is not the words that bring comfort but the manner and expression. So Ben Gunn calmed down and looked at me.

'Can I tell you a great secret, Doctor?'

'Of course, Mr Gunn.'

'And will you keep it secret?'

'Yes,' I said, 'provided that no innocent persons shall be harmed.' Ben Gunn frowned at that, and thought very hard. Then he sighed most desperately.

'You'll be judge of that, Doctor,' he said. 'But don't tell Silver! Don't tell him, 'cos telling him is telling Flint, 'cos they're mates, them two!'

'As you wish,' I said, judging that this was not the time to unroot a fixed belief, however false, and also I was intensely curious to know the nature of this secret.

'You swear?' he said. 'You swear on something sacred? Something you love?'

I hesitated, because I thought instantly of Charlotte. 'Swear!' said Ben Gunn fiercely. 'Swear to keep my secret, or I'm off and you'll not see me never again, nor have no help from me, nor nothing!'

'I swear!' I said, and Ben Gunn leaned forward and whispered something into my ear that changed everything from that moment on.

'Good God in Heaven!' I exclaimed.

'Aye, and the saints and angels too!' said Ben Gunn, and he smiled happily. He was like Christian in *Pilgrim's Progress* when his burden of sin fell away. So he stood up straight and saluted. 'Permission to make my report, Doctor, sir?' he said.

'What report?' I said.

'On Flint and his crew,' he said. 'I run up and down this island on the high ground, and I goes faster than goats, and I sees everything, and here's what's happened aboard *Revenge*.'

'*Revenge*?' I said.

'Flint's ship, Doctor sir!'

'Go ahead, Mr Gunn,' I said, and so he did. Indeed he did, and I listened and knew that I must instantly tell my comrades. 'Mr Gunn,' I said, when he was done, 'will you come to the blockhouse and repeat what you have told me?'

'Not I,' he said, 'not in there!'

'Then will you wait at the fence while I speak to the others?'

'Aye,' he said, 'so long as you don't drag me in.'

So we went back, and he waited at the palisade, and I went back to the house and told everyone what Ben Gunn had said, and they listened in silence until I was done.

'So Flint's alive?' said Trelawney.

'Yes,' I said, 'wounded in the knee, but alive.'

'I *knew* the ball went low!' he said. 'And Flint's got the map? Got it from Hawkins?'

'Map and papers both,' I said. 'Ben Gunn got close enough to hear men talking.'

'Is he going to live?' asked Trelawney. 'Flint?'

'Aye?' said everyone.

'Yes,' I said, 'he's getting better. He'll live.'

'Damn Flint,' said Silver. 'Why couldn't he die, or lose a pin like me?'

'And there's more, Mr Silver,' I said. 'Ben Gunn says there's a woman aboard *Revenge,* a young woman, a woman of colour…'

'WHAT?' shouted Silver.

'…a very lovely woman, a very—'

'WHAT?' Silver shrieked once more. 'It *can't* be. She's safe home in England. I left her safe in the old Spyglass!' And he turned and hopped out of the house at great speed, with all of us after him. 'Where's that swab Ben Gunn?' Silver cried. 'I'll have the truth or kill him!' And he was down the hill to the fence at great speed, but all he saw of Ben Gunn was a quivering of the bushes. So Silver turned to me as I ran down. He turned and seized the lapels of my coat. He was a very tall man and loomed over me like a tree. 'What's he done to her?' he yelled. 'What's Flint done to her? Is she a prisoner? Is she hurt?' He shook me hard.

'No!' I said, 'she's free, and she's well. *She's safe*, Mr Silver,' and I pushed his hands away. 'She's safe and Ben Gunn has been listening to the men aboard *Revenge*. They were talking about the treasure, and all of them were waiting for Flint to get out of bed, now he's got the map and papers, and take them ashore to dig up the treasure.'

'So?' said Silver.

'So?' said everyone.

'So,' I said, 'Ben Gunn thinks we could take the ship, *Revenge*, while Flint's out of it, if we board her quietly.'

'How?' said several voices. 'How can we do that?'

'Aye,' said Silver, 'after such rain as we've had, this island'll be all swamp between us and the north. So we can't get there on foot, and we've got no boats.'

'But we *have*,' I said, 'we've got Ben Gunn's boat, and he says it will carry six men.'

'What boat?' said Silver.

'Ben Gunn has made a boat from skins and branches.'

'Will she swim?'

'He says she will,' I said, 'and he says he can get us into the northern anchorage and alongside *Revenge* without being seen.'

'Then, by thunder, we'll take her! Six is enough if there's only an anchor watch aboard and I'll not leave my girl with Flint, not if I have to die ten times in trying!'

'I'm with you, John!' said Israel Hands, and everyone looked at me.

'And so am I, Mr Silver,' I said. 'Because I would not leave *my* lady in his hands, and because *Revenge* is the only ship on this island, and I hope someday to return to England.'

CHAPTER 32

From Dr Livesey's journal:

Six of us went. First Ben Gunn himself, who was vital to navigate the boat, which did not behave anything like a timber-built vessel with a proper keel. Also we needed him to make good his promise of getting us alongside *Revenge* quietly. John Silver and Israel Hands came too, together with myself, Squire Trelawney and Abe Gray. The whole blockhouse company came down to the anchorage, by the tall white rock, to see the skin boat launched, though the boat was so light that two men could easily carry it, or Ben Gunn alone who knew its ways and was used to getting it on his shoulders.

We took drinking water in a skin bag made by Ben Gunn, plus food from our stores, some dried goat meat — again from Ben Gunn, and a musket and pistols for each man and as many cartridges as we could carry. We would have taken more muskets, ready loaded for rapid fire, but the skin boat had room for no more.

One thing we did not take, was Silver's parrot.

'She don't like boats,' he explained, 'and she don't like men fighting, do you my lovely?' And he kissed her green head, and tickled her feathers, and whispered to reassure her, and she squawked quietly and nibbled his ear, and he passed her to one of those who was staying. 'You take care o' that bird,' said Silver.

Finally, with the boat in the shallows, and all of us aboard, and in fair weather with a hot sun and clear skies, Ben Gunn got into the stern with an oar to steer by, and Abe Gray took first turn at the oars. There were only two pins to brace oars, since Ben Gunn had never imagined anyone in the boat than himself, pulling a single pair.

The boat swam well. We were all greatly reassured, and Ben Gunn was delighted. We made far more leeway than in a conventional boat, and Gray had constantly to rest one oar and pull the other to maintain a straight course, with Ben Gun heaving on his steering oar besides. But when we emerged from the anchorage and came round to larboard, past the southern cliffs of the island, and with the great, honking sea lions wallowing in the surf, the boat truly proved her worth by riding the waves with splendid buoyancy, and was a comfortably dry craft that shipped no water.

'Here's the current, Doctor sir,' said Ben Gunn, who had the habit of addressing me alone rather than all of us, because he was still in fear of John Silver, and would not speak to him nor look him in the eye. 'Hold hard, Doctor sir,' he said, 'she rolls! She rolls!' And we all took hold of the thin bough that served as a gunnel, since the skin boat rolled heavily in the powerful current, and the current spun us around, and played with us, until Ben Gunn and Abe Gray together got her head the right way, and mastered the current and made it our servant. Then it carried us on our way like the wings of angels.

After that the journey was easy, the smooth-running current was almost without waves, and the sea birds sang, and we saw dolphins and tuna, and we ran up the coast of the island at great speed, relieving one another at the oars from time to time. So it should have been a pleasant voyage, even with a fight coming at the end of it; at first I thought I was alone in feeling a depression upon me as I looked at the island. Then looking at Silver, Hands, the squire and Gray, I saw them too, glance at the island and sigh.

Only Ben Gunn remained jolly, pleased to have companions and an important task. So he manned the steering oar, and grinned and caught my eye, then nodded at our companions, and whispered since I was closest to him.

'It's the island, Doctor sir,' he said, 'it takes everyone like that. It drains the joy out of them, and no scholar knows why, unless'n you do, Doctor sir?' But I shook my head.

Finally, we rounded the northern coast of the island, where the current faded and there was work to be done at the oars, and Ben Gunn began to justify his place among us, by steering not into the mouth of the northern anchorage, but into a deep cove to the north of it. There was a great expanse of sand, and thousands of birds like puffins with coloured bills, though not actual puffins which live further to the north. They inhabited holes in the cliffs that encircled the cove, and were never still or silent.

'We have to lift her from here,' said Ben Gunn, as the boat ran aground with a hundred yards of sand between us and where the shore rose in bare rock with trees above. 'Out we get, mates,' he said. 'She's an easy load, 'cos that's what she was made for.' She was indeed, and Ben Gunn would have carried her alone, but I thought we must conserve his strength, so we took turns to share the load, which greatly amused him, and he capered all around the boat, as if amazed to see it move without him lifting.

When we got into the cover of the trees, we stopped and I spoke.

'Now gentlemen, let's all attend to our priming, and make sure our pieces will fire at need.' So we all took a good look, the squire fiddled with the flint of his rifle-lock, then everyone nodded. 'So,' I said, 'Mr Gunn! We look to you for our next move. How shall we come alongside *Revenge* quietly, and in daylight?'

'Aye-aye, Doctor sir!' he said, touching his brow. 'Knowing what you know,' he said, then put a hand to his mouth in horror, because he was referring to the great secret we shared and he looked at John Silver, as if he, Ben Gunn, had just divulged it.

'Go on, Mr Gunn,' I said, to reassure him, 'all's well.'

'Aye-aye, Doctor sir,' he said. 'Well first I'll get myself over this rise,' he pointed to the high ground shielding us from view of the anchorage, 'for a look at what *Revenge* is doing, and whether Flint's gone after the treasure.' Again he looked at me and blinked.

'Go on, Mr Gunn,' I urged him.

'T'f he ain't gone yet, and took his crew with him, we must wait till he does.'

'Yes,' I agreed.

'But if he has gone, then we must wait till noon, when it gets so hot in that anchorage that all aboard will be sleeping.'

'T'ain't much of a plan,' put in Silver.

'No,' said Trelawney. 'Should not we wait until dark?'

'Oh, no!' insisted Ben Gunn.

'No!' I said. 'In case Flint and his men suddenly return.'

'Aye!' said Ben Gunn.

'But they've got heavy labour to perform,' said Trelawney, down at the burial site. They'll be heavy laden, they might not be back for days.

'But they might be back soon!' said Ben Gunn, most insistent.

'Indeed,' I said. 'We should listen to Mr Gunn, who knows the ground.'

'Aye!' he said. 'But first I has to see if they've gone.'

'Oh yes,' said Trelawney.

'Aye,' said Silver.

'Off you go, then, Mr Gunn,' I said.

He was off at great speed, running uphill as easy as on the level. He was soon gone, and we had hardly got sat down to wait, when he came running back.

'They've gone! They've gone!' he panted. 'Only two men and some boys on deck, and boats beached on the southern side. They're gone, shipmates, and noon's a-coming!'

So we got up, and followed Ben Gunn to the crest, which we reached just as the sun was climbing to its highest. We lay behind bushes for cover and looked down into the northern anchorage, which was very different from its southern brother. There was high ground all round, it was entirely closed at the western end, where a river flowed into it. The water was a deep and lovely blue, a fine, large brig was anchored just below our viewpoint, an old wrecked ship beyond that, and the heat was already tremendous, with no breeze in the enclosed space, and the warmth of the sun reflected from the encircling hills. Even the birds were resting, and the only sound was a great chirruping of insects such as is heard in the Mediterranean lands: that and the booming of the surf.

'Look, Doctor sir,' murmured Ben Gunn. 'Only one man on deck, and he's half asleep by the transom, under a shade rigged of sailcloth.'

'No!' said Silver, 'by thunder, look there!' And we saw Jim Hawkins come up on deck, presumably looking for a breath of air. 'Little rat!' muttered Silver. Then he pointed. 'And see there, Doctor? That's a line of swivels on the quarterdeck rail. Could be nasty!'

He was right. On each side of the quarterdeck, four swivel-guns were mounted on the rail: light pieces throwing one or two pounds of shot, which meant several dozen of pistol balls at each discharge. Any one of those swivels, if fired into our boat, would be the end of us.

'Will they be loaded?' I asked Silver.

'What,' he said, 'aboard Flint's ship? Huh! They'll be charged and primed, and with matches ready to fire. That was ever my way, and it was Joe Flint's, too!'

'Mr Gunn,' I said. 'They can't fail to see us coming, there may be more of them below, and we don't know how many. So can you make us a diversion to draw their attention?' He thought, and grinned and nodded.

'Give me two turns of the watch glass, and I'll run round the high ground and be on the other side, where them boats is beached. I'll go fast and I'll make 'em look my way, and when you hear me, you get my boat in the water and pull like the Devil!' Then he was off, before another word, and running at top speed.

After that it seemed a long wait. We brought up the skin boat to be ready, we drank some water, and the anchorage cooked in heat, and the figures on *Revenge* got under the shade, and some boys came up to join them, and finally there were three seamen on deck as well as Jim Hawkins. So we did right to send Ben Gunn on his mission. We waited and waited, and shed our coats and even our shirts for the tremendous heat that rose out of the anchorage. And then, with everything still, there came a weird and unatural wailing from the far side of the anchorage.

'Fifteen men on the dead man's chest! Yo-ho-ho! And a bottle of rum!'

It was Flint's song, but delivered with such a mournful voice that it sounded uncanny. 'Drink and the Devil have done with the rest! Yo-ho-ho! And a bottle of rum!'

'It's Ben Gunn!' I said.

'Sounds like the Devil himself,' commented Trelawney.

'It sure ain't Flint!' said Silver.

'It's Benn Gunn,' I repeated, 'and all aboard *Revenge* are looking that way, and this is our chance!'

So off we went, at top speed, carrying the boat and our firelocks, and scrambling across the sand, and launching the boat and getting in, Abe Gray pulling and pulling, and Silver at the steering oar.

'Pull, me hearty!' roared Silver in encouragement. 'Pull, me boy!'

'Go on! Go on!' cried the squire.

'Huzzah!' cried Gray.

'Huzzah!' I shouted, because there is a madness in attack that makes men charge and cry out when they should creep and be silent.

'Huzzah!' we all cried, and 'heave away!' And the skin boat shot across the narrow gap, and we were almost alongside *Revenge* and were clear out of sight of those aboard, unless they came and looked over the rail, and the whole thing done without powder burned or blade drawn, right up to the last instant.

'Ware boarders!' called a voice, and a head appeared over the rail. Two pistol shots sounded from *Revenge* and two puffs of smoke appeared, and then another head, and two more shots, but all missed. Then a loud voice, 'man the swivels!' and we saw the dreadful sight of a swivel gun swinging towards us, with a man's head in clear view, taking aim down the barrel before putting a match to the touchhole, and surely blowing us all to rags. We fired our pistols but all missed, then *whoof-bang*!

The squire proved as good at snap shots as deliberate aim, and the man behind the swivel dropped from view.

'By the main-chains!' shrieked Silver, and Abe Gray heaved, and we were alongside and climbing aboard, with our muskets slung over our shoulders, onto the deck to see two men standing by the main mast, one cocking a musket, one with a boarding pike, who both went down in a volley from myself, Gray and Silver. Three boys were howling, but then there was another pistol shot, and we all looked round. Israel Hands was climbing the fore shrouds and yelling at Jim

Hawkins who was up above him, having run up into the fore top, away from the fighting. Hawkins had a pair of pistols in his hands, one still smoking.

'Come down, you little swine!' shouted Israel Hands. 'Come down or I'll flog the arse off you!'

'No!' yelled Hawkins, and fired the second pistol.

'You little sod!' said Hands, and his pistols being fired, he drew his seaman's knife and threw it at Jim Hawkins in rage, pinning the boy to the topmast by his shoulder. Hawkins screamed, and Israel Hands hung on to the shrouds and clenched his teeth in effort. But then his eyes closed, his face relaxed, his grip failed, and he fell from the shrouds, down and down, and over the side, and into the blue water with a great splash.

'Oh, no, no, no!' cried Silver. 'Not you too, mate? Not Israel Hands?'

One-legged man that he was, he was up in the fore top like lighting, and wrenched Jim Hawkins, shrieking, free from the knife, and dragged him down to the main deck, and beat him savagely until the rest of us united our strength to pulled him off.

'All right, you little swab,' hissed Silver, heaving and panting with effort. 'You can bless these gentlemen as your sea-daddies, but tell me this or I'll do for you the moment their backs is turned: where's my girl? Where's my Selena? I hear she's aboard this ship. So you just tell me she's alive, or God in Heaven help you!'

'She's alive! She's alive and well!' said Hawkins. 'She's gone with Flint, after the treasure,' and Silver first breathed deep in relief, and closed his eyes in thanks.

But then he looked at Hawkins and frowned.

'Gone, says you?' he said. 'Gone *willingly*? With Flint?'

'Yes,' said Hawkins. 'Gone willingly because she likes him.'

'You bloody liar!' roared Silver, and we had to restrain him again, or he really would have done for Jim Hawkins there and then.

So we stood together, in joy and sorrow, triumph and despair, having at least got ourselves a ship again. But still there was more to come.

So I went to the side of the ship facing the spot where Ben Gunn had been singing, and I slowly waved, and saw a small figure waving back.

It was him. It was time to finish this miserable business.

CHAPTER 33

From Dr Livesey's journal:

We should have gone straight after Flint once Ben Gunn came aboard in one of Flint's boats. Certainly he was hopping from one foot to another and pleading with me to do so.

'Doctor sir! Doctor sir!' he said. 'What if Flint comes back? He'll be back! You *know* he'll be back! And he's got more men than us, and he'll lay aboard of us and kill us all!'

But we could not go at once, because John Silver would not leave Israel Hands floating dead in the anchorage, and was gone with Gray in the skin boat to recover the body, while Jim Hawkins was in dispute with Squire Trelawney, trying to climb out of the pit he had dug with his treachery, and in this he proved to be a most fluent and inventive liar.

'Oh, sir,' said Jim Hawkins, bloodied and battered and knelt at Trelawney's feet, 'I was only acting on your orders!'

'What orders?' demanded Trelawney.

'I fled the blockhouse because you told me to run, to save my life and save the map, and then I hid in the jungle to keep it safe.'

'*What? I* told you to run?' gasped Trelawney. 'I never did!'

'You told me! In the blockhouse!' insisted Hawkins. 'You did!'

He said it with such absolute-seeming honesty, that Trelawney searched his memory and was unsure...

'And what about waving to Flint with that palm leaf, on the beach?' I asked.

'But I was waving to *you*, Doctor,' he said, without the least hesitation, 'and Flint saw me and came and captured me, and later when you came aboard this ship, I saw only John Silver and Israel Hands and thought they were pirates too, so I defended myself.'

'But didn't you see *me*?' said Trelawney. 'Or the doctor?'

'No,' asserted Hawkins. 'I did not!'

'Oh,' said Trelawney.

Then Silver and Gray came aboard, and saluted me as if I were captain.

'We took Mr Hands ashore, Doctor,' said Silver.

'Aye,' said Gray.

'And we laid him under the trees like we did for Tom Morgan,' said Silver, 'and covered him with a ship's blanket, and we'll bury him proper later on.'

'Indeed we shall, Mr Silver,' said Trelawney, in hearty agreement. 'You did right to attend to Mr Hands in such fashion, just as I would do for my own people.'

'Thank 'ee, Mr Trelawney, sir!' And Silver saluted him too. Then everyone looked to me again.

'Gentlemen,' I said, 'we've won only half a victory. Half or less, because we have covered our backs by taking this ship, but might not be able to hold her if Flint returns, and our best hope remains with falling upon him in ambush.'

'Yes! Yes! Yes!' cried Ben Gunn, and the rest nodded.

'So let's gather our arms, and be off in pursuit!'

'What about them?' asked Silver, looking at the three ship's boys, stood gaping at us with their hats in their hands, and for once I was confounded. I did not know what to say. But Silver did. He hopped over to them, and stood like a giant glaring down with fierce eyes.

'Listen well, my lads!' said Silver. 'Flint's your enemy now. His ship's been took, and he'll be in a rage, and looking for someone to blame, and you three'll do very nicely, and God help you if he comes aboard!' The boys cringed in terror. 'So you must all be true to the doctor and squire,' said Silver, and he turned and took off his hat to us, 'cos those gentleman are your only hope.'

'Aye-aye, sir!' said the boys. 'Aye-aye, sir!' They bowed and saluted, and were terrified into believing what Silver had said, because Flint *was* perfectly capable of punishing those he could get hold of, rather than those who were guilty.

So we left them aboard, and had to trust that they would take no action against us, since we could not drag them with us, it was unthinkable to do them harm, and we had already wasted too much time to spare more for searching out keys, locks and chains. So we left them aboard *Revenge* with three dead men for company, one of whom, I later learned, was Gilbert, the ship's surgeon who had attended Flint's knee. So even if Gilbert had been my enemy, I hoped that it was no shot of mine that had killed a fellow practitioner.

After that, with *Revenge's* boats now ours, we set aside the noble skin boat, as having done its duty, and made preparations for another expedition. Since we would be pursuing a party which outnumbered ourselves, we loaded every firearm in our possession, and raided the brig for as many more as we could, giving a cutlass, two muskets and as many pistols as we could carry for Silver, Gray, Trelawney, Ben Gunn and myself, though Trelawney of course kept his rifle. Also, I had a private word with Ben Gunn concerning the way in which we should chase Flint through the jungle.

Then, as a final precaution, we took Jim Hawkins with us.

'We cannot leave him behind,' I said, 'for fear he might work mischief.' Everybody agreed. Then we pulled the brief distance to the shore, and got our arms and ammunition aboard ourselves, and Jim Hawkins was secured by a length of line between his wrist and Long John's belt. This was at Silver's suggestion and insistence.

'It'd best be me that brings the little swab,' he said, ''cos this way, he knows what he'll get if he don't behave.'

'Squire!' said Hawkins, to Trelawney. 'Will you permit this?' And by George, I saw Trelawney dither, so I spoke fast.

'Consider yourself lucky to be alive, Jim Hawkins,' I said. 'Better men than you have fallen all round you.' Then I spoke to everyone, with Ben Gunn at my side. 'Gentlemen,' I said, 'we must now trust to Mr Gunn, whose knowledge of this island, and whose skills as a tracker can take us after Flint and his men, and catch them by surprise.

'Good!' said Silver and Trelawney together, both having friends to avenge.

'So this shall be the way of it,' I explained. 'Mr Gunn will go ahead, and will follow the tracks left by Flint's party. He will then return to lead the rest of us forward to a stopping place. He will then go ahead again, and come back to lead us onward, and so on. Also, Mr Gunn has asked me to insist that we maintain silence, not speaking to one another, and paying attention to signals that he will give by hand.' They nodded, they understood — and the method proved good.

So into the jungle we went, and the sunlight darkened into mottled light and shadow, and the heat sweltered, and the ground was soft underfoot, and insects crept and buzzed. A stone statue would have dripped with sweat in such a place, and we all laboured to move forward, burdened with our arms: especially John Silver with his crutch and with Jim Hawkins in tow, who started to moan after a few steps. But he stopped sharply when Silver whispered some threat in his ear which caused Hawkins to gasp and fall silent.

Then at the first stopping place, a clearing which Ben Gunn obviously knew, our method of progress changed because he wanted me with him all the time. I suspect that he feared for his precious secret and never entirely trusted me to keep it. So when he waved at us to stop in the clearing, he put a finger to his lips for silence, waved everyone else to sit and wait, and took my hand and inclined his head into the jungle, and tugged at me. So I shrugged, and would have gone with him, but he shook his head, took my cutlass and firearms and handed them out among the rest of the party, and likewise he gave up his own weapons, and grinned at me and tapped the knife in his belt, and once more put a finger to his lips. I nodded. We must go lightly and not weighed down with a load.

So, with a nod to the rest which I hoped was reassuring, I followed Ben Gunn, and began to marvel at his wood craft. I cannot begin to know what it was that he saw, that indicated a party — Flint's party — had gone ahead of us. I suppose he had learned these mysteries over the years tracking goats, and was like the Iroquois of the American colonies, who can follow any creature that passes through their native woods. He moved fast, too: bending to stare at who knows what, then darting forward without a sound, and beckoning me, and myself doing my best to follow and make no noise. In this way we must have spent some hours, constantly advancing then going back to bring up our comrades. In a military sense, we were the light company and they were the grenadiers, because we moved fast but they were our fighting strength.

Then finally, when Ben Gunn and I were out in front, and moving along a crest of high, dry ground, he stopped dead, waved a hand at me to stop, listened hard, then grinned. He winked at me and cupped an ear with one hand, and I did the same… and I heard voices. I heard grumbling and complaining.

Ben Gunn nodded, and beckoned me to follow, and I noticed that we were in a pathway — presumably made by goats — which curved to the left into a semi-circle of rocky ground that looked down on another path below. Urgent hand signals from Ben Gunn made me crouch down, just as he did, and the two of us sat in total silence, ignoring the mosquitoes and ants, and looking down on a party of men coming along the lower path, actually from behind our position. Ben Gunn had got us ahead of them, guessing their destination, and provided we kept silent, those below would never see us, so much were they toiling, heads down and burdened with spades, picks and arms.

But we could see them, and I took my first close look at the notorious Joseph Flint, of whom I had heard so very much. I recognised him instantly both from his having a heavily bandaged knee — the bandages stained by seeping blood — and his needing a stick to walk with. I likewise knew him for the fine features of his face, and the manner of his bearing, because he had a swagger about him that even wounds did not abolish. That was Flint, and he was in the lead, looking down constantly to a notebook of instructions, which I supposed were his fair copy of the papers that attended the treasure map.

I also recognised the woman that followed close behind him. She was Silver's wife Selena, a most remarkable young woman, dressed in men's clothes, and obviously not under restraint but going of her own free will. I frowned. Silver would not like that.

'Keep up, my jolly boys!' called Flint, turning back to his men.

'How much longer?' came a voice. 'We been going for hours.'

'And it may take hours yet,' said Flint, 'and any man who chooses to give up his share may go now, straight back to the ship.' He laughed and there was more grumbling, but nobody turned back, and they were indeed a large company.

Then, Ben Gunn became almost hysterical with glee. He nudged me and nearly smothered himself not to laugh. He reached out, took my head and turned it so that I looked somewhat in advance of Flint, and he stabbed a stained, dirty, crack-nailed finger at what Flint was almost treading on.

'Ah-ha!' said Flint in surprise, because he had just noticed that immediately in front of him, at the foot of a great pine and wrapped in a green creeper, there was a mouldered and desiccated corpse. It was almost a skeleton, but not quite, with shreds of tanned skin and sinew remaining, and scraps of clothing and belongings. Then Flint recovered and laughed. 'See here my lads,' he said. 'Here's one of Flint's markers. I left a few of these on this island!' His men pushed forward and clumped around the remains, which lay perfectly straight in a most unatural position, with the arms raised over the head, like a diver's. Flint put away his notebook, produced a small compass and took a bearing along the skeleton.

'Ah,' he said. 'East-south-east, by east! Exactly as it says in my notes.' And he laughed again.

'Look,' said one of his men, 'there's earrings by the head, and a tarred pigtail. This here was a seaman!'

'So, what should you expect to find on an island?' asked Flint. 'A cabinet-maker?' Flint laughed again but nobody else did. They were seamen one and all, and seamen are superstitious.

'This ain't right,' said one of them, and they began to murmur among themselves.

Then Ben Gunn shook my arm, signalled me to stay put, and was off at high speed, and I wondered where he was gone. Soon I heard his voice from some high place, all thin and warbling and slow.

'Fifteen men on the dead man's chest! Yo-ho-ho! And a bottle of rum!'

Even I thought the singing was strange, but Flint's men were horrified. They clung together and fumbled for weapons, while Flint stood straight, and frowned and stared in the direction of the voice.

'What is it?' said Selena, taking his arm. 'That's your own song!'

'I know,' said Flint, 'so who's singing it?'

'Spirits!' said one of his men. 'Dead spirits.' He pointed to the corpse. 'It's his'n! Him what's lying there!'

'Aye!' agreed the others.

But the voice sang on, and then finally ceased, apart from a brief echo, which made Flint laugh in triumph.

'There, my boys!' he cried, 'did you hear the echo? A spirit casts no shadow, and can have no echo!'

'*Can't* it?' someone asked.

'Of course not!' said Flint. 'Everyone knows that!'

The nonsensical argument worked. The men smiled and nodded, and then Flint was inspired. 'Ben Gunn!' he cried, 'It'll be Ben Gunn, the maroon! He was left in this place, and it must be him. It's only Ben Gunn and nobody's afraid of *him*!'

Indeed, nobody was, because I could see from the expressions on the faces of Flint's men that they had never heard of Ben Gunn. But so cheerful was Flint and so confident, that his cheerfulness and confidence inspired the rest. 'Follow me lads,' he said, and looked at his notes and led on.

Ben Gunn was soon back, and not pleased. He was clearly angry at what Flint had said. He signalled me to follow, and took a new path that overtook Flint's column, which was now on the same level as ourselves, but off to one side. He signalled me to stay put, and was off yet again.

308

I waited and heard nothing, and he was soon back, and he looked hard at me and drew a finger across his throat and held up two crooked fingers. Then we were off and back to where we had left the others, with Ben Gunn talking to me on the way, once it was safe to do so.

When we reached the others we had a council.

'We're close to the treasure burial site,' I said.

'How do you know?' said Silver.

'Ben Gunn knows the island. He says that where Flint's heading, there's only swamp to either side, with a patch of dry ground by spyglass hill. So the burial must be there.' They accepted that and nodded. 'So here is our plan,' I said. 'Ben Gunn will take us to a place near the likely spot, and we will wait while he scouts ahead to find the actual site, which he will know, when Flint's men stop, and commence digging.'

'That makes sense,' said Trelawney and the rest nodded.

'Then we must take great care,' I said, 'because Mr Silver's wife is among them.'

'Is she?' he said. 'Is she safe?'

'She is, Mr Silver,' I said, 'but she keeps close company with Flint.' Silver groaned and shook his head.

'I can't believe it,' he said, 'not my lass.'

'Now gentlemen,' I said, 'this is the hard part. We are outnumbered by armed men.' Everyone nodded. 'They are led by a cruel master,' I said, 'who would kill every one of us if he could, and would treat prisoners with atrocious barbarity. And so, gentlemen, there can be no honours of war. We must take our first chance, to pour volleys into them from cover and without warning.' I looked at Trelawney. 'Do you understand, Squire? Are you with us?'

'I am, sir,' he assured me, 'and I shall personally mark Flint, so you may leave him to me.'

'Thank you, sir,' I said. 'But we must take care not to fire, if Mrs Silver is among them.'

'By thunder we shall!' said Silver, 'I'll not see her hurt!'

'So all of you,' I said, 'do not fire until I give the command.' Everyone nodded. 'And there is one more thing.' I turned to Ben Gunn and put my hand on his shoulder. 'Mr Gunn has recently decreased the number of our enemies by two.'

'Oh?' they said.

'Aye!' said Benn Gunn. 'Tickled their windpipes I did,' and he grinned. 'They was the last two in the line, and the rest didn't even know.'

'Mr Gunn,' said Silver, much impressed, 'I see you are a gentleman of fortune, and I hope we may be friends.' He offered his hand to Ben Gunn, who took it and bowed, though he was still afraid of Silver, as anyone could see.

Then we were back in the forest, going forward leapfrog as before, with myself and Ben Gunn out in front. After some further hours, and a necessary stop for food and water, we reached another patch of high ground, which Ben Gunn said was close to where the treasure must be buried. Although we were on the crest of a low hill, the ground was soggy wet, and full of the roots of trees.

Entirely with gestures, Ben Gunn signalled the rest to stop and sit and wait, then he and I went onward. We went straight and directly onward, up rising ground to where the trees changed from tropical jungle to dense thickets of thorn and brushwood without a feature to mark the terrain, or give guidance.

But Ben Gunn and I crept low, and with his guidance we reached a hidden hollow, something like the arenas of the Romans, but only twenty or thirty yards across. There were some rocks and sandy ground, but no vegetation. Hidden among the surrounding jungles of the island, it was a place no man would come across by accident.

Ben Gunn looked in all directions. He listened hard. He sniffed the air. He smiled. Then he beckoned and we went back to fetch our comrades — to witness a most remarkable piece of theatre.

CHAPTER 34

From Dr Livesey's journal:

We were ready when Flint and his men came out of the undergrowth. The five of us were deep hidden by thorn bushes and the crest of the hollow such that we were in the most perfect position to fire. We did not even have to lie flat, but could crouch on our knees, with two muskets each, saving only the squire with his rifle, and Jim Hawkins sat behind us. Hawkins had been cast loose from Silver's line, but with Silver's promise to slit, gut and fillet him should he misbehave. The squire frowned at these words, but I certainly did not.

Then, most intense excitement fell upon us as Flint himself appeared, with Selena at his side, and a long, straggling line of followers coming after him, out of the undergrowth and into the hot sun and the open air. We who lay in wait, felt the thrill of every hunter who sees his prey come into view, whether he be a savage with his bow, or a gentleman with his fowling piece. But I reached out and touched each man that I could reach, and shook my head emphatically lest anyone should fire. We absolutely could not do that, because Flint's men were grouped all around him with himself in the middle and Selena beside him.

He looked around, and then spoke, and we heard him clearly, and I record to the best of my ability what he and others said.

'Is this everyone, my lovely lads?' he said, and one of the others looked round and counted.

'Two short, Cap'n,' he said and touched his brow.

'And where are they, Mr Hitchin?' asked Flint.

'Stragglin' behind, Cap'n,' said Hitchin, 'shall I send after them?'

'No,' said Flint, and smiled. 'If they don't want their shares, they needn't have them.'

The rest laughed, then Flint raised a hand for silence.

'This is the moment, my boys,' he said, and they raised a cheer. Flint held up his notebook. 'According to my own notes, made at the time of the burial, we have now found the resting place of eight hundred thousand pounds of treasure!'

They gasped, and stretched their limited minds even to comprehend such a sum.

'Eight hundred thousandpounds,' said Flint, 'to be shared among us all. So I shall sit and take the load from my leg, while you my boys shall take up spades and picks and dig, right here,' he pointed into the centre of the hollow, 'right here, and let us see what you may find.'

This brought a great cheer from Flint's men, then a casting aside of arms, and a throwing off of coats and shirts, and a grabbing of tools, then a furious, mad effort of digging, with stones and sand thrown in all directions. Those unfortunates left without tools were down on their knees and digging with their hands. They made so much noise that Trelawney, next to me, whispered.

'I have Flint in my sights, Doctor. Just give the word.'

His rifle stock was at his shoulder, the barrel rested steady on the bough of a thick bush, and Trelawney's entire concentration was focussed on his aim. So I was tempted. But I shook my head because at that moment, Flint got up and Selena with him, and they went to drink from a water canteen laid down among the clothes and muskets. Flint stayed there, with Selena beside him. So I might well have trusted Trelawney to hit Flint — and Flint only — but I feared that the discharge of his rifle would cause others to fire, who did not have his precision of aim.

Then little by little, the merry mood among Flint's men began to change. It changed as the excavation grew deeper and neither chests, nor any other sort of container was found.

'How far down is it, Cap'n?' asked one man, leaning on his shovel, with sweat running off him, looking up at Flint.

'Is that yourself, Mr Kerr?' said Flint. 'My friend from our adventures fighting John Silver?'

'What fighting?' said Kerr. 'And how far down is it?'

'A little further yet, I would guess,' said Flint. 'So why not keep on digging?'

'It'd better be here!' Kerr was tired, and his expression said that he had not gone to sea to become a digger of holes in sand.

'Aye!' said the rest.

'Eight hundred thousand,' said Flint deliberately, and smiled, and that started them digging again, though now they were tired, and growing angry.

Then there was a shout of delight.

'Here's *something*, mates!' said Kerr, because he was the lucky one, and he turned to the rest. 'Bring a crowbar!' he yelled. 'There's a damned great box here and I can't shift it!'

This caused a great surge of excitement, and men crowded in, digging and scraping, and a crowbar was found and levered against a half-revealed sea-chest some three feet long. It was formed of heavy leather, bound with wooden bands and closed with lock and clasp.

'Hurrah!' The men cheered as the chest came free, and then it ripped apart, being rotten, and its lid came off. There was a united groan because all that poured out was sand.

But then:

'Back your topsails, mates!' cried Kerr, and dived forward and picked up a gold coin. 'It's a two-guinea piece!' he cried. 'We've found the treasure!'

'Three cheers, boys!' cried Flint, 'Hip-hip-hip…'

But there was no response, and already Flint was backing away from the diggings, drawing Selena with him — still squarely in our line of fire — as his men fell to their knees and scraped and scraped with their hands, and failed utterly to find anything else than limitless quantities of sand and a few round pebbles. The lure of gold is mighty, so they kept this up some while, but finally they ceased digging and growled and scowled, and climbed out of the diggings, and picked up their arms and turned on Flint.

'Is that all?' asked Kerr, waving the coin. 'Two blasted guineas? Is that Flint's treasure? Is that what you've brought us round the world for?'

'Aye!' said the rest, even Hitchin the quartermaster.

'Watch your tongue, Mr Kerr,' said Flint, 'or you might find it cut out, and yourself forced to eat it.'

'Oh no!' said Kerr, 'that don't work no more, Joe Flint, 'cos you ain't so quick now, not with your busted leg!'

'Aye!' roared his men.

'And you ain't so clever, neither,' said Kerr, 'not with killing your own men! You shot our mates what you wouldn't take aboard the launch, and you left the rest to drown!'

'Aye!' they roared, still frightened of Flint but gathering for support and raising their muskets.

'And you pulled bits off that poor devil we took off Silver,' said Kerr, finding the courage to advance on Flint, musket in hand, 'you pulled bits off him with pincers, and you cut him and burned him horrible, and then you killed Elmore.'

'And now I'm killing *you*, Mr Kerr,' said Flint, and drew a pistol and shot Kerr in the belly so that he fell, wriggling and screaming into the sand, almost at Flint's feet.

'Oh do shut up, Mr Kerr,' said Flint, 'you're unsettling the men.' And he drew another pistol, leaned forward and shot Kerr deliberately through the brow, at a range of inches, spattering blood and brains on the sand.

'And who else wants to die?' said Flint. 'Is there anyone else of Mr Kerr's persuasion?'

It *nearly* worked, because Flint had charisma, and was a bold and fierce leader able to strike fear into his followers, if not affection and respect. So he stood on his one good leg, with blood oozing out of the other, dropped his walking stick, stood with his hands on his two smaller pistols and faced his men in this dire, dreadful circumstance when all was lost and the treasure gone, and he stared at them without obvious fear — or at least I supposed that to be the case, because he had his back to me, and Selena still with him.

But it did not work. Flint's luck was out. He had pushed his men too far, and done too many things they disliked, and now he had failed to deliver the treasure, and his followers were raising their guns against him such that he pushed Selena with his left hand, sweeping her behind him to shield her from harm, except that he pushed too hard, and she stumbled and fell, grabbing at him, and taking him over with her.

'Now!' I cried, 'Fire!'

So we fired, then up came our second muskets and they were fired too, then our pistols, till our target vanished in smoke. 'Charge!' I cried. 'Cold steel and at 'em!' And we dropped our guns, drew cutlasses and ran down whooping and yelling, and fell on Flint's men, who were still cowering from our fire. We laid on left and right, and Gray even broke his blade on a man's head and snatched up a shovel as a weapon, while Silver clashed blades with Hitchin the quartermaster, who did not run but stood his ground until Silver cleaved him from brow to chin with a tremendous down-stroke. This, even as Ben Gunn leapt on a wounded man who was trying to crawl away, got his knife under the man's chin and finished him.

So ended the battle of the sandy hollow. We looked round, saw smoke everywhere, and heard the sound of Flint's men running off into the undergrowth having mostly dropped their arms as they fled. Laid in the sand at our feet were five men stone dead, two more badly wounded, and weapons and tools dropped higgledy-piggledy. But some of our enemies had escaped and might return.

'Muskets, lads!' I cried. 'Re-load!' I saw Gray and Ben Gunn run to retrieve their firearms. But Silver was looking over my shoulder.

'Let her go!' he shouted. 'She ain't yours, Joe and never can be.'

I turned and saw that I must have run over Flint, and he had now got up, and was raising Selena to her feet. Flint looked wild and mad. He had a knife in one hand. He was hopping and swaying on his one good leg.

'Let her go!' said Silver.

'For you to enjoy, John Silver?' Flint taunted him. 'For a one-legged cripple? You never were half the man that I was.'

'And what *are* you?' cried Selena to Flint, trying to shake free of him. 'You're all lies, Joe Flint. It was nothing but lies, everything you told me. You're no man at all, and if John Silver had no legs at all, he'd be worth a thousand of you.'

Flint howled. Even his recent tremendous self control had limits.

The woman he loved despised him, he was broken and wounded, and now everything was gone. Everything, absolutely. He stared at Silver. He asked the only question that made sense.

'Where is it?' he asked. 'Where's my treasure?'

'Damned if I know, damned if I care,' replied Silver. 'I never wanted it. I came after *you*, Joe Flint, not a pile of gold.'

'So where is it?' Flint asked again. 'Where in the name of God and the Devil is my treasure?'

I looked at Ben Gunn. He looked at me.

'Tell him,' I said. 'Tell him our secret, Ben Gunn.'

So Ben Gunn nodded, then he stepped forward as close as he dared to Flint, and snapped his fingers in Flint's face.

'I'm rich,' said Ben Gunn, 'I'm rich, rich, rich. I am, and you *ain't* Cap'n Flint!'

Flint howled, and in his despair — and with actual tears in his eyes — he pulled Selena towards him and raised his knife.

'No!' shrieked Silver, and started forward, though he could never have reached Flint in time.

'No!' I cried, and stooped in the sand for someone's pistol that had not been fired, though I had not the marksmanship to hit Flint and not Selena.

I had not, but someone else had.

Whoof-bang! Trelawney's rifle sounded from the crest of the hollow, among the thorn bushes, and I heard the sharp *crack* of a speeding rifle ball as it passed close over my head. Then Flint staggered, and lowered the hand that held the knife. His grip on Selena failed and she shook him off and ran to John Silver, who folded her in his arms. Then the two of them and all the rest of us watched in silence, as Flint turned and looked at the puff of smoke above the bushes at the crest of the hollow.

'Is that you, Squire Trelawney?' he called. 'Trelawney, the celebrated marksman?'

'It is, sir,' said Trelawney, standing up with rifle in hand.

'A coward's blow,' said Flint. 'You shot me in the back.'

'And would do so again,' asserted Trelawney. 'Like stepping on a cockroach. I was only waiting for the chance of a clear shot.'

Flint fell to his knees. The shadow of death was on his face but he fumbled with the pistols still in his belt.

'Beware of him!' warned Silver.

'So you should be,' said Flint, 'though alas, my fingers will not work.' He blinked and stared, and then rallied his strength in a last great effort. He got to his feet, teeth clenched in pain, and stood and swayed. His face contorted in rage and he poured out a string of such threats and curses, as I shall not report, except to say that they included his promise to rise from the grave and come to us in the night for revenge, when we fancied ourselves safe in our beds.

Then his strength failed, and Joseph Flint, a man of huge talents and damaged mind, a man who should have been a fine sea officer but was not, a man who was a lieutenant in King George's navy, and then a gentleman of fortune beside John Silver, and finally a loathsome pirate... Joseph Flint, of tremendous though foul reputation, fell face down into the sand and was dead.

CHAPTER 35

From Dr Livesey's journal:

There was much weary work to do after that: much work, and many explanations which I give here in one piece rather than reporting the individual conversations in which different parts were expressed.

Ben Gunn had found the treasure long before our expedition landed on the island. He was marooned

for so long that he slowly acquired his tracking skills, as well as an intimate knowledge of the island's geography, through his ceaseless wanderings. More than that, he had enough knowledge of the history of Flint and Silver to know that a great treasure was buried somewhere on the island, and he had the time and patience to look for it.

'What else should I do, Doctor sir?' he asked me. 'Poor Ben Gunn all alone with not a soul to talk to? So I ran and I looked, and it was years and years, and I got lucky too, 'cos Flint left them markers.'

By this, he meant the bodies of no fewer than six men with whom Flint had gone ashore to bury his treasure, all of whom he had killed once the labour of shifting and burying was done: a morbid act which preserved the secrecy of the burial site. But he then went beyond practicality, and in cruel humour laid out their bodies as pointers along the pathway to the site, which to my mind surely contravened his original aim, of preserving secrecy. But Flint's mind was diseased, so who knows his entire motives?

Then, once Ben Gunn had found the burial site, and the many chests and boxes below ground, it was the work of endless days for him alone to move what he had found to a safe place: a labour he relished as giving purpose to his aimless existence.

Since Ben Gunn knew exactly where the treasure had been buried, then when it came to tracking Flint and his men from the north anchorage to the burial site, Benn Gunn did actually follow their tracks for a while, but knowing their destination he was easily able to get himself, myself and our companions to the sandy hollow, to be ready and waiting for Flint.

So to the practicalities: we buried Flint and his men where they fell, and I defy any reader to conceive of a more appropriate place to lay Joe Flint! The two wounded men soon followed the rest into the grave, being shot in the body and hacked about the head in the fight. One died soon after the battle, the other on the very next day, even though we carried him back to *Revenge* for some attempt at treatment. That still left unknown numbers of Flint's men running wild in the forest, so we took care to carry away the weapons and ammunition they had dropped, and never went about the island ourselves except heavily armed.

On our return to *Revenge* after the battle, even though the light was failing, we likewise buried Mr Israel Hands, master gunner, and marked his grave with a cross inscribed to that effect. Not having a Bible to read from, we would have been without formal words, except that Abe Gray happened to know the Royal Navy's prayer which he recited to the satisfaction of all present, and doubtless to the spirit of Mr Hands, who was always proud of his navy service.

We spent the night of the battle aboard *Revenge* and found her a fine ship, well provisioned and in all respects fit for the voyage back to England. Silver and Selena spent much time alone, talking and talking, since both were concerned to heal the wounds that these adventures had inflicted on their mutual affection. But we ate and drank well, and were merry. Cap'n Flint the parrot was back on Long John's shoulder, and Ben Gunn was able to gorge on cheese to his heart's content, and took so many thimbles full of rum that his snoring that night was like thunder.

I must also record that once aboard *Revenge* Jim Hawkins very near worked himself to death, at the vast labour of climbing back into the affections of those of us who now despised him: running to and fro, serving food and drink, and doing all the cooking and cleaning, always with so cheerful and open a smile that it was almost believable as truth. He had a mighty work to do in this respect, but I must also record that Squire Trelawney was beyond salvation where Jim Hawkins was concerned.

'What did he actually *do*, David?' he asked me that night, as we smoked our pipes under the stars, with the insects chirruping from the shore. 'What did he actually *do*, other than run away in fear?'

'Taking the treasure map and papers with him,' I added.

'Yes, but he thought — he really did think, David — that I had told him to do so!'

'Oh John,' I sighed, 'do you believe *everything* he says?'

He ignored that and pressed on. 'And as for Mr Hands, Jim thought he was a pirate and so...'

I gave up at that point, because I knew that Jim Hawkins must come home with us to England, and I also knew that I would not — could not — be the one who told his mother exactly what he had done. So in that respect, even if for different motives, I was as bad as Trelawney.

The next day we began the task of bringing up from the southern anchorage all those left in the blockhouse, including Captain Smollet who was soon ready to resume duties, being definitely out of danger. This we did with two of *Revenge's* boats, going round the eastward side of the island for the passage to the blockhouse, and taking advantage of the strong, north west current for the return. The work was done in a day, and a joyful reunion was had by all hands, and another evening passed in feasting.

Then, on the day after, we finally had sight of the great treasure that had caused all the misfortunes listed above, and which — as I have already made clear — I never wanted, while Silver's wife outright condemned it as evil. She said so loudly, before all hands on the quarterdeck of *Revenge*, as a party of us were about to go down into a boat with Ben Gunn.

'It's cursed,' she insisted. 'It was taken by violent force in the first place.' She glared at John Silver, who looked away, and I knew that this matter might still divide them. 'It was stolen from honest men, and has caused nothing but murder and shame ever since.' She said that, and she looked each one of us in the eye and as she did so, small as she was and a woman besides, we all found it hard to meet her gaze because she was telling the truth. But Trelawney protested.

'It's up to us to make good of it, ma'am!' he said, still preserving the romance of treasure-hunting that had brought him here from Cornwall.

'Aye!' said the hands, who all wanted their shares.

'Aye!' said Ben Gunn. 'It'll put a roof over my head and bread in my mouth!'

'And cheese!' added someone, and there was laughter.

Then, whatever Selena said, the appointed party went into the boats including John Silver, the squire, Abe Gray and myself, and of course, Ben Gunn. The route was down the north-eastern side of the island again, to one of many small bays and inlets, all very similar, but which Ben Gunn unfailingly knew. We beached the boat, pulled it clear of the tide, and walked up the beach — which sloped steeply — to what looked like a wall of rock covered in green creepers.

Even within ten feet of the greenery I could not find Ben Gunn's cave — because that was our destination — but he cheerfully ran forward, burrowed into the hanging fronds, then turned back and beckoned us to follow.

So we entered the cave, which was large and airy with a round entrance, and other holes that let in the light. There was a little spring and a pool of clear water, overhung with ferns. The floor was sandy, and there was a ring of neat, round stones that showed signs of regular use as a fireplace. But none of us looked at those things. What drew our sight like iron to a lodestone was a vast pile of gold coin, and quadrilaterals built of gold bars. It gleamed and shone, and beggared the imagination with the size and wealth of it. And there was more than just gold coin. There were great piles of Spanish dollars, there were gold chains, and there were twinkling gemstones separated out from the rest and put into great sea-shells by Ben Gunn.

This then, was Flint's treasure, that we had come so far to seek, which had cost so many lives on our expedition alone. But who knew how many more had died in the amassing of it? What blood and sorrow? What ships sunk in the deep? What broadsides of cannon? What shame and lies and cruelty? I sighed and thought of what Selena had said, and knew that she was right. Yet gold does indeed have a mighty lure, and I hoped that good might be made out of evil, because even after all these reservations there was not the slightest possibility of this great wealth being left where it was.

So we set to, with Captain Smollet now in command and myself only too pleased, because I am happy as a magistrate and fulfilled as a doctor, but I had eaten my fill of being a general. Also, he more naturally re-established the ship's hierarchy than I could have done, making clear who was lower deck, and who was quarterdeck, and who saluted whom.

Thus even before we moved the treasure there was a task to do in building containers to carry it, since the original chests and casks had long since rotted away. So boxes were contrived with skill, from the nails, planks and wreckage of *Hispaniola,* to Captain Smollet's orders. Then the treasure was loaded into our boxes, and each box slung under a spar with two men to carry it, and the boxes loaded into a boat, and taken to be stowed under hatches aboard *Revenge.*

In this way, and with boats passing up and down the coast, we eventually got everything aboard ship, and once again the boy Jim Hawkins was outstanding in his willingness to take a share of the work, whether sorting coin into guineas, doubloons, dollars and the rest, or in taking a man's share of the load in carrying our boxes down to the boats. Cunning little devil that he was, his charm worked well on the hands, who never questioned his motives and saw only a young lad doing his best, as indeed Squire Trelawney never ceased to do.

I myself took no part in the counting and hauling of the treasure. Captain Smollet insisted on this when I would have gone with the first boat to carry boxes back to the ship.

'No, Doctor!' he said, now fit enough to walk the deck in an officer's coat and hat. 'You'll not sweat like a common hand, sir! T'ain't good for ship's discipline. You're ship's doctor and a learned man. So you must berth aft, and not sling a hammock with the men.'

'Aye-aye, Cap'n,' I said, and touched my hat. I had been a seaman long enough not to question orders. Conversely, Smollet insisted that Trelawney *must* go with the hauling parties, regarding the squire as a more robust person than myself.

'There needs to be a gentleman in command,' he told Trelawney, 'and I can't go just yet, since I'm not fully fit.'

'I see,' said Trelawney, nodding. 'And am I to take my share of the load?'

'No, sir! Not you, sir!' said Smollet. 'You're there to keep coin out of the pockets of the lower deck hands. You shall go, and Abe Gray with you, whom I rate as coxswain.'

In this way I came to spend time with John Silver and Selena, who were given no hauling duties: he for his wooden leg, and she because she was a woman. I have said before that I liked Silver, and it was in some of the conversations that we had aboard *Revenge*, that I learned more of him.

Revenge was running sea-going watches by then, and the bell had just struck the turn of the morning watch, and the latest hauling team gone away in boats, when Silver, Selena and I were alone on the quarterdeck. Smollet was below and studying *Revenge's* charts and instruments, in preparation for our voyage home. The full heat of the day was not yet on us, the weather was fine, the anchorage was bright and clear, and we fell into conversation.

I should point out, that by then it was tacitly agreed by all sides that it was best to pretend that no mutiny had ever occurred, and that all aboard *Revenge* were loyal hands, fit to take a share in the treasure. So Silver asked what I should do with my share, on my return to England, and I said that I hoped to do some good

'And what of you, Mr Silver,' I said, 'and Mrs Silver?' Selena looked at Silver steadily.

'We'll take no part of Flint's goods,' said Silver, and Selena nodded firmly. Silver shrugged, ''cos it's tainted money, and we don't want it, and we don't need it and never did.' She nodded again.

'Oh,' I said. 'And shall you go back to Bristol? And the Spyglass tavern?'

'Never!' said Selena. 'I'll not sleep in that house again.'

'No, Doctor!' said Silver.

'Then where shall you go?'

'To America,' he said. 'All my old shipmates is gone, and I want a new place, a new name and a new life.'

She nodded and squeezed his hand.

'America?' I said. 'But there's slavery in the colonies.'

'And I'm black,' said Selena. 'You noticed?'

'Yes,' I said, and laughed, and Silver put his arm round his wife.

'Aye,' he said. 'But she's free, and she's married, and she's rich.'

'Rich?' I queried.

'Rich *enough*,' said Silver, and tapped a finger against his nose.

'How is that?' I said, and he looked at her.

'We've come to an agreement, my lass, haven't we?'

'Yes,' she said.

'What goods I had before Flint, shall stay mine,' he said, 'but nothing after.' She nodded.

'What do you mean?' I said.

'I took some goods… a lot of goods. In the old days. And I stowed the loot a bit here, a bit there, and all in different places.'

'But if you go to America, how can you take your wealth?'

'Have you heard of the Brotherhood of the Red Shield, Doctor?'

'No.'

'The *Roth Schild* in German,' he said, 'The Rothschilds, and they shift gold with a paper letter.'

'Do they?'

'Aye, Doctor, they shift it round the world, and have done so for me, for years.'

'It sounds like magic,' I said, and he nodded.

'It is, Doctor,' he said. 'They do such magic as I wonder they can't give me back my leg and I could be free of this ugly crutch!' He laughed at the impossibility of that, but I answered as I would to any patient who had lost a leg.

'You don't have to use a crutch,' I said. 'You could go on a cork leg, and then with britches, stockings and shoes you'd look the same as any other man.'

'Would he?' asked Selena.

'Yes,' I said. 'I'll take measurements and draw a plan for you if you like. Then it's a thing any good craftsmen could make: a shoe-maker or a joiner, for instance.'

Silver shook his head, but his wife nodded. 'Yes,' she said, 'we'd like that.'

Then finally when everything was stowed aboard, we filled *Revenge's* water casks afresh, and fitted out Ben Gunn with a good suit of seaman's clothes. He combed his hair and shaved his beard, and looked twenty years younger.

We hoisted anchor, and crept out with just enough breeze to move the ship, and with a boat ahead sounding the way. Of the thirty-seven men who had come aboard *Hispaniola* in Bristol, seventeen were now dead, but we had enough hands to take *Revenge* to sea, though far too few to man her guns properly, if any pirate should learn that we carried the richest cargo since Anson took the Manila galleon in '43.

Fortunately none did, and our moment of greatest danger came just after we hoisted our boat aboard, and rounded the larboard mouth of the anchorage, when a ragged group of men appeared on the headland above us. They were the remains of Flint's crew, and they begged us to take them on board. They were close enough for voices to carry, and we heard them moaning and groaning, then saw them fall to their knees with arms raised, imploring us to save them. But they were too many to risk among us and Captain Smollet simply shook his head, and ordered the helmsman to hold his course.

At this, and seeing our determination to leave them behind, they produced at least three muskets which they had kept hidden, and fired down on us such that two balls smacked into the deck at Smollet's feet, and another punched a hole in the binnacle.

Aside from that, the voyage was without incident. We met no great storm, the winds were fair, and we sailed north and into the Caribbean which we *could* do since there was not yet any war with France or Spain, and which we were *obliged* to do since it is impossible for a ship to sail straight to England from the latitude of the island, and necessary to sail north to find westerly winds. We stopped briefly at Port Royal in Jamaica to replenish supplies, and also as a courtesy to John Silver who declared that he would not return to England, which held nothing for him now.

'I'd warrant you're an Englishman through and through, Doctor,' he said. 'Am I right?'

'I am, Mr Silver, ' I confirmed. 'English and proud of it, and loyal to my King.'

'Ah,' he said, 'there's the rub! I'm nearly thirty-six and I went to sea at nine years old, and hardly lived ashore at all. While as for King George, for most of the time he would have hanged me if he'd got hold of me! So England ain't my home, I've got no use for Kings, and I'm bound for Boston, in the colony of Massachusetts. But I'm known in Port Royal and can take ship from here. Then it's a new name and a new life for me and my lass.'

'What about the Spyglass?' I asked, and he smiled.

'The Rothschilds will sell it for me, and send on the gelt. They don't work cheap but they work honest, 'cos they work on trust.'

Finally, and just before Silver and his wife went over the side, they were persuaded to take a sum of money from the treasure, strictly on account and to be returned in due course. Selena frowned at this, but it was practical necessity. But then Abe Gray stepped forward, with a small, highly-polished wooden box in his hands, and saluted her and spoke.

'I'm a deputation, ma'am,' he said. 'I speaks for all hands in saying that such a lady as yourself has been our light and inspiration, each hour you was aboard.'

'Aye!' said the crew all together, and grinned and nodded, including myself because she was a remarkably lovely woman, and had been in every man's dreams.

'And therefore,' said Gray, 'we begs that you take this, which is out of all our shares combined, as a remembrance of ourselves, one and all.' And he opened the box, which had been lovingly made by the men, and took out a slim gold chain with an enormous ruby in the centre.

'Oh,' she said, with profoundly mixed emotions. But Silver was quick to speak.

'The lady accepts with gratitude,' he said, and that was that.

Then we sailed for England, and in God's good time came safe into Bristol, and we arrived in triumph since Trelawney blabbed to all the town, and we became the sensation of the hour. In due course the treasure was shared, and every man became rich and able to choose his own path from that day on.

But as for that entire adventure, and though it made me an exceedingly wealthy man, the worst dreams that I ever have are when I hear the surf booming about the coast, or start upright in the night for fear that Flint is at the foot of the bed, and I swear to myself every time and yet again, that not oxen and wain-ropes would ever drag me back to the treasure island.

EPILOGUE

BEN GUNN

The considerable congregation gathered at St George's Church, Polmouth, for this Sunday's christenings, included the well-known Mr Gunn, philanthropist, who is recently raised to the rank of verger.
(From the '*Polmouth Clarion and Recorder*' of Monday 30th August, 1756.)

The congregation was very large, there being present numerous luminaries of the town, bringing their infants for baptism, including masters of the trade guilds and the lady wife of the vicar himself with their first-born. The day was fine, with hot sunshine and a chorus of birdsong. The red stone church tower, with its crenelated crest, bore the flag of Saint George against a blue sky, and a great file of humanity — dense as a column of infantry — made its way along the winding, upward path that led through mown grass and tumbling gravestones, to the wide-open church door, with a constant sound of merry conversation and laughter on this happy day.

In the dark interior, lit by handsomely coloured glass of lovely hues, the folk stepped forward, leaving the front rank of pews vacant for the proud mothers and fathers and for the bawling infants, with their fat red faces, tiny fists and long draperies of lace.

As the couples and families entered, they were met by the new verger, Mr Benjamin Gunn, dressed for the first time in his black robe and clerical band. Mr Gunn bore himself well, with a straight back, and bowed to each paterfamilias as he handed out orders of service, and with all proper deference, directed the leading citizens to their own pews.

'Thank you, Mr Gunn,' said the master cutler.

'Glad to see you, Mr Gunn,' said the master tailor.

'A happy day, Mr Gunn,' said the master butcher, and even the gentry smiled their acknowledgement of the man who had paid for lead sheeting of the entire the church roof. Then, with the congregation assembled, and the vicar before the altar, the reverend announced:

'We shall first sing that fine and resounding hymn of praise: *Oh God our Help in Ages Past!*'

Everyone stood, with a resounding rumble, some at least of the infants ceased bawling, the organ stuck up the tune, and many hundreds of voices bellowed out the hymn, led by the choir which included Mr Gunn, who sang with joyful strength and happiness, being complete and whole in life's satisfaction, and whose voice was so nearly in tune, that all who knew him, most willingly forgave him.

ABRAHAM GRAY

Entered this day into the COMPANY's records, the names of the

*following candidates as fit and proper persons for THE COMPANY's
SEA SERVICE...*

(From the 'Minutes of the Proceedings of the Sea Service
of the Honourable East India Company', Vol IX Paragraph II,
Tuesday September 2nd, 1756.)

Abe Gray stood in London's Leadenhall Street, suddenly struck with
nerves. He looked across at New East India House, headquarters of
the East India Company, which company owned the biggest and finest
merchant ships in the world, and was making a colossal fortune out of its
monopoly trade with India and the orient beyond. Gray gazed at the fine
building that rose behind its iron railings: four stories, noble columns,
huge windows, balustraded roof, and huge oaken doors guarded by
two servants with laced coats, shiny badges, big hats — and big fists to
keep out unwanted visitors.

Gray summoned courage. He knew he looked the part, in good
clothes with a long coat, silver buckles to his shoes and a new hat. He
walked across the road, taking care of the fierce London traffic, and
managed to avoid being trampled by two horses the size of elephants,
drawing a Whitbread's dray loaded with vast barrels of beer.

He touched his hat to the livery men, they touched their hats to him.
He gave his name, they consulted a list, and they bowed and showed him
into a high, bright foyer: marble-clad, lined with statues and hung with
expensive paintings. There he sat and waited on one of a line of chairs
against a wall, along with a number of other young men, who like himself
were postulants seeking a berth aboard one of The Company's ships.

Gray sat and fiddled with his hat. The nerves came on again. But
he did not have to wait long because, very soon, another livery man
appeared. He had a white wig rather than heavy fists and he earned

his living inside a book of accounts. He came down the big staircase in the middle of the room, and paused on the last but one step, and called out a name.

'Gray?' he said. 'Abraham Gray?'

'Aye-aye, sir!' said Gray, standing up.

'Quite,' said the white wig, not quite sneering at sea talk. 'You will follow me, Mr Gray.'

So Gray followed and was taken upstairs, and a pair of big, mahogany doors were thrown open in front of him, then closed behind him, and he was alone in a huge, high room with one chair in front of him, and a table behind that, and five gentlemen sat behind it, and a big window behind them, that shone so much light into his eyes that he could scarcely see their faces.

'Ah,' said the man in the middle, who was the chairman. 'Mr Gray! Sit down, Mr Gray, we are most pleased to see you.'

'Aye-aye, sir!' said Gray and sat down.

'Aye-aye, sir?' said the chairman. 'Good! You are a seaman, sir, a seaman indeed.' The rest smiled and nodded, and the tide came in on the flood for Abe Gray. 'I have here your letter of application, Mr Gray,' said the chairman.

'Aye-aye, sir,' said Gray.

'And I have letters of character reference,' said the chairman, and all the others nodded emphatically. 'Letters from Squire Trelawney of Trelawney Hall, and from Dr David Livesey, magistrate, physician and surgeon. And best of all, Mr Gray, I have here,' and the chairman held aloft a letter, 'I have here a reference from Captain Alexander Smollet, master mariner, who is known to this board, and who affirms that you are a sound and steady man, who has already begun study of celestial navigation.'

'Indeed,' said the board members.'

'Therefore, Mr Gray,' said the chairman, 'this board is pleased — nay, *delighted* — to offer you a warrant as third mate aboard the company's ship *Castle of Gwent* now loading for a voyage east, with an injunction upon her captain that you be fully trained in all manners fit to advance you to high rank in the company's service.'

'Indeed, indeed!' said the board. But the chairman was not done.

'Furthermore, Mr Gray,' he said, 'I see from your letter that you wish to take a substantial share in the trading value of our cargoes.'

'Yes, sir,' said Gray, now avoiding sea talk because he thought that it was time to become a man of business as well as a seaman.

'In that case, Mr Gray,' said the chairman, 'I can promise you the most splendid and profitable future.'

CAPTAIN SMOLLET

Led in by the Right Worshipful, Lord Mayor Marshe Dickinson M.P., Captain Smollet entered the dining room, to the applause of a great concourse of elevated persons including those of Royal and noble blood, and senior princes of the Church.

(From the 'Westminster Chronicle and Gazette' of Saturday July 31st 1757.)

The Lord Mayor of London arose, splendid in velvet and fur, and draped with chain of office. Behind him, an usher raised a white wand and beat it three times to the floor for silence.

His Worship looked round the huge dining hall of the Mansion House, heart and soul of the financial capital of the city. Noble Corinthian columns rose on either side, the coffered ceiling was ornate with floral relief. Great lamps of polished silver were suspended from chains, and the whole long chamber was lit by a magnificent round-top window, one of the biggest areas of glazed panelling in London.

Long tables ran in rows, lavish food had been eaten, and vast quantities of wine served. Only the best wine. Flushed and satisfied, the great and the good of London sat back with their jewel-bedecked wives and gazed at the Lord Mayor at the high table with the elite of the elite around him. Servants stood to frozen attention, since the Lord Mayor was about to speak.

Also profoundly silent was a choir of two dozen little boys, rigged out in blue coats with shiny buttons, and who stood in the minstrels' gallery half way up one of the walls, with a band of musicians behind them.

'Your Royal Highness, Your Grace, my lords, ladies and gentlemen,' began the Lord Mayor, then he turned to the gentleman on his right, 'and yourself, Captain Smollet — the gentleman of the hour!' The Lord Mayor turned to the room and raised his hands, inviting applause, which came first in waves of clapping, and then, by degrees, in cheers, as first one man, then another stood and others followed, and there was a great bellowing of Smollet's name, since it was well known that the dinner and wine were all entirely at the captain's expense, and the wine in particular had been exceedingly generously served, and exceedingly generously consumed.

The Lord Mayor beamed, and waited for silence, and for all those who had missed their chairs in sitting down and who were sprawled on the floor, to pick themselves up and regain their dignity.

'We are here today,' cried the Lord Mayor, 'to celebrate the foundation of *Smollet's Academy*, and since the captain himself has begged me to be a man of few words, I now ask him to stand and address us!'

Smollet rose, the Lord Mayor sat, great applause followed then died away in anticipation of a speech.

'Your Royal Highness, Your Grace, my lords, ladies and gentlemen,' began Smollet, and he stood straight-backed, in the plain blue coat that he always wore. 'His Lordship is right,' said Smollet, 'I'm a man of few words, and here they are. A wound has sent me ashore from the sea. So here I am, and in going through this great, rich city, I was dismayed to see poor boys hungry in the streets, barefoot in winter, and as thin as starvation.' He looked around with stern gaze, and the audience became distinctly uneasy, as any audience does when charity tries to shame it into giving. 'So,' Smollet continued, 'having recently come by a certain sum of money,' great laughter followed, and much drumming of feet on floor, 'I decided to build and equip: entirely at my own expense...' great cheers greeted these five words, '...an academy whereby young orphan boys might be taken in, and clothed and fed and trained up for the sea life. And this I have now done, and the building stands in Southwark Square, and there are my boys up there,' he pointed to the minstrels' gallery, 'who are waiting to sing *God Save Great George our King* — and I hope you will all stand and sing with them.'

So the musicians played, the boys sang, the entire company joined in, and Captain Smollet's Academy thrived ever after, and he was welcomed into London's highest society.

DR LIVESEY AND SQUIRE TRELAWNEY

Squire John Trelawney gave away the bride, radiant in silk taffeta and acknowledged as the reigning beauty of the county, whose marriage to the renowned Dr David Livesey was celebrated with joy by the entire populace at a vast and magnificent feast.

(From the *'Bristol Mercury and Telegraph'* of Saturday July 31st, 1756.)

The squire easily obtained the special license for the marriage to be celebrated at Trelawney Hall, and kindly providence delivered fine weather upon such a scene of beauty as only nature can display, with soft green hills, noble trees, broad fields, ancient hedges, grazing sheep and the green and rolling majesty of England.

The gardens and grounds of the Hall were trimmed immaculately, and the mansion wonderfully decorated within, not only by the squire's servants, but by a host of willing tenants who came in to prepare for the great day. Though their generosity was hardly surprising, since from the moment of his return from the treasure expedition, the squire had ridden from one end of his estates to the other — and beyond, in the case of relatives of his tenants — cancelling debts, paying off mortgages, repairing everything that was broken, sending promising sons to good schools, buying tools, stock and seed for farmers in need, and in general becoming the universal benefactor.

In addition, Squire Trelawney took the most particular care that the wives and families left by Tom Redruth, Rob Hunter and Lewis Joyce were lavishly pensioned, and taken care of for the rest of their lives.

In discharging all these happy duties, it should be noted that if the squire had responded with enthusiastic vigour to the smiles and profound gratitude of some of the younger women on his estates — including some undoubtedly married to husbands — then no word of censure was heard in any house between Trelawney Hall, Polmouth and Bristol.

On the great day, Dr Livesey — nervous as any bridegroom — had spent the night at the mansion, and struggled manfully to avoid the squire and his friends quite entirely drowning him in wine. But finally,

Livesey and Trelawney, backed by a phalanx of servants and accompanied by the entire gentry of the county, stood on the steps of Trelawney Hall, as a glazed white carriage came up the drive, drawn by matched white horses, to cheers of the local people en masse.

'What a shame the boy Jim can't be here,' said Trelawney to Livesey. 'His mother would have been so proud of him, and he of her.'

'Yes,' said Livesey.

'I saw you talking to him, the day he went to London,' said the squire.

'Yes,' said Livesey.

'You were talking quite a while, and with some passion,' said Trelawney.

'Hmm,' said Livesey.

'You didn't...' asked Trelawney, 'you didn't... ah... you didn't *say* anything to the lad?'

'A-hem,' said Livesey, as if clearing his throat.

'I mean... say anything to make him unwelcome?'

'Squire,' said Livesey, 'we have received Jim Hawkins' letter regretting with sorrow, that pressing business prevents his leaving London, where he is obliged to remain for some considerable time. So what more is there to say?'

'But—'

'Ah!' Livesey interrupted him, as the white carriage swept round in front of the mansion, and the footmen leapt down from their posts at the back and opened the door, and threw down the steps, and Charlotte Hawkins was handed down from the carriage, and every heart that beat on that day was pierced with her loveliness, and the flowers and ribbons of her gown seemed to shine in radiance around her.

'Whoa!' said the squire, as Livesey stepped forward with arms outstretched. 'I'm supposed to take her in, not you. That's protocol.'

'Damnation on protocol,' said Livesey, and took Charlotte in his arms and kissed her.

'My darling,' he said.

'My love,' she said, and Squire Trelawney sniffed as the tears rolled down his cheeks for the happiness of his good friend, and he wondered if it wasn't time that he got *himself* a wife.

Meanwhile it was universally felt to be a pity and a surprise that Jim Hawkins had been unable to attend his mother's wedding to Dr Livesey, especially as the large and splendid free hospital, built and lavishly equipped by Dr Livesey, was named the *James Hawkins Hospital* in his honour.

It was almost as if some agreement had been made.

JIM HAWKINS

The by election for the Trelawney West constituency, following the sad and sudden death of Sir Robert Smyth-Collins M.P., was marked with a vast public celebration entirely paid for by the successful candidate, Mr James Hawkins, standing in the Whig interest.

(From the *'Polmouth Clarion and Recorder'* of Monday July 20th, 1761.)

The band blew loud and hard: bassoons, serpents, horns and pipes, to the solemn beat of a great drum that gave the time for Cornwall's traditional and immemorial Furzle dance:

Boom! Boom! *Ba-boom-boom-boom!* The dancers pranced and swayed, couple by couple, men and women, passing in and out of shops and houses, stepping forward to the monotonous beat, and the tune that hardly varied and was constantly repeated, as the mighty host crammed into Polmouth's George Street, rolled along in time to the music, and roared out the melody such as it was:

'Dah! Dah! Da-da-da-dah, Diddle om-pom-diddle-diddle doodle dah!'

Every kind of humanity was present, from gentry to beggars, from lost children crying for their mothers to townsmen, countrymen, servants and raucous apprentices. Dogs howled, pigs grunted, chickens clucked. Beer went down by waterfalls and gin went down by buckets. Fights broke out, pockets were picked, girls' arses were pinched, and those who could not find the privy piddled hard into the gutters.

Aside from the novelty of the Furzle dance, with its progression in and out of houses, the scene was the perfectly ordinary, completely typical celebration of any parliamentary election, anywhere in England, whereby the victorious candidate was carried through the town, raised up on an armchair lashed to poles, such that eight or ten men might bear him, with the number varying dependent upon how many got up again after falling down drunk. It was also typical of such occasions in that it was best for supporters of the losing candidate to keep off the streets, for fear of being battered by the cudgels of those whose candidate had won.

But this was Cornwall, and the Furzle dance was a necessary part of the celebration, which meant that Mr James Hawkins, the new member of parliament, had to be carried along with the dance, dipping and swaying, pitching and rolling, and got under the thresholds of the shops and houses, as best as could be without entirely braining Mr Hawkins, now vastly wealthy and deep into politics.

'Down!' cried his bearers, and they stooped to get Mr Hawkins through the latest door.

'Mind yer 'ead!' they cried, and laughed as Mr Hawkins' brow came smart up against the lintel over the door jamb of a grocer's shop, and 'Ooooh!' they cried as Hawkins yelped, and there was a brisk fight, as some of Mr Hawkins' supporters fought for a grip of the chair-poles, considering those in place to be incompetent.

Later there was a victory dinner, at the Royal Oak Inn, where Mr Hawkins had his head bandaged, and sat at the head of an enormous table, laden with gross quantities of food, surrounded by sweating faces, guzzling mouths and busy-shovelling knives and forks, while a great numbers of persons shoved forward through the noise and press and stink of the room, hoping for a word with Mr Hawkins. But of course, Mr Hawkins' agent introduced each and every one to Mr Hawkins, because each and every one wished to make obeisance, beg favours and offer bribes.

Mr Hawkins received all this entirely and completely sober, and he smiled and smiled and smiled. He knew that he had made a mistake with Flint. But he would never make the same mistake again. Nor would he ever go to sea again, nor risk any other kind of danger. He had found his world and he would stay in it. London beckoned. Parliament called.

JOHN SIMPKINS

Spy reports that this morning, Governor Thomas Pownall, representative of his Britannic Majesty, condescended to receive a delegation of colonial persons, whose only qualification for addressing him regarding the government of free men, was the fact of their having been freely elected, in a free election, by free men.

(From *'Spy's Boston Monitor'* of Wednesday 28th February, 1770.)

Mr Simpkins led the delegation out through the eastern end of the Boston State House, seat of Government of the Province of Massachusetts Bay, where the Governor held council, the Supreme

Court sat, and the Colonial Assembly debated.

Mr Simpkins was a very tall man, who walked with a steady gait and the aid of an ebony stick, going first on his right leg then swinging the left forward. His face was broad and blond, with strong features and fair hair going grey. He was fifty years old, vigorous, energetic and widely respected in Boston as a ship-owning merchant whose ventures stretched up and down the coast and across the Atlantic.

Nearly two dozen men followed him out of the door then gathered round him and looked up to him. They were the leading men of Boston, and they were all tradesmen, because it was trade that brought reputation here, not accidents of birth, nor patronage of a monarch.

'So, gentlemen,' said Mr Simpkins, 'look there.' He pointed up to the roof of the elegant four-storied, brick building that was the State House. 'There's the lion and the unicorn of England up there, all shiny and bright!' Everyone looked up and nodded at the great, gold-leafed images that stood, one on each upper corner of the building. 'They look like solid gold,' said Simpkins, 'but they're only wood inside, and wood can be burned.' They nodded, but they were not quite sure.

One of them spoke: Mr Samuel Adams, who had been a brewer and a newspaper owner, but who was now turned philosopher and politician. He was a man in his late thirties and was clever. Very clever.

'Not everyone is with us, sir, there are many who doubt we could declare independence and survive.'

'So there are, Mr Adams,' replied Simpkins, 'but look all around.' He swept his arm to indicate the streets of modern buildings that surrounded the State House. 'Look at them houses,' he said, 'on the outside there's bricks, lead pipes, window glass and iron door-knockers. On the inside there's clocks, cutlery, printed books and bed linen. So what does that tell you, Mr Adams?'

'That Boston is rich!' said Adams, and everyone laughed.

'So it does, Mr Adams,' Simpkins concurred. 'But it says more than that, because all these things…' he paused, 'and muskets too: muskets and cannon! All those things we can make right here in America, and we don't need England to rule over us and tell us what to do.'

Most of them nodded, but another man, Mr Paul Revere, the young silversmith, had another question.

'What about the Governor? What about Pownall? He's a good man, and he was on our side.'

'Yes!' they all said.

'You're right, Mr Revere,' said Simpkins. 'Governor Pownall is a good man, and he agrees we shouldn't be taxed without seats in the London parliament. But he don't run that parliament, and he can't get us those seats.'

'So what do we do?' said Samuel Adams. 'We don't have a majority in the Assembly.'

'I'll tell you what we do, Mr Adams,' said Simpkins, 'because we don't need all hands on our side just yet. But we do need a band of brothers, like ourselves,' they all nodded, 'we need a band of brothers to act together, and never give up, and persuade the rest to follow us as true companions, united in the common cause.'

'Yes!' they chorused.

'And we need something else,' continued Simpkins. 'We must, every man of us, keep a musket under the bed and ready, because King George won't give up America without a fight!'

'Well spoken, sir!' said Samuel Adams.

'Indeed,' said Revere, 'there's war coming. The British are coming.'

Then a carriage rolled up towards the group of men and came to a halt. It was a glossy-bodied, open landau in deep maroon, drawn by two horses. The driver and footmen wore livery, and a fine lady and a little boy sat in the carriage. The lady was black, as was the child beside her. She was extremely beautiful, she wore Paris fashions, and she kept a salon visited by the best ladies in Boston. Thus the gentlemen swept off their hats and bowed to the lady as the carriage stopped.

'Good day, ma'am!' they said. 'Good day, Mrs Simpkins!' She waved and acknowledged them.

'Daddy!' said the little boy, and Simpkins smiled. But there was still another occupant of the landau. A big, green parrot, flapped into flight and settled on Mr Simpkins' shoulder, and nibbled his ear.

'Good day, Cap'n Flint!' said Samuel Adams.

'Good day, Captain,' said the rest, smiling.

'We'll talk more tomorrow,' said Simpkins. 'I have to be gone, now. It's my boy's birthday!'

'Good day, sir,' said Adams and shook Simpkins' hand. 'I've heard all the rumours of your past life, sir,' he said, and everyone laughed, because they had too, 'but you're an inspiration to us, Mr Simpkins! You are a man who's faced the enemy's shot and never flinched.'

'Right kind of you, Mr Adams,' said Simpkins, 'but all I ever was, was a seaman: just a hand before the mast.' Everyone laughed even more at that, then Simpkins tipped his hat and got himself up into the carriage, pulling with his two hands and pushing with his right leg.

'Home!' said the lady.

'Ma'am!' said the driver, and cracked his whip, and the carriage moved off, through the ever-growing streets of Boston.

'Did they agree?' said the lady.

'Not all of them,' said Simpkins. 'But they'll come round in time. Then things is going to be exciting.'

AFTERWORD

LONG JOHN SILVER'S ARTICLES

The 'articles' so constantly mentioned by Long John Silver appear in one of the documents in Dr Livesey's collection. They are a voluntary code whereby a company of men banded together to capture ships and towns for profit, and they are similar to articles drawn up by other famous pirates like Henry Morgan and Bartholomew Roberts.

Silver's articles are typical in being vigorously democratic, with provision for election of a captain and in their insistence that 'brothers' should be armed and should keep their weapons within reach: the very opposite of the situation in naval ships where the hands, who might be pressed men, were denied weapons and were dominated by armed marines. Thus, it is easy to understand that a man so dedicated to the concept of democracy and who had no ties of loyalty to King George, would support the Declaration of Independence by the American colonies, at a time when the colonists were denied representation in parliament by the British Government.

Note that there is no article thirteen, perhaps because the number was considered unlucky. Also note that articles sixteen and seventeen may sound quaint but they reflect practical reality, in that wooden ships crammed with men had to be kept clean, and that the musicians had to get a rest some time, despite the need to keep the crew cheerful with music.

Article six is highly unusual, presumably reflecting the personality of Long John Silver, while article eighteen undoubtedly defines his deepest belief. The articles are as reproduced here, as follows:

John Silver's articles which every man shall sign, who would be a gentleman of fortune, but signing only after having read these articles , or if not a scholar to hear them truly read before witnesses, and then having pondered them well.

1. Every brother shall swear allegiance to these articles to the exclusion of all other loyalties, and there shall be neither nation nor religion to divide the company, and allegiance to all such is forbidden and condemned.

2. Every brother shall have an equal vote in all matters of dispute.

3. Any brother guilty of offences against these articles, if guilt be proven before a council, shall be punished as the company shall agree, which punishment may include flogging, loss of shares, marooning or death by hanging.

4. The company shall be led by a captain who shall be elected in a free vote of brothers and shall remain in power until deposed by black spot, given after a council of brothers.

5. Until deposed, the captain shall have full authority over the brothers and his orders shall be obeyed with willing cheerfulness.

6. Any brother in dispute of the captain's orders when no black spot has been given, shall meet the captain face-to-face with cutlass drawn.

7. Every brother shall have an equal share of goods taken, saving only the captain who shall have three shares, and the quartermaster and boatswain who shall have two, and other officers one-and-a-half at the captain's will.

8. Every brother shall keep his arms clean and fit for service and forever within his reach, likewise his powder and shot.

9. No brother shall fight another brother aboard ship.

10. No woman shall be carried to sea and no woman shall be abused if she be unwilling.

11. No brother shall dice or play at cards for money.

12. No brother shall render himself unfit for duty by drunkenness.

14. No brother shall display cowardice in the face of the enemy.

15. No brother shall carry a light below decks, nor smoke below decks, nor snap a firelock below decks other than those charged by the captain to do so.

16. No brother shall piss or shit in the ballast below decks, but only in the buckets provided.

17. The musicians may rest on the sabbath day, but the other six days and nights, they may not rest without leave of the captain.

18. Brothers shall in all things behave as jolly companions, united in the common cause and caring more for their fellow brothers than for themselves.

No copy is known of Joseph Flint's articles although he frequently addressed his men as 'brothers'. Judging from his behaviour, if such articles ever existed, they were either very different from John Silver's, or Flint simply ignored them and ruled by terror.

ALCOHOL IN THE EIGHTEENTH CENTURY

Twenty-first century readers may be surprised at the constant reference to alcoholic drink in *'Traitor of Treasure Island'*, but this is an authentic reflection of eighteenth century seafaring reality. For instance, the Royal Navy's drink allowance for common seamen was, according to Note 66 of *'Countdown to Victory'*, by Peter Godwin, then Curator of HMS Victory (Manuscript Press, 2000):

'...eight pints of beer, or two pints of wine, or half a pint of rum or brandy (diluted 1:4 with water) per man per day.'

The rum or brandy did not contain our meagre 40% alcohol but something far stronger: eighteenth century 'proof' spirit contained c. 57% alcohol.

As for the officers, I quote from chapter two of *'The Wooden World'* (William Collins, 1986), which is naval historian Dr Nicholas Roger's definitive account of life in the Georgian navy:

'The amount of alcohol the officers took on board was prodigious.'

So here's to ourselves, and hold your luff, plenty of prizes and plenty of duff!

READY MONEY IN THE EIGHTEENTH CENTURY

Readers may also be surprised that I have valued Flint's treasure in billions (see the Introduction), although I have said that one Georgian pound equals one thousand modern pounds. So if the treasure was worth £800,000 Georgian, why not £800,000,000 modern?

The reason is that eighteenth century England ran on debt. Everyone paid late, and everyone ran up long term bills, led by the aristocracy and nobility who ran up the biggest debts of all. This was partly due to the method of payment by 'bill of hand' which meant a piece of paper, hand-written with such words as:

I, John Smith, owe James Jones £1,000. Signed by John Smith, 1st January 1755

That piece of paper was a legally binding contract. John Smith could be sued for the money or imprisoned for debt until he paid up. It was as easy as that, and was therefore much abused. There may have been other reasons for chronic debt, including a scarcity of gold to be struck into coins, but the *fact* is that chronic debt existed. Thus, gentlemen paid their tailors years in retard, and ladies paid their stay-makers years in retard. Likewise the butcher, the baker and candlestick maker all had to wait to be paid.

So imagine yourself to be a horse dealer with a splendid stallion to sell. Along comes His Grace the Duke of Dunabunk with his retinue in tow and a seat in the House of Lords. He wants the horse and proposes to pay by bill of hand, so you bow and smile, but you know he is a bad payer like all his kind, and you ask the exorbitant figure of £5,000 in the hope that you might get *some* of the money, someday, before you die of old age. But next through the door is Squire Trelawney, who famously dug up Flint's treasure, and who can pay right now in actual gold coins, and who offers £1,000.

Ask yourself: who gets the horse? Then imagine a similar deal for everything you might ever want, and that explains why Flint's treasure, nominally equivalent to £800,000,000 (admittedly an enormous sum), was worth far more in the 1750s, because it was entirely in ready money.

THE ROYAL NAVY'S PRAYER

This is the prayer that Abe Gray recited over the grave of Israel Hands, master gunner. It is still the prayer of the Royal Navy, with the name of our own dear Queen (God bless her!) taking the place of her Georgian ancestor, and I hope that you the reader may be as moved by it as I am.

> *O Eternal Lord God, who alone rulest the raging of the sea; who has compassed the waters with bounds until day and night come to an end; be pleased to receive into Thy almighty and most gracious protection the persons of us Thy servants and the fleet in which we serve.*
>
> *Preserve us from the dangers of the sea, and from the violence of the enemy; that we may be a safeguard unto our most gracious Sovereign Lord King George and his dominions, and a security for such as pass upon the seas upon their lawful occasions that the inhabitants of our Empire may in peace and quietness serve Thee our God; and that we may return in safety to enjoy the blessings of the land, with the fruits of our labours and with a thankful remembrance of Thy mercies, to praise and glorify Thy Holy Name, through Jesus Christ our Lord,*
>
> *Amen.*